Regency Romance

The Regency Spring and Valentine Hearts Collection

Arietta Richmond

ARIETTA RICHMOND

Dreamstone Publishing © 2016 to 2020

www.dreamstonepublishing.com

Copyright © 2020 Dreamstone
Publishing and Arietta Richmond,

ISBN-13: 978-1-925915-50-1

Dedication

For everyone who had the grace to be patient while this book, and every other book that I have written, was coming into existence, who provided cups of tea, and food, when the writing would not let me go, and endured countless times being asked for opinions.

For the readers who inspire me to continue writing, by buying my books! Especially for those of you who have taken the time to email me, or to leave reviews, and tell me what you love about my books, and what you'd like to see more of – thank you – I'm listening. I hope that you enjoy this new series (which features some appearances by old favourite characters from the His Majesty's Hounds series), just as much as my other books.

For my growing team of beta readers and advance reviewers – it's thanks to you that others can enjoy these books in the best presentation possible!

And for all the writers of Regency Historical Romance, whose books I read, who inspired me to write in this fascinating period.

Introduction

This anthology brings you five of my Valentine's Day or Spring related stories in one collection! Each story has a relationship to Spring or Valentine's Day, either for the whole story, or by the way it ends at that time of year, and with the associated emotional effects for the characters.

This is your chance to immerse yourself in Spring and Valentine's reading, and sample stories from my most loved His Majesty's Hounds series while you do. Each story can be read standalone, but each story also has intertwined relationships with others in the series.

All of these stories are clean.

The table on the next page summarises it for you, as well.

Book	Series
Giving a Heart of Lace	His Majesty's Hounds (3) – Valentine's Day
Being Lady Harriet's Hero	His Majesty's Hounds (4) - Spring
Loving the Bitter Baron	His Majesty's Hounds (11) – Valentine's Day
Falling for the Earl	His Majesty's Hounds (12) – Spring
Restoring the Earl's Honour	His Majesty's Hounds (17) - Spring

I hope that you enjoy reading this collection of Christmas stories! (and if you do, please try some of the other books in the series – I'm sure that you will love them too!

Arietta Richmond

Table of Contents

Books by Arietta Richmond

His Majesty's Hounds

Claiming the Heart of a Duke   Intriguing the Viscount
Giving a Heart of Lace   Being Lady Harriet's Hero
Enchanting the Duke   Redeeming the Marquess
Finding the Duke's Heir   Winning the Merchant Earl
Healing Lord Barton   Kissing the Duke of Hearts
Loving the Bitter Baron   Falling for the Earl
Rescuing the Countess   Betting on a Lady's Heart
Attracting the Spymaster   Courting a Spinster for Christmas
Restoring the Earl's Honour
From Soldier Spy to Lord (contains the first three books in one volume)
To Love a Determined Lady (Contains Books 4, 5 and 6 in one volume)
Love Heals a Lord (Contains Books 7, 8 and 9 in one volume)

A Duke's Daughters – The Elbury Bouquet

A Spinster for a Spy (Lily)
A Vixen for a Viscount (Hyacinth)
A Bluestocking for a Baron (Rose)
A Diamond for a Duke (Camellia) (coming soon)
A Minx for a Merchant (Primrose) (coming soon)
An Enchantress for an Earl (Violet) (coming soon)
A Maiden for a Marquess (Iris) (coming soon)
A Heart for an Heir (Thorne) (coming soon)

The Nettlefold Chronicles

The Duke and the Spinster   To Dance with the Dangerous Duke
A Duke in Autumn   A Christmas Bride for the Duke

The Regency Gothic Series

Lord of the Storm
Lord of the Darkness (coming soon)
Lord of the Lost (coming soon)
Lord of the Shadows (coming soon)

The Regency Scandals Series

The Gift of a Christmas Scandal   Lady Mariel's Scandalous Love
Christmas with *That* Duke (coming soon)

Lady Canterford's Conspirators (The Mayfair Ladies Poetry Society)

A six book series (coming soon)

The Derbyshire Set

A Gift of Love (Prequel short story)
A Devil's Bargain (Prequel short story - coming soon)
The Earl's Unexpected Bride
The Captain's Compromised Heiress
The Viscount's Unsuitable Affair
The Count's Impetuous Seduction
The Rake's Unlikely Redemption
The Marquess' Scandalous Mistress
A Remembered Face (Bonus short story – coming soon)
The Marchioness' Second Chance
A Viscount's Reluctant Passion
Lady Theodora's Christmas Wish
The Duke's Improper Love (coming soon)
A Gentleman's Unconventional Courtship (coming soon)
The Derbyshire Set, Omnibus Edition, Volume 1 (the first three books in one volume.)
The Derbyshire Set, Omnibus Edition, Volume 2 (the second three books in one volume.)

Other Books

The Scottish Governess
Her Summer Duke
The Earl's Reluctant Fiancée (coming soon)
The Crew of the Seadragon's Soul Series, (coming soon - a set of 10 linked novels)

Themed Collections

The Regency Christmas Hearts Collection
The Regency Spring and Valentine's Hearts Collection
The Regency Summer Hearts Collection (coming soon)
The Regency Autumn Hearts Collection (coming soon)

His Majesty's Hounds– Book 3

Sweet and Clean Regency Romance

Giving a Heart of Lace

Arietta Richmond

ARIETTA RICHMOND

Chapter One

The coal box was empty. The larder contained some cheese, some bread, and very little else. Serafine walked to her room with a heavy heart. In her dresser drawer there was a small metal chest – the sort that, in another life, she might have used as a jewellery box.

She turned the key, and opened the chest. She stared at the contents, as despair gripped her. The box contained only ten pounds. Ten pounds that were their last remaining money. And, carefully wrapped in a scrap of silk, a heart made of lace and ribbon and beads, all sewn onto a piece of parchment.

Lace that was all she had left of her grandmother. Everything else had been sold. Sewing that heart had been just for fun, then – it seemed an eternity ago – before *'the fall'* as she thought of it. Before her fool of a brother had gambled away everything, drawn into a tawdry gaming hell by that demon Pendholm, and bled of everything that had any value in their lives. Before her brother had committed the ultimate betrayal, and killed himself because of it.

Before the *ton* had shunned them for the scandal of a suicide in the family. Before.....

She shut the thoughts away. At least they had the house. It was small, and in a rather unfashionable part of town – not quite respectable at all – but it was her mother's outright, left to her by her aunt, shortly after Serafine's father's death. Although an unheated house, with no servants, and little furniture left was not exactly the most pleasant place to live, at least it was theirs.

She took out two pounds, her finger absently stroking the lace as she did, then shut and locked the chest, hiding it away again. Today, she could buy food and coal. What would she do on the day when there was no longer any money to do so?

~~~~~

Serafine sighed, holding the bag of food close against her. It was heavy, but she treasured the weight – it was the substance of survival, at least for a little longer. The coal would be delivered later in the day – enough for a month, if she was very careful. The food would not last near so long.

Passing the shop on the corner, she paused to look in the window a moment. Once, she would have thought such a shop beneath her – now, what it contained was as far beyond what she could afford as the moon was above the earth. Yet she still liked to look at pretty things. A little collection in one corner of the window caught her eye. A pile of what might be called favours – little cards and items, decorated with ribbons, lace and sometimes paste gems or feathers.

Pretty little nothings that a man might give his mistress, or a woman he was courting.

One, in particular, a little stained on the edges, but still pretty, reminded her of the heart with her grandmother's lace – it was the sort of thing that some called a Valentine. She stared at it for a while, feeling as if it was important, but not knowing why, then shrugged, lifted her bags again, and went home.

~~~~~

The next day was clear and bright, but very cold – they would likely have snow on Christmas Day. Serafine sat at the window of the parlour, sewing. She was nearly finished embellishing the gown for Mrs Johnson, which was a relief, for it meant that she would be paid for the work, but also a worry, for there were no more dresses waiting her attention. And her sewing was their only income –the only way to stretch out what money they had, for a little longer.

The ladies of the merchant classes, who lived all around them, those who had some money, but were not rich enough to ever consider going to a modiste in the heart of London, they were her customers. They found the idea of a Lady born sewing for them somehow satisfying (not that anybody ever called her 'Lady Serafine' any more – that manner of address belonged to *before* – now she was just 'miss' most of the time. And to those who knew her name at all, she was Miss Sera – Serafine had seemed a lovely name to her mother, who was fascinated by old mythology and similar, but now it was simply out of place for her current station in life.).

The merchant ladies appreciated her fine sense of fashion. But more than that, they appreciated her affordable pricing. She hummed as she worked, her clever fingers sewing beads onto a tracery of lace on the hemline of the dress, but her mind was elsewhere.

Her thoughts kept going back to that sad little pile of favours in the shop window. She wondered if they sold well, and what sort of people bought them. She'd seen a few things like that... *before*... but she'd never thought much of it. She thought of it now. They were such little things, and sewing them was, she suspected, not so different from sewing embellishments onto dresses.

Were they a thing that members of the *ton* might buy? Perhaps – if someone important bought one, or gave one to someone noticeable... if that happened, then others would follow – there were always those who simply copied everything the arbiters of fashion did, or the royal family did. She brought her attention back to sewing the last few beads onto the dress – what a goose she was, dreaming about the royals and the *ton*! They had nothing to do with her world now, nothing at all.

Chapter Two

Mr Raphael Morton was bored. That was a terrible thing to admit, when what he was doing was going over the business ledgers with the man he employed to do his accounts. Mr Manning was excellent at his job, and the ledgers were neat and clear. They showed just how wealthy Raphael was — just how well Morton Empire Imports was doing. Most men would be excited by what they saw — not bored.

But, bored he was. For Raphael, the exciting part was the planning, laying out the path that led to this, that ensured that, if all the steps were followed, the wealth would grow. After years at war, the inactivity of sitting in an office, or walking the warehouse and speaking to customers, was slowly driving him mad. To make it worse, his ship's captains came back not only with cargoes of exotic goods to make him even wealthier, but with tales of distant lands, strange sights and different people.

He envied them. He wanted to see those places himself. No amount of wealth and rich living here could change that. London was a gilded cage.

For, no matter what they had vowed to each other, the world would go as it did – his friends, those who had been closer than family for those long years of war, would be forced away from him. It was simple fact. They were all titled, and he was not. He was, in fact, that worst of things (from the *ton's* point of view), a Cit – a merchant, one tainted by dirtying his hands with trade. No matter that it had made him wealthier than most of them, no matter that they craved the luxuries he imported, he was, to the *ton*, to be disdained for his lower class existence.

How could his friends ever overcome that? He would not wish them shunned by their peers for associating with him. Yet he missed them sorely. Better to travel the world alone, than to live here in luxury, so close, yet never able to see them.

"That will do for today, Manning. Your work is excellent, as usual. Make sure that the Captain of the Morton Venture receives a suitable bonus – he has done far better than I expected with this cargo."

Manning blinked in some surprise, for they were barely half way through the review of the ledgers, then nodded, closed the books, and left the office.

~~~~~

Two hours later, Raphael was still sitting there, thinking. He had reached the rather depressing conclusion that there was no easy answer to his boredom, or to his sense of being trapped. Perhaps it might be more bearable if he had something new and different to do, some new venture?

At least then he could sink himself into the planning, into bringing something new to life, and making it profitable. But what? He had warehouses full of exotic materials, objects, spices and other things – was there some new way that he could use them, something new he could create, that could be cleverly brought to the attention of the most influential of the *ton*, or perhaps even the Prince Regent? Raphael knew that, for something new to become a profitable venture, it would have to draw the attention of those with money to spend.

The idea took hold, it was a puzzle to be solved – what new thing could he create, using goods that he already had, which could take the fashionable people by storm, and make him even wealthier? (not that he cared about the money, he had enough – it was the challenge that mattered...)

He spent the next few days stalking through his warehouses, looking at everything, terrifying his managers and warehouse labourers, who were certain that he must be seeking evidence of wrongdoing on their part. He could feel an idea, an insight, at the edge of his thoughts – but it refused to surface. He went home to toss and turn in restless sleep, dreaming of exotic oddities.

~~~~~

With Mrs Johnson's dress completed and delivered, Serafine took a little of the money that she had been paid, and went to the market. She would add some more food to their supplies while she could, and getting out and walking felt good, after the last few days of sitting and sewing.

At the little shop on the corner she stopped, looking at the items in the window again. Surprised at what she saw, she considered a moment, then turned and entered the shop.

"What can I do for you, Miss?"

The shopkeeper looked at her, obviously assessing her possible wealth from her clothes.

"In the window – those little... favours? I noticed them the other day, and meant to come in earlier – I particularly liked the heart shaped one, but I can't see it now – has it been sold?"

"Oh yes Miss, you've got to be quick to get a nice one of those – they sell all the time, any that I get. The young gents are always looking for tokens to give the girls they're courting. The heart shaped ones go fastest – seems they like it to be obvious what they mean when they put it in the girl's hands. Don't often get a young lady asking about them though."

Serafine thought for a moment, as the shopkeeper waited, his expression curious.

"Where do they come from? I mean, who do you buy them from?"

"Well Miss, it's not always the same. Used to be my old mother made some for me, but she's gone to God now, and m'wife don't like to sew fiddly things. So now it's only when someone brings some in, that they want to sell, that I can get any. Pity, because there's always those as wants to buy 'em."

"How much do you sell them for?"

Serafine waited for the answer, almost holding her breath.

When the shopkeeper, after some time thinking, named a figure, she was pleasantly surprised, even though she suspected he might have inflated the number, because he thought she looked like she could afford more. That idea almost brought a bubble of bitter laughter to her, but she repressed it. An idea was forming – maybe there was a way for her to earn more, to keep them surviving a bit longer.

"What if I had some to sell you? New ones, heart shaped ones with pretty beads or ribbons, not just lace?"

The shopkeeper's eyes narrowed with avarice, and Serafine knew, instantly, that her instinct was right – this *was* a way to earn more.

"Likely I'd be interested in buying… if the price was right…"

Twenty minutes of haggling later, Serafine left the shop, with a bounce in her step that hadn't been there for a long time. They had agreed that she would bring him three as a sample, in a few days' time. For those, he would give her about half of the price he normally sold them for. If they sold well, he would buy more – and give her a better percentage of the price, especially if she made things that he could sell for a higher price to begin with. By her calculations, she could earn as much from making four or five of the pretty little favours as she could from embellishing a dress – and she would need to use less materials to do so. After a quiet luncheon with her mother, who declared it far too cold to go out, and wanted only to huddle by the fire and read, Serafine went out again – to buy beads and lace, and some heavy paper. It was time to get to work.

~~~~~

Some hours later, tired but satisfied, she carefully put away the collection of beads, laces and little paste gems that she had bought – the amount it had cost her, even buying mismatched and second-hand (for small favours did not need many beads, unlike dresses!), worried her, for it had taken far more of their money than she was comfortable with, but there really was no choice – she had to earn money somehow, and that meant spending some first.

If these did well, though, she would need to find another source of materials – both to get better quality, and because, with today's purchases, she had quite exhausted the supply from the places she usually shopped.

Chapter Three

Christmas Day arrived with a deep fall of snow overnight, after which the day dawned clear and beautiful, the winter sun making the icicles on the trees and eaves sparkle like decorations. For Seraphine and her mother, it was a day of sadness – their second Christmas since '*the fall*' - and now they were considerably poorer than they had been for the first one. They missed James, her brother – for no matter how much Serafine might curse what he had done, he was still her brother – and his absence hurt.

There was enough coal to warm one room of the house – it had to be enough. And, taking Serafine completely by surprise, Mrs Johnson, and two of the other ladies whose dresses she sewed, had sent their servants to her door bearing a hamper of Christmas food and a bottle of good wine. The simple kindness had brought her to tears.

Between that, and the success of her first few favours, the money would last a little longer, and that was, at least, something to be grateful for.

Curled by the fire, Serafine was thinking about favours. The first few that she had made were Christmassy – in the hope that young men might buy them to give to their sweethearts for the Holiday. She had tried, as much as possible with the cheap materials, to make them look expensive, to make them look like the sort of thing that a member of the *ton* would not be ashamed to give.

It seemed that she had succeeded, for Mr Tanner at the shop had been impressed, and she was sure that he had sold them for even more than he had originally thought he might. She had seen his eyes narrow with avarice again, when she unwrapped them from the box she had brought them in. She might have pushed for more than he had paid her, but she was grateful for what she received – and anyway, if she wanted him to buy more, it was best not to make that too hard for him.

She had gone back two days later to see if any of them had sold, and been startled to discover that they all had – and that he would like more, as soon as she could make them. So she had. And now she had used up almost all of the materials she had bought. The money from those favours would, with care, keep them in coal until the weather got a little warmer. But she would need to make more – Mrs Johnson and her friends only had so many dresses in need of work, and there was nothing else to provide an income.

So she stared into the flames and worried. She worried about what sort of favours she should make next – what holidays or events might there be, that would encourage people to buy favours for their mistresses or for the girls that they courted?

And even more, she worried about where she would get some more suitable materials, without having to use money

14

that they would need for food. Whatever else happened, she would not see her mother starve, after all that they had been through. She dreamed of the sort of shop that she used to buy her ribbons and gloves and bonnets from, before, when she was a Lady, when she had money and no idea of what it was to be poor, or reviled. Oh to have even a tiny bit of the sort of ribbons and lace that could be bought in such a shop!

As her eyes drifted shut in the quiet room, a tiny thought floated through her mind, just before sleep took her:- *'where did those shops get their stock from?'*

~~~~~

For Raphael, Christmas was also strange – there was the joy of actually being there to celebrate it with his mother, sister, and brother, yet the sadness of his father's empty chair. He missed his father with an intensity that had caught him off guard – and he deeply regretted that war had taken him away, when the business had grown so astoundingly in his father's talented care. There was so much that he might have learnt, had he been at his father's side.

There was also the truly odd feeling of not even knowing exactly where the other Hounds were. After more than four years together at war, their tight knit band of specialists, called 'His Majesty's Hounds' by most of the rest of their troops, for their uncanny ability to find and deal with French spies, and to predict French troop movements, they had become almost more family than his family.

Christmas without them seemed somehow wrong, somehow a betrayal of the bond between them.

He felt cast adrift, trying to be a serious merchant, running what had become a vast empire of trade, yet totally unsure of his own place in the world, now that he had to deal with the rules of society. Over the last few weeks, since the day when he had realised just how bored he was, he had repeatedly thought about his wish to travel – and the complete impossibility of doing so. And the puzzle that he had set himself that day, of finding something new to sell, some new way to leverage what he had, still nagged at him. He had no answer. He would find one yet.

"Raphael's not listening, Mother. I don't think he heard any of what I just said!" Isabella's voice was somewhere between teasing and petulant, for, after so long of not having Raphael there, she could not truly be angry with him.

Raphael realised, with a start, that he had, indeed been wool-gathering – had been drifting off into his puzzle, oblivious to the conversation around him.

"I wasn't completely ignoring you, Bella. I do know that you were talking about dresses and Balls, and eligible young men, and bemoaning the fact that we are not of the aristocracy, so that you will not be invited to any of the truly fashionable events." The fact that he could not remember anything of exactly what she had said did not prevent his summary from being accurate. She turned her huge dark eyes upon him and proceeded to look like a hurt puppy.

"Well, it isn't fair! We can afford dresses and jewellery just as beautiful as theirs – why should not being titled matter?"

His sister had an alarmingly revolutionary attitude to some things, he thought with chagrin. Whilst he could rather sympathise with her sentiment, that attitude could make her life somewhat difficult, given the oh so rigid rules of society.

16

Gabriel was uninterested in his sister's complaints – at 16, he was just growing into himself, with the shape of the handsome man just beginning to emerge from the boy. He was, however, most interested in doing justice to the remarkable Christmas Feast that their chef had produced. Raphael watched him with affection, and prayed that Gabriel need never go to war, need never see any of the things that he had seen, need never know the terrible things that men could do to each other. He hoped that Gabriel would join him in running the business – but that was at least two years off, for he would have the best education possible before then.

Isabella was speaking again, and he had missed part of the conversation... again.

"...quite beautiful – so intricately worked – a little heart, with ribbon and lace and little bells and holly berries on it. It must mean that he truly cares for me, mustn't it, mother?"

What on earth was she talking about? Raphael wondered, as the conversation continued.

"Now my dear, perhaps he does have a *tendre* for you... or perhaps he simply wishes to outdo your other admirers..." Their mother's voice was filled with affection and amusement and she watched her daughter consider that comment.

"No, no, he must really care. You don't understand – I will have to show you!"

Completely ignoring any sort of ladylike behaviour, Isabella rose and ran from the room, to return a few minutes later, with something cradled in her hands.

"You see?"

She deposited it on the table for them to examine.

Raphael, curious, scooped it up. It was a piece of heavy, parchment like paper, folded in two so that a message could be written inside, and decorated on the outside with lace, ribbon and gems (which were almost certainly paste), with tiny paste holly berries in a cluster, and two even smaller dangling bells. The whole thing was cut to a heart shape. It was, he had to agree, charming. He had seen things like this before, on the occasion of Saint Valentine's Day, and at other times attached to bouquets and gifts. This was both more elaborate and, strangely, more elegant than any he had seen before.

Just as he went to open it, and see just what message had been written for Bella, she snatched it from his grasp.

"Oh no – that message is for me, it's private. You can't read it!"

"As you wish." Raphael made great show of turning away and becoming uninterested, which only made Isabella make a little huff of expelled breath in exasperation. Tilting her nose up, she turned away.

"I think I shall remove myself to the parlour." He watched her leave the room with a fond smile. But the image of that exquisitely wrought little piece of frivolity stuck in his mind. Why did it seem significant?

Chapter Four

Within a few days, the pristine white snow of Christmas morning had turned to half melted muddy piles of icy slush on London's busy streets. People ventured on their way with care, in boots or with pattens on their feet if they could afford it. Serafine set out that morning in her best remaining winter dress, with the pelisse that was still mostly respectable over it. She had woken from her nap on Christmas Day with the memory of that passing thought.

And now she felt compelled to investigate – *where did the shops that sold pretty trifles to the nobility buy their goods?*

She went back towards the more fashionable parts of the city, back towards her past... She sought out the shops that were close to, but not on, the most fashionable streets. Shops that would have been beneath her... before... And therefore, shops where she would not be recognised. She could not bear to face the cut direct from those she had once called friends – she would not allow herself to risk that again.

At least she must have managed to look like a Lady should, for a scruffy crossing sweeper leapt out to sweep the snow and detritus from her path as she crossed the street. She tossed him the smallest coin she had – she could ill afford to, yet she would not see anyone starve – not now that she knew the feel of true hunger herself.

She received a few curious looks – a young gentlewoman out without a maid beside her - but she ignored them. Just ahead was exactly the sort of shop she was seeking.

Inside, the shop was small, yet full of many beautiful things. An older woman, well dressed, yet in garments some years out of fashion, was seated behind a small counter. She rose as Serafine entered.

"Good day to you, my Lady, what may I help you with today?"

Serafine almost laughed – it was so long since anyone had called her 'my Lady' that it almost sounded wrong. She looked around, and wandered through the shop, drawn from display to display, with so many beautiful items to explore.

"I am not sure – I would like to simply look for a little – to see what appeals to me most."

"Certainly, my Lady, do ask me if you wish to know about anything, or see anything else." The woman sat again, quietly waiting, and watched her every move.

In the back corner of the shop, jumbled in a little basket on a shelf, she found a collection of scraps of lace, short pieces of ribbon, broken pieces of paste jewellery, little feathers, and other interesting things. She took it to the counter.

The old woman looked at her in surprise, but waited for her

to speak.

"This basket of things – how much? I know it may seem strange, but I like to make small things, for my friend's children's dolls, and other little things – all of these pieces are interesting, and I can use tiny amounts like this."

The woman smiled at her, seeming to find the explanation reasonable – for many ladies of the nobility amused themselves with charitable works and most embroidered or sewed small trifles. Waiting for the answer, Serafine ran her fingers through the tangle of items – some pieces were unusual – in colour or texture, or in the shape of small silver or carved stone beads.

"Where do these come from?" She hoped that her question sounded casual enough.

The woman looked at her again, and named a price for the little basket – a remarkably reasonable price, considering the location of the shop. As Serafine produced the money to pay, the woman went on, finally getting to the answer that Serafine really wanted.

"Where do they come from? Things come from all over the world, from India and beyond – China and the East Indies, from Africa, from many places – sometimes materials are brought here, and made into things here, sometimes they are imported complete. The merchant companies get very wealthy finding exotic trinkets to keep the *ton* happy. I buy things from only the better importers – I like to sell quality to the quality!"

She gave a small laugh at her own words, and Serafine joined her.

"I've never thought about it before, but when I saw all of these things, and touched them, I couldn't help but wonder." She smiled at the woman, hoping that she might say more.

"You'd be a rare one to think about it. Most of the young Ladies I sell pretty things to don't care where they come from. There're some good merchants now. Now that the war's over, more goods can get here, shipping's safer, they tell me. The good ones even charge a bit less, now there's less risk in their business. For those who've got a taste for the exotic or the unusual, and good quality, I buy from Morton Empire Imports. That's a sad tale though. Old Mr Morton, God rest his soul, the poor man died before his son got home from war – such a sorry thing!"

It seemed that Serafine had unleashed a flood of words. Perhaps the woman rarely had anyone to talk to – anyone who had the slightest interest in her business or her life, that is.

"There's other companies, but Morton is the best of the bunch – never had a faulty shipment from them, not once!"

After letting the woman ramble on for another twenty minutes, Serafine finally extracted herself from the shop, her purchases in hand, and took herself home. Now she not only had some more materials to work with, but a name. What if she could buy materials direct from the importer? Surely that would be cheaper, or at least better quality for the same amount of money. She would have to find out where this Morton Empire Imports had its office.

~~~~~

A few days later, when Serafine delivered the next batch of favours to Mr Tanner's shop, he greeted her with great enthusiasm.

"Good day to you Miss, I do hope that you've got some more of your excellent work for me?"

That was more flattery than usual from him – she wondered why.

She didn't have to wonder long – he could hardly contain himself.

"Those last few – the Christmas heart ones – I sold the smallest of them to young Jemmy – works as a groom at the Arbuthnot place – they're the second wealthiest merchants around, don't you know. You'll never guess what happened next! Mr Arbuthnot – Porter his name is, he's the son of the house – saw it, and he liked it so much he actually came here, to buy one for the girl he's sweet on. Now that's the sort of customer I like! He bought the biggest one – that nice one with the little bells - didn't even blink at the price." Mr Tanner was so excited at the idea of such a wealthy customer that he was almost rubbing his hands together with glee. "The wealthy merchants' sons, they're always trying to outdo one another – all except Mr Morton that is – he has no need to outdo anyone, he's the wealthiest of the lot. If any of the others hear of this, they'll likely come looking to buy something similar – so I hope you've got some quality work for me."

Silently, Serafine placed her basket on the counter, and lifted out her latest work.

There were 5 favours, each unique, some heart shaped, some not, made using a mixture of ordinary ribbon and lace, and some of the unusual bits and pieces she'd bought from the fashionable shop.

"I think that these would please the most exacting customer. I will have to ask you for a slightly higher price for these, Mr Tanner – for the materials are a bit more expensive – but if you want to tempt the wealthy, the items have to be of a suitable quality."

She waited, outwardly looking calm, serene, but inwardly terrified that he would refuse to pay extra. He looked closely at the favours, obviously wanting them, unconsciously narrowing his eyes in that characteristic expression of avarice. Eventually he looked up.

"I do agree Miss, things need to be obvious quality to sell to the better class of customer. I like these – I'll give you a better price."

Serafine nearly sagged from relief. And so the haggling commenced – for Mr Tanner couldn't agree to anything without some haggling. When they were done, Serafine was happy, for she had secured his agreement to a standard price twenty percent higher than that which he had paid for her previous work. Mr Tanner looked happy too – so she suspected that she could have pushed him for more, and succeeded. But haggling was exhausting – at least they were both happy with this outcome.

Now that she could stop worrying about the money, something of what he had said earlier came back to Serafine.

Surely that richest merchant family he had mentioned – Morton wasn't it? Surely she'd heard that name recently? Then it came to her, a clear little bubble of memory in her mind. The old woman in the other shop – she'd said she bought from Morton Empire Imports – it had to be owned by the family Mr Tanner spoke of, for the chances of two wealthy merchant families of the same name were low. Taking a deep breath, she spoke as casually as she could.

"This Mr Morton you mentioned – the wealthiest merchant? What does his business do, that they are so wealthy?"

Mr Tanner was always happy to show off his knowledge of

everyone and everything, and especially when he could make himself look important by association. He puffed his chest up with that supposed importance, and launched into a long, gossipy explanation.

By the time he was done, Serafine knew all about the last two generations of Mortons, about how sad it was that the old man had died before his son Raphael returned from the war, how the son was a war hero, even if he didn't speak of it, how the mother was Italian, and her three children all strikingly good looking as a result, how young Mr Arbuthnot was sweet on Miss Isabella Morton, but Mr Tanner doubted he stood a real chance there, and she had also been treated to what seemed an exhaustive list of the sort of products that the firm imported, from the far reaches of the empire and beyond.

Her face and neck were aching from nodding and smiling as he talked and Serafine thought, with wry amusement, that she seemed to have developed rather a talent for gossiping with shopkeepers.

Taking advantage of a break in his conversation, she thanked him, and, escaped into the cold afternoon.

She was now absolutely certain that she needed to seek out the offices of Morton Empire Imports as soon as possible.

ARIETTA RICHMOND

Chapter Five

Raphael rode through the streets, observing as the morning bustle gave way to quiet, the closer he came to Hyde Park. The *ton* did not rise early, unlike the merchants, even the wealthy merchants, who lived nearer his home. He felt the need to let his horse stretch out and shed its excess energy, to feel the wind on his face, to be moving.

His head was full of cobwebs and an ache that came from imbibing a little too much, yet he was happy – happier than he had been for many weeks. The previous evening he had, for the first time since their return, spent time with the rest of the Hounds, who were, with the start of the Season approaching, all in town. It had been wonderful – not just to see them, to feel at home again, in a way that he had deeply missed, but also because it had gone a long way to assuaging his fear of losing them.

He was still very cynical about their ability to continue to associate with him, as, should the *ton* become aware of it, they would most certainly show their disapproval pointedly.

But for now, all was well. He reached the park, and gave Foxfire his head. The rush of fresh air blew the last of the effects of the drink away, and the day was beautiful as the soft winter sun lit the frosted grass and trees in a sparkling glitter.

Two hours later, relaxed, and refreshed, he turned to make his way home, ready to tackle the day. He was preoccupied as he rode, still worrying at the challenge he had set himself before Christmas, to find a new project, which would leverage his existing stock, yet be unusual and attractive to the wealthy. It was proving a much bigger challenge than he had expected.

As he reached the Grosvenor gate, he was startled to see, perched on the high seat of a fashionable phaeton, his sister. She was laughing in delight as the young man beside her drove in through the gate at a rather indecorous pace. Who was Isabella with? He had not known that she intended to go out, and an early drive with a young man, with no more chaperonage than a very young looking tiger, who clung with some desperation to the back of the speeding vehicle, was not the sort of behaviour that he expected from her. He would not want her thought fast.

As they came closer, he realised that he knew the young man – it was, surprisingly, Porter Arbuthnot. His family had not been on good terms with the Arbuthnots for many years – not since his father's skilled handing of the business had brought them to wealth and prominence, quite eclipsing the Arbuthnots, who had, hitherto, been acclaimed as the wealthiest of merchants.

He wondered, as he moved aside, unnoticed by Bella and Arbuthnot, if this had been going on for any length of time.

Was Porter Arbuthnot courting Bella, seriously? Or was this merely an amusement to him? Or worse, some attempt at disadvantaging his family through disgracing his sister, in revenge for their mercantile success?

Raphael turned his horse, and followed them, at a distance, keeping amongst the trees and out on the grass, simply watching. After a half hour or so, they turned back, and Raphael, relieved, followed as they proceeded, at a more sedate pace, through the streets towards his home. He had half expected them to stop in the park, and descend to walk in some secluded spot – which he could not have allowed.

As Arbuthnot deposited Bella at the front door of their home, Raphael slipped quietly into the lane at the rear, and delivered Foxfire to his groom. Striding into the house, he was in time to catch Bella still in the Hall, as she removed her fur pelisse and scarf.

"Is that the first time that young Arbuthnot has taken you for a drive?"

Bella startled, her cheeks flushing a charming pink, which could charitably have been attributed to the cold wind outside, but which, to Raphael, more resembled guilt than anything else.

"N.. nnooo. It was the third time."

Her voice had that edge of defiance that he recognised from many moments in her childhood. Her chin came up, and he could see that she was waiting for a reprimand. Intentionally choosing to disconcert her, he smiled genially.

"I would prefer, in future, that you have a maid with you, should you grant a gentleman the honour of taking you for a drive in the park. I would not have you thought fast, or your reputation called into question."

Obviously surprised, and expecting more, she glared at him for a moment.

"Yes Raphael, if you so insist."

It was too easy an acquiescence.

"Is he courting you? And do you wish it so?"

Bella flushed again, before half shaking her head. She answered with the honesty that was the essence of her, which endeared her to him more.

"I do not truly know. He is flattering, and amusing to be with. He flirts with me, but I am not sure that I would call it courting. I like it well enough, but… I am not sure if I wish it to become more."

Raphael did not allow his face to show the relief that he felt. A sudden insight made him ask, "Was it he who gave you that pretty Christmas favour?"

Bella nodded, blushing again, and said nothing more.

"Be careful Bella – best that you discover his true intentions before things go any further. After all, our families have been on less than friendly terms, ever since father began to do better than they, in business – it seems odd that he should be so friendly now.

She nodded again, and fled to her room to think.

Raphael went in search of a light meal, before turning his attention to the business of the day. Pensively, he considered the conversation with Bella, and, unbidden, the image of that Christmas favour rose in his mind again. He remembered her delight at receiving it, and their mother's admiration for its prettiness, as well as his own recognition, at the time, of the quality of its design.

Now there was a simple thing, which could yet be made in many different designs, which might interest the *ton*, as easily as it did his sister – so long as the quality of materials and manufacture was high enough. For the *ton* loved fripperies and extravagant gestures... the thought led to the very beginning of an idea.

~~~~~

Serafine took a deep breath and pushed open the door, causing a bell attached to it to ring. Inside was a small seating area, and a counter, off to one side. Behind the counter, in an exquisitely constructed glass fronted case, were samples of fabrics, beads, feathers, and a range of other items. As she stood there, feeling nervous and unsure, the door to one side of the counter opened, and two men entered.

The first appeared to be a clerk, well-dressed but ordinary. The second was another thing entirely. They were mid conversation as they entered, but stopped immediately upon noticing her presence. The second man turned towards her, taking her in with a single pass of his dark eyes, and she felt suddenly unable to breath, a flush of heat rushing through her entire body.

He was tall, lean, and elegant, moving with the fluid economy that spoke of skill with weapons and military experience. His hair was dark, and his skin tanned as if from long exposure to the sun.

She thought that he looked somehow foreign, just a little – perhaps Italian? This must be Mr Morton - hadn't Mr Tanner said his mother was Italian?

She had never seen a man so handsome, so understated in his dress and manner, yet so utterly sure of himself.

He looked like he would have been completely at home in the ballrooms of the *ton* – yet, if he was here, and so obviously in a position of authority, if he was *the* Mr Morton, then he could not be of the nobility.

He waited, eyebrow raised, while she stood there, stunned to silence. When it became obvious that she was not about to speak, he approached her and asked, "Can I help you my Lady?"

She felt a ridiculous sense of relief, that she still looked enough of a Lady for him to grant her that status of address immediately. Would he still think her a Lady when she asked the questions she had come to ask?

"I hope so, Mr....?"

"Mr Raphael Morton, at your service, my Lady."

He swept a courtly bow over her hand, his eyes sparkling with some amusement.

"Welcome to Morton Empire Imports – how can we assist you today?"

Serafine's heart beat harder – she had not imagined the owner of such a large merchant business to be so young and good looking – somehow, she always expected successful merchants to be old, and bent from poring over ledgers.

"I... I would like to ask some questions about the materials that you import – to see if they may be suitable for a project of mine." Sera watched his reaction, hardly daring to breathe.

This was obviously not quite what he had expected her to say, but, being both a consummate gentleman, and a clever merchant, he simply waved her to the seating area and turned to the clerk.

"Jenkins, if you would, some tea and biscuits for Lady.... "

He looked at her enquiringly.

"Lady Serafine Parkington." She managed, just, to keep her voice steady as she spoke, waiting for the condemnation to appear in his eyes – for surely a merchant as wealthy as he would be aware of the gossip of the *ton*, would know of her disgrace.

He simply nodded, and waved Mr Jenkins on his way. She let out the breath that she had not realised she was holding, and lowered herself to a chair, depositing her basket on the floor at her side. He turned back to her.

"So, Lady Serafine, tell me more about your project, ask your questions, and let us see if I can supply what you wish for."

Wickedly, her internal voice suggested that he could supply many things that she wished for, in her most secret thoughts. She pushed it away, and began.

"First, Mr Morton, I must make an admission that may shock you, coming from a well born Lady."

At her words he looked most interested, and raised that enquiring eyebrow once again, but said nothing, waiting for her to continue.

"I… create… things. It began as a hobby of sorts, some years ago, but, in more recent times, it has become more… commercial… in nature. My family are in rather… straightened… circumstances, and I have been forced to supplement our income in small ways."

She waited, again, for an expression of horror or disgust to cross his face – for Ladies were not expected to sully themselves with work. It did not appear. He simply nodded, and she had the most peculiar feeling that, even wealthy as he was, he truly understood what it was to be poor.

33

At that moment, Jenkins returned with the tea tray, and placed it on a small table before them. She was forced to wait until Jenkins had left, and tea had been poured. It felt strange to have a man pour tea for her, but this was his premises, after all. At last she could continue.

"I am finding that I need more materials for my creations – materials of a better quality than those I have been able to source to date. It seems that there is a demand for my work – but a demand for items of the best materials. I only need very small amounts, as the items I make are quite small, but the materials must be unusual and high quality. I purchased some offcuts and other items from a shop selling trifles to Ladies of Quality, and the proprietress informed me that she purchases such things from your business. Hence my visit."

In her need to get her explanation out, Serafine had quite forgotten to be nervous, somewhere in the middle of speaking – perhaps because he seemed so genuinely interested in what she had to say. There was something about him that made her feel respected, safe, in a way that she had not, since... *before*. He appeared to consider for a moment, then spoke, his voice warm and positive, wrapping around her softly.

"It certainly sounds as if I may be able to assist you – but to do so, I believe that I will need to see an example of these items that you create, to better understand your needs. For I must confess, at this point I am at a loss to guess what they might be."

As he said it, she felt like a complete goose – how had she managed all of that long-winded explanation, without ever actually telling him the core of it? She lifted her basket to her lap. Folding the cloth cover back, she lifted out the last of her most recently made favours, and, pushing aside the tea tray, laid them on the small table before them.

A small gasp escaped his lips, and he reached out a hand to lift one up and examine it, touching it as if it were some precious thing. She was not sure that her work deserved such reverence. Silently, she waited until he had completed his examination. When he looked to her again, his face was alight with what appeared to be excitement, with a smile that lit his eyes, and transformed him from merely handsome to utterly breath-taking.

"The perfect solution!" His exclamation confused her, and she waited for him to say more.

"Did you, perchance, make some of these just before Christmas, Lady Serafine? Including one with tiny holly berries and bells?"

She nodded, wondering how on earth he had seen it, when it had been purchased by that other merchant – Arbuthnot, if she remembered Mr Tanner's ramblings aright.

"Excellent! A hopeful swain gave it to my sister, and I was most impressed with its elegance and workmanship when I saw it. So was my mother, whose taste is quite beyond compare."

It was as if he had read her thoughts. She still could not fathom why he was so delighted, for surely the small amounts of materials that she might buy would be but the tiniest pittance compared to what most highborn Ladies might buy from him.

"Lady Serafine, I have a proposition for you." At the look of shock in her eyes, he gave a light laugh and continued, "A business proposition only, let me hasten to assure you, nothing of any impropriety, one which I most sincerely hope will be of monetary profit for both of us."

She found herself laughing with him, and a ridiculous, giddy bubble of hope was fluttering about in her chest. "Please, Mr Morton, you intrigue me – tell me more."

"I have been looking, this past month or more, for a new venture, a new way to use materials that I already have, or import often, to create something new to catch the interest of the *ton*. For the wealthy of Quality love to outdo each other with fripperies, and fads, and I would profit from that shallowness."

She nodded, fully understanding what he meant, for the outrageous fashions taken up by the *ton* had always both fascinated, and repelled, her even whilst she was one of them, and oblivious to how the world truly went on.

"Ever since I saw my sister's Christmas favour, it has niggled at the back of my mind – I felt it important, but did not know why. Now I do. For surely, this sort of thing, created with high quality materials and workmanship, and using exclusive, exotic imported materials would appeal to them. I need only gift a few select pieces to the current arbiters of fashion, or perhaps to the Prince Regent himself, and, should they like them, they will be all the rage overnight, and will be sent to young Ladies as often as hot-house flowers are."

Excitement shot through her, for this was her vision, multiplied tenfold. The thought that one day, a piece made by her hands, her, a shunned and disregarded member of society, might reach the hands of the Prince Regent was both satisfying and sublimely ridiculous. Still she must take care.

"That seems a wondrous concept, Mr Morton, yet... even with the best of materials, I can only make so many, for each takes some time. Should your vision come to pass, I could not keep up with such a demand."

Nervous again, she reached up from habit, tucking the escaped tendrils of her rich dark brown hair back. His eyes followed her movement, and she found herself caught in them. They simply looked at each other, until he broke the spell by speaking again.

"Ah, but I have a solution to that problem too."

Serafine was suddenly utterly conscious of everything around her, in fine detail – the colours of the fabrics on display, the subtle scent of oriental spices that pervaded the place, the pine and leather scent that could only be from Mr Morton himself, the muted sounds of movement in the back rooms of the shop. It was as if her future turned on this moment. She waited.

"It would be possible for you to teach others to make these, would it not?"

She nodded again.

"But... if I should do that, how would that make income for me?"

Perhaps her question sounded greedy, but she had to ask – her mother's survival, and her own, turned upon the answer.

"Because, Lady Serafine, you will not simply be a pair of hands to sew, you will be a business partner with me, and the business that you will own half of, will be a manufactory for these. I have a small building nearby that we can use, and we will employ poorer girls from hereabout, helping their families survive, and you will teach them how to make these to the exacting standards required for us to sell them to the *ton*. You will help me understand exactly how to make them something that the Ladies of the *ton* will crave – for of that world, you have much greater knowledge than I."

His eyes were alight with excitement again, and she found herself caught up in it, swept away by the scale of his idea. This was beyond all her imaginings.

There was only one thing that she could do.

"Yes, Mr Morton, I accept your business proposition."

"Wonderful! We will need to move fast, for I believe that our best opportunity to launch this endeavour approaches. In but a month, it will be St. Valentine's Day, and people of all classes will be giving love tokens to those they admire. Can you design some suitable favours, that girls could make, in time for us to have them on sale before then?"

He was sweeping her along, and she felt like a leaf on a torrent, caught in the enthusiasm of his ideas. It was terrifying and exhilarating at once.

"I will most certainly do my best – but there is much to be done, and for some of it, I have no idea where to start, for I find that the education of a gently reared Lady is sadly lacking in the area of setting up a manufactory."

He laughed, delighted at her gentle wit, and reached to take her hands.

"My Lady, I will have a contract drawn up, immediately, so that you can be assured of your security in this enterprise. And I will arrange staff to assist you. If you will return here tomorrow morning at 10, all will be ready – you will have the contract, your staff, and the building at your disposal." Stunned, she simply nodded, for the heat flowing through her from the touch of his hands quite fuddled her brain, his nearness leaving her more flustered than that of any man, ever before. He looked at her again, as if considering whether he should speak further. Then, apparently, he decided that he should. "I will understand should you be offended at what I am about to say, but I feel that I must say it, nonetheless."

The old dread curled in her – was she, after such a wonderful few minutes, about to meet the rejection again – had he, perchance, just remembered the scandal attached to her name?

"I sense, Lady Serafine, in what you said, and what you did not say, that your financial position is, at present, very difficult? I must commend you for your initiative in acting to change that, for many young women of the aristocracy would simply retreat into tears and depression, and starve."

She could do nothing but nod, again (he must be beginning to wonder if she had a weak neck, for she had been nodding stupidly through half of this conversation!). She was embarrassed at the truth of his words about her poverty, yet elated to find that he actually respected her for taking action. It was a novel experience for a man to regard her that way. When he continued, it was tentative, as if he expected her to push him away. Startled, she realised that he still held her hands.

"Lady Serafine, in recognition of the enormous effort that you have agreed to put in, over the next weeks, before our enterprise will begin to make sales, I wish to offer you an amount now – an amount that I regard as being fair compensation for the licensing of your idea and knowledge, for use in this business. Can you see your way to accept such a thing?"

She understood his concern, for a 'true Lady' would reject such apparent charity with scorn.

She was long past such scruples.

'Mr Morton, that is a more than generous offer, in the light of all that you have already agreed to do, and to contribute to this business. But, I am somewhat embarrassed to admit, you have assessed it correctly. My situation is somewhat dire. So, for my mother's sake, I will most gratefully accept your offer, in the spirit it is made."

"You, Lady Serafine, exhibit great courage and sense, as well as beauty. I cannot imagine a better person as a business partner!"

After a short further conversation, which she barely managed, so dazed was she by the fact that he spoke of her as beautiful, as she was about to turn and leave, he shook her hand, just as if she were another gentleman of business!

Then he drew forth a purse and handed it to her, saying quietly, "An advance, Lady Serafine – I will have a draft on my bank for you tomorrow, along with everything else. But I do not wish to see you in any difficulty. Please, take a hackney home, for your safety - it grows dark."

"Thank you." What more could she possibly say?

All the way home she replayed the afternoon in her mind, hugging it to her as if it might dissolve in the winter rain outside. But the purse was real, as was the scent of Mr Morton, which clung to her hands where he had held them, and seeped, dizzyingly, into her senses.

~~~~~

Raphael watched her leave, feeling at once bemused, confused, and more excited and alive than he had since arriving home from the war. She was a stunning woman – rich dark brown hair, thick and a little unruly, curling into tendrils from the winter damp, eyes that were almost golden, that seemed to glow from within when she was caught up in an idea, a figure that no worn and slightly outdated dress could hide, and lips that should, oh definitely should, be kissed.

And she was intelligent, resourceful, and loyal. It was a

40

seemingly impossible combination, but, improbable as it was, it existed. His friends might think him mad, but he had no doubts about the decisions he had just so impetuously made. He was quite, quite certain, with the instinct that had kept him alive in Spain, that she was everything she said she was, and that this would work.

And, he had to admit to himself, the thought of days with a woman like that, to create a new venture, was arousing – in more than one way – he would not at all object to spending time working with such a beautiful woman at his side.

Chapter Six

That night, Serafine slept better than she had for months. Her sleep was threaded through with dreams of Mr Raphael Morton, whose handsome face and compelling dark eyes seemed even more so in dreams. The purse he had handed her was under her pillow, and the subtle remnants of his personal scent which clung to it surrounded her.

The money it had contained was safely locked in her little metal box, along with the heart of lace which had begun all of this. She had been astonished, when, upon reaching home, she had dared to investigate just what the purse contained. More than thirty pounds! Enough to keep them, in their current excessively frugal lifestyle, for months! And this was his idea of a small 'advance' on what he intended to pay her for agreeing to join him in a business venture! A venture which would, later, also return her a share of the profits!

It all seemed too good to be true, yet she knew that it was true. She had never felt more certain of a man's honesty and good intentions in her life.

Her mother had been abed when she had returned, and she had not disturbed her. Now, as the weak morning sun shone through her somewhat grimy bedroom window, she rose and dressed, eager to tell her mother of the momentous events of the day before.

In their little breakfast room, they sat to a plain repast of bread, cheese and a little cold meat. Serafine ate, then, unable to wait any longer, she began.

"Mother, I have such news! Wonderful news. News which, it is my hope, will solve our precarious financial situation forever."

Her mother looked up, startled, and was overjoyed to see the light in her daughter's eyes, and the enthusiasm in her expression – neither of which had been present since her brother's death. As Serafine went on to explain, her mother's face showed at first doubt and uncertainty, but swiftly moved to a hope equal to Serafine's. When Sera spoke of the funds already received, her mother's amazement and relief were obvious, although deeply coloured by embarrassment at having their severe financial straits known.

"This Mr Morton sounds a positive paragon – you are quite certain that he is being honest with you? That he will not try to take advantage of you in... inappropriate ways?"

"Quite certain – he is everything a gentleman should be – much more so than many of those young rakes and fops of the *ton*, who panted after me, then were the first to turn away."

"I would meet him. Might I accompany you this morning, to see that all is in order, and set my mind at ease?"

Serafine was most glad of her mother's interest – it had been many months since her mother had set foot outside their house, her depression had been so deep.

"Why certainly mother, if you will not be embarrassed to be seen about without a maid to accompany us."

"As we have no maid, I will have to be content, will I not? You have seemed to do well enough in these circumstances Sera, much though such things might once have horrified me."

Both smiling, they rose from the table and went to prepare for the day.

~~~~~

From the moment she had walked out his door, Raphael had swept into action, summoning his man of business to draw up the contract, arranging staff to be allocated to support of this new project, and sending Jenkins to arrange a cleaning of the building they would use, which had recently come into his possession as payment of a debt from a Lord who was financially embarrassed at present, but whose wife had spent rather excessively on the silks that Raphael imported.

He fell into a deep sleep, late in the night, and woke with the dawn, feeling full of energy. For the first time since his return, there was no trace of boredom in his thoughts. After Garrett had assisted him with dressing (a situation he still found peculiar after years at war, looking after himself), and he had broken his fast, he gathered up his hat and gloves, and slipped on his caped winter coat.

As he turned to the door, Bella came down the stairs, just beginning her day. He went to her and took her hand a moment.

"Bella, dear sister, I must thank you."

She looked at him, startled at this pronouncement.

45

"You see, dear sister, that pretty Christmas favour you showed me, it has given me a new business idea, which I hope to find most profitable. I shall tell you more this evening, but for now, my thanks."

He swept on his way before she could do anything but smile. It was typical of Raphael, she thought, to leave her with a tiny bit of information, and expect her to wait all day to hear more!

~~~~~

At precisely the hour of ten, the door to Morton Empire Imports opened, and Lady Serafine entered, followed, Raphael was surprised to see, by an older woman. A woman who could only be her mother, he thought, for the resemblance was clear. The older woman's hair was streaked with some grey, but was still thick and shining, and the sharp lines of her high cheekbones were a clear echo of the softer lines of Lady Serafine's face.

Raphael bowed over their hands.

"Lady Serafine. And this is...?'

"My mother, the Dowager Lady Galwood."

For a moment, as she spoke, fear flickered across Serafine's face, and that of her mother also. More than a year of being treated to the cut direct, as soon as people discovered who they were, had left its mark. Raphael wondered at the fleeting expression, but let that go to think about later.

"Delighted, my Lady. I am Mr Raphael Morton, owner of Morton Empire Imports. Your daughter is most talented and enterprising. I count myself fortunate to have found such a person to be my partner in this business venture."

He waved them to the seating area.

"Please be seated, I will have everything brought momentarily. Might I offer you some refreshment? Some tea, perhaps?"

"Thank you, Mr Morton." Lady Galwood was, suddenly, the elegant aristocratic woman that Sera remembered, rather than the shadow that she had lived with for the last year.

By the time another hour had passed, Serafine was in possession of a signed contract, making her the half owner of a new business, to be called Parkmorton Gifts, a signed bank draft for a remarkable amount of money, a business manager in the form of Mr Jenkins, who had agreed to take on this new challenge, a housekeeper in the form of Mrs Jenkins, who would assist with hiring domestic staff, as well as finding girls to employ in the manufactory, as she was well known in the surrounding area, and an assistant, a Miss Emily Nunn, who would help with identifying suitable materials from the vast stores of exotic items in Morton Empire Imports warehouses.

Once again, she felt like a leaf tossed on the torrent.

It was wonderful, exhilarating and positively the most frightening experience of her life. Her mother appeared to feel the same way, as she watched all of this happen with amazement.

There followed a visit to their new building, which was only a few blocks away, where Sera could barely contain her excitement – for it was large, larger than she had ever imagined, and, whilst still being cleaned after some time unused, was most suitable, with rooms for offices, sitting rooms for meetings, a tidy kitchen, storerooms, and a selection of large rooms with excellent windows where the light would be suitable for girls to sit and do the fine sewing necessary.

There was also a small stable at the rear, where the yard opened onto a lane between the buildings. And... the stable contained a small town carriage, two horses, and a cheerful groom/coachman named Alf. Mr Morton casually informed Sera that they were for her use – she was now an important merchant, and should look the part, apparently.

At the end of the visit, when Mrs Jenkins had arrived and been introduced, Alf drove Lady Galwood and Mrs Jenkins back to Sera's home, to begin on the hiring of staff and the planning there, and Sera returned to Morton Empire Imports office with Mr Morton, and Mr Jenkins, to begin planning in earnest.

By evening she was elated, and exhausted, and still only just beginning to believe that this was real. The sense of unreality was heightened when she reached home (driven by Alf!) and a footman opened the door for her.

Mrs Jenkins greeted her in the hall, and introduced the shy looking young girl standing behind her as, "Polly, your new maid, my Lady."

As she dropped into sleep that night, the thought drifted through her mind that it was incongruous, and rather amusing, that the thing that should give her back something almost like her old life was to 'sully her hands with trade' – that idea most reviled by the nobility. After a year of barely surviving, she would take practical and comfortable over poverty and ridiculous concepts of noble behaviour every time.

~~~~~

Over dinner that evening, Raphael had, as promised,

explained his new venture to Bella, and the rest of his family. His mother thought it an excessively clever idea, and praised his astuteness in capturing Lady Serafine's skills before anyone else saw the potential. Gabriel thought it boring – girls sewing fripperies held no interest for him – he would rather listen to the sea captain's tales of exotic lands.

Bella thought it wonderful, and romantic, that making love tokens should transform the life of a woman fallen on difficult times, as well as make what should be the coup, for their own business, of starting a new fashion. Perhaps she would tell Porter Arbuthnot what a wonderful chain of events his gift of the favour had set in motion.

She was still unsure how she felt about him, but she had agreed to another drive tomorrow, albeit insisting that it be in a vehicle where Liza, her maid, could accompany them.

Indulging in a quiet glass of port with his mother, after the meal was done, Raphael was surprised when she spoke, breaking into his thoughts of business.

"Raphael, Lady Serafine... you said that her mother is the Dowager Lady Galwood?"

"Yes, that was the name." He wondered where this conversation was going.

"I seem to remember something about that name. From more than a year ago, whilst you were still at war. Before your father..."

Her voice caught, for she still missed her husband fiercely, although she rarely let that show. He waited, sipping his port, letting the stresses of the hectic day slide away, as she paused, seemingly sifting through memories. Eventually, she spoke again.

"I remember now. There was a scandal, young Viscount Galwood, that would be Lady Serafine's brother, killed himself. Gambling debts, I believe. He had gambled away everything not entailed, and left his family ruined, so he took the coward's way out and killed himself. His mother and sister were cut dead by the *ton*, for the scandal of having a suicide in the family, and the title went to some distant cousin. That would explain their straightened circumstances, and her need to create an income."

"Whilst I cannot see that suicide should ever be a choice for a man of any class with any honour, I also cannot see why the *ton* must cast aside the family of such a man. Surely they suffer enough in losing him, without needing disgrace added to that."

"Raphael, I must agree with that sentiment. The poor women, this last year must have been hell. It does, however, amaze me that this Lady Serafine has the vision and the courage to have even considered working, and going into business – for most members of the *ton* would surely actually starve before they did so!"

"She is, indeed, most unusual." As Raphael spoke, the image of her rose in his mind, as she had been that morning, flushed, excited at what they had begun, golden eyes alight, rich dark hair escaping its pins to lie in tendrils around her face, and full of intelligent questions. She was beautiful in an unconventional kind of way, for he found that her beauty came as much from her keen intelligence as from her fairness of form.

He also remembered, in that instant, the fleeting expression that had crossed both Lady Serafine's and her mother's countenance – could it have been fear? Did they fear that he would act as the *ton* did, and reject them for the actions of her brother, actions over which they, personally, would have had no influence whatsoever?

With him, they had no need for fear, he would never behave that way. But... he wondered, how the other Hounds would respond? They were of the *ton* (although Gerald had only recently risen to such high estate), would they reject her? Or see it as he did? It was the first time that he had ever had to consider a situation where their opinions might be so divided. He did not like the possibility at all.

"Thank you for the information, Mother, I will bear that in mind as we proceed with this."

Soon after, he took himself to bed, to dream of golden eyes and hair the colour of rich mahogany timber from the East Indies.

ARIETTA RICHMOND

Chapter Seven

Two days later, whilst Serafine and Raphael were immersed in a whirlwind of arranging the manufactory, hiring girls, choosing materials, and starting to teach them how to make the favours, Isabella was nervously awaiting the arrival of Mr Porter Arbuthnot, her maid, Liza, standing patiently by her side.

When she saw, peering through the curtains of the front parlour, the small but elegant open carriage draw up outside, Isabella breathed a sigh of relief – she hated waiting... for anything.

A moment later, there was a knock on the door, and the footman ushered Mr Arbuthnot in.

"Miss Isabella, you are beautiful as always." He took her hand, and performed an exaggerated bow, his lips barely brushing her glove. Liza stifled a giggle. Isabella glared at her, sidelong.

"Why thank you sir!"

He offered her his arm, and led her out to the carriage, Liza dutifully following. Once they reached the park, and he could take some of his attention from the task of avoiding collisions, he asked her how she had been, declaring that he had missed her terribly since they had last met. Isabella blushed, not entirely convinced, but certainly flattered.

"Why Mr Arbuthnot, I believe you are gulling me. For, surely, your duties in your father's business must occupy your thoughts the majority of the time?"

"Ah Miss Isabella, nothing can completely distract me from thoughts of you." She was beginning to find his approach rather overdone, now that she considered it. Still, perhaps he was sincere.

"Well... I have mostly been rather bored, for it has been a little too cold for my liking, to walk, or even to visit my friends. Still, I do have one bit of news that may please you. You remember, I am sure, that delightful Christmas favour you gave me?"

He looked at her, puzzled by this turn in the conversation, and nodded.

"Well, it was so beautiful that I showed it to my family at the time. My mother, and my brother, both thought it most elegant and well made – a very nice sentiment. And now I find that it has inspired my brother to a new enterprise. He plans to arrange the making of such things, to sell through our business! Your romantic gesture has resulted in good fortune for us, and for a Lady who has agreed to assist with this venture. Isn't that wonderful!"

Whilst Isabella was enamoured of the romantic nature of the whole concept, it seemed to her that Mr Arbuthnot was not. As she spoke, it had seemed to her, for a moment, that an expression of annoyance, almost anger, had crossed his face – but... surely not? For what was there, in what she had said, that might conceivably annoy him?

After that, for the rest of their drive, whilst he spoke most amiably to her, he seemed a little distracted, and flattered and flirted considerably less than usual – a development that Isabella was not sure she appreciated at all. Still it was a pleasant outing, and she returned home happy enough with the day.

~~~~~

Two sennights later, Sera regarded the shelves of the storeroom with satisfaction. Neatly laid out, each wrapped in a delicate bag of sheerest muslin, the shelves contained the first 200 favours of their manufacture. Ten girls now worked for her each day, and they were proving most adept at learning the required skills to produce very high quality favours.

The selection of exquisite silk ribbons, fine laces, beads of exotic woods and metals and highest quality paste gems which had been chosen from the warehouses of Morton Empire Imports had proved of perfect suitability to bring the designs that she had envisaged to life. Tomorrow, Raphael... Mr Morton, she sternly corrected herself... intended to send a selection of the best favours to the Prince Regent, and one or two of the *ton's* most acknowledged arbiters of fashion.

The thought of it was both immensely satisfying and utterly terrifying – for what if they did not take the fancy of these important people? Then all of this work might be for nought, and, if their venture did not succeed, what would become of her income, or the income that this work now provided for the girls?

Raphael had taken the ones that he had selected to his home, to sit, this evening, and write carefully crafted letters to accompany the gifts. Now, all was quiet. She had sent the girls home, with her enthusiastic thanks for their hard work so far, and was, as she usually did, taking a bit of quiet time to herself, tidying things away, and assuring herself that all was well, and ready for the next day.

She had locked the doors, all but the little one at the rear, and sat, now, appreciating the peace, still astounded at her good fortune, and at how much the last weeks had changed her life. All because one man had chosen to listen to her, had seen the potential in her idea, and, rather than simply stealing it from her, had given her the great gift of treating her as he might another man, and taking her on as a business partner.

He was a remarkable man. She found herself wool-gathering, dreaming of him – his deep dark eyes, his lean elegant face, his strong hard body and his voice that flowed over her like a rich wine. As if that wasn't enough, he was a good and kind person. So much for the disdain that the *ton* held for those of the merchant class! Her experience with Mrs Johnson and the other ladies had begun the change in her view of the world, but Mr Raphael Morton had quite totally turned those views upside down.

If she was completely honest with herself, she was half in love with the man. Which was ridiculous – to him, she was a business partner, nothing more. He insisted on treating her with the full deference due to a Lady of Quality, no matter her circumstances. She felt it like a wall between them – no matter how they might speak of the business, and converse freely and happily, it was as if the invisible barrier of the difference in their birth grew stronger over time, not weaker.

It saddened her, yet she supposed it was the way of the world.

~~~~~

Raphael sat back, shaking the sand from the last carefully penned letter. Leaving it aside for the ink to completely dry, he turned to the small stack of boxes on the side table, and began to pack the favours carefully into each, counting them as he did so. After three checks of his count, he huffed a frustrated breath. There was one too few. He had been a fool, and allowed himself to be distracted by watching the afternoon sun draw deep red lights from Sera's... Lady Serafine's, he corrected himself... beautiful hair and had miscounted when collecting the favours.

There was nothing for it. This had to be perfect.

He locked the door to his study, collected his hat and coat from the footman on duty at his door and set out to walk the moderate distance back to the manufactory, to select the final required favour.

~~~~~

Some sound brought Sera out of her dreaming, and she flushed, a little embarrassed at having been mooning over a man like a love-struck young girl. Glancing around, she realised that more time had passed than she had thought – the windows showed only the deepening dusk outside - her mother would be expecting her home. It was odd, though – normally Alf would have come to find her by now, keen to drive her home before it got too late and cold. She wondered where he was.

A sound came again, and an odd, reddish light tinted the dusk through the window. Alarmed, she stood, and ran to look. From the window she saw, to her horror, the flickering light of flames – she ran to the rear door, and went to open it, but the heat of the metal door handle nearly burnt her palm, and she backed away in fear. She grabbed for her keys and ran to the front of the building, through the small kitchen.

Her skirt caught on the logs waiting near the kitchen hearth, and she was spun by the tug, the keys flying from her hands and down into the grated drain near the washtub under the small window. She froze, staring at where they had disappeared, terror taking hold deep inside her. She had seen what fire could do to houses, had seen people barely rescued in time from a burning building. At that instant, she saw her death before her.

She could hear the fire now, burning the door, and the window frames – she ran, again.

Perhaps she could force open a window at the front, and attract some passer-by's attention. But the windows were all secure, with strong bars – they had put great effort into protecting this property, and their new venture. Despairing, she crumpled to the floor against the front door, then shook herself out of the stupor, and pulled a pin from her hair. She had heard tales of hairpins being used to pick locks – this was the time for her to attempt such a feat, if ever.

~~~~~

Three blocks from the manufactory, a rough looking man stepped out of the shadows, and approached the well-dressed young gentleman who stood in the pool of dim light from a nearby street lantern.

"It be done, just like ye wanted. Ye can see the colour from here." He pointed and, indeed, the red flicker of light from flames was visible on the wall of a tall building some distance away. The rough man held out his hand, and, unspeaking, the young gentleman deposited a heavy purse upon it.

"Always happy to oblige, Mr Porter, if'n ye should need me again." He sketched a parody of a formal bow, turned, and faded into the shadows.

The young gentleman stood a while longer, watching the colour on the wall, then nodded to himself, turned and was gone.

~~~~~

Raphael took the shorter way to the manufactory, ducking through the lanes to the rear, in a hurry to get the favour and get home, to have all in readiness for the morrow. He turned the last corner and stopped in shock for a second, before launching himself forward at a full run. For the back wall of the manufactory was wreathed in flame, and the yellow and red tendrils of it were licking towards the stable.

Surely Sera and Alf were both safe, for by now Alf should be driving her home, but he would not let all of their work be destroyed – not when they were so close to a great success!

He reached the stables and ran inside, grabbing a horse blanket from the rack and soaking it in the horse trough at the door, then used the wet wool to beat out the flames which were just reaching the stable wall, carried on the few wisps of spilled hay and straw that had not been swept up – he thanked the Lord God that they kept a neatly swept yard at all times.

As Raphael turned to thrust the blanket into the trough again, he heard a moan from inside the stable.

He glanced at the door, then at the manufactory building – the flames were gaining strength – he had little time, but... if that was Alf, he needed help. And, if that was Alf, could it be that Sera was still inside? His heart beat harder than it ever had in his life, and horror froze him to the spot. Then his battle reflexes took over, and the judgement honed on the field of war took him into a cold calm space where he assessed his options in an instant, and acted.

As Raphael turned to the stable door, Alf staggered out, unsteady on his feet, and clutching his head. His face, already white, turned ashen when he saw the flames.

Alf pointed, shaking, and croaked in a harsh voice "Lady Serafine...."

In that moment, Raphael was utterly grateful for the cold calm of battle, for under it, he felt fear greater than ever before – fear of losing a woman that he had come to care for, well beyond the respect a man might have for a skilled business partner. Despite the difference in their stations in Society, she had, in these last few sennights, become central to his life.

Grabbing the soaked horse blanket, he threw himself at the building like a madman, beating at the flames. Moments later, water splashed past him to land at the base of the flames where grass and straw, and a scatter of refuse reeds from the kitchen floor gave the fire enough fuel to keep it hot on the timber of the door. Alf turned and was soon back with another bucket full.

Raphael beat at the higher flames, spending all of his effort to stop it spreading further, working along the wall as best he could, and desperately wishing for more hands to help. He kicked aside the neatly piled stack of logs kept for the kitchen fire, scattering them into the icy slush of the yard, satisfied that they would not burn further there. The blanket began to burn, and he ran back to the water trough to soak it again.

As he did, three young men rushed past him into the yard, buckets in hand, and a small spark of hope filled him. With extra hands, they had a chance. A fraught fifteen minutes later, the fire was out. The rear door and window frame were nearly burnt away, the window broken, and all of the mortaring of the stone of the wall would need redoing, but the building stood.

His elegant clothes charred and blackened with soot, Raphael stood a moment, quickly bowed, and thanked the young men, then threw himself at the door, breaking through what remained of the still smouldering timber. His three young assistants looked at Alf quizzically, as if to ask if the man was mad. Alf shook his head, and again, pointed.

"Lady Serafine."

Horrified comprehension spread across the faces of the men.

"No… She give me sister a job there, we'd be close to starving without that – we came to help because a' that. I nivver thought the Lady might be trapped."

Alf just waited, quietly praying. He had faith in Mr Morton. But what if Lady Serafine was hurt… or worse?

ARIETTA RICHMOND

Chapter Eight

Sera struggled with the hairpin, but the lock was stubborn, and her fingers began to hurt from the effort of trying. At first, apart from the fear, it was not so bad – this far from the back of the building, there was no heat, but she could hear the flames, hear cracks and thumps as the building suffered its assault. But, after a few minutes, there was a loud cracking noise, and a tinkle of falling glass. The kitchen window must have shattered in the heat.

That was enough to start a flow of air into the building – air laden with thick smoke. As the smoke began to fill the rooms, Sera coughed and struggled to breathe, to concentrate on the lock – surely she could manage to pick it! But it stubbornly refused to open. And she began to feel light headed, her vision blurring as the smoke made her eyes shed continuous tears.

It was no good, she thought despairingly. She had tried so hard. That everything she had worked for should end like this, and her with it, was insupportable. But it was happening.

She sagged against the front door, barely able to breathe any more, and wished desperately that she might see her mother to say goodbye, that she might see Raphael, to tell him how she felt about him – whether it be foolish of her or not. But that was a fever dream – the reality was the darkness closing in and the air no longer supporting her breath.

Just as she slipped into the blackness, she thought she heard a resounding crash – surely her exit from this life was not to be announced with a clash of drums? Then there were arms around her, and she was lifted against a hard chest, which was surely real, for she could feel it move as its owner coughed in the smoke-filled room.

Moments later, sweet fresh air filled her lungs, and, subtly underlying it, she recognised the pine and leather scent that could only mean that it was Raphael who held her so tightly against him, even as he staggered a little, passing through the burnt doorway and into the yard. It seemed that her prayer had been answered. He staggered as far as the stable, still holding her, and collapsed on the bench just inside.

Sera opened her eyes, to find his only inches away. A magical stillness overcame them both, and everything else but his eyes seemed to fade away. She had never seen anything so wonderful in her life.

"Sera." His voice was a smoked strained croak, but her name on his lips was sweet nonetheless – for no-one but her mother usually called her Sera, not since James…. And then those lips were upon hers and a sweet heat rushed through her body. She felt alive, intensely so, most especially because, short minutes ago, she had expected death.

After some unfathomable length of time, the kiss stopped, and they found themselves simply gazing at each other.

"Raphael…"

Her voice was a smoke shattered whisper, but he heard in his heart what she had no voice to say.

He pulled her tight against him.

"Alf…"

"Yes, Mr Morton?"

Alf stuck his head around the door, looking pleased when he saw her still in Raphael's arms, but with her eyes open and obviously not badly hurt.

"Please arrange with the helpful young men outside to have a guard mounted on the building until we can arrange repairs tomorrow. They will be amply rewarded. And then, if the horses are alright, please hitch them up – I think that we will need the carriage to take Lady Serafine home."

"Yes, Sir!"

Once Sera was safely settled in the carriage, Raphael stepped back.

"One moment – there is one more thing that I must do, before we are on our way."

He turned and went back into the building, making his way carefully to the storeroom, and selected the one extra favour that he had come for. And a blessing it was that he had miscounted to start with – for had he not, Sera might now be dead, and all their work in ashes. The thought that he might have lost her was a band of agony on his heart.

Climbing into the carriage, and meeting her enquiring expression, he explained, in his roughened voice, just how he had come to be there, to save her.

She was beginning to think that the favours were the signposts of change in her life. What might they bring to her next?

Chapter Nine

For the first time in a very long while, Raphael was nervous. It was an odd sensation, and not a comfortable one. He had seen the carefully and elegantly wrapped boxes, each containing a number of the Saint Valentine's Day themed favours, and a carefully penned letter, dispatched for individual delivery by footmen in his employ, each dressed in new and impressive livery.

Now there was nothing but waiting – for the men's return, and then for the reaction of the recipients.

He turned the nervous energy to good effect, and set about arranging the repairs to the building, so that business might go on as before. He had arrived to find that the young men had been true to their word, and diligently guarded the manufactory overnight. He handed each of them a sizeable purse, and sent them off home to rest. They were effusive in their gratitude, but he brushed it aside, assuring them that their efforts in helping him fight the fire, and then as guards, were worth that and more.

As he settled the last of the girls to working, and saw the last of the workmen off to obtain the required repair materials, he was surprised when Sera arrived. He had expected her to spend today recuperating from her experience – but obviously she was made of sterner stuff. He was unreasonably pleased to discover that to be the case.

He was not sure how to approach her – he had kissed her yesterday, and she had most certainly not pushed him aside, yet today, it was as if nothing, and yet everything, had changed between them. Did she regret that kiss now, in the light of a new day? Did she think it presumptuous that he, a merchant, should have kissed a Lady born? He certainly did not regret his actions, and if truth be told, he would happily sweep her into his arms immediately, and kiss her again. But all of his training made him wait to see her reaction, for he was utterly unsure of how she might respond.

So he held himself back, drinking her in with his eyes, seeing just how beautiful she was, and feeling again that sense of how lucky he was not to have lost her. He bowed, allowing himself to take her hand.

"My Lady, I am surprised, and very glad, to see you looking so well today. I had feared that your terrible experience yesterday might have left you less than well today."

A brilliant smile lit her face, and she shook her head.

"Oh no Mr Morton, I will not let such a thing prevent me from being here – for we must not let this stop us. This venture must succeed, and I fully intend to be here to do my utmost to ensure that. Even if my voice is frightfully unmelodic at this point."

It was true that her voice still suffered from the effects of the smoke, but he found the low, slightly roughened tone of it seductive, indeed, almost erotic, rather than unpleasant in any way. She flushed a little, as if suddenly unsure how to go on with him, and turned away, going to each of the girls in turn, to reassure them of their continued employment and to see to their work in progress.

Feeling suddenly unnecessary, Raphael turned away, and took himself home, hoping that his deliveries had, by now, all been made.

~~~~~

All but one of the footmen had returned, and reported that each parcel had been received with curious interest, delivered, as per his instructions, only directly into the hands of the persons he had so carefully selected as his targets. The one who had not yet returned had been tasked to deliver his parcel to the Prince Regent – a challenge which, it was entirely possible, might take him days to achieve.

Raphael could not settle to anything, and found himself prowling the house like a caged tiger, looking for something to distract him from the tension of the waiting. There was no point him going to his offices, for he would only disturb his perfectly efficient shop and warehouse staff, yet simply waiting would drive him quite mad. He entered the parlour, and discovered Bella, curled inelegantly in a chair, a book in her hand – a book it was quite obvious she was not actually reading.

Upon his arrival, Bella heaved a dramatic sigh. Raphael repressed his amusement, and, instead, asked her casually, "What causes you to sigh so, dear sister?"

"Oh Raphael! I am so bored. For this last sennight, Mr Porter Arbuthnot has not seen fit to invite me for a drive. I may not be entirely sure that I desire his interest, but at least he has provided me with some amusing conversation, and the chance to get out. And now he has abandoned me! Not even a message for days!"

"Perhaps, Bella, he feels that you have not shown any great interest in him, and has decided to not press his attentions if you do not wish him to?"

"But... surely any man who truly cared for me would not be so easily discouraged?"

"Perhaps you have simply confused him, then?"

"You are no help at all!" Bella dropped the book onto the table at her side, with rather more force than was seemly. Watching her, amused, yet sympathetic, he decided to act.

"Bella, if you so wish to go for a drive in the park, I shall take you. For I find myself with some free time this afternoon." She spun to him, a smile claiming her face.

"Raphael! That is most kind of you. Yes, I would love to go for a drive, please, may we go now?"

Nodding his agreement, he led her from the room.

~~~~~

When the final footman had returned, it was to report his mission a success – he had actually managed to deliver the parcel into the hands of the Prince Regent himself. It seemed that fortune had favoured him, for, as the footman had made his request for audience, he had been overheard by Cecil

Carlisle, Baron Setford, who had, at mention of Raphael's name as the sender, turned back a moment, and whispered something to the Prince Regent. Suddenly, the footman had been waved forward, and given the chance to deliver the elaborately presented favours.

Raphael was elated – for if the favours were a success, orders would follow. He did wonder, in passing, what Setford had said. He had not seen the man since leaving the military, yet he suspected that Setford would be aware of his movements still. Within the day, the whispers of gossip began to make their way back to him, reported faithfully by his employees and household staff – for many of them had sisters and brothers, or other relatives and friends, working in the houses of the nobility. For a merchant, the gossip was valuable, and allowed him to most effectively supply the desires of his highest paying customers.

But this time, the gossip was newly precious, for it told of the progress of the favours. Being items designed to be given, those he had sent them to were now doing exactly that – giving them to the women they admired. It seemed that Ladies of all stations had received them, from actresses to the daughters of the nobility. And, most pleasing of all, the current most favoured mistress of the Prince Regent.

Although this was what Raphael had intended, it was succeeding faster than he had expected. By the following day, he heard of shopkeepers in Bond Street receiving enquiries from members of the *ton*, who were seeking to purchase these newly fashionable favours, in time for the coming Saint Valentine's Day. Raphael, smiling, sent forth messengers again, this time bearing missives to all of the most exclusive shops, offering them the chance to obtain a supply of the favours – for a premium price, of course.

By the end of that day, they were sold out, and had a waiting list.

Chapter Ten

Serafine's life became a whirlwind of hiring and training more girls to make the favours, creating new designs, ensuring that everything was made to the best quality, packed, and sent to the right addresses, occasionally remembering to eat, and falling into exhausted sleep each night.

The success of the venture astounded her, and she was impressed at the cleverness with which Raphael had brought the favours to the attention of the *ton*.

Each time she saw him, her heart beat harder, her breath came a little short, and the memory of that kiss filled her mind. He was, to her, even more handsome and desirable when tired and somewhat dishevelled; carrying boxes along with his staff, being fully engaged in making sure that their venture was as successful as possible. She could not imagine any other gentleman she had met, of whatever station in Society, willingly doing such work. She certainly did not despise him for it, as convention said she should – indeed, she admired him instead.

After all, Society's mores said that she should also despise herself, for sullying her hands with work and trade. And that, she had long decided, was ridiculous – to have the funds to live in comfort, she was more than willing to work like this. A year of living in fading genteel poverty had impressed that on her, quite thoroughly.

They never touched, beyond the brief moment when he would gallantly greet her by bowing over her hand. She wished for more, but knew no way to breach the gulf that seemed to have opened between them. That kiss almost might not have been real, so distant, so unreachable did he seem now.

She had little time to think of it, however, except in the drifting moments before sleep took her each night, but it left her with a permanent little ache of sadness in her, nonetheless. Perhaps she had dreamed some of it – perhaps her smoke hazed brain had imagined the care in his voice when he had spoken her name, or the tenderness in his eyes when he had kissed her. She no longer knew what was real, beyond his presence every day, and the chaos of attempting to produce as many favours as the *ton* wished to buy.

~~~~~

Raphael ached. Somehow, he was fitting everything into the days – the running of Morton Empire Imports, the coordination of the distribution of the favours, making sure that Serafine was safe, that the building was repaired and guarded, and that everything that should happen, did happen, and nothing else.

He fell into bed each night, slept for not enough hours, and did it all again. He had not slept this little, and felt this worn, since Spain. Yet, at the same time, he revelled in it. For he was not bored, he was much too busy to feel trapped, as he had before, and everything that he did was succeeding, beyond his expectations.

There was, he had to admit, one thing that he was unhappy about. Serafine haunted his dreams, all golden eyes, pale skin and rich dark hair, soft in his arms, and pressing into his kiss. Over and over, he relived that moment in the stable – but only in dreams. He wished, with startling intensity, to make it more than dreams, but saw no way to do so. She was a Lady born, no matter that she chose now to engage herself in trade. He was not of her station. He might do business with her, but he could not expect to ever have her attentions in any other way.

Her family had suffered enough scandal – she did not need it added to, by an association with a merchant, beyond that of an astute investment in business. He would not do that to her. He was not certain, anyway, if she had truly, in any sense welcomed that kiss, or if her reaction at the time had only been the natural relief at finding herself alive, when she must have thought that her death was imminent.

So he watched her, his eyes drinking her in, his mind finding joy in her kindness and cleverness as she worked with the girls in the manufactory, transforming their lives, even as she transformed her own, his body aching to touch her, beyond that single touch he allowed himself each day – the torture of the moment when he greeted her and bowed over her hand.

He would never press his attentions on a woman who did not wish them – he had seen too much of the worst of that at war, so he suffered, not knowing if she even noticed him, beyond his existence as a business partner, and threw himself into the work to dull the pain.

And then, somehow, sennights had passed since the fire, and Saint Valentine's Day was upon them.

~~~~~

The last boxes were settled into the cart, and his delivery man drove off, keen to get them delivered and be done for the day. Raphael turned, wiping a hand across his brow, and stepped back into the building. Sera sat at the little kitchen table, her hands around a mug of slowly cooling tea.

They had sent all of the girls home, with a bonus payment each, and declared that the manufactory would be closed tomorrow. The day after that was Saint Valentine's Day – there was no more time to make and deliver favours for that day's benefit. What they made hereafter would be for other occasions.

Raphael sank into a chair opposite her, a sigh escaping his lips, to echo softly in the empty room. The silence, after so many days of busy work and voices, seemed wrong, deafening in its own way. Their eyes met, and time slowed. They sat, as the afternoon light faded into evening, simply drinking each other in, with no words said. It was a companionship of effort shared, and of words that neither dared speak.

In the end, it was Raphael who broke the spell. He stood, stretching a little, with the same grace and strength that a cat does, and held out his hand.

"Come Lady Serafine, let me drive you home. Your mother will be glad to see you, and the dark circles under your eyes tell me just how much you need to rest."

"Why Mr Morton," she smiled, "how very ungallant. A

gentleman should never indicate that a Lady looks anything less than radiantly beautiful." That she had the energy left for even mild repartee after the last month astounded him, and yet it was typical of her tenacious character.

But she took his hand, the first true touch they had shared since the kiss after the fire, and rose from the table to accompany him out the door. And he thought, as she did so, that to him, dark circles or no, she would always look radiantly beautiful.

He delivered her to her door, and accompanied her in, greeting Lady Galwood with genuine pleasure, seeing before him a changed woman, a woman restored to her rightful state of health and comfort. A woman who might not say so in words, but whose expression told him just as clearly how much she appreciated what her daughter, and Raphael, had done to transform her circumstances.

"Good Evening Lady Galwood. I fear that Lady Serafine has quite exhausted herself, and needs a day of rest. We have agreed to close the manufactory for tomorrow, so that all can rest after the hard work that has been done."

Lady Galwood nodded approvingly.

"I would like to invite you, Lady Galwood, and Lady Serafine, to a dinner at my home, tomorrow evening, in celebration of our most successful business venture. Will you do me the honour of attending?"

Lady Galwood inclined her head regally, and smiled, drawing Sera to her side.

"We shall be delighted Mr Morton."

"Excellent – I will send Alf to collect you at seven."

He took Sera's hand, and bent to kiss it, his lips lingering longer than usual, as he breathed in the unique scent of her, clean and fresh and touched with something faintly exotic.

"Until then."

"Thank you – for everything, Mr Morton." Sera's voice was soft, thready with exhaustion, rich with sincerity. He wondered if that 'everything' included the kiss.

Chapter Eleven

Sera stood in the foyer with her mother, awaiting Alf's arrival. She smoothed the soft wool fabric of her dress, and settled the silk shawl around her shoulders, her fur pelisse close to hand for when they must step out the door. New clothes, which she might once have barely regarded, were now a thing to treasure and appreciate – a year of poverty had taught her that. The wealth that had come with her business venture had given them back comfort, and dignity – she would never let herself forget the lessons of the last year.

It felt most odd to dress as a Lady for a dinner party, after so long. She wondered what Raphael's family would be like, and if her dress was appropriate. Her mother, it seemed, had no such doubts or questions, she simply stood, elegant as always, and waited, watching her daughter fidget with a fond smile.

There was a tap at the door, and Alf was there, ushering them to the carriage cheerfully, surrounded by a faint but pleasant scent of hay and warm horses.

It was not far, yet she was most glad of the carriage, for the chill of late winter was still sharp as the day closed in. Her fingers closed around the strings of her reticule, reassuring herself that its contents were still secure. Perhaps she was a fool, but perhaps this was the right decision. She would see.

~~~~~

They drew up outside a most impressive residence, considerably larger than their respectable but unfashionable dwelling. The sheer size of it made her nervous, but she pushed that aside. The doors opened onto a marble tiled hall, and a respectful footman took their outer garments. Another ushered them into a parlour.

It was a beautiful room, part panelled in rich inlaid timbers, part papered with a delicate Chinoiserie pattern of birds and bamboo, all in delicate gold tones, with tiny highlights of red. The chaises were covered in gold toned brocades, and a magnificent painting hung above the mantle. It resembled paintings by the Flemish masters, with late afternoon light on golden hills and fields, all under a sky of dramatic storm clouds with just a trace of blue. It was, she suspected, worth a fortune.

The door opened behind her, and she spun, somewhat embarrassed to have been caught gawking at her surroundings like someone who had never seen an elegant room before. Raphael was followed into the room by his mother, sister and brother, but, at first, she did not even see them. He looked as she had never seen him before.

In evening wear of the highest quality, of a cut that was both elegant, and yet displayed his form to perfection, he looked more the gentleman than any man of the *ton* she had ever met.

Her lips parted in a little gasp of admiration, and her eyes locked with his, their dark depths drawing her in, the warmth of his gaze unmistakable.

He hesitated a moment, then, blinking, looked away.

The rest of the room, and the people with him, came rushing back into focus.

His mother was most definitely Italian, and age had in no way diminished her beauty. Sera could see immediately that Raphael's face echoed the elegant lines of hers.

"Mother, may I present the Dowager Lady Galwood, and her daughter, Lady Serafine Parkington."

Sera chose to honour Mrs Morton with a curtsey, although their respective ranks did not demand it. Raphael's eyes glowed with appreciation at her gesture.

"And Lady Galwood, Lady Serafine, may I present my mother, Mrs Sophia Morton, my sister, Miss Isabella Morton, and my brother, Mr Gabriel Morton."

Isabella performed a curtsey to match Sera's, and Gabriel managed a creditable, if slightly wobbly, bow.

Gabriel showed all the signs of equalling Raphael's handsomeness in a few years' time, and Isabella was already a beauty – had she been a daughter of the *ton*, she would have quite been the toast of this Season.

There was a moment of silence, into which Lady Galwood smoothly inserted a gracious thanks for their invitation.

Mrs Morton swept forward to capture Lady Galwood's hands, and spoke, the lilt of Italy still in her voice, even after all the years that she had spent in England.

"I am delighted to meet you at last. My son has been full of extravagant praise for your daughter, and I must add my gratitude to you both. For Raphael was quite blue-devilled at first, upon his return to us – feeling the loss of his father, and readjusting to civilian life – this business venture has completely cured him of that state. Now, come, pray be seated, let us be comfortable together."

Sera blinked in some surprise at her words. Extravagant praise? For her? It was a startling concept. She found herself liking this forthright woman – very much. Raphael had, on hearing his mother's words, actually blushed – something she had not thought it possible to see. Perhaps, after all, she had made the right decision – her fingers unconsciously patted gently at her reticule, reassuring herself that its contents were safe.

They fell into comfortable conversation with ease, with Isabella excited to learn about how she had come to have the ideas for such beautiful designs, Gabriel asking slightly wistful questions about how young men of the *ton* spent their time and Mrs Morton setting them completely at ease, with witty and intelligent discussion on an astonishingly wide range of topics, including some rather tart, but accurate commentary on members of the *ton*.

It was a great insight for Sera, into how the merchant class saw the nobility, and on just how much they knew about the lives of the upper ten thousand, just from the goods sold to them.

It was, in fact, rather humbling. The courtesy and good cheer in this house quite outshone that of those of the Quality who had been her supposed friends... *before*... As dinner was announced, and they rose to proceed to the dining room, Sera came to a realisation which left her shaken to the core.

These people knew so much of the life and the gossip of the *ton*, it was impossible that Mrs Morton, at least, was unaware of their family scandal. Yet she had received them with sincere pleasure and grace, and seemed truly happy in their company. The kindness of soul demonstrated here nearly brought her to tears on the instant. For surely, if Italian, it was quite possible that Mrs Morton was of the papist church – who held taking one's own life as an even greater sin than did most. That she could look past that terrible blemish upon their family, and receive them with genuine warmth was a great gift.

As the dinner proceeded, Sera found herself relaxed and enjoying herself, engaged in discussions that ranged from the business plans for the next year to the comparative virtues of different fabrics, or the qualities required in a superior cologne or perfume, to Isabella's wistful desire to attend society Balls, even knowing that she would be looked down on. Although, as had often been commented in Society drawing rooms, *sotto voce*, a merchant's daughter with a very large dowry to accompany her beauty might often be forgiven her birth and seen as a suitable bride for a Lord in need of funds.

Raphael relaxed as the evening went on – he had, at least a little, been concerned that his family might not take to Sera – which would have made him most unhappy – although he did not inspect his reasons for that too closely. The last course was removed, and the ladies retired to the parlour. As an acknowledgement of his growing maturity, Raphael retired to the library with Gabriel, and provided him with a glass of port. The boy's eyes lit up at being treated as an adult, and they sat for a while, talking of horses and vehicles, of boxing and fencing and other 'gentlemanly' topics, and only a little of business.

Eventually, though, the port had its effect, and Gabriel's eyes drooped. Raphael smiled at him, glad to see his brother happy.

"Off to bed with you, Gabriel, before you fall asleep in the chair."

Gabriel started, then placed his near empty glass on the side table with exaggerated care, nodded, and rose.

"I like her, Raphael, and I rather think that you like her more than you say, too. That's good, you should have someone to care about that way. Good night to you." Yawning, he left the room.

Raphael stood, open-mouthed in surprise for a moment, before turning and pouring himself a brandy that he felt a sudden need of.

Epilogue

It was very late, and the enjoyable evening would end soon. If she was going to do this, now was the time.

Sera rose and asked for the direction of the necessary, then quietly exited the room. But she did not follow the directions given. Instead, she made her way down the hall to the slightly ajar door of the room that she had seen Raphael enter, when they left the dining room.

Her heart beat hard, thumping almost painfully in her chest, and her palms felt damp with nerves. But she was determined. He might reject her gesture – if so, at least she would know where she stood. But he might not, and in that case, the future might hold things she had once though lost to her forever. At least there would be a chance.

She pushed the door open gently, stepped in, and just as gently pushed it closed behind her. The soft click of the closing door brought him round, from where he stood staring into the flames of the fire, to gaze instead, at her.

The soft amber colour of her gown made her golden eyes glow more brightly than usual, and the deep red highlights in her hair shone in the lamplight. He waited, bemused, as she walked to him and stopped.

"Raphael..." her voice had the same soft huskiness he had heard in the stable, but this time it was some emotion, not smoke, that had roughened her voice. He shivered at the sound, feeling it deep within him, in the place that had ached for her, all these sennights.

"I... I wanted to give you something." Her voice shook a little, but her smile was breath-taking. She lifted her reticule and undid its strings. Raphael watched, intrigued, waiting. Sera opened the reticule to its fullest extent, reached in, and very carefully withdrew something. "Your hand, if you please."

Still bemused, he complied, holding out an open palm.

Delicately, as if handling a tiny bird, or something equally fragile, she laid something on his hand.

He dragged his eyes away from her face, and looked. On his hand lay a tiny favour, a heart made from beautiful antique lace, adorned with tiny beads of crystal and ruby, all stiffened by a piece of old, old vellum of the highest quality. If he had thought the favours that she made for their business exquisite, then this was a step above and beyond them again.

He raised his eyes to hers, and she smiled, shyly, with uncertainty, but with something in her eyes that he had dreamed of, and barely hoped could ever be real.

"I made this some years ago... *before*... I put all of my wishes and longings into it, all of my memories of my grandmother, and the good things in my life, into this, made with her lace. It was a promise to myself, through all of the bad things. The heart of me. Now, I want to give it to you. It is near midnight. In but a few minutes, it will be Saint Valentine's Day. Please, accept my Valentine."

She stopped, and simply stood, watching his face. She was afraid, shaking, terrified that he would reject this, more vulnerable than she had ever felt in her life, and by her own actions. But she would not presume – she would wait upon his response.

Raphael lifted the tiny thing and studied it. It was imbued with the scent that he had come to know as hers, it was, in its way, as utterly beautiful as she, as much from its simplicity as from its complexity. He brought it to his lips and kissed it gently. Then he slid it carefully into the pocket inside his jacket, close against his heart. Perhaps his dreams had a chance, after all.

"Thank you. This is a gift beyond price. I will treasure it, as I treasure you, always."

He held out his hand again, and this time she placed her own in his. He drew her to him, enfolding her in his arms as he had in the stable, and tilted his face against her hair, the silky softness and the scent of her arousing him, as no other woman had. After a moment, he raised his hand, and tilted her head up. Her eyes sparkled with unshed tears, and something more. Her lips were soft and inviting, reddened where she had nibbled at them in her nervousness.

He bent his head and kissed her, gently at first, his lips exploring the shape of hers, his tongue caressing, and then, after a moment, she responded, her lips opening to him, her body pressing to his, her hands coming up to encircle his neck, to tangle in his hair. The kiss deepened, and everything faded away, but the feel of her in his arms, and the taste of her on his lips.

As the clock gently chimed midnight, and it became Saint Valentine's Day, towards which they had both worked so hard, they explored each other in a kiss that went on, and on, and on. Neither wished to stop, for stopping might require words again. For now, the possibilities for their future, which were contained in touch, taste, and scent, were all that they wanted, perhaps all that they would ever need.

The End.

Number 1 Bestselling Author

Arietta Richmond

Being Lady Harriet's Hero

His Majesty's Hounds - Book 4
Sweet and Clean Regency Romance

His Majesty's Hounds – Book 4

Sweet and Clean Regency Romance

Being Lady Harriet's Hero

Arietta Richmond

ARIETTA RICHMOND

Chapter One

Lord Geoffrey Clarence tapped on the rickety door before opening it carefully. No matter how many times he had been here, the whole place still felt fragile to him – he was a big man, and worried that, if he pushed too hard, the stairs or the doorframe would simply break.

On the other side of the door, the room was warm as the early winter afternoon's sunlight streamed in through the large glass windows. Cecil Carlisle, Baron Setford, waved him to a chair and handed him a cup of coffee, which was, as usual, perfectly prepared, and exactly as he liked it. One day, Geoffrey thought, he would find out how Setford managed that – the miraculous appearance of perfect hot coffee, when there seemed no-one else in evidence, and there had been no exact time for the meeting.

For now, he simply accepted the cup, and sipped with pleasure. This was a place in which he could be totally relaxed, certain that there was no danger – which was a sensation to treasure.

"You've done well these last few months, m'boy. The Prince Regent appreciates still being alive."

Geoffrey raised an eyebrow, a somewhat cynical expression on his face.

"Is that 'appreciates' in a 'here's your reward' way, or in a 'since you're so clever at this, here's your next nasty job' way?"

Setford guffawed and leant back in his chair, his piercing pale grey eyes sparkling. Once the laughter had run its course, his face took on a more serious expression.

"You always were damn sharp – straight to the crux of it. And you're right about it being able to go either way. But in this case, it's actually a bit of both. There's a reward, but there's also another 'nasty job' as you so aptly put it."

He reached over to the table beside him, and produced a folder. From the folder, he withdrew a large sealed document. Sealed with the Prince Regent's seal, if Geoffrey wasn't mistaken. Silently, Setford passed it to Geoffrey.

"That's the reward."

Geoffrey broke the seal carefully. A minute's perusal of the document revealed that he was now the owner of a rather large estate, located not too far from Charlton's country seat, Pendholm Hall. An estate called, apparently, Witherwood Chase. He wondered what it was like. Gifts from Prinny had an alarming potential to come with 'issues'. Who knew if the estate had been well maintained or not? He may have just been gifted an expensive repair and maintenance bill.

"Do you know anything about it?"

Setford shook his head.

"Nothing at all, beyond the fact that it has reverted to the crown after the previous owner proved treasonous. So you may find interesting things within its walls. And that's the 'nasty job' bit. We are not at all sure that we have all of the conspirators in the treason. So, you need to develop a sudden desire to look into your new property – in VERY great detail. I would personally be extremely grateful if you manage to find the papers and other evidence that we believe are hidden there."

Geoffrey grimaced – digging through dusty cellars and trying to find secret compartments in wainscoting might have amused him when he was a boy, but it certainly wasn't exactly appealing now! Still, a decent estate wasn't a gift one received every day. It might even turn out to be a pleasant place. With Charlton's family nearby, he'd even have good company if he wanted it. And... far better to spend the next few months, and then the holiday season, in a place of his own, rather than in his miserable brother's house, watching him bicker with his miserable wife. Alfred's opinion of what Geoffrey should do with his life stopped at 'being a good heir and doing everything the way I do'.

Setford watched him carefully, and smiled wryly as the expressions flowed across Geoffrey's face.

"Yes, I rather thought you'd appreciate having a bolt hole of your own, and a damn good reason to stay there."

"Astute as ever, sir. I just hope it's not quite a crumbling ruin – this 'reward' doesn't happen to come with any convenient cash, to help deal with any repairs needed, does it?"

Setford laughed again.

"A gift from Prinny, that came with money?? Surely you know better!"

Geoffrey sighed, and went back to the excellent coffee.

~~~~~

Five sennights later.

Lady Harriet Edgeworth arrived in the morning room at Pendholm Hall like a whirlwind (which was not an uncommon occurrence...). Her brother looked up with an amused smile on his face. Charlton Edgeworth, Viscount Pendholm, was quite used to his sister's tendency to be all energy — behaving like a good little society miss was challenging for her at the best of times, and here at Pendholm Hall, where they had grown up, she simply didn't try most of the time.

The two dogs lying by the hearth looked up, their sleep disturbed by her arrival, but, after a few thumps of their tails, they settled back to rest.

"Did you have a good ride Harriet?"

"Wonderful! Thank you again for buying Moonbeam for me — she is just the best horse that I have ever had! Poor John can barely keep up with me, and Miss Carpenter quite refuses to ride with me anymore."

Charlton knew that the last statement was the most important to Harriet. His sister's long-suffering companion had never been much of a rider, and Harriet had been making her life miserable by causing her to ride as often as possible during the last year.

"Where did you ride to today?" Lady Pendholm asked her daughter, smiling at her exuberance.

Harriet's face took on an expression which could be described as 'false innocence', if one was to be uncharitable.

"Oh, just across the park to the river near Witherwood Chase." Whilst her tone of voice was casual, the whole effect was spoilt by the blush that coloured Harriet's cheeks. Her mother's eyes sparkled with a mischief that made it quite obvious where Harriet's volatile demeanour came from.

"It's a lovely ride, isn't it? You didn't, perchance, happen to see Lord Geoffrey did you? I wanted to invite him to dinner tomorrow."

Harriet's blush deepened, to a colour that was not exactly flattering against her dark gold hair. Her family teased her about her interest in Lord Geoffrey. They were sure that she would grow out of it. She was equally sure that she would not. It was not a childish infatuation, not at all.

She had decided, when she had first met him, just after he had heroically saved her brother and mother's lives, as well as the lives of four other people, that he was wonderful. He looked like the hero he was. And he was going to be her hero. No matter how long it took for her to convince him.

Whilst she had been the toast of the Season earlier in the year, and had been flattered by the attention of a large number of eligible gentlemen, she had not wanted to marry any of them. She had shuddered at the thought. She knew what she wanted, and she planned to get it.

"He did ride by, in the distance. Unfortunately he didn't see me." She sighed in disappointment, firmly telling herself that he had NOT ignored her, that he simply hadn't seen her. "So you'll have to send a footman over with a message to invite him."

Watching Harriet's eyes light up at the thought of Lord Geoffrey coming to dinner, her mother had a hard time not laughing.

But it really wouldn't do to belittle her daughter's *tendre* for the man – that would, of a certainty, only make her more stubborn.

"I will do so this morning."

Harriet produced a large smile at her mother's words, and whirled out of the room again, to change from her riding habit to a gown suitable for luncheon.

Chapter Two

Lord Geoffrey's first sight of Witherwood Chase had not been inspiring. The gates were uneven and looked not to have been shut for a very long time, the drive was rutted so badly that he feared for the wheels of his carriage, and the winter bare trees that lined it did nothing to improve the prospect.

The house itself was larger than he might have expected – a graceful and well-proportioned H shape, where the side wings enclosed a formal garden and a grand approach to the porticoed entry at the front. Between the wings at the rear was a terrace onto a once elegant herb and scent garden, which was protected from the elements by a decorative wall between the ends of the wings. An impressive four stories of windows had looked down on him as he alighted from his carriage and approached the doors.

Everything had shown signs of some recent neglect, but not so much as he had feared might be the case. He had discovered, upon his arrival, that the property had come with staff – a point which had not been mentioned in the missive granting him ownership.

The staff (a butler of a rather venerable age, a housekeeper, an estate manager, two footmen, a cook, two maids and two grooms, plus a gardener) had responded to his arrival with courtesy, but obvious suspicion. Now, a month later, as Christmas approached, that had at least faded to them treating him with cordial distance. That suspicion and distance was not aiding his investigations one bit.

He had added another two footmen, and a valet, to his staff – men who came well recommended, via Baron Setford, and who had skills and knowledge not commonly found in footmen or valets – which they took great care not to reveal to the other staff. The house had also seen a continuing parade of persons in the business of providing various types of repairs, cleaning services, furniture supply and restoration, and more. The costs were rather alarming, but the ledgers presented by the estate manager had at least given him hope that the place might actually be capable of funding itself, with a little attention to the tenant farmers.

That realisation had led to a round of visits to the village, and all of the tenant's cottages, to assess what repairs would be needed, and to start the long process of building their trust. It was increasingly obvious that the previous owner, apart from having been foolish enough to commit treason, had never been a very likeable man, and had never put the slightest effort into caring about those whose work generated much of his income. Geoffrey hoped that, eventually, the tenants would trust him enough to actually reveal exactly what they had so disliked about the previous master of Witherwood Chase.

On this particular day, Geoffrey had just returned from checking on the repairs to various farmers' cottages. He was well pleased with progress, as the fact that their cottages had been restored to a weatherproof state, before the worst of winter, had led to a markedly more positive attitude from the farmers and their families.

The day was brisk, and the early snow had partly melted in the weak sunlight. He had enjoyed being out and moving, as he always did. At one point, in the distance near the small river that bounded one side of his land, he had seen Lady Harriet riding that quality grey mare that Charlton had bought her a few months ago. He had admired her seat, and, if he was honest, her fine figure, from a distance, but had carefully pretended not to notice her. However attractive the chit was, she was only eighteen, and the sister of one of his closest friends – definitely not a girl that he should be getting interested in!

Handing Rajah to the waiting groom and leaving the horse to his well-earned rub down, Geoffrey took himself inside, via the kitchen door – why walk all the way around the house in the cold and the sleet which had begun to fall? Cook gave him her best disapproving look, glaring at the small trail of wet slush left on the floor from his boots. He swept her a somewhat mocking bow.

"I must apologise, Mrs Chester, for trailing mud in here. But I quite refuse to freeze for any longer than necessary. I am certain that the maid can manage to deal with it expeditiously."

Her expression suggested that his frivolous attitude was unsuitable for a Lord, but she said nothing of it, simply turning back to the preparation of what looked like a sumptuous meal.

As he stepped into the hall, on his way to his study to warm up with a glass of good brandy in front of the fire, his butler intercepted him.

"Good afternoon, my Lord. A letter has just been delivered for you." Barnstable proffered the letter on an aged and elegant silver salver.

"Thank you, Barnstable."

Geoffrey swept the letter up as he continued towards the study, determinedly ignoring Barnstable's rather pointed look at the final drips of muddy snow which had fallen from his boots onto the patterned marble floor. This having a collection of staff was still a strange experience. So many years of looking after himself during the war had made him unused to needing others, or paying any heed to their fussiness. Still, there were some advantages – such as the excellent meals that Mrs Chester produced each day. Brandy in hand, he dropped into his favourite chair with a sigh, and brought his attention to the letter. It was addressed simply 'Lord Geoffrey' in a hand which he recognised. He wondered what Lady Sylvia wished of him.

Opening it, he smiled. It was, for a letter from a member of the *ton*, utterly short and to the point. It invited him to dine with Lady Sylvia and her family, at Pendholm Hall, the following day. A relaxing, and likely entertaining, evening in Charlton's company was definitely appealing.

Lady Sylvia was also an excellent conversationalist, and a pleasure to speak with, as she was intelligent, and not afraid to have opinions. The only thing which gave him a moment's pause was knowing that it would also be an evening spent in Lady Harriet's company.

Since the unfortunate incidents of early in the year, when he had been forced to dispose of some ruffians to save the lives of a number of people, including Charlton and his mother, Lady Harriet had conceived a vision of him as some sort of hero. Which idea rather horrified him. He was certain that she harboured a *tendre* for him, and he found dealing with her somewhat obvious regard difficult. Especially as the girl was so damned attractive!

So be it. He would not let the chit's obsession with making him out as a 'hero' stop him from spending time with Charlton. Charlton Edgeworth, Viscount Pendholm, was, like Lord Geoffrey, one of a group of six men who had, during their service in France and Spain, come to be called 'His Majesty's Hounds' for their tenacious ability to sniff out French spies and troop movements, and deal with them. For all of those years, they had been closer than family – each owed the others his life, multiple times over. Geoffrey was overwhelmingly glad that Witherwood Chase was so close to Pendholm Hall.

Leaving his brandy on the side table, he went to his desk and quickly dashed off a reply, accepting the invitation with pleasure. Once his note of acceptance was sanded and sealed, he rang for Barnstable and settled back into his chair. The door opened rapidly and Barnstable came into the room at a rate that belied his appearance of great age.

"Yes, My Lord?"

"Please have Peterson deliver this letter to Pendholm Hall immediately."

Barnstable took the letter, bowed, and left the room.

Staring into the flames, and sipping his brandy, Lord Geoffrey contemplated his progress with his mission. Digging into the secrets of the house had become more of a pleasure for him than he had expected. For, as he did, he discovered fascinating things about the building, and he was, as well, making it his own. He had not quite realised, until he came to Witherwood Chase, how soul destroying it had been to live in his brother's house, dependent upon him. The gift of Witherwood Chase may have come with a mission which was frustrating and slow, but it had been a gift without price as far as its impact on his state of mind.

He was beginning to realise just how deeply blue-devilled he had become after his return from war. Working for Setford had begun to turn that around, but the simple fact of having his own place had been the biggest factor in shifting his view of the world. He still had days when it all seemed pointless (usually after digging through yet another few rooms of the house, and finding nothing more thrilling than mouse droppings and tasteless paintings), but they were less now.

He was, however, beginning to be annoyed. Setford was so certain that there was something here to find, yet he had been singularly unsuccessful, to date, in finding any trace of either papers, or possible hiding places. But, he reminded himself, he had barely begun.

He had searched, in detail, barely more than a quarter of the house so far – he could not expect this to be easy, or Setford's men would have found everything when the treasonous previous owner was captured. The house was old – at least 500 years old - and had been extended many times. There was a warren of cellars and a tangle of tiny attic rooms, as well as the large quantity of rooms on the main floors. Add to that all of the outbuildings, and the scope for potential hiding places was extensive.

He had the feeling that some of the staff knew more about the house, and the events here before the conspirators had been caught, than they were telling him – he would simply have to find a way to get them to talk of it. He wondered, not for the first time, if the house had hidden passages and rooms. It was old enough to have been here at a time when hidden rooms, priest holes or secret passages and tunnels might have been needed, to escape the ravages of civil war. But if those things were there, he had yet to see any sign of them.

Perhaps, tomorrow, he would take a different approach. Leaving the rooms in the main part of the house for later, he would start with the attics, and see what interesting things he found there, then work his way from there down, a floor at a time, until he reached the deepest cellars. Attics in houses this old often contained items stored generations ago, so, if nothing else, he might actually have fun discovering items from bygone eras. And, should they include further truly ugly paintings, at least he could sell the damn things, to recoup some of the costs of putting the place back in order!

Having a plan made him feel more cheerful about it all.

Leaning back, he eyed the faded tapestry on the wall in front of him and sighed – another thing needing cleaning and care. Now that the drapes on the windows to the side of it had been replaced, the sad state of the tapestry was very obvious. Oh well, it could wait for now. Right now, as he sipped the last of his brandy, food was the most pressing thing on his mind.

Barnstable, as if he had heard the thought, chose that moment to appear at the door, announcing that dinner was served in the dining room. Lord Geoffrey rose and followed him from the room.

ARIETTA RICHMOND

Chapter Three

The following day Lord Geoffrey took himself up to the attics, much to Barnstable's horror.

"My Lord! The attics are full of... um... a... rather historic... collection of... things... not to mention dust, dirt, and probably rodents! Surely a gentleman like yourself doesn't wish to dig about in all that!"

"Oh, what fustian, Barnstable, stop fussing. I will, eventually, stick my nose into every nook and cranny this rather curious construction of a house has to offer. A little dust and dirt never hurt anyone. I might even find something of value – at least I can hope. If nothing else, I can ascertain whether the roof is leaking anywhere!"

Barnstable managed to look both offended and dignified at once (rather an achievement, Geoffrey thought) and, bowing stiffly, took himself out of the room. Geoffrey followed. As he entered the hallway, he saw one of the footmen moving hurriedly in the direction of the servant's stairs. Idly, he wondered what the rush was.

Putting that from his mind, he made his way up a rather impressive number of stairs, finally arriving at the door into the attics. It was a rather small door, and Lord Geoffrey, being a rather large man, squeezed through it carefully. He noted, with amusement, that Barnstable was right – he had already acquired smears of dust and dirt on his clothing – and that by just going through the door.

The attics proved to be a warren of rooms, spread across the under-roof space of all of the main part of the house and the wings, sometimes in multiple levels, with small flights of stairs between them. To start with, all he did was wander from room to room, trying to get a feel for the scale of it. He found a section with a large rainwater cistern – no doubt responsible for the luxury of running water which was present in parts of the house, and a multitude of rooms full of stored furniture, paintings, and God knows what else, all covered in dust sheets.

Mid-afternoon, just as he was contemplating returning downstairs in search of luncheon, Lord Geoffrey opened another door. All thought of food left him instantly. This room, unlike the others, was ordered. Its walls were covered in carefully structured racks, stands and display cases were placed neatly about the space, and, on every rack, in every case, on every stand, were weapons and armour.

This one room was a museum collection of weaponry from centuries past and times recent. It was, in one room, more weapons that Geoffrey had ever seen before – including the armoury tent in their field camps during the war!

For a man whose distinguishing ability was consummate skill with weapons, this was the ultimate find. He felt rather like a small child presented with a room full of toys.

The swords, in particular, called to him. The light of his lantern reached into shadowy corners, drawing sparkling glints from sharpened metal. Even through the light layer of dust, he could see that they had been well cared for – as if someone, until very recently, had come here often, dusted, polished and oiled everything, to keep it in the best of condition.

He wondered who. It did not matter.

The next few hours disappeared into a haze of delighted exploration, as he opened cases, lifted weapons down from the wall, and generally did an inventory of the contents of the room. This was certainly not what Setford wanted him to find, but, for himself, this alone was reward enough for all of the tedious time he had spent, and would spend, searching for the blasted treasonous papers.

"My Lord! My Lord?? Where are you?" Barnstable's voice came to him, distantly echoing through the attic rooms.

"Here Barnstable – in the north-west wing, I think."

Footsteps approached after a few minutes, and Barnstable peered through the door.

"Oh my!"

Barnstable's shock was obviously not feigned, as he stared in some awe at the contents of the room.

"I gather that you were not aware of this collection?"

"No, my Lord, not at all. It is… impressive, isn't it?"

"Quite. Even if I find nothing else of interest in the entire house, this is worth any amount of dust dirt and poking about. Now, what was it you came to tell me?"

"My Lord, it is nearly five – I believe that you are due at Pendholm Hall at seven, for dinner?"

"Is it? I quite lost track of time up here, with no light but my lantern. I'd best hurry then. Thank you."

Lord Geoffrey turned, and, with a last longing look at the beautiful collection of weaponry, closed the door and followed Barnstable out of the attics.

~~~~~

Lady Harriet was fidgeting. She had tried to read, and found herself unable to concentrate, even on the new novel that had just arrived. She had considered embroidery, and instantly discarded the notion – she did not do it well at the best of times. So now, she was wandering about the family parlour, randomly picking up the various small statues and items on the mantle and shelves, fiddling with them a few moments, then replacing them, just to keep herself busy. For sitting still was an impossibility, when, at any moment, Lord Geoffrey might arrive.

Had they been in the morning room, she might have sat at the pianoforte, and allowed herself to release her tensions into the music. That always worked. But, alas, this room did not contain an instrument, so she was left to fidgeting beneath her mother's amused and tolerant gaze.

Lady Sylvia observed her daughter with interest. Harriet had, it seemed, put more effort into her appearance this evening than usual, even allowing for the fact that they were expecting a guest. That would be because of who the guest was, she surmised. She was still quite uncertain about Harriet's obsession with Lord Geoffrey – he seemed to be of a temperament rather more quiet than Harriet's bright volatility. Perhaps that was part of why he appealed to her? But, for a man like that, would Harriet seem appealing, or merely childishly annoying?

For now, given that Lord Geoffrey's behaviour had always been utterly correct and polite, and that he was a man to whom she owed her life, as well as being one of Charlton's closest friends, she was willing to simply let things proceed as they would. Her thoughts were interrupted by the sound of the front door knocker, followed by the measured tread of the butler's feet on the marble foyer floor.

At those sounds, Harriet froze, arrested in mid motion as her hand reached for yet another trinket, and she stood a moment, a flush rising to her cheeks, and her heart beating hard, as she composed herself, ready to greet Lord Geoffrey when he was shown into the room. Then, with a deep breath, she moved again – turning to face the door just as it opened.

Lord Geoffrey was, as always, immaculately presented. The dark blue superfine of his perfectly cut coat displayed his powerful shoulders in a manner that quite stole Harriet's breath. It was ever so – no matter how much she prepared herself for his presence, each time the impact was just as great. Her breath stalled, her heart beat harder, and her ability to think became alarmingly dimmed.

He advanced into the room, bowing over her mother's hand, then hers. Somehow, she stammered a greeting in response to his. He turned to greet her brother. Her eyes drank him in as he spoke with Charlton, who was laughing at some comment Lord Geoffrey had made.

They all settled into the comfortable seats around the fireplace, and conversation flowed freely. As the initial effects of his presence wore off, Harriet regained her ability to think, and found that she had missed, apparently, quite a bit of conversation – it seemed that Charlton and Lord Geoffrey were discussing the events of the last year.

"It seems so surreal to me, Charlton, that it is, this week, a year since we returned from the war. So much has changed! Then, we were exhausted, heartsick from years of war, and unsure of how to go about life again, here. Now, we are all so much more settled, Hunter is married, you will be married in little more than a month, Raphael is off travelling and actually enjoying life, Gerry has been given a title – deservedly so – and Bart thinks he's found the perfect place to breed his horses. And as for me – I am finding that Witherwood Chase is far more interesting than I had expected. Having a place of my own has its challenges, but it is infinitely better than living on Alfred's sufferance."

Lord Geoffrey's rich, deep voice flowed over her, and she had to agree with his sentiments – it had been a remarkable year. It seemed that Charlton also agreed.

"Indeed, Geoff, it is hard to believe that Christmas is almost upon us. I will be glad to see the others at Meltonbrook Chase for twelfth night, although it seems that Raphael will not return in time – he will be sorely missed!"

"I have to assume that there is some great profit to be had from this venture, for it to have dragged him away for so long. We will simply have to wait to find out though – he's been remarkably close about it all. It's bad timing from my point of view – being purely selfish – Witherwood Chase, it turns out, is full of a great hoard of things that have been shoved away in its attics, rooms and cellars forever – perhaps centuries! Including the largest collection of ugly paintings that I have ever seen. I will be selling them, with Raphael's help, I hope. With a bit of luck, our canny merchant can help me actually make the place pay for all of the repairs I've done since I got here!"

"The previous occupant had bad taste then?" Lady Sylvia's

voice was amused. "I never met the man, even though we were close neighbours. He never seemed to be here when we were. The villagers did sometimes remark on the state of his tenants' cottages though – it seems that he was not a good manager at all, and certainly not popular with his tenants, or anyone else in the district."

"That is very much true my Lady, this month has been one long tale of woe as far as the condition of the cottages, and of the house and outbuildings. I don't think the man had spent a penny on maintenance in the last few years at all. The tenant farmers are beginning to at least talk to me, now that I've had their cottages repaired in time for the worst of winter. How they survived last winter I've no idea, some of those cottages were so run down."

"I'm glad to hear that you're making progress – no-one deserves to go through winter without adequate shelter."

Charlton spoke emphatically.

For both Charlton and Geoffrey, the memory of nights on cold winter ground, and peasant cottages ravaged by war, was close to the surface at that moment. Each knew, without words, what the other was thinking.

After a moment's silence, Lord Geoffrey chose to turn the conversation to lighter things.

"Witherwood Chase has turned up some things rather more interesting than ugly paintings, disintegrating drapes and mouse droppings."

"Oh?"

Charlton raised an eyebrow and waited for Lord Geoffrey to continue.

"Yes. Today, I decided to explore the attics – well, to start on that, at least – they are enormous, with rooms full of the discarded possessions of centuries of inhabitants. I found yet more ugly paintings – I can only assume that generations of that family had matching poor taste! But, late in the day, I found something quite wondrous." His voiced conveyed a sense of excitement that Lady Harriet had never heard in it before, and she gazed at him in some astonishment, suddenly desperate to hear more.

"There is a room up there which might best be described as a museum. A museum of perfectly cared for, neatly stored and displayed weaponry! Enough weaponry to outfit a regiment or more. I could spend weeks exploring the possibilities of what's in that room."

A boyish enthusiasm lit up Lord Geoffrey's face. Charlton smiled, caught up in the energy emanating from him.

"Well – it's yours now – you've got weeks to play with your new toys." Charlton grinned, and Lord Geoffrey laughed at his teasing.

"If only that was all I had to do! I've barely touched on the place, even though I've been digging into it for over a month now. I've made it my mission to explore every inch of it before I allow myself to indulge too much – God knows what the place has hidden in its crevices!"

As he spoke, his eyes were on Charlton's, and there was a slight emphasis on the words 'mission' and 'hidden' – an emphasis that Charlton did not miss. Unfortunately for Lord Geoffrey, Lady Harriet did not miss it either, as her adoring eyes were soaking in his every move. She found herself, when in his presence, unable to look away for too long – her eyes simply found their way back to him, as if that was the only natural place for them to rest.

She decided that there was more going on here than the apparent. And a puzzle was not something that she could leave alone. Nor was a secret. The idea of things hidden in Lord Geoffrey's house, of a potential treasure trove to be discovered, took her right back to her not-so-long-ago childhood. Before she could stop herself, words were falling from her mouth.

"Oh! I love digging through old things and finding treasures! Can I help? I am sure that Miss Carpenter would love to help too. If the house is that big and full of old things, surely more people going through them will get it done faster – and give you more time to explore those weapons." Harriet understood the value of bribery... surely he would agree to let her help, if it got him what he wanted, faster?

Lady Sylvia watched, fighting an urge to burst out laughing. The moment of what was almost terror in Lord Geoffrey's eyes did not escape her.

"Err, I... I am sure that you don't really want to get covered in dust and spider webs?" Lord Geoffrey spoke hopefully, having, for a moment, obviously forgotten that Lady Harriet was not your ordinary genteel young Lady.

Harriet laughed.

"Oh I don't mind dust and spider webs – it's no worse than I've found in the stables and the garden outbuildings, and I've been poking around in those all my life. I especially don't mind if there's something interesting to find!"

Lord Geoffrey glanced at Charlton, then at Lady Sylvia. When it was obvious that neither of them intended to rescue him, he took a deep breath, silently promising Charlton retribution for this later, and spoke.

"Well, umm…, in that case, I errr… I will be glad of your assistance, when you can spare the time. But you must be certain to bring Miss Carpenter – you must have a suitable chaperone with you, after all."

Lady Harriet tried, almost successfully, to repress her grin of triumph. Her heart beat faster at the very thought – she would get to spend whole days in his company! Surely, with such proximity, she could get him to start seeing her as a woman, not a child?

~~~~~

Unbeknownst to Lady Harriet, at that very moment, Lord Geoffrey was most decidedly seeing her as a woman.

He had been, quite unsuccessfully, trying to avoid looking at her all evening. From the moment that he had been shown into the parlour, he had been acutely aware of her – of the sensation of her leaf green eyes following him, of the delightful shape of her beautiful body, the flushed red of her lips, the slightly dishevelled fall of her dark gold curls, that seemed never to stay quite as tidy as her maid had intended, and the subtle rich floral scent that she wore – a mixture of rose, and daphne, with perhaps a tiny touch of lemon sharpening the sweetness.

He had never met another woman who used that combination of scents – a combination that instantly took him back to the scent garden of his grandmother's house, so long ago. It made him want to simply soak it in, for it brought him a sense of peace and safety that he had not felt since his childhood years. Which felt odd to him, as, at the same time, her presence roused in him a much more carnal appreciation of everything about her. No matter how often he told himself that such an appreciation of his closest friend's sister was not a good idea, his body refused to obey his mind, and flamed into awareness the instant he found himself in the same room as the delectable Lady Harriet.

Her childlike manipulation of the conversation had charmed him, even whilst it brought him a sensation of sheer terror – for how could he possibly carry out his mission to search the house for evidence of the traitors if he was to be continuously distracted by her presence? He would have to make sure of her safety, and still somehow search, whilst concealing what he was really looking for. His head hurt at the very thought of how hard that would be.

For Lady Harriet's keen intelligence and bright curious nature would ensure that she cheerfully investigated everything…

He had been sure that Charlton would save him, but the rogue had just sat there, and let his sister gull Geoffrey into doing as she wanted. They would have words about that later!

Still, he couldn't help but be warmed by the sight of the glowing smile on her face, now that he had agreed to allow her to help. Perhaps it was worth it, to make her look that happy.

Chapter Four

The staff at Witherwood Chase has greeted the additional two footmen and the valet with suspicion, having all been working at Witherwood Chase for many years. They had their own routines, their own unstated, but agreed, divisions of authority, and had, largely, got over interpersonal politics years ago. Which wasn't to say that there were no secrets, or that they all trusted each other.

Newcomers, however, had caused them to silently close ranks and defend their territory, without any discussion required. Peterson, as one of the newcomers, was acutely aware of the wall of silence that they presented to him. Cold politeness hid secrets, but whether those secrets were a previous complicity in treason, or simply a resentment of the invasion of the place that they saw as their own, he had not yet discovered.

In time, he would do so. Baron Setford had chosen him for his skills, which included things unusual in a footman, such as weapons training, lock-picking, tracking and investigation, amongst other things.

Lord Geoffrey was a man he could respect – a man who appreciated his capabilities, and left him to get on with things. There was nothing soft or foppish about Lord Geoffrey, and his reputed skill with weapons was something any man would admire.

This evening, with Lord Geoffrey away visiting Viscount Pendholm, Peterson was using the time to apply those investigative skills of his. Most of the staff were in the servants' hall, enjoying a quiet evening. But at least two were not. After Peterson had excused himself from the gathering, supposedly to take to his bed early, he had quietly waited in a small storeroom just outside the servants' hall.

His patience was rewarded when Jobs, one of the grooms, and Ashley, one of the footmen who had long been with the house, quietly left the room. They paused a moment, not far from the storeroom door, and spoke in whispers.

"Ash, if his Lordship keeps a'diggin around like this, he's sure to be findin a door soon. Things aren't safe. Not up here. They'll have to go deep with t'others."

"Aye, but how'll we get 'em moved? Can't be a'doin it now – we don't know when His Lordship'll be back, and you'll have to be in t'stable to take his horse when he gets here."

"So I'll be in t'stable. But you go now and make sure all's still where it ought to be, and pack em up so's we can move em the next time he's away – or sooner, if'n he gets too close."

"I don't like it, but ye have the right of it, we can't do more'n that tonight."

The two moved on, from the sound of their steps in two different directions, and moments later Peterson heard the door to the back garden open as Jobs headed back to the stable.

A lone set of footsteps echoed along the corridor towards the servants' stairs.

Peterson eased out of the storeroom, moving along the corridor on silent feet, listening to the footfalls ahead. With great care, he followed Ashley up the servant's stairs to the floor above, and along the servants' corridor there. The corridor turned, a short distance after exiting the stairs, and Peterson paused at the corner, peeking carefully around to assess Ashley's progress. The corridor was empty. Peterson shook his head. That wasn't possible – there were no doors off this corridor for quite some distance – he couldn't have gone that far yet. Yet the corridor was empty.

Peterson eased around the corner, and walked the length of the corridor – no door, no sign of Ashley. He shook his head and took himself to his bed, mulling over what he had heard, and seen – or rather, not seen.

~~~~~

The next morning brought two visitors to Witherwood Chase. One was expected – Lady Harriet, with the long-suffering Miss Carpenter (who, unlike Lady Harriet, **did** object to dust and spider webs...) in tow, and one was unexpected, but most welcome.

Barnstable, still recovering from the shock of Lady Harriet's somewhat energetic arrival, turned in surprise at the second knock on the door.

Upon opening it, he discovered a sprightly gentleman of middle years, dressed in fashionable clothing better suited to a young dandy, on the doorstep. The gent stepped inside, doffed his hat, and presented his card.

Winston Featherstonehaugh Esq.

Valuer of Artworks

Bowing, he looked Barnstable in the eye and declared -

"I am here to see Lord Geoffrey Clarence. Sent, at his request, by Mr Raphael Morton. Please let his Lordship know that I have arrived."

Barnstable, rather flustered by this apparition, showed him into the visitors' parlour, and went in search of Lord Geoffrey.

Lord Geoffrey, who was just in the process of settling Lady Harriet and Miss Carpenter into the morning room, and offering her tea (whilst he worked out how on earth he was going to keep her occupied and entertained, without giving up on his own investigations completely), was as startled as Barnstable had been, when handed the gentleman's card and told of his arrival.

After the surprise wore off, however, he was rather pleased. He had written to Raphael shortly after arriving here, when he had come to the conclusion that the place was packed with horrible art, asking if he might advise on getting it valued, as a step towards disposing of it profitably. It would appear that Raphael had gone one better than simply advising, and had, before setting off on his travels, engaged a valuer on Lord Geoffrey's behalf.

How typical of Raphael! He was always generous, and often chose to simply act, rather than fuss about anything. And, perhaps, this was also a solution to occupying Lady Harriet, at least for a while, and doing so in a way where he did not have to be in her presence (and thus tortured by his awareness of her). He turned to her, smiling, and waited a moment whilst a maid delivered the tea, and left the room. Once the maid was gone, he spoke.

"Lady Harriet, might I ask you to carry out an important task for me?"

"Why of course, Lord Geoffrey – what can I do to help?"

She sounded genuinely delighted that he had a task for her, and he found himself charmed yet again by her positive, energetic nature.

"I am sure that you heard me mention, yesterday, that this house contains a vast quantity of artworks that are... not to my taste... shall we say?"

She nodded, wondering what was coming next.

"A gentleman has just arrived, whose skill is in valuing artworks. I have need of someone to go from room to room with him, and to take down notes for me on what he says about each painting, and to also make those notes very clear about the exact position of each painting, so that, later, we make no mistakes when sorting them for sale. I can provide Peterson, my footman, to be guide and escort from room to room, if you, and Miss Carpenter, will be my scribes, and capture this information for me?"

It wasn't exactly the sort of task that Harriet had hoped for, but still, it was a start. And Lady Harriet found, rather to her own surprise, that, because it was Lord Geoffrey who was asking, she was willing to take on this task, even if it sounded rather less adventurous than what she had been imagining.

"Certainly, Lord Geoffrey. I would be pleased to assist."

Had his shoulders just sagged with relief? Surely not, she pushed the thought away. That must have been her imagination at work.

"One moment."

Lord Geoffrey left the room, and went to greet Mr Featherstonehaugh. As he stepped into the room, he suddenly better understood Barnstable's reaction. The man was unusual, to say the least. Still, Raphael had recommended him. A few minutes conversation confirmed Lord Geoffrey's faith in Raphael.

However eccentric the man might appear, he seemed to know his field, providing a rapid and somewhat passionately enthusiastic assessment of the painting on the parlour wall as demonstration of his knowledge. And the number he named as a value for the painting left Lord Geoffrey a little shocked, and very pleased. If all of the paintings had similar values, he was about to be a wealthy man indeed.

After enquiring as to Mr Featherstonehaugh's arrangements, and sending a footman to pay off his driver and bring in his luggage, then to see the housekeeper about having a room prepared, he led the man into the morning room.

Upon introducing Mr Featherstonehaugh to Lady Harriet and Miss Carpenter, he was surprised to see that, within minutes, Lady Harriet had charmed Mr Featherstonehaugh, and that Mr Featherstonehaugh had charmed Miss Carpenter – which, based on his past observation of the woman, was quite an achievement! Leaving them chattering enthusiastically about the paintings on the morning room wall, he sent Peterson to fetch some pencils and suitable paper, as well as a slate to rest the paper on. Stepping back into the room he breathed a sigh of relief – perhaps his day would contain useful work after all, for the ladies appeared to be forging a firm friendship with Mr Featherstonehaugh already.

When Peterson returned, he explained the requirement,

and that Peterson should, for the next few days, or until such time as the inventory was complete, place himself at Mr Featherstonehaugh and Lady Harriet's command. Given that the inventory would also need to deal with those paintings currently in the attics, which would need to be brought down for inspection, it was likely to take some considerable time.

As they set off into the house, Lord Geoffrey breathed a sigh of heartfelt relief – even though a traitorous part of him regretted letting Lady Harriet out of his sight.

~~~~~

Lady Harriet was delighted when Lord Geoffrey actually seemed to be taking her wish to help seriously. Expecting a tedious task, and quite prepared to be a martyr to her regard for him and do it anyway, she was pleasantly surprised.

For the gentleman valuer was entertaining, passionate about his subject, and quite willing to treat a Lady's assistance with respect. He was, she suspected, the only other person that she had ever met, who was quite as... vigorous... a personality as she herself was. And, even better, Miss Carpenter appeared to actually like him! Perhaps she might not moan about the whole process after all.

Therefore, when Peterson has supplied her with pencils, paper, and a slate, she was happy to leave the room and begin the apparently extensive task of cataloguing the paintings in this rather large house. Happy that is, all but a little anguished regret at not being able to stay in the same room as Lord Geoffrey, who, it seemed, had other work to do, elsewhere. She was sure that it was important. He would surely not, after all, be avoiding her company.

ARIETTA RICHMOND

Chapter Five

Two sennights passed, and Christmas was upon them. It was two sennights of tedium, interspersed with moments of humour, frustration, and delighted discovery. Lady Harriet, in a manner that quite astounded her family, stuck to her stated intentions, and went, accompanied by Miss Carpenter, every day, to continue the work. Such persistence, from the normally volatile Harriet, made her mother begin to think that, truly, it was possible that her *tendre* for Lord Geoffrey was more than a passing infatuation.

What astounded them all more (including Harriet herself), was that Miss Carpenter also went willingly and cheerfully, without complaint. For once she seemed to actually be happy with being dragged along by Harriet, willy-nilly. No-one mentioned either fact. But the general interest in what might be found in the rooms and attics of Witherwood Chase was high.

Lord Geoffrey was both pleased with the progress and utterly frustrated.

Pleased, because Mr Featherstonehaugh's valuation list was providing growing evidence that the dusty collection of paintings, antique furniture and tapestries in the house represented an astounding amount of wealth – even if Geoffrey only sold a small portion of them.

Frustrated, because he was still only marginally closer to fulfilling his mission for Baron Setford. Peterson had confirmed that at least two of the staff who had come with the estate, appeared to have been party to the treasonous conspiracy, and that he suspected the house contained secret passageways or rooms. But he had been unable to find an entry, or to get enough detail of the men's involvement for Lord Geoffrey to take any action.

In addition, the daily interaction with Lady Harriet was a source of constant stress. The more he saw of her, the harder it became for Lord Geoffrey to think of her as 'Charlton's sister', and the easier it became for him to see her simply for herself – an attractive young woman, who had more determination and less fussiness about her than any other woman of his acquaintance. That she stuck at the dusty and somewhat boring work impressed him, and his respect for her grew daily. As did his attraction to her. He wanted to know more about her – how she thought, what on earth possessed her to want to do this for him, why she saw him as anything more than her brother's friend. Surely she could not still be casting him as some fairy-tale hero, based on the events of nearly a year ago?

Her scent had subtly infiltrated the house, and he was, even when in another wing of the building entirely, always aware of her.

They had fallen into the habit of gathering in his study each afternoon, to go over the achievements of the day – the latest finds in various rooms, as far as paintings and other items of value (for they had, some time ago, dealt with the items he had already seen, and headed into previously unexplored territory in the long unused wings of the house), the progress of repairs and renovation of many parts of the house, and the plans for the morrow.

When it was but a few days to Christmas, Mr Featherstonehaugh spoke up, after reporting his latest finds.

"Lord Geoffrey – I would like to make a pause in this work. Whilst I am keen, extremely keen, to see this through to the end – for never before have I had the privilege to assess such a remarkable collection -..." his eyes shone as he spoke, and he almost bounced on the spot, his enthusiasm still as bright as the day they had begun, "- I am also keen to return to my family for this holiday season. Now that my wife is gone, whilst they are happy in my mother's care, my children will want to see me at this time If it is agreeable to you, my Lord, I would take leave of you until just after twelfth night, then return to your most gracious hospitality to continue this work."

Whilst Lord Geoffrey felt ready to grind his teeth in frustration at the thought of another few sennights of delay to his mission, he could not, in good countenance, refuse such a request.

Added to that, he, and Charlton's family, had committed to spending twelfth night at Meltonbrook Chase, where most of the other Hounds would be present.

He would need to devise a way to ensure that the servants suspected of being conspirators had no chance to remove anything in his absence.

"That seems, Mr Featherstonehaugh, to be an admirable plan. I must commend your good work to date, and that of Lady Harriet and Miss Carpenter in documenting your findings. I wish you the best of the season and will gladly release you to your family for now. Peterson will see to making travel arrangements for you."

He turned, unable to prevent himself, aware, as always, of Lady Harriet. She was watching him, her face a picture of conflicting emotion. Her emotions often showed on her countenance, and he was beginning to understand more of her thoughts, just from watching her face. It seemed that she felt as he did – both glad of the rest and the holiday, and reluctant to lose the excuse to spend each day, at least partly, in company with him. He most certainly felt that way with respect to her.

He had come to look forward to her arrival each day, to her bright enthusiasm lifting his spirits and to watching her sparkling green eyes light up with delight each time some new and interesting treasure was unearthed, revealed by the removal of a tattered dust sheet, or the unlocking of a previously locked chest. When she spun about exuberantly with childlike joy in the discoveries, he sometimes had to stop himself from sweeping her up and spinning with her. The impulse rather shocked him, for he had never been one for such outward show of his feelings. But stop himself he did, for he suspected that, should he take her into his arms like that, it would not stop at simply spinning about.

He was terrifyingly certain that, should he gather her to him, he would be unable to stop himself from kissing her.

At this moment, watching the flicker of sadness cross her face, followed by what seemed... could it possibly be... like longing... he wanted more than ever to kiss her. Propriety be damned. Somehow, in the last month, he had come to care for her in a new and different way. He pushed the thoughts aside and firmly repeated to himself, mentally *'Charlton's sister – not for you!'*.

Lady Harriet took a deep breath and the normal bright smile appeared on her face. She spoke politely, granting Mr Featherstonehaugh a curtsey.

"I wish you well of the season, Mr Featherstonehaugh, and your family. I will look forward to making new discoveries with you when you return."

Her words were followed by another soft voice, hesitant but clear, surprising Lady Harriet into turning slightly to look.

"As do I Mr Featherstonehaugh – this has been a most enlivening few sennights, which I have much enjoyed."

Miss Carpenter actually blushed slightly as she spoke.

Lord Geoffrey and Lady Harriet shared a startled look, and both, at the identical moment, raised an eyebrow. The understanding between them was instant, and they found themselves then repressing laughter. It would seem that the usually somewhat stiff-necked Miss Carpenter had been charmed rather more than might have been expected!

Mr Featherstonehaugh swept them all a flourishing bow, thanked them for their words, and took himself off to pack.

~~~~~

As they swept up the drive of Meltonbrook Chase, Lord Geoffrey felt a little ridiculous. Here he was, arriving in his own new carriage, with a groom, two footmen and a valet.

After all of those years at war, this entourage seemed excessive, yet he had no choice. He had left Walters, the other unusually skilled footman sent by Setford, at Witherwood Chase to keep an eye out for anything suspicious. With him, he had Peterson, his valet Hurst, Ashley as the second footman, and Jobs as groom and driver.

He had concluded that the simplest way to prevent his two suspect conspirators from removing evidence while he was away, was to take them with him. They could scarcely refuse his command, but their surly expressions upon being told that they had been chosen to accompany him had seemed a good indication that Peterson's suspicions were correct.

His thoughts were brought back to the present as the house came into sight through the winter bare trees – magnificent, and imposing. And a scene of mild chaos, with multiple carriages vying for space before the doors.

It would seem that everyone had arrived at once.

When he alighted from the carriage, he was swept up into exuberant greetings and laughter, leaving poor Peterson and Hurst to deal with unloading and managing the distribution of his belongings to the appropriate places, whilst he tried to keep straight all of the new faces and names through a whirlwind of introductions which only slowed down once they were all ensconced in the parlour with refreshments.

With a few exceptions, they were a far happier group than they had been a year ago.

The year had wiped the outward traces of war from the lines of their faces, had softened the edges of their bodies a little and removed the gauntness of years of hard living, and, most importantly, had brought love and family back into their lives.

Hunter Barrington, Duke of Melton, was a transformed man – he had returned grief stricken and lost in so many ways, yet here he was with his delightful new Duchess and obviously very happy. Charlton was equally happy, and was seated beside his betrothed, Lady Odette, who, with her aunt Lady Farnsworth, had been invited to their gathering as well. Bart and Gerry were tucked away in the corner, probably talking horses – but, whilst they were the quietest in the room, and perhaps still carried the strongest after effects of the war in their minds, they too looked cheerful. Hunter's sisters, Lady Sybilla and Lady Alyse, had joined their conversation and appeared to be holding their own on the topic of horses.

The Dowager Duchess of Melton and Lady Sylvia had settled with Lady Farnsworth, and seemed deep in discussion of the plans for Charlton's wedding. The only others in the room were Lady Harriet and Miss Carpenter, Hunter's brother Charles was away, apparently dealing with estate matters elsewhere, much to his mother's displeasure. Lady Harriet had settled on the seat of the pianoforte near the large windows to the rear of the room, her hands stroking its surface almost reverently. Miss Carpenter seemed rather lost, but, faithful shadow to Lady Harriet, she had settled on a small elegant chair off to one side, and simply watched.

It seemed wrong that Raphael was not there too. What could be so important that he would sail off and miss this gathering? The thought was fleeting and Lord Geoffrey found himself drawn into conversation with Hunter, Charlton and their Ladies and the afternoon disappeared into the flow of discussion.

Somewhere along the way, Lord Geoffrey realised that a quiet, yet beautiful thread of melody was winding its way through the room.

Not loud enough to disrupt any conversation, but soothing and relaxing in the background. He was drawn, as always to watch Lady Harriet, whose fingers on the keys were producing the marvellous sound. She seemed more still, more relaxed than he had ever seen her, and her eyes were closed – she played from memory, by feel alone, seemingly unaware of her audience, just lost in the music. He had not thought it possible for her to look more beautiful than she usually did – but like this, she was stunning.

With a start, he realised that one of the others had addressed him – had possibly spoken his name more than once.

"My apologies – I am a little... distracted."

"So I see." Hunter laughed good-naturedly and returned to the topic. "I must show you Nerissa's plans for the grounds – come spring, you won't recognise the gardens. We will have the most beautiful park of any estate in the county. But enough of us – what have you to tell us about your new estate? How goes your restoration of Witherwood Chase? I hear that it's a huge rambling place that needed quite a bit of maintenance."

"That is an accurate, if rather understated summary! It's five or six hundred years of rambling additions to the building worth of unmaintained mess."

Hunter laughed at his expression, whilst Charlton added his own commentary.

"It is, at least, an elegantly proportioned building – through all of those additions, and no matter how tangled the interior layout is, at least they managed to keep the exterior attractive!"

"True." Lord Geoffrey turned to Lady Nerissa, "I believe you would enjoy the gardens, my Lady, for the front between the wings of the house is a lovely formal pattern, and the rear, enclosed between the other wings has been a well-designed herb and scent garden. They appear to have had little good care for some years, yet retain the evidence of their design. I would be honoured should you be willing to apply your skills to helping me plan their restoration and improvement."

The young Duchess favoured him with a glowing smile which lit up her face and clapped her hands together in delight.

"Nothing would please me more, Lord Geoffrey – I will be sure to inspect them in great detail when we gather at your estate for Easter."

Conversation flowed, and Lord Geoffrey drifted from one group to another, more relaxed than he had been in months, yet always aware of the music winding through the room, his eyes drifting, again and again, back to Lady Harriet as she played. This was something of her that he had not known, and it intrigued him that one who was normally so active and energetic could be so still and peaceful.

Eventually, dinner was announced, and Miss Carpenter stepped forward, diffidently, and gently touched Lady Harriet's shoulder, bringing her back to awareness of the room. Lady Harriet flushed, and looked rather surprised to find that so much time had passed. She stood, composed herself, and stepped forward.

Somehow, Lord Geoffrey found that he was in the perfect position to offer her his arm, and lead her in to dinner – and to discover himself seated between her, and Lady Odette. Dinner was both delightful and torture, for Lord Geoffrey was acutely aware of Lady Harriet's presence, so close beside him, her scent winding its way around him, and of the fact that he should not be reacting to her the way that he was, the way that he always did, no matter his resolve to not do so.

To add to his discomfiture, Lady Odette insisted on thanking him, yet again, for his actions in saving her life, and Charlton's, earlier in the year, even though those actions had meant the death of her father. Lady Harriet's eyes shone with that alarming hero worship again, as the story was told for those who had not been present at the time. And he had been hoping that she had stopped seeing him that way! How could he ever live up to such a perception? He was no hero, he was simply a man who did what must be done, when it was needed.

By the end of dinner, he was heartily glad to escape to the library and a glass of port with the other men.

With only Hounds present, Lord Geoffrey felt comfortable enough to discuss, a little, his mission for Setford, and his current frustrating lack of progress. They all agreed to keep an eye on the behaviour of Jobs and Ashley whilst the men were at Meltonbrook Chase. Charlton regaled them with the tale of Lady Harriet trapping Lord Geoffrey into letting her help with the exploration of Witherwood Chase, and great merriment and teasing resulted. But it was not without sympathy.

Geoffrey followed up with a description of the findings so far, including the weapons 'museum' in the attic – a find that they were all keen to see for themselves. His tales of dust sheets and mouse droppings, ugly paintings and archaic furniture were greeted with less enthusiasm, until he mentioned some of Mr Featherstonehaugh's astounding valuations of the pieces. He was slapped on the back and congratulated on his luck. In his opinion, it was only fair compensation for all his, so far fruitless, searching for hidden compartments or passages.

They settled to talking about possible places a door could be hidden, or a mechanism to unlock one, in a room or a hall. Lord Geoffrey took careful note of their ideas – anything was worth a try if it got him a step further towards finding the blasted papers for Setford.

This was the point at which, again, he missed Raphael's presence – for Raphael was the one who would have immediately 'seen' a logical plan of attack to test for, and undoubtedly find, the hidden passages. His sharp mind had always been able to lay out an approach better than any of them could.

Ah well, surely he would see Raphael at Charlton's wedding, although, God willing, by then he would have found the papers and be done with this mission.

~~~~~

Lady Harriet had excused herself from the parlour and gone in search of the necessary. That urgent business dealt with, as she returned along the hall, she heard the murmur of the men's voices through a door she was passing.

She stopped. Eavesdropping was wrong... but... she wanted to know what they spoke of... what was men's conversation about, when they were by themselves?

Feeling guilty, she applied her ear to the door. They were discussing the many ways that hidden doors and passages, rooms and compartments could be made or unlocked, in a house! What a remarkable thing to talk about. But wait... they seemed to be discussing how Lord Geoffrey could find such a thing in _his_ house! At the faint sound of a servant's footfall, imagination aflame, she stepped away from the door, and returned to the parlour.

~~~~~

Peterson, leaving Hurst to wait for Lord Geoffrey in his guest suite, went out to the stables to make sure that the carriage and horses had been suitably cared for, and to check on Ashley and Jobs.

The two had been given a small room to share in the stable block, whilst Hurst and Peterson had been given an equally tiny room in the servants' quarters of the house. With this many people, and all of their staff, in attendance, space was at a premium.

He stepped into the shadowed stables and paused. The two men were there, alone, at the far end of the row of stalls, talking quietly. Peterson froze, easing back into deeper shadow behind a rack hung with horse rugs, the scent of horses and hay rich around him, and listened. They were not speaking loudly, yet the words carried to him clearly by some trick of the building's structure.

Horses snuffled, but apart from that, there was only the men's voices to hear.

"It'll be right 'til we's back. He can't be a'searchin through the place while he's here." Ashley didn't entirely sound like he believed what he was saying.

"True, and that silly lookin' little art man's gone off home for the holiday too. So with Lord Geoffrey and Lady Harriet here we should be good."

"Still, soon's we's back, we'd better git 'em moved. 'E might find the top spot, but 'e's not like t'find the deep one."

"But Ash, what about later like. D'ye reckon any of them fancy blokes'll be ever comin' back? 'R we hidin this stuff fer nuthin?"

"Shut that thinkin Jobs! Old master paid us good to keep t'stuff safe, 'n we will. That's all there is to it."

"Right then. What'll we do if'n he gets close then? D'ye reckon as we could scare 'im off the place?"

"Not likely. 'E's a tough one – you seen 'im with them swords. Right scared me proper that. We don' wanna be buying any trouble. Just keep the stuff hid. We can worry about what to do else when we has to, 'n not afore."

At that, Jobs absently stroked the nose of the nearest horse, and the two took themselves off through the row of stalls and out the door into the grooms' quarters.

Peterson waited a few minutes, then eased out of shadow, checked on the horses, and the carriage in the next section of the building, and headed back to the house. It was good that the men had, apparently, seen Lord Geoffrey at weapons practice, and been scared by his skill. So they should be!

He was no closer to knowing what it was, exactly, that the men had hidden, but the conversation at least confirmed that it was still at Witherwood Chase, and that they wouldn't be taking it elsewhere any time soon.

They were canny, but they'd have to eventually make a mistake – one way or another, Peterson intended to find the entry to the secret passages – he was, more than ever, convinced that the papers, if that was what they were 'keeping safe' must be hidden in secret rooms or passages somewhere in the upper floors of the house. By now, there wasn't a lot of the main area of the house left unexplored, so secret places became more and more likely.

ARIETTA RICHMOND

Chapter Six

With Christmas and Twelfth Night gone, Lord Geoffrey was ready to tackle the mystery of the hidden papers again. His conversations with the other Hounds had filled him with renewed determination to prod and poke at every possible piece of the walls and framing, until he found a way into the hidden passages – for he was convinced that such passages existed. What Peterson had overheard whilst they were at Meltonbrook Chase had just added to that certainty.

They were watching Ashley and Jobs closely since their return, in the hope that the two might accidentally reveal an entrance. At this instant, though, Lord Geoffrey's biggest concern was Lady Harriet. For, once the nearly complete assessment of all of the paintings and antique furniture was done, how was he to keep her occupied? If she should insist on continuing to 'help', so that she was always with him, how could he prevent her from noticing his rather eccentric looking behaviour, when he started poking and prodding at the walls of his house?

As if his thoughts of Lady Harriet had summoned her, she and Miss Carpenter arrived at that moment.

Mr Featherstonehaugh had arrived just a few hours ago, and settled in, newly enthused about his task, and keen to finish the assessment. Although, it had seemed to Lord Geoffrey, he was rather sad that it was coming to an end. He had asked, with studied casualness, if any new rooms, or storage spaces, had been discovered?

'I wish' had been Lord Geoffrey's internal thought, although he wasn't wishing for quite the same sort of new hoard of treasure that Mr Featherstonehaugh seemed to be.

Interestingly, Miss Carpenter blushed like a schoolgirl when Mr Featherstonehaugh greeted her with his customary flourishing bow and a kiss on her hand. Lady Harriet observed it with a raised eyebrow again, and said nothing.

A plan was devised, mapping out which parts of the house had yet to be checked for paintings, cleaned and set to rights, and they all set about their appointed tasks. Lord Geoffrey stood in his study, staring, unseeing, at the faded tapestry before him, as he decided where he would start.

Perhaps, given the conversations that Peterson had overheard, with mentions of down, and deep, he should work in the cellars and the servants' belowstairs rooms. It would be braving the wrath of Mrs Chester, and possibly disrupting his dinner, but it had to be done.

~~~~~

Days later, he was no further advanced, and had achieved little but convincing most of his staff that he was mad.

His obsessive need to have seen, touched and inspected every single corner of his home utterly puzzled them —no member of the nobility they had ever met before had given a damn about such things.

And so it went. Mr Featherstonehaugh, with the able assistance of Lady Harriet and Miss Carpenter, and the guidance of Peterson, worked steadily through the remaining rooms, as well as the large quantity of paintings and objects which Lord Geoffrey had instructed be brought down from the attics, for their convenience.

Lord Geoffrey, with ever increasing frustration, worked steadily through the entire house, for what felt like the thousandth time, poking and prodding at walls, carvings, architraves and anything else, likely or unlikely, which might conceivably conceal a mechanism to open a hidden door or panel. He drove the frustration from his mind by spending a few hours at the end of each day on weapons practice, trying out progressively, all of the remarkable collection of swords and other weapons that the room in the attics had provided.

Meanwhile, repairmen came and went, new items of furniture were delivered, old ones were repaired, rooms were painted, or papered with new, brighter and more appealing colours, drapes were replaced and the house was generally being brought back to the state it deserved to be maintained in.

The tenant farmer's cottages were in better condition than they had been for many years, and the farmers themselves had come from grudging politeness to cheerful respect and liking for their new Lord. Were it not for Baron Setford's mission, he could almost be happy. Almost... for a traitorous voice in his mind whispered that, without the mission, he would have no excuse to spend so much time in Lady Harriet's company.

~~~~~

A month passed, and, with only a few days' work remaining on the assessment of valuables, the neat ledgers of Mr Featherstonehaugh's findings, so ably written in Lady Harriet and Miss Carpenter's hands, showed totals so large that it made Lord Geoffrey's head spin. Gifts from Prinny might rarely come with cash attached, but this one had certainly come with more wealth included than anyone might ever have imagined.

He was now so wealthy that it might even bring him close to the wealth enjoyed by Raphael, or by Hunter, now that the mismanagement of his estates in his father's time had been corrected. It gave him great satisfaction – satisfaction that he really should not indulge in – to realise that he was now, in no way whatsoever, dependent upon his miserable brother. Alfred would be livid. He would have no leverage left, to use to try to make Lord Geoffrey behave *'as my heir should'*.

Hopefully, Raphael would be at Charlton's wedding – Geoffrey couldn't imagine him missing it, but who knew, with the sea, when ships would come in.

If Raphael was there, then it should be possible to get him to stay at Witherwood Chase a few days, to see the remarkable collection, and put in place a plan for its sale to the right buyers. There were, actually, a few pieces that Lord Geoffrey might keep – amongst the ugly paintings there were a small number of attractive ones – ones that Lady Harriet had expressed admiration for. Perhaps he would gift them to her.

With the wedding only a few days away, the pace of final organisation at Pendholm Hall was intense. When Charlton had decided to be married at Pendholm Hall, rather than in the crush of London as the Season began, Lord Geoffrey had been relieved.

Not only would he be able to continue his mission with less interruption, but he would not have to face the fluttering sea of hopeful young ladies seeking a wealthy war hero, who was heir to a Marquessate, to marry. Nor, whispered that part of his mind that he chose not to listen to, would Lady Harriet be surrounded by the sea of young fops who sought an heiress to marry.

The approaching wedding had, perforce, caused work to stop on the painting assessment, to a large extent. The last few rooms worth, carted down from the attics, would have to wait a week or so.

Lady Harriet and Miss Carpenter were required at the Hall to assist with the preparations, so Lord Geoffrey had asked Mr Featherstonehaugh to review his work so far and confirm his valuations as listed in the ledgers, adding some notes on which pieces he felt might sell fastest, and which pieces he believed he knew of specific potential buyers for.

With typical generosity, Lady Sylvia, upon hearing that Mr Featherstonehaugh would still be in residence, had invited him to the wedding as well.

After a hurried consultation with Peterson, Lord Geoffrey had solved the issue of how to limit the activities of their two suspect conspirators, whilst they were at the wedding, by volunteering the men to Lady Sylvia as extra help, to assist with the influx of horses, carriages and guests which would descend upon Pendholm Hall. Putting aside his annoyance with the stubbornness of his house, in not giving up its secrets, Lord Geoffrey chose, instead, to spend some time in sword work.

The weapons from the attic were fast becoming old friends, to the extent that the two swords he liked best now graced the wall of his study, in easy reach whenever he felt the need to work off his frustration.

Chapter Seven

As Lord Geoffrey dressed for the wedding, standing obediently still for Hurst to force his cravat into a complex style with military precision, he wondered what it would feel like, to want a woman so much, that you chose to marry her, and commit for life. He had seen, in both Hunter and Charlton's faces, the certainty that they had made the right choice, that happiness would be the outcome. Yet still, when he thought of the concept, what came to his mind was the image of his brother, bickering with his wife, both of them always miserable, trapped with each other forever. He shuddered.

Maybe happiness was possible – but for him? He wasn't sure. Perhaps his family was cursed. His parent's marriage had been no better than his brother's.

~~~~~

The wedding ceremony was done, and the day was drawing to a close.

Lady Sylvia and Lady Farnsworth had settled onto two chairs in the corner of the ballroom at Pendholm Hall, for a well-deserved rest. As they sat, watching the younger people dance, they discussed the events of the day.

The wedding had been wonderful, the celebration a success, and now Charlton and Odette were waltzing together, so obviously in love that it quite lit up the room. But wait, there, beyond them – Harriet was waltzing with Lord Geoffrey – the little minx, so she had finally persuaded him to at least look at her as a young woman. All that persistence with trudging through dusty rooms and taking notes about ugly old paintings must have achieved something for her. Lady Sylvia had to admire her daughter's sheer willpower. She was definitely beginning to think that Harriet's fascination with Lord Geoffrey had gone beyond mere infatuation, for surely, after a year, a simple infatuation would have faded.

Lady Sylvia still wasn't sure that she approved – after all, he was considerably older than Harriet, and a rather serious man – still, who knew what might come of it? He had proven himself, over this last few months, to be a man of integrity, a man who cared for his tenants, and stuck to his word. Perhaps that serious, caring nature was just what was needed as a foil to Harriet's bright volatility.

Turning further, she saw Mr Raphael Morton, the only one of the Hounds that she had not met before today. He had arrived just in time for the wedding, apparently having come almost straight from his ship, and been greeted with great joy by his fellow Hounds. She thought he looked pensive, sad, as if something troubled him, but his eyes followed Charlton and Odette wistfully. She wondered what that was about.

Lady Sylvia had liked him immediately, no matter his lack of title and the fact that he was a merchant. Any man who was a close friend of her son was welcome in her home. He was, she believed, planning to stay with Lord Geoffrey for the next few days – something to do with arranging the sale of all of those ugly paintings that Harriet had been helping to catalogue.

Her eyes found Harriet and Lord Geoffrey again, as they swirled past her on the dance floor. Harriet gazed into his eyes with that adoration which had, from the day that she had first met him, as the hero of the hour, never faded. And, most interestingly, Lord Geoffrey appeared to be gazing back into Harriet's eyes with an expression of wonder, as if he had only just discovered something new about her.

Lady Sylvia smiled to herself, well pleased with the day, all over again.

~~~~~

Lady Harriet had planned her campaign carefully. She had tracked, as subtly as she could, Lord Geoffrey's movements in the room, and made quite certain that she was close to him, when the orchestra struck up a waltz. As he looked around, apparently considering escaping the room, she had simply stepped in front of him, smiling, and waited. He had gulped, glanced around, and apparently, having now known her for some time, concluded that she had, yet again, trapped him neatly. He had offered her his hand, raised an enquiring eyebrow, and, at her nod of acceptance, swept her on to the floor.

She looked stunning. Her gown of a vibrant rich green (a colour officially unsuited to so young a woman, according to the disapproving old biddies of the *ton*) made her eyes shine, and made their green even brighter.

Her rich dark gold hair was swept up into a pile of artful curls, which tumbled to the side, drawing the eye to her shoulders and the creamy expanse of her décolletage. His eyes were most happy to be led there.

As he took her into his arms, her unique scent surrounded him, a scent which he found arousing, yet the scent of safety, of home, of childhood delight. After the long day, and a glass or two of celebratory wine, she was intoxicating to his tired senses. He wanted to kiss her. He had known, for so long now, that should he take her into his arms, he would want to do just that. He forced himself to remain a gentleman, guiding her through the flow of dancers, letting the swirling steps of the waltz carry them smoothly around the room. She was light on her feet and sure, seeming made to fit against him, somehow perfectly matched, even though he was large and tall, and she was quite petite of height, and slim.

She was gazing into his eyes, her face full of that adoration that he found so alarming, however flattering it might be to be regarded as a hero. He found himself gazing back, and the room faded away around them, until it seemed it was only them, and the music. Her eyes, seen close up like this, were a mixture of shades of green, like sunlight through leaves in spring, and they shone with her pleasure in the moment. He was lost in their depths. How had he ever thought her a child? Once, that might have been the case, but no more. The woman he held in his arms was well shaped and grown, and well aware of her own desires.

In that moment, even the fact that what she desired was him, suddenly seemed less frightening. But, cold reason insinuated itself into the moment, she was still Charlton's little sister! He should not be looking at her like this, with eyes that heated with desire, that traced her delectable lips and wished to kiss them. He needed to escape, or he would, of a certainty, do something he would forever regret. As soon as the waltz ended, he would deliver her back to that companion of hers, and find Raphael.

As if the thought had magically caused her to appear, he saw Miss Carpenter. But she wasn't standing patiently on the sidelines, as was usually expected of a companion and chaperone. She was swirling past them on the floor, in the arms of none other than Mr Featherstonehaugh. Well, if that was the lay of the land, things might soon be most interesting!

~~~~~

Harriet had lost all sense of time and place. The feeling of being in Lord Geoffrey's arms was better, oh so much better, than anything she had imagined. She gazed into his dark storm grey eyes and simply soaked up the moment. She knew well that her heart was quite likely on her face, her feelings spelled out for anyone to see, and she didn't care one whit. So long as he saw and did not instantly abandon her, she could cope.

His eyes connected with hers, and the warmth, and... was that desire?... that she saw in them made her heart race and her breathing come short.

She had no idea how long the music played, only a wish for it to never end.

But, of course, it did.

He had appeared as caught up in the moment as she, but as the music stopped, he swirled her to the side, and quickly delivered her to Miss Carpenter's company, before bowing elegantly.

"Thank you, Lady Harriet. If you will excuse me, I must have a word with Mr Morton."

He turned, leaving her feeling somewhat lost and bereft, and walked away from her rapidly, as if escaping some terrible fate. Her mouth fell open in shock a moment, before she forced her best bright smile back onto her face. How could he? How mortifying! She had thought, for a little there that he… but no, obviously not.

She was still determined. There was hope. She would not give up. There was no-one else for her. She would convince him yet.

Chapter Eight

Three months! He had been searching through the entirety of the damn house for three whole months now! It had delivered him enormous riches in artworks, antique furniture, tapestries and trinkets. It had provided a magnificent collection of weapons. It had delivered him a new perspective on the world, and a new sense of self-worth, as he restored farmers' lives, as well as their cottages. It had delivered him the delicious torture of seeing Lady Harriet nearly every day. But the one thing it had not delivered him was the papers that Baron Setford required him to find.

And now he was at wits end. He could not imagine where else to look, yet he had not found the secret passageways or any other hidden spaces. And today, Mr Featherstonehaugh had finished the last of his assessment. In a few scant minutes, he, Peterson, and the Ladies would appear in this very room to report the final discoveries.

What was he to do once that was done?

Raphael had been amazed at the paintings and other objects, and had readily agreed to arrange sale of the items. The first shipment was packed, and would be collected tomorrow, or the following day, by a specialist carrier that Raphael had engaged to transport it to his London warehouse.

Raphael had raised an eyebrow at Lady Harriet's involvement in the search and assessment of the contents of the house, but Lord Geoffrey had studiously ignored the implied question. Raphael let him be, but went away looking very thoughtful. So everything was in order. Everything except the reason that he was here in the first place, the reason that he had been given the place. The place that he had now made his home. What was he to do?

Barnstable chose that moment to knock, and ushered Mr Featherstonehaugh and the Ladies into the room, closely followed by a maid with the tea tray. Barnstable was becoming remarkably attuned to his habits, and he nodded his gratitude to the man as he quietly left the room.

"Lord Geoffrey. Today has been a quite marvellous conclusion to this work." The man's voice vibrated with excitement, despite his surprisingly bedraggled appearance. Obviously, he had managed to discover one of the last remaining caches of dust and mouse droppings in the house!

"We discovered another twenty paintings, in a tiny store room near the entry to the servant's stairs, just down the hallway here. And they are magnificent. I believe at least two to be by renowned masters, pieces thought lost to the world, now recovered! They alone may be worth nearly as much as all of the others together."

If Lord Geoffrey had been stunned by the wealth found so far, this statement tipped him into a state of total incomprehension of the numbers involved.

Then, quite spoiling the effect of his pronouncement, Mr Featherstonehaugh sneezed – violently and repeatedly. Miss Carpenter rushed to his side, concern writ large on her face. She proffered a dainty handkerchief, which he gratefully took.

"I must apologize – the dust you see – in my excitement I managed to pull the entire dust sheet down on me, from the largest canvas. I fear my attire is not at its best, nor are my nasal passages. If you will excuse me, I will go and change." He took himself from the room, Miss Carpenter fussing at his side.

Lord Geoffrey found himself alone with Lady Harriet, and a short but difficult silence ensued. Dragging her eyes from his, she spun away, looking for whatever distraction was available. There, right in front of her, across the room, was a large faded tapestry.

Why had she never noticed it before? They had certainly not yet listed it on their inventory. Stepping forward, she examined it closely. It was certainly old, but appeared to be of exquisite workmanship. The threads were unfrayed, the edges mostly firm.

It seemed, to her untrained eye, to be simply in need of a careful cleaning. There was so much dirt on it that, in parts, the picture was hard to make out. Stepping forward again she lifted one side of it, studying the only spot that she could see where the edge did seem a little frayed – as if that spot had been touched more than any other part of it.

As she stepped, her foot caught on the edge of the rug, and she stumbled against the wall, one hand tugging on the tapestry, and the other slamming into the whorl of carving on the top of the wainscoting beside it.

Except that the wall seemed to have suddenly become insubstantial, for she kept tumbling forward. Lady Harriet gasped and righted herself, just as Lord Geoffrey reached her and took firm grip on her shoulders to stop her fall.

Even in her moment of shock, she felt the warmth of his touch and a little burst of joy ran through her. He cared enough to catch her!

At the same second, they both realised what had happened, what they saw before them. For the wall had opened. The tug on the tapestry had caused it to slide to one side, and the hit on the whorl of carving had somehow opened a door – a door which swung inwards to a narrow passage. Their eyes met, and his lit with such joy that she knew there was something important about the opening wall, some secret.

But, when he whooped, and swept her into his arms to spin her around in an exuberant display of delight, she quite forgot about anything else but his touch, at least until he put her down again.

"Uhh, I apologize, that was uncalled for, but... I have been looking for something like this – I was so sure that the house had secrets yet to show us, and I was right! And you, most cleverly, have found it!"

He pulled her to him again for a moment, and kissed her full on the lips. She melted against him, heat flooding through her body.

If this was how he reacted to secret doorways, she would endeavour to discover one every day! Then he released her and stepped back, seeming suddenly embarrassed by his actions.

Lord Geoffrey looked into her flushed face, and wanted to kiss her again. He did not – what he had already done was unforgiveable, no matter how much he wanted to repeat it. She was not for him. Quickly, he turned to the matter in hand – the door in the wall. Grabbing a small decorative stone urn off a side table, he used it to ensure that the hidden door could not close, before stepping inside the space.

"Perhaps a lantern... or at least a candle... would be useful? Lady Harriet's voice penetrated his excited contemplation of what he saw. She was correct. He turned, to find her already offering him a lit taper. Resourceful as always.

The light showed that the space within the walls was not large. It appeared to be a small room, not a passage at all. He felt a moment of crushing disappointment – he had been sure it would be more than this! Perhaps it was. He set to examining it minutely. One end of the space appeared to be a cabinet built into the wall – that was the side towards the windowed wall – which made sense, for there was nowhere in that direction for a passage to fit.

The cabinet door was, as could be expected, locked. He huffed his disappointment again, turning to examine the rest of the small space. Nothing of significance that he could see. Lady Harriet peered in through the door.

"Oh, a cabinet. Is it locked?"

"Yes, unfortunately, it appears to be quite solidly locked – and no sign of a key."

She nodded, and squeezed in beside him. His body tightened at the press of hers against him and he gasped. She crouched, putting her face at a level with the lock (and also, alarmingly for his peace of mind, at a level with certain parts of his anatomy, which were very aware of her presence).

She pulled a hairpin from her tangled locks as she did so.

"Hold the light down here please."

Shocked, he did as requested, and watched in open admiration as she swiftly picked the lock.

"How... where... did you learn to do that?"

She looked back at him, flushing, perhaps embarrassed?

"I... when I was a child, Michael – my horrible, now deceased elder brother, you remember? Michael used to lock away anything I treasured, just to be mean – he was like that. So I learned to pick locks to get my things back. Jimmy taught me. He was our stable boy in London. I think he'd been a thief before we took him on. But he never stole from us."

"Lady Harriet, I am doubly indebted to you. And impressed by your resourcefulness."

She flushed again, definitely embarrassed this time, at receiving praise from him, and squeezed her way back out of the space to allow him to investigate the contents of the cabinet.

The brush of her body against him brought a new rush of desire, but he pushed it aside. Right now, the contents of that cabinet were his first priority. She took the candle from his fingers, and held it for him, so that his hands were free to pull forth the roll of pages within. Shaking, he unrolled it. And, for a few moments, was hit hard by disappointment again. Not a set of incriminating letters or lists. Just a collection of maps or diagrams.

And then his brain caught up with what he was seeing. In his hands was a full set of maps of his house – every floor, of every wing, and the attics, and the cellars. Neatly drawn, well noted with names of rooms, and with some odd symbols in various places. Most importantly, these maps showed a large number of passages and rooms that were not part of the normally accessible parts of the house. It appeared that he held a full set of maps showing the hidden passages and rooms in the house, and under it. This was a prize indeed. He stepped back out into the study, and allowed the hidden door to close, after carefully studying the mechanism. Then he opened it again, to be sure that he could, closed it, and took the maps to his desk. Lady Harriet followed, her face alight with curiosity.

In that instant he realised – there was no going back now, no keeping her out of it – she had found the secret, opened the door, unlocked the cabinet – she knew that the maps existed. After all that, she had a right to see them. But what could he tell her, without revealing the detail of his mission? Thinking carefully about that very pertinent question, he spread the maps out on the desk. They were old, and appeared to have been added to and annotated at various times over many years. He wondered who had first drawn them. Whoever they were, he owed them a debt of gratitude.

Lady Harriet stood close and peered over his shoulder to better see the detail. The brush of her body against him, the touch of a tendril of hair against his cheek, made him nearly groan aloud. He forced his mind back to the drawings in front of him. The longer he looked, the more excited he became.

There were, it seemed, secret passages and rooms on every floor except the ground floor. After some thought he concluded that one of the symbols used indicated the locations of doors into the passages. He was not entirely sure about some of the other symbols, but perhaps they might indicate the locations of peepholes, which would permit a person lurking in the walls to spy on the occupants of the normal rooms? It was a likely possibility.

By far the most fascinating thing was the drawing of the cellars. For, not only was there a sheet for the level of the cellars he knew of, where root vegetables and wines and other comestibles were stored, but there was another sheet, which appeared to show not just one, but two further levels of cellars below that. At this rate, he would be spending the next few weeks exploring secret rooms and passages, and still be lucky to get through all of them!

And... if the conspirators knew of these, if, as Peterson had surmised, they had hidden the treasonously incriminating papers somewhere in this warren of hidden passages, what action might they feel forced to take, once they realised that he was exploring them??

Chapter Nine

With a start, Lady Harriet pulled back, removing the contact between her, and Lord Geoffrey. She could still feel the heat of him, as if they yet touched. What she truly wished was to throw herself into his arms, to regain that moment when he had kissed her. Instead, she stepped back, considering the maps of the house, and what they had just revealed. She wondered how the mechanisms for the other doors worked.

The thought of exploring the passages was beyond exciting – who knew what they might find within, given what had been there to find in the open parts of the house!

"When will we…"

"No-one must know of…"

They both spoke at the same instant, and stopped at the same instant, startled. He was the first to recover his composure.

"No-one must know of this. It must be kept between us for now."

"Why?"

And here was the moment. The moment that he was still not truly prepared for. What could he say? Could he trust her with the truth? Or would that simply endanger her more than this knowledge already did? Her bright green eyes watched him, waiting.

He gulped for air, his throat suddenly tight, and made an impetuous decision, perhaps an unwise one, yet it seemed, in the moment, the only decision to make.

"Because, my dear Lady Harriet, these hidden rooms and passages may, nay, almost certainly do, contain evidence of treason against the crown, perpetrated by the previous owner of this house, and an unknown number of other conspirators. Some of whom are, I believe, still here in the house, in my employ. If they were to realise that we have discovered this, they might choose to act precipitously. Speaking of this would be to endanger your life."

Her face had paled as he spoke, and she stared at him in some shock. But her eyes shone with intelligence, and it seemed that she was thinking, rather than about to faint away in a ladylike swoon. Minutes passed, while she absently twirled a tendril of hair around her finger, and thought, then she spoke.

"I see. If that is the case, then we will simply have to take the utmost care as we explore them. For surely, whatever is hidden there is what you have been seeking this last three months. This information makes sense of your insistence on seeing every crevice of the house – am I correct in my deduction?"

She showed no sign of fear, and her usual enthusiasm for life was undimmed – before him, what he saw was excitement.

She was quite a remarkable woman.

In that instant, he realised that she had just, neatly, trapped him again – for he had no choice but to allow her assistance, if he wished to ever complete his mission. She would get what she wanted, in this, at least.

"Yes, you are correct. That is what I have searched for, and yes, I must reluctantly allow you to assist me in searching these hidden passages. I have already stepped beyond the bounds of what I should reveal to you, and, if Charlton knew of this, he would never forgive me for involving you, but I see that I have little choice. For now, I must lock these away in my own safe, before anyone sees them. Miss Carpenter is sure to soon realise that she has left you scandalously unchaperoned, and return in a fluster!"

He stood, and went to a small cabinet near the desk, opening compartments and locks to secure the plans. Lady Harriet had, until then, quite completely forgotten about Miss Carpenter, and prayed that her *tendre* for Mr Featherstonehaugh would keep her distracted a little longer.

"Then how will you explain to me what we must do? How will we plan, if we are never to be alone?"

It was an excellent question, to which Lord Geoffrey was sadly lacking an answer. All manner of thoughts flooded his mind, in the context of being alone with Lady Harriet.

None of them had the least to do with his mission.

He forced the inappropriate thoughts aside and considered.

"Perhaps, tomorrow, you should ride here, rather than take the carriage. I could then take a little time out from ugly paintings and dust to show you around the property – I believe that you have yet to see the extent of the grounds in the direction away from Pendholm Hall?"

She nodded, waiting for him to continue.

"Of course, Miss Carpenter would accompany us, for reasons of propriety. It would, I am sure, not prevent her chaperonage from being effective, even if her lamentable riding abilities meant that we were well ahead of her most of the time – not out of sight, but certainly out of earshot."

Lady Harriet's face lit with delight and amusement. So, he had noticed her rather naughty tendency to make poor Miss Carpenter struggle to keep up with her when riding! It was a very clever solution, especially as she loved to ride, and, now that the weather was warming, she would enjoy a chance to see the grounds. It would be the perfect way to talk privately. And Moonbeam needed the exercise after the last few months when Harriet had sadly neglected her to spend her time at Witherwood Chase.

"What a brilliant idea!" She clapped her hands together, and spun across the room, all energy and impatience for the morrow. At that precise instant, Miss Carpenter, looking flushed, embarrassed and guilty, all at once, entered the room. Finding Lord Geoffrey and Lady Harriet on opposite sides of the room, and most obviously not engaged in anything scandalous, she breathed a sigh of relief, and chose to say nothing. Lady Harriet smiled, and her eyes lit with devilment.

"Miss Carpenter! We are to have a treat tomorrow. Lord Geoffrey has most kindly invited us to ride over, and he will ride with us to show us the farthest reaches of the Witherwood Chase grounds. Is that not most delightful, after all of these days amongst dusty paintings?"

Miss Carpenter paled, then squared her shoulders with a long-suffering sigh. "Delightful indeed, Lady Harriet." Her tone was dry, and Lord Geoffrey looked at her in surprise. Perhaps the companion was not so mousy as he had supposed.

~~~~~

All around, the ride was a great success. Miss Carpenter, whilst not exactly happy about it, managed to cope quite well, and was just slow and sedate enough to allow them the perfect opportunity to talk. Lord Geoffrey discovered himself having fun, even whilst discussing a topic of such a serious nature.

Lady Harriet rode extraordinarily well, and Lord Geoffrey thrilled to the chance to ride with a woman who could not only keep up with him, but potentially even outride him. He explained, in as minimalist a way as possible, that he was working secretly for a representative of the crown, to find and neutralise the last of the treasonous conspirators. That he was searching for a cache of incriminating papers, and possibly other items, and that Ashley and Jobs seemed the only possible guilty parties amongst the staff that had come with the house. He also explained that Peterson, Walters and Hurst were to be trusted absolutely, but that everyone else was not. The difficulty was going to be finding a way that Lady Harriet might assist in the search, whilst staying within the bounds of propriety. The only possible option seemed to be taking Miss Carpenter into their confidence. A step that Lord Geoffrey was loath to take, for every extra person who knew was another person at risk.

In the end, they agreed to think on that for a few days, whilst Lord Geoffrey studied the maps, and began to identify the places in the rooms and corridors, which corresponded to the points on the map marked with the symbol which they believed to represent doors. For they had to find those locations, before they could work out how to open the doors.

Lady Harriet prayed that all of the doors would have similar mechanisms, for if they did not, the search would be slow and difficult.

Chapter Ten

Three days later, Lord Geoffrey was ready to start opening doors – if he could work out how. He was fairly certain that he had discovered the doors, less certain of the mechanisms controlling them. Lady Harriet, unable to bear the thought of missing out on exploring, approached Miss Carpenter carefully.

Fifteen minutes later, a combination of appealing to Miss Carpenter's patriotic nature (which was not difficult, as her father and brother had both perished as soldiers in the war) and threatening to tell Lady Sylvia of her *tendre* for Mr Featherstonehaugh, and the hour that she had spent in his company, leaving Lady Harriet unchaperoned, had persuaded Miss Carpenter to co-operate.

Once convinced, Miss Carpenter was surprisingly enthusiastic about the project, for which Lady Harriet was immensely grateful. The plan was simple, and still rather risky, but it was the best they could do. Miss Carpenter would continue to work with Mr Featherstonehaugh, sequestered in the library, working through his final notes.

They would all pretend that Lady Harriet was also working with them, and, if asked by a servant, or anyone else, Miss Carpenter would report that Lady Harriet had simply left the room to use the necessary. Miss Carpenter was quite confident that Mr Featherstonehaugh would, because she asked it of him, also ask no awkward questions.

Meanwhile, Lady Harriet and Lord Geoffrey would be exploring the passages. The doors, between the map allowing them to be found, and the fact that the mechanisms were all very similar – in each case there was a whorl of carving of some sort to push, and a drape, tapestry or painting to pull on, at the same time – proved remarkably easy to open. Lord Geoffrey felt rather foolish that he and Peterson had not found even one of them in those three long months of searching – they seemed so obvious now that he knew what to look for!

~~~~~

Over the next two sennights, Lord Geoffrey and Lady Harriet discovered two things – that lurking in corridors and poking at walls, then disappearing through them, was remarkably difficult to do without drawing the notice of servants, and that hidden passages contained even greater amounts of dust and mouse droppings than long unused rooms. What they did not discover, was the cache of incriminating treasonous documents which they sought. It also became, as they worked at checking the passages and tiny hidden rooms, at first together, and then separately, obvious that there were more passages than those shown on the maps - which depressing fact just made the work harder.

There were moments of amusement, and moments of great surprise, as they discovered yet more paintings and other minor valuables, long forgotten in recesses in the hidden rooms and passages, or looked through peepholes to discover which rooms they allowed one to spy on.

Lady Harriet took especial delight in discovering a peephole which let her spy on Miss Carpenter and Mr Featherstonehaugh. They were studiously working away, whilst each casting surreptitious longing glances at the other, when they though the other wasn't looking. It took enormous effort for Lady Harriet not to burst into a fit of the giggles watching them. More seriously, she took note of all of the rooms for which she found peepholes, and they compared them to the symbols on the maps. It seemed that they had guessed the symbol correctly.

Each day provided another chance for Lady Harriet to be as close to Lord Geoffrey as she could manage, without actually throwing herself at him. Which was what, if she was honest, she truly wished to do. Now, more than ever, he took her breath away. Not only was he heroic by his actions, but also by his nature. His steadfast refusal to take advantage of their scandalous proximity, even whilst his storm grey eyes followed her and, in unguarded moments, revealed what she dared to hope was desire for her, was demonstration of his honourable character.

She found his dedication to his mission, and his willingness to suffer months of dirt, dust, and tedium impressive, and worthy of respect. Especially when compared to the town fops who had clung to her side this Season past.

Still, for both of them, the lack of result for their efforts was wearing, as was the continual subterfuge required to keep their actions secret. By the end of the second sennight, the novelty of peepholes and hidden passages had quite worn off, and frustration had set in.

~~~~~

As it happened, their explorations had not gone entirely unnoticed. Late one evening, after Lady Harriet and Miss Carpenter had returned to Pendholm Hall, and Lord Geoffrey had locked himself away in his study, with the maps, and a glass of good brandy, two figures slid quietly through the shadows at the back of the house. They made no sound until they reached the run-down shepherd's cottage at the edge of the boundary woods. Once inside, by the light of an only partially unshuttered lantern, Ashley and Jobs looked at each other with fear on their faces.

"What'll we do Ash? He's found the passages – least some of 'em anyway. The dust's all disturbed and some of them old pictures in there's been moved." Jobs' voice quavered as he spoke.

"We'll move them things from up top down with the rest tomorrow – one way or t'other - we can't wait any longer. I don't think he's found the hidden door down the bottom – even if'n he has, he won't find the second one." Ashley put as much confidence as he could into the statement, but, in truth, he wasn't sure it was true.

"What if he does? What if'n we runs inta him in the passages?"

"Then we'll deal with it. Whatever it takes. If he catches us, we're dead – we'll hang or worse for those papers. If'n he finds us, he'll have an 'accident' – I'll make sure of it."

"I dunno about that. I nivver signed up fer no killin. But… if'n it's his neck or mine…"

"Exactly Jobs, exactly. I'll send a message ter Nobby first thing. Have him ready to cart off whatever might need to be... removed, if'n ye take me meaning."

"Aye, that be best then. Nobby won't be askin' any questions, 'n if'n he's not needed, no-one'll know."

They talked for a while longer, about the best way to get from the top passages to the very bottom, without being seen, or making any noises in the wrong places. Finally, satisfied that they'd done all they could to prepare, they disappeared back into the night.

~~~~~

Lord Geoffrey locked the maps away again, satisfied with the day's work. There were only two areas of the upper floors hidden passages left to search – even allowing for possible extra bits that weren't marked on the maps. Tomorrow Lady Harriet would take the top floor, just below the attics, and he would take the one below. Surely they would find the papers in one of those two places.

If not, they would move on to the cellars. Which would be more difficult, for access to those meant moving into the servant's' domain, and staying unnoticed would be nigh on impossible. He prayed that would not be necessary. Every day of this work was more fraught with the risk of discovery.

His admiration for Lady Harriet's resourcefulness, determination and persistence had grown with every day of the search. Had she truly been still the tantrum prone child that Charlton had described to him so often, she would have long ago lost patience with the whole thing.

But she had not. She had stayed true to her commitment to helping him, and applied her keen intelligence to searching, and to their efforts to update the maps as they did so.

And every day he spent in her company, especially when they had searched together in the tight confines of the passageways, it became harder and harder to convince himself that he should not be attracted to her.

She was like no other woman he had ever met. When she gathered up Miss Carpenter and went home at the end of each day, he found himself oddly bereft. The house felt infinitely emptier without her bright presence. He pushed those thoughts away, for the thousandth time, and went back to considering what he would do when they did, finally, find the damn papers.

It startled him to realise that he had no idea exactly what those papers would contain. No doubt Setford had a very clear idea. Which was all that mattered. Lord Geoffrey couldn't wait to find the things, pass them to Setford, along with his traitorous employees, and be done with the mission.

He had come to like Witherwood Chase, to feel at home there, in a way that he had not felt at home anywhere since he was a boy of eight or ten, and his parents and grandmother had still been alive.

He wanted the dark stain of treason gone from the place, to make it completely his.

He wanted that done before the rest of the Hounds, and their families, came to stay at Eastertide, so that it might be a time of joyous celebration of the bonds they shared, with no shadow hanging over it.

Chapter Eleven

Lady Harriet was determined. This was the day when she would find what they sought, and bring this tedious process to an end. *'But'*, whispered the stubborn small voice in her mind *'how will you then find cause to see Lord Geoffrey?'* She ignored it. That was a problem for another day. For now, Lord Geoffrey desired to find those papers, so searching for them was her first priority.

She stood in a small parlour on the upper floor, with windows which overlooked the herb and scent garden in the rear courtyard area of the house. This wing was one of the oldest parts of the house, and, along this side of the floor, the rooms all opened into each other, in the manner of centuries past, with the doors close to the windows in each case.

The centre of the floor contained servants' corridors, but also secret passages, accessed through the apparently blank walls which faced the windows in each room. At the far end of the floor, there was an area which was not clearly explained by the maps.

Lady Harriet held high hopes for what that area might contain. Once certain that no-one was near, she stepped to the rear of the room and, with careful coordination, shoved hard on a carved leaf at the edge of the mantle above the fireplace, whilst also pulling on a shelf of the adjoining bookcase. The shelves pivoted out to her pull, and she stepped into the dark passageway revealed, partially unshuttered her small lantern, and pulled the door closed behind her, taking careful note of the placement of the lever which would allow her to open it later.

She worked her way down the passage, looking through peepholes, poking into crevices, seeking any evidence of other doors, of cabinets skilfully laid into the walls, or of any other possible hiding places. For a long distance, there was nothing of interest beyond the peepholes. Eventually, she reached what appeared to be an end to the passage. Frowning, she retraced her steps to the last peephole. Looking through it confirmed her suspicions – the passage should continue, for the room she saw was the second to last room on the floor, not the last.

Returning to the blank wall, she ran her fingers over its surface, and traced its edges, as well as the walls to either side. Finally, when she was beginning to think that she might be wrong, that the passage might simply end, her gloved fingers caught on an uneven area of the side wall. A few moments poking and pushing at it experimentally, and the blank end of the passage shifted slightly, with a soft click. She pulled it open and slipped through, impatiently pulling at an errant tendril of hair as it caught on the door frame.

~~~~~

Jobs had come into the kitchen for a quick bite of food, taking advantage of the left-overs from the nobility's luncheon.

He turned away, as if about to return to the stables, catching Ashley's eye as he did so. At Ashley's quick nod, Jobs stepped out of the kitchen, but, when sure that there were no eyes upon him, went quickly up the servants' stairs, rather than out the side door to the stables. Not long after, Ashley also quit the kitchens and casually took the same path.

One floor up, they took separate ways, Jobs slipping into the walls as soon as possible, but Ashley continuing in the servants' corridors, looking for all the world just like any footman might, going about his appointed business. Closer to the end of the old wing, he also slipped into the walls, finding Jobs waiting. In careful silence, they climbed up another two floors of narrow hidden stairs.

They emerged into a dusty room, tucked right at the end of the wing, close below the attics. Unlike most of the hidden spaces, this had a tiny amount of natural light from a narrow strip of dusty window.

From outside the house, it seemed just another window in the row along that floor, a bit smaller for being right at the end, but nothing unusual. From the inside, it let in just enough light, past the aged velvet drape that hung over it, to show a tiny table, a single chair, a rough pallet on the floor and a small crate in one corner. On the crate stood a pitcher of water, and some battered cups, just below an odd looking tap on the wall.

The room was just below the rainwater cistern – as a bolt hole, it had the superior advantage of a water supply. Incongruously, beside the crate stood a largish basket full of dirty looking dust sheets, topped by a tangle of old ropes or curtain pulls.

"Right then, let's be about it." Ashley strode across the room and lifted the rough timber tray with the pitcher and cups.

Setting it on the small table, he turned back to the crate. A few minutes work, and the apparently nailed together crate was in two pieces, revealing a smallish strongbox nestled at its core. The box was old, of ebony or some similar wood, banded in iron. It was locked, and heavy.

Jobs had pulled half the dust sheets from the basket, and Ashley carefully settled the box in amongst the remaining ones, and set to reassembling the crate, whilst Jobs reached for the dust sheets to cover the box. A sound shocked them to stillness. Their eyes met, with fear their uppermost emotion.

The other entry to the room – a secret door, behind a secret door, at the far end of a hidden passage, a door that no-one else should be able to find, opened, and Lady Harriet stepped through. The dim light from the window was enough to momentarily blind her after the deep darkness of the passageway, and she stood, blinking in confusion at the sight of the two men before her.

Ashley recovered from his shock first, and, just as Lady Harriet's eyes fell upon the box, and lit with startled comprehension of its importance, Ashley grabbed her, clamping one hand across her mouth, and the other around her body, trapping her arms against her sides. He hauled her back against him.

"Jobs!" Ashley's voice broke Jobs from his shock, and he leapt forward to grab Lady Harriet's legs before she could try to get away. Five minutes later, Ashley and Jobs bore bruises and scratches from Lady Harriet's failed attempts to escape.

They stood back, breathing hard from the effort, whilst Lady Harriet lay on the pallet, bound and gagged, her dress a little torn, and her eyes blazing her anger at them as clearly as if she could speak. If looks were daggers, they would both have been dead.

"Guess we'll be needin' Nobby then." Ashley's voice was flat, but not displeased. Rather be found by this little piece than by his Lordship with his bloody swords or a pistol. This way, they'd turn a nice profit too. Nobby had contacts. There'd be a few competing to buy something this pretty, if he wasn't mistaken. The high class houses of pleasure had a taste for quality fresh goods like her. They'd just have to be sure they got her out and gone tonight, and kept it so no-one suspected them.

But who would? She must have found the entry to this room by blind luck – and if she was alone, that meant no-one else knew where she was. For now, she could stay right there on the pallet, while they got the other valuables stowed away in the deep.

"Let's be getting this down t' the deep then. Once tis stored away with t'other, we c'n worrit about mileddy here."

Jobs piled the scattered dust sheets over the box, throwing aside the few pieces of old rope which had not been used in binding Lady Harriet, and Ashley lifted the basket. He looked at Lady Harriet, a touch regretfully.

"We'll be a seein' you later mileddy. Tis a pity we'll get a better price for ye untouched, or I'd be a tastin' the wares before we ship em, if'n ye understands me."

~~~~~

Lady Harriet watched as they exited the room, through a tiny door near the window. She'd think about the meaning of those words later. For now, once she was sure that they were gone, she would concentrate on trying to escape.

Lying still, she listened carefully. Their steps receded – it sounded as if there were stairs beyond that door. And then there was silence. Drifts of disturbed dust floated in the air, turned to sparkling gold by the faint rays of afternoon sun coming through the tiny window. She would have thought it pretty, were her situation not so dire.

Once their footsteps faded into the silence, she let herself move. She pulled and twisted her hands and feet, but only succeeded in abrading her wrists and ankles on the rough bits of rope that they had bound her with. She panted for breath, revolted by the taste of the dusty cloth that filled her mouth. She refused to think about what that taste might be caused by. She would especially not contemplate any thought whatsoever of mouse droppings. Definitely not.

Shouting was impossible, and anyway, it was extremely unlikely that anyone would be near enough to hear – for this was the furthest end of the least used wing of the house, and behind three layers of secret doors as well. She could but hope that Lord Geoffrey would become alarmed when she did not return for their late afternoon discussion of the day's achievements, and would come seeking her. The hours between now and then loomed ahead of her, an interminable opportunity for despair.

Resting before another attempt at loosening the ropes, she finally allowed herself to consider the import of the footman's parting words. Try as she might to discover another, she could only find one possible meaning in what he'd said. She might be physically an innocent, but she was certainly not ignorant about what men did with women, or of the existence of places expressly for allowing men to satisfy those needs. Her deceased elder brother, terrible man that he had been, had made quite certain of that by his actions. When her mother had, after his death, rescued the girls that he had abused and left with child, Lady Harriet had discovered many things that she might have wished not to know.

She loved Mary, Polly and Sally, and their children, just as much as she would have had they been legitimate, and so did her mother, for her brother's behaviour had certainly not been the fault of the girls. But, being of curious mind, she had asked them, once they trusted her, about their experiences. Their answers had been quite an education.

And, applying the understanding gained from those conversations to the footman's words, she was left with a single stark conclusion. Those men were going to take her somewhere, and sell her to a house of pleasure, to be used by men, against her will. The thought terrified her.

She well knew that, if there was love, or even respect, between a man and woman, as was the case with Charlton and Odette, and had been the case with her mother and father, when he still lived, then the physical activities carried out between men and women could be acceptable, or even pleasant.

But she also knew, from what her terrible brother had done to the girls, that it could be very unpleasant indeed.

She lay there shaking, exhausted by her struggles and close to tears. But she refused to give up hope. After all, this room was at the top of the house. They still had to get her out unseen – which would mean late at night.

So, there was time. Time for her to think, time for her to keep working at the ropes, and, she fervently prayed, time for Lord Geoffrey to find her.

He was a hero. He was the most capable man she knew.

Surely he would save her. She had to believe, and to keep trying to escape her bonds.

~~~~~

Lord Geoffrey was irritated and dispirited. It was late afternoon when he slipped carefully from the hidden passages into his dressing room, and allowed Hurst to assist him with a change from clothing which was much the worse for wear from his explorations, for the last passages on this floor had been, it turned out, quite the filthiest of all of the areas that he had yet explored. Thank God that Hurst was one of the men provided by Setford, and knew of the mission.

The mission. The mission that was still incomplete. For he had found nothing but filth this afternoon. Exploring the hidden parts of the cellars was looking inevitable. Cleaner, but no happier, he went down to his study to await Lady Harriet's return, praying that her search had been more fruitful, and less filth-encrusted than his.

Settled into his favourite chair, with a warming glass of brandy in hand, he wondered what his days would be like, once this mission was finally done with. What would he do with his time, when the search was complete? *'What would he do, when he no longer had a reason to see Lady Harriet every day...?'*

He would wait until she was here to pull out the maps, for them to update any of the detail of the passages they had explored today. For now, he would simply rest, and try to improve his mood.

He took down the beautiful old swords from the wall, and ran his fingers along the blade. It was now not only clean and polished, but sharp, as it should be. The balance was wonderful, and, had he not been waiting for Lady Harriet, he would have been tempted to take the blades straight to the drawing room which he had cleared of furniture to use as a *salle*. A little sword work always cleared his thoughts of any frustration – weapons required a clear and focused mind.

An hour later, he began to be concerned. Surely she should have returned by now? Even if she had found another unmapped section, surely it would not have taken this long? Generally, she and Miss Carpenter departed by dusk at the latest, and it was past that hour now. The darkness was closing in.

What if something had happened to her? He would never forgive himself should she be hurt. It was one thing to talk of the risk involved in this mission, and to speak of accepting it – it was quite another to meet that danger head on.

In that instant, he saw his own feelings for her clearly. No matter how much he might have been denying it, he did care for her, with an intensity that was almost frightening. The thought of any harm coming to her was like a blade to his heart. How could he have allowed her to place herself at risk? How could he have been so selfish, wanting her company and the success of his mission above her safety?

At that moment, there was a tap on his door. He breathed a sigh of relief – but his relief was short-lived. The door opened to admit Miss Carpenter and Mr Featherstonehaugh – who looked surprised, and then concerned, when it became apparent that Lady Harriet was not in the room.

"She hasn't returned." Lord Geoffrey broke the silence.

"What shall we do?" Miss Carpenter's voice was soft, and she twisted her hands together as she spoke.

"I am going to look for her. Miss Carpenter, please get Walters to take a message to Pendholm Hall – tell them that I have invited you, and Lady Harriet to stay for dinner. Let us not concern her family unduly. Should I not return by the time dinner is called, please, eat, and assure the staff that I am simply busy."

He strode out the door, and, seeing Peterson on duty in the hallway, called him to follow.

It was only when Peterson looked enquiringly at the sword in his hand that he realised he still held it. Well and good then. A weapon in hand was not a bad thing, should there be trouble.

They began on the top floor, searching through each room, then moving into the hidden passages.

Some hours later, they had covered every inch of the place twice over, and found nothing. Outside the walls, dinner had come and gone.

The candle in their lantern was burnt down to a nub, casting little effective light, and Lord Geoffrey had reached a state of internal turmoil unlike anything he had ever felt before. The fear of losing Lady Harriet forever ate at him. Not knowing where she was, or what she might be suffering was torture of the worst kind.

He slumped back against the passage wall, close against the blank wall where it simply ended. Peterson lifted the lantern, to better see Lord Geoffrey's face, and opened his mouth to speak. Lord Geoffrey's hand whipped out to arrest the motion of the lantern.

"I thought so! Look, Peterson – just there, caught at the edge of that piece of wall."

Peterson peered at the spot Lord Geoffrey pointed to, at first seeing nothing. Then he reached out a careful hand, and touched the dark gold hair that had glinted in the lantern light. He tugged on it gently, but it seemed trapped – trapped between the blank wall and the side wall that Lord Geoffrey leant on.

"Her hair!" Lord Geoffrey's voice was rough with emotion. "But… how is it trapped? What is it caught on?"

"I think, my Lord, that this wall is not a wall. It must be another door, for the hair appears to go into the crack along its edge…"

Without a word, Lord Geoffrey pushed away from the wall and began to push and prod at every part of the surrounding surfaces.

Chapter Twelve

Lady Harriet had worn her wrists and ankles raw, but had not succeeded in loosening the ropes enough to slip out of them.

The light was fading from the tiny window, and, with full darkness, she knew that it would not be long before they came for her. But unless she could somehow escape the ropes, there was nothing she could do but pray that Lord Geoffrey found her, before she was beyond his reach forever. She wished, most fervently, that she had, at every opportunity, thrown herself into his arms, propriety be damned.

She remembered that one kiss, and wished for more. If she was never to see him again, she wished for more to remember. She had known, for more than a year now, that he was the man for her. These last few months had simply deepened that feeling, deepened her love for him. Did he realise? Did he know how much she felt for him? Did he care for her in return? Or were those momentary flashes of desire she had seen in his eyes only that – desire, not anything deeper?

Her thoughts were interrupted eventually, long after the window had gone dark, by the sound that she had been anticipating with dread. The sound of feet upon the hidden stairs. As the door opened, she abandoned the last of her hope. It was too late. Lord Geoffrey could not save her now, they were here to take her away, to a life too horrible to contemplate.

"Had a comfortable afternoon, have you mileddy?" Ashley, the footman, smiled at her as he spoke. It was not a pleasant smile.

"Let's get movin Ash, the quicker she's off and gone, the happier I'll be." Jobs stepped towards her, then paused. "How's we gonna carry her Ash? Them stairs is narrow and steep. If'n she wriggles too much, we could all end up at the bottom with broken bones."

"Carefully – we's carryin her carefully. We wants to protect our investment here, doesn't we? And you, mileddy, you'll a be keeping still for us, won't ye? Cause I'm thinkin ye've no more wish than us to fall, have ye?"

Lady Harriet shook her head. She most definitely didn't want to fall – alive and unhurt, there might still be a chance to escape – injured there would be none.

"Right then. I'll get her by the legs, and you be liftin under her arms. I'll go down them steps first, backwards and slow, and you'll keep pace wiv me, wiv her between us."

Ashley bent to lift her legs. Jobs looked at the door to the stairs uncertainly, then shrugged and shoved his hands under her upper body, hindered by her hands tied behind her.

She flinched at the feel of their uncaring hands on her, but did not fight. She chose, instead, to be as limp and heavy as possible. With two older brothers, she had learnt, long ago, that limp and heavy was much harder to lift and carry than wriggling and screaming.

The men grunted and hauled her up awkwardly, making so much noise that she did not, at first, notice any other sound. But she did notice something else. The air in the room had moved, stirred like a light breeze across her face, drifting a fine tendril of her hair into her eyes. She gave no sign of anything having changed, but inwardly she prayed. *'Please, let that touch of moving air mean what I think it might.'*

And then she heard it – definitely a sound. A sound she was deliriously happy to hear – the sound of the other door moving, ever so slowly. Let it be him, let it be Lord Geoffrey come to save her. The men started to cart her towards the door to the stairs, and for a moment she thought that she must have been mistaken.

~~~~~

Lord Geoffrey was ready to give up poking about and simply batter at the door, when his fingers found an odd bump, low down on the wall. A bit of pushing at it, and the wall popped open, just a crack, releasing a gentle puff of air that sent Lady Harriet's golden hair drifting to the floor.

"Finally!"

He pulled it open, and stepped through into another dark and empty passage. A short passage. With no visible exit.

Geoffrey groaned aloud, then began the process all over again. There had to be another way out. She had come in here, so she had to have gone out of here. He just had to find it.

The walls were rougher here – more possible bumps and lumps to push and prod at. He worked along the passage on one side, whilst Peterson took the other. Just as they reached the apparent end of the short length of passage, he stopped, and froze in place, touching Peterson to make him stop too.

There was a sound, he was sure of it. From the other side of the wall. Creeping forward, he pressed his ear to the rough plaster and listened. Men's voices. Two, he thought. He couldn't make out what they said. Then a thump and a bump, as if they were moving something heavy about, and bumped into a chair or similar, then a muttered curse – he might not be able to hear the exact words, but the tone and emotion in it were clear enough.

As he pressed harder against the wall, desperate to hear more, his fingers caught on a simple latch. He lifted it, and the door shifted gently. The disturbed air carried a scent to him from within the space on the other side of the door. A scent he would recognise anywhere. Lady Harriet's perfume, that unique mix of rose, daphne and lemon. He closed his eyes, as much from horror as relief.

She was here – but she was in the hands of the traitors – was she hurt? Why was she silent? He could not imagine Lady Harriet going anywhere quietly, if it was against her will. He eased the door open a little, and peered into the room. Ashley and Jobs were struggling to lift a completely limp Lady Harriet, moving awkwardly towards a door on the other side of the small room.

His fear for her drove him to immediate action. He could not, as much as he wished it, simply drive his sword through Jobs' back, even though it was presented nicely before him – for the sword could just as easily penetrate the man and harm Harriet, limp in his arms, as well. He leapt forward and drove the hilt of the sword towards Jobs head, hoping to knock him out with one blow.

But as the blow landed, Jobs staggered under Lady Harriet's weight, and what should have been a solid collision with the man's head became a glancing blow instead. Jobs dropped her and spun, roaring in anger. Ashley, after one look at Lord Geoffrey, sword in hand and eyes wild, with Peterson behind him, somehow hauled Lady Harriet up and over his shoulder, then staggered to the stairs. For one second, before Jobs rushed him, fists windmilling in panicked attack, Lord Geoffrey found himself looking straight into Harriet's beseeching eyes.

Then she was gone, and he heard a bolt shot into place on the other side of the door, as Ashley carried her away. Desperation drove him. He would not lose her now! He would not let her down – that look had told him she believed in him – that she had the utmost faith in his ability to save her. To her, as always, he was a hero. Well – it was time he lived up to that then, though he had never sought it.

Then all thought disappeared, as battle reflexes honed at war cut in. He became a coldly focused fighting machine. A minute or two later, Jobs found himself flat on the floor, Lord Geoffrey's sword at his throat, as Peterson used some of the remaining scatter of old rope on the floor to bind him tightly.

"Where is he taking her?"

The sword still hovered at Jobs' throat, and Lord Geoffrey's voice made it clear that anything but the truth would result in pain or death. Jobs gulped, flinching as the movement of his throat caused the sword point to break his skin. Stammering from fear, he spoke, with a last spark of defiance.

"You'll be too late. He'll have her out and away afore ye can get down t'ground. Once she's in the cart, ye'll nivver see her agin."

Lord Geoffrey looked at Peterson, and they reached a silent agreement. Geoffrey ran to the now bolted door that Ashley had carried Harriet through, and began to batter it, using anything to hand. The bolt might not break – but the wood was old – batter it enough, and surely it would splinter.

Peterson spun and ran back the way they had come, through the hidden passages and out into the main part of the house. He flung himself down the stairs, yelling to Walters, who was stationed in the foyer, to get Hurst and follow, then charged out into the night. Where was the nearest lane to the estate? Where might a cart be hidden?

Meanwhile, the door had finally shattered under Lord Geoffrey's onslaught. Geoffrey slid down the narrow stairs, perilously close to falling, uncaring of his own safety in the desperate need to get to Harriet in time. Unregarded, in the room above, Jobs muttered pathetically about being abandoned, bound hand and foot. He was quite unaware of the appropriateness of him being left exactly as he had left Lady Harriet all day. He did, however, realise after a while that, unless he could escape now, he was dead – for he would surely hang for treason. He began to struggle against the ropes.

Reaching the ground floor, Lord Geoffrey sprinted through the servants' corridor. Shoving a startled maid aside, he charged out the door towards the stables, sword still in hand, silver in the moonlight. Skidding to a halt, he looked around. Where had Ashley gone with her?

Then he saw it – a moment's glint of moonlight on the gold of her hair. Near the edge of the trees, across the wide lawn. He had to be heading for the rutted lane that led to the old shepherd's cottage.

Geoffrey ran, ran as he had never run before in his life, glad that he heard Peterson's footsteps on the gravel behind him, before he hit the smooth grass of the lawn. In that instant, he blessed his gardeners – they would all be getting an increase in their wages, for the immaculate lawn made it easier to run. And he, a fit, large man, trained to fight, could run considerably faster than an older, somewhat unfit footman carrying a full grown woman.

He was gaining on them, but they were still ahead, and nearly at the small stone wall that marked his boundary. When Ashley reached the stile over the wall, another man leapt up onto it from the other side, reaching for Harriet.

"No! no, no, no, no!" The words were muttered, for all his breath was spent on running. But his heart's agony was in every one of them. As other hands lifted Harriet away, Lord Geoffrey swung his sword at Ashley's lower leg, waiting only a second to see him fall screaming, before leaving him for Peterson to deal with. He vaulted the stile and launched himself onto the back of the cart as it lurched into motion in response to the driver's desperate whipping of the horses.

He paused a second to touch a finger to Harriet's face, where she lay tumbled in the bed of the cart, and realised, as he did, that the driver had thought the shudder of the cart as he landed on it to be simply part of the violent lurch into motion. The man didn't know he was there!

Moving with infinite care, he felt his way down Harriet's arm and used the sword edge to cut the ropes that bound her. She bit down on the gag at the pain of returning circulation, but made no sound.

He eased down to trace her leg to her ankles, silently wishing he was doing so in any circumstances but these, and sliced the ropes from her ankles too. As he did so, she was already pulling the gag from her mouth.

He crept up past her, pausing only long enough to press a kiss to her lips, and edged towards the front of the cart. He felt, rather than heard, Harriet easing her way after him. He turned to look at her, and her green eyes sparkled in the moonlight. She motioned towards the man, then to Geoffrey. Then she pointed at herself, and mimed her hands holding reins and driving.

His heart bursting with love and pride, he nodded once, and turned back to his task. She edged to one side, close against him, but not enough to prevent his movement. He tapped her hand three times, and launched himself. His arm went around the driver's throat, cutting off his air, and the sword came around to hang before the man's face, the threat obvious.

The driver squirmed desperately, the ribbons falling unregarded from his fingers, then froze in place when he saw the sword.

As he dropped the ribbons, Harriet launched herself from the back of the cart onto the seat, snatching the falling ribbons of leather from the air, a fraction of a second before they fell into the gap between cart and horses.

She teetered a moment on the brink of falling herself, and Geoffrey felt his heart stop in his chest, then she grabbed the seat with one hand and hauled herself back, already beginning to bring the racing horses under control. She was, it seemed, as good at driving them as riding them.

"That thrice damned bastard's name is Nobby. He had a deal with them, to sell me to a house of pleasure, and split the profits. I'd happily see you skewer him now, but I suspect we'd better turn him over to the law."

Her voice was a little shaky, but not, he realised from fear. It was anger he heard, pure and simple. She was, quite simply, magnificent.

"Oh. That wasn't very ladylike language was it? I am sorry, but in this case, I rather think I'm entitled to swear."

He laughed, a shaky, almost hysterical edge to it.

"I believe you're right."

He kept the sword to Nobby's throat, while Harriet brought the straining horses back to a walk, then turned them carefully in a wider bit of the lane, before driving them back toward Witherwood Chase at a smart clip.

~~~~~

By the time they reached the stile again, Peterson had bound the bleeding Ashley, and Walters and Hurst were ready with ropes to bind Nobby. They hauled the screaming Ashley on to the back of the cart, and Harriet drove them all back around through the gates and up the drive to the stables.

Once the horses were held by the grooms, Lord Geoffrey slipped from the seat, supervising the traitors' removal from the cart, and the field dressing of Ashley's wound. He didn't want the man dying on him from an infection, before he'd had time to tell him where the papers were. Satisfied that things were under control, he turned back to the cart.

Lady Harriet was simply sitting there, staring ahead. She was, he realised, shaking, quivering like a leaf in the wind.

He knew this reaction – he had seen it after battles, when the aftershock of action set in. Gently, he stepped up as close to the cart as he could, and, reaching out, slid her into his arms and lifted her down. She came willingly, sliding her arms around his neck, and burying her face against his shoulder. He thought she whispered something, but it was so faint he wasn't sure. It had sounded suspiciously like *'My hero'*.

He carried her into the house.

Chapter Thirteen

Lord Geoffrey settled Lady Harriet onto a chaise in the parlour, rang for tea, and brandy, and sat quietly beside her. She said nothing, but simply reached out and twined her fingers with his.

When the maid brought the tea and brandy, it was obvious that the staff were agog to know what was happening. They would have to wait. He shooed the maid out and poured a cup of tea, adding a generous drop of brandy. Harriet accepted it gratefully, and sipped.

Peterson knocked and entered when bidden, reporting that the traitors were bound and locked up in a secure room in the stables, with Walters guarding them. Lord Geoffrey nodded his thanks. Peterson turned to go, when Lady Harriet spoke.

"Please stay, Peterson. For you should hear what I have to tell, given your part in this mission."

Peterson hesitated, and, at Lord Geoffrey's confirmatory nod, stepped back into the room.

Her voice hesitant at first, then growing stronger as she spoke, and the brandy took effect, Lady Harriet described the events of the day. When she spoke of the box that she had seen, just before Ashley and Jobs had bound and gagged her, Lord Geoffrey sprang to his feet, pacing about the room. Could it really be over? Was that box the end to this mission? But where had they taken it? He broke in on her tale.

"Was there anything in what they said to indicate where they took the box?" She stared at him a moment, face blank, and he castigated himself for behaving in such an inconsiderate way - here he was, expecting her to have taken detailed note of what the men were saying, when she had just been roughly set upon, bound, gagged and threatened!

"I am so sorry! That is completely unreasonable of me to ask."

Lady Harriet looked up at him and smiled. His heart turned over at what he saw in her eyes.

"Ah, but I did listen to them. I was so utterly, blazingly angry, it hadn't yet occurred to me to be truly afraid. That came later. Just before they left the room, Ashley said something about taking it down to *'the deep'* and putting it with *'the other'*. It was just a single comment, before they left me there. They had put the box in a basket of dirty linens and covered it up. Probably so that they could take it down into the cellars somewhere, and be thought to be just adding a basket to the laundry pile. But beyond down in the cellars, which seems logical, I've no idea where *'the deep'* might be."

Frustration laced her voice. They might have the conspirators, but they didn't yet have the evidence. Lord Geoffrey thought a moment, pacing about the room, then spun back towards her.

"Wait – they spoke of 'another' something?"

"Yes – they definitely were going to put the box with *'the other'*."

"But that's wonderful! Forgive me, I know that sounds terrible of me, but had today's events not happened, we would never have known of this second thing that is hidden. If we had found this box when they were not there, we would most certainly have believed that we had found all that there was to find."

Lord Geoffrey fell to his knees beside her, and pulled her into his arms, pressing a kiss to her lips as he did so. She clung to him, a little puzzled but delighted by his actions. Peterson met her eyes over Lord Geoffrey's shoulder and smiled. Lord Geoffrey pulled back and gazed at her.

"Oh Harriet, you are truly wonderful! Whilst I would never wish for you to have suffered what you have today, I am beyond grateful for what you have discovered. Your courage and resourcefulness never cease to amaze me. When any society miss might be expected to have fainted dead away, you were alert enough to listen and take note. And then on the cart! You are magnificent, magnificent!"

He had spoken her name! Without the 'Lady' in front of it! Her heart suddenly beat harder, the intimacy of her unadorned name on his lips leaving her even more flushed than the kiss.

Peterson cleared his throat, whilst feigning great interest in a book which had been left lying on a side table.

Lord Geoffrey, who had, for those moments, completely forgotten Peterson's presence, dropped Harriet's hands, and leapt to his feet, a flush of embarrassment on his face.

"Ah, Peterson, it seems that we will need to interrogate our prisoners. I am sure that one of them can be convinced to tell us where the box is hidden. That would be considerably quicker than searching every hidden part of the cellars that the maps show, and probably parts that exist, but aren't on the maps."

Lord Geoffrey shuddered internally, even as he spoke. He hated interrogations. A good clean fight was one thing, but the process of drawing information forth was a dirty thing. Gerry had always been the one amongst the Hounds who dealt with that – expertly and efficiently. They were all beyond grateful that he had done that dirty work for them. Tonight, Geoffrey would have to deal with it himself.

"Yes, my Lord, I will arrange that – tonight – the less time they have to think about it, the more likely they are to tell us. Will you wish to be present?"

Lord Geoffrey took a deep steadying breath.

"Yes, it is my duty to do so."

Peterson nodded, having expected nothing less.

"And, my Lord, shall I arrange for Lady Harriet and Miss Carpenter to be conveyed home? And what message do you wish delivered to Viscount Pendholm to explain all of this?"

Harriet paled. The thought of explaining all of this to her brother and mother did not appeal at all.

They were reasonable people, and Charlton, she knew, had dealt with traitors before, but neither of them would be happy about her involvement in this mission, especially when they heard the details of today's events. But hear they would, for it was now past any reasonable time for her to be returning, even after a supposed dinner.

"I think that, before we consider returning Lady Harriet to her home, we must first call for some ointment for her poor wrists and ankles, which are, I now see, worn quite raw from her struggles. I do apologise, Lady Harriet, for not having that attended to sooner. Also, I suspect that some food would not go amiss, as you have had nothing since breaking your fast this morning."

Harriet looked positively enthusiastic at the suggestion of food. It was, at least in part, because that would delay facing her family, but the embarrassingly loud growl of her stomach was a pointed reminder of her actual need to eat.

"Whilst those matters are addressed, let us deal with our prisoners. Once that is done, I will personally escort Lady Harriet and Miss Carpenter to Pendholm Hall."

Harriet met his eyes, her gratitude and relief showing clearly.

"Thank you, Lord Geoffrey, your escort will be most appreciated."

~~~~~

The three prisoners, when asked questions separately, demonstrated rather different reactions. Nobby refused to say anything, knowing full well that there was enough wrongdoing in his past to deliver him to the hangman's noose no matter what he said now. Lord Geoffrey let him be – for he had, as far as they could tell, no knowledge of what had gone on inside the house. Ashley and Jobs were another matter. Threats of immediate violence had little effect on Ashley, but Jobs was quickly persuaded that cooperation might, perhaps, save him from the hangman's noose.

Compared to death, transportation seemed a far better option. Lord Geoffrey gave his word that, if Jobs provided them a guide to the location of the hidden box, he would do his best to ensure that transportation was the sentence. But only once they had recovered the box – if Jobs gave them falsehoods, he would make certain the sentence was death.

"Jus' one other thing, milord. If'n I tells ye, don' ye be putting me back near Ash. If'n he knows I've ratted him out, I'm a goner for sure."

"That can be arranged. Now speak."

Peterson took careful notes as Jobs described the path to the secret doors in the cellars, and the exact location of the hidden boxes. Lord Geoffrey was startled to hear that below the cellars, there was not only a priesthole, dating back to the time of Cromwell, but below even that, a secret chapel with an ancient altar. The boxes were, sacrilegiously, it seemed, hidden in a cavity within the altar itself. Finally, when Lord Geoffrey was satisfied that they had all of the information needed to recover the boxes, Jobs was locked away separately, still securely bound.

But confirming the truth of his words would need to wait for the morning. For now, he must face Lady Harriet's family, and admit to the terrible danger he had placed her in, by allowing her to assist him. He would understand should they forbid him from ever seeing her again. At least his mind would. His heart was not so sanguine about that possibility. The ache in his chest at the very thought suggested that such a possibility would leave him empty forever.

~~~~~

Harriet perched on the edge of the carriage seat, desperately wishing that she could lean against Lord Geoffrey's temptingly close shoulder. But fear of the coming conversation kept her from moving. Miss Carpenter had exclaimed over her poor wrists and ankles, and tutted about the battered state of her dress, but said nothing further. Harriet knew that she would honour their agreement and support her.

When they alighted before Pendholm Hall, Lord Geoffrey graciously offered her his arm, and led her inside. The warmth of the strong muscle beneath her hand reached her, even through the layers of his shirt and coat, making her feel safe and protected somehow, as she had felt in his arms when he had lifted her down from the cart.

Lord Geoffrey, at that moment, was feeling quite as nervous as she was, if not more so, although he strove to keep his manner steady and calm, for her. Her scent wrapped about him, bringing, as it always did, that sense of safety and care. They would manage this conversation, together.

When they were admitted to the house, they were shown to Lady Sylvia's private parlour. As was their habit, Charlton and his mother had settled for a late evening coze, to talk through the events of their day. Lady Odette had already retired, happy to allow Charlton this time with his mother, knowing that he would not stay away from her long. Charlton took one look at Lord Geoffrey's face, and his sister's dirtied and torn morning dress, and leapt to his feet. Miss Carpenter followed them into the room, and the door closed behind her.

"What has happened?"

"Oh my poor child – your wrists – what has happened to you?"

Charlton's voice tangled with Lady Sylvia's as they both spoke at once.

"It is rather a long story, I am afraid, but it must be told now, despite the late hour." Lord Geoffrey sounded more nervous than Charlton had ever heard him. Geoff didn't do nervous – in all their years at war, he had always been cool and steady, no matter what happened. This would be most interesting.

"Do sit then, and I'll call for some tea." Lady Sylvia was as practical as ever. In that moment, Harriet thanked God for her mother's nature. They sat, Geoffrey and Harriet instinctively staying together, sinking gratefully onto a comfortable chaise. Miss Carpenter settled on a small chair in one corner of the room, and tried hard to be invisible.

A somewhat strained silence ensued.

Once a maid had delivered the tea, and left them with it, Charlton's patience failed him.

"Out with it Geoff – I can see that there is a lot to tell, so please get on with it – or... is it Harriet's story to tell?" He looked at Harriet, waiting. Harriet looked at Lord Geoffrey, and some unspoken communication passed between them, which Lady Sylvia observed with great interest, then Geoffrey spoke.

"I'll start at the beginning. Charlton, you know I've been working for Setford. Lady Sylvia, I'll repeat this part for your benefit. You already know that I received ownership of Witherwood Chase as reward for services to the crown during last year. What you don't know, but Charlton is at least a little aware of, is that along with the property, I received a mission. The previous owner of Witherwood Chase was part of a treasonous plot. When it was discovered, he was dispossessed of all his belongings and incarcerated with many of his conspirators. But not, Setford suspected, all of them. So the price of me receiving the property was to ferret out any evidence still hidden there, and the remaining conspirators."

He paused for a sip of tea, feeling a little better now that he had begun.

"Hence my obsessive poking into every corner of the house, and taking inventory of everything I found. Which, I must say, has proved a capital idea. One which is set to make me a remarkably wealthy man, when all of those ugly paintings are sold. When Lady Harriet volunteered..."

At this description, Charlton snorted, and Lady Sylvia smiled in amusement. Geoffrey fixed them with a baleful look.

"As I said, when Lady Harriet volunteered to assist, I was most grateful. For, whilst she and Miss Carpenter trailed around with Mr Featherstonehaugh, taking interminable notes about the obvious contents of the house, I was free to search for hidden things. Things which I conclusively failed to find."

"Ah," Charlton broke in, "which was when you sought our suggestions at Meltonbrook Chase, about ways in which hidden rooms or passages might be concealed, and how to find them."

"Correct. Shortly after that, accidentally, Lady Harriet stumbled, quite literally, on a secret door, and opened it. Only I was present at that moment. Inside the room revealed, we discovered detailed maps of the entire house, showing most of the secret passages and rooms as well. We initially kept it between ourselves, but then found ourselves forced to draw Miss Carpenter and Mr Featherstonehaugh into our confidence to some degree."

At mention of her name, Miss Carpenter squirmed uncomfortably on her chair. So much for not being noticed....

"The last few weeks we have searched, usually separately, through every hidden passage we could. And found nothing but more dust and mouse droppings. This morning, we moved into the last two sections of the passages, except for the cellars. I admit, I was not hopeful, and searching the cellars, with access through the servants' areas was not a task I looked forward to."

Lady Sylvia nodded, listening to Lord Geoffrey, but watching Harriet's face.

"By late afternoon, I had finished searching my allocated section of the passages, with no better luck than on any previous day. I waited in my study for Lady Harriet's return. But today, she did not appear at the expected time. I waited, thinking that perhaps she had found some extra passages, and it was taking longer. But then I realised that it was far too late. I sent you that message – I do wholeheartedly apologise for the subterfuge – so as not to worry you unnecessarily, and set out to search for her."

Lady Sylvia had gone very pale, and was looking, again, at Harriet, and her bandaged wrists. Geoffrey continued, telling the tale of his frustrated and increasingly fearful search, the discovery of Harriet's hair trapped in the passage, and his reaching the room where she was held. When he spoke of noticing the hair and thus finding the door, Harriet gazed at him with open adoration.

At that point, Harriet spoke up, taking over the telling of the tale, describing her day, how she had stumbled upon the secret doors, and walked in on the conspirators, only to be captured and bound. When she spoke of the plans they had made for her, Charlton's face went hard as stone. When she reached the point in the story where Geoffrey had arrived at the room, he joined her in the telling of the rest, their voices interweaving as they shifted from one part to the next, instinctively finishing each other's sentences until the tale was complete.

Lord Geoffrey spoke of her heroic capture of the ribbons and controlling the horses, Harriet spoke of Lord Geoffrey's heroic disabling of Ashley, his leap to the cart, and the capture of Nobby.

To Charlton and Lady Sylvia, watching them, it was very obvious that the bond between them was extraordinary, and that something remarkable had been forged that day, beyond the achievement of capturing the villains. Lady Sylvia wondered if Harriet and Geoffrey had admitted their feelings to each other yet.

"So there you have it. A sordid and distressing tale. I can only most humbly beg your forgiveness for ever placing Lady Harriet in such danger. I will never forgive myself. At that moment when she teetered on the cart, I knew that my life would not be worth living if I had lost her. Now, to complete this damnable mission, all that remains is to go into the cellars tomorrow morning, and retrieve the hidden boxes, confirm that their contents are what Setford seeks, and allow him to carry off the conspirators and the papers."

"I insist on being the one to open that altar and remove the boxes. After all of this, I think I'm entitled to that." Harriet's voice was strong, and her bright cheerful manner was returning, even after all the shocks of the day.

Geoffrey looked at her a moment, then nodded.

"Charlton, would you do me the honour of being there as well? I would like another witness to this, one that Setford knows and trusts."

"Certainly, I wouldn't miss it!"

"You're not leaving me out of this either! After what my daughter has been through for those boxes, I want to see them with my own eyes."

Lord Geoffrey, seeing a glint in Lady Sylvia's eyes that was a rather clear echo of her daughter in a determined mood, inclined his head in acknowledgement. She smiled.

"Good, we are agreed then. We will bring Harriet to Witherwood Chase in the morning, and see this thing complete. And Lord Geoffrey – of course I forgive you – I am fully aware of how difficult it is to prevent my daughter from doing anything that she truly wishes to do. I do not blame you in the least. But I am overwhelmingly glad that you were there to save her – as you saved us all last year."

Lord Geoffrey flushed at Lady Sylvia's words.

"You are most gracious my Lady. I will look forward to your arrival on the morrow."

He turned to Lady Harriet, took her hand a moment, and bent to kiss it, before standing and bowing to the others, then took his leave.

~~~~~

In the carriage, he allowed himself to relax, and discovered, to his chagrin, that he was shaking. He had been so afraid that they might blame him, might cast him from their house, that he might never see Harriet again.

The relief was overwhelming. He could not bear to never see her. He loved her, he wanted to...

What! What had he just thought? He rewound the thoughts

and there it was. He loved her. It was a startling idea, yet it seemed utterly right.

But... how did she really feel about him? What if her affection really was just the infatuation that he had always thought it? What would he do?

Chapter Fourteen

Harriet had barely slept, between the aching in her arms and legs from the long hours bound in awkward positions, and the exertion afterwards on the cart, and the feverish dreams of Lord Geoffrey's arms about her, and his lips on hers, all mixed in with more terrible dreams of being bound in the darkness. She tried to sit patiently whilst her maid dressed the wounds on her wrists and ankles again, wincing a little at the pressure on the sensitive flesh, then found herself still ravenous after the exertions of the previous day. Lady Sylvia was happy to see that Harriet's appetite was undiminished by her adventures.

Once in the carriage, she fidgeted, anxious to see Lord Geoffrey again, desperate to finally see the papers that had brought them all so much trouble, and, at the same time, afraid of what would follow. The days ahead looked bleak and empty if she should no longer have an excuse to spend them in Lord Geoffrey's company. She had thought, last night, when he had cared for her, held her, that she saw something in his eyes, in his manner, that she had longed for, this year past and more.

In the grey morning light, she was no longer sure. Did he care for her, truly, or was it just her wishes making her see what wasn't there? If he did not care for her, what would she do? For she loved him. She had from almost the first time she had met him. That would not change. She had known that he was the man she wanted, been quite certain of her feelings from the start – but how would she live if he never returned her love, or even affection?

As Witherwood Chase came into sight, she pushed those thoughts aside – first, the cellars, and the boxes of papers.

They were shown into the study and Lord Geoffrey greeted them a little seriously, although his eyes locked with Harriet's the moment she stepped into the room. That moment seemed to last forever, and to be gone too fast. He dragged his eyes away, and, showing them to seats placed near the desk, he brought forth the maps of the house.

Peterson had been busy, and had marked, on the map of the cellars, the places described by Jobs. Once they were all clear on the path before them, Lord Geoffrey rose.

"Shall we get this over with?"

"By all means. I would like to see these papers that are so precious as to be, apparently, worth my life and more." Lady Harriet rose from her seat. Lord Geoffrey led her from the room, followed by the others. The servants were shocked at the procession that entered their domain, and scurried aside.

At the back of the root cellar, Peterson led them to a section where sacks of various vegetables hung on hooks, and larger barrels of potatoes and onions stood below. Once the barrels were shifted aside, a push and pull on two of the hooks at once caused the panel to open, exposing dark steps beyond, steep and uneven. Lantern in hand, he led them downwards.

The steps turned, and finally deposited them in a small room carved out of the earth. Nooks carved into the wall served as shelves, and a space for a narrow bed. A trickle of water fell from a small hole in the rocks to one side, no doubt fed from the rain water cisterns above, and pooled in an old earthenware bowl, before overflowing to trickle out again through a crack in one corner of the floor. It was well constructed as a place in which a man could hide for a long time, given a supply of food. Harriet shuddered at the thought of priests being forced to hide in such places, those many years ago.

Turning, they studied the space. Where was the secret entry to the chapel, which Jobs had described? Lord Geoffrey, eyes narrowed, strode forward and swept the mouldering blanket from the boards that covered the earth in the nook designed as a bed. Grasping the boards, he lifted, and revealed, not the beaten earth that was to be expected, but a small space and more stairs leading down into inky darkness.

Again, Peterson took the lead, checking the steps for safety, and holding the lantern, as best he might, to allow them to see where they stepped. Lord Geoffrey assisted Lady Harriet, and Charlton assisted Lady Sylvia, who grimaced a little at the smears of earth now decorating their clothes.

When they reached the bottom, they gasped in awe. Whoever had built this had spent much effort and care. They stood in a small chapel, the walls lined with stone, plastered and decorated with paintings – religious imagery in a style many centuries gone, the colours still beautiful, only lightly touched with mould in a few places. Small gems embedded in parts of the pictures glinted in the lantern light, and silver candlesticks shone in nooks and on either end of the plain altar.

The altar was built of stone and wood, carved with elegant simplicity. Harriet stepped forward, and walked around it, wondering exactly where it opened.

"On the end, my Lady. The two floral pieces to either side of the cross in the carving. According to Jobs, they must both be pressed at once, and the timber panel on the end will open. In these old altars, they made these cavities to store relics – often the bones of saints, I believe." Lord Geoffrey's voice was muted. This might be long unused, but they all felt the sense of the intended sanctity of the place.

Harriet, praying that no bones of a saint graced this altar, sharing their housing with sacrilegious boxes of traitorous information, did as instructed. The panel popped out as they had been told it would, and she lifted it aside. Reaching in, she pulled out two boxes – one that she had seen upstairs, one which was larger and heavier, and passed them to Peterson, who sat them on the single simple pew.

They looked so insignificant, yet, for what these contained, men had been willing to destroy her life. Charlton tested each box.

"Locked. As was to be expected. How do we plan to open them."

"I have no key, and Jobs didn't know of the key's location either, but…" Lord Geoffrey had turned towards Lady Harriet, with a hopeful expression. He smiled when he saw that she was already pulling a pin from her soft gold hair.

She pushed past her brother and sank down onto the pew.

"Peterson, the light, if you would."

Peterson brought the lantern close and both Charlton and

Lady Sylvia watched in some astonishment as Lady Harriet carefully picked the locks on both boxes. With a satisfied expression, she replaced the pin in her hair and turned shining eyes to Lord Geoffrey.

"There my Lord. If you would open them now, we may at last see what all of this fuss has been for."

Lord Geoffrey was watching Lady Harriet with unfeigned admiration. He bowed elegantly to her, with a flourish worthy of Mr Featherstonehaugh, and stepped forward.

The boxes proved to contain, as Baron Setford had expected, a collection of papers detailing meetings, conspirators' names, plans, and other deeply damning evidence of treason. They also contained a few small bags of coinage, and of gemstones, which was not expected. In the larger box, a small ledger listed payments made – a source of information that would delight Setford and no doubt lead his men to many of those who had supported the plot, however peripherally.

Papers. So innocent looking, and yet enough to send many men to their deaths. Lady Harriet shuddered, and gently closed the lids.

"Let us be out of this place. That so many should have plotted against our country leaves me feeling sickened." No-one disagreed.

~~~~~

Urgent messages were sent, and, three days later, Baron Setford arrived. He brought a second carriage, with barred windows and armed men to guard it.

The prisoners were handed over to his guards, and the carriage departed, taking them to their fate. Lord Geoffrey, true to his word, told Setford of his promise to Jobs, and the Baron agreed that, under the circumstances, he would most likely be able to get the man transported, rather than hung.

Late in the evening, Lord Geoffrey, Charlton and Baron Setford took their ease in Geoffrey's study. Brandy in their glasses, and the boxes resting on the desk in front of them, they went over the events of the last few days again, for Setford's benefit.

He listened intently as Lord Geoffrey told the tale, leaving nothing out. He examined the contents of the boxes, and nodded, pleased. This would leave no loose ends. This matter would finally be done, and he could now report it as such to the Prince Regent. He hefted the bags of coin and gems, his shrewd grey eyes considering. Then he turned, and dropped them into Lord Geoffrey's hands.

"Excellent work. How convenient that these boxes contained only the papers we sought, and all of the papers we sought. And, from your description, I am most impressed with young Lady Harriet. She would, I suspect, have the talent to make an excellent contribution to our work. I don't suppose you'd consider recruiting her?"

"No!"

"Definitely not!"

Charlton and Geoffrey spoke at once, both glaring at Setford, who laughed.

"That's what I thought you'd say. But you can't blame me for asking – it's not often we find a woman with courage, and useful skills like lock picking!"

"True. It's not a talent I was aware my sister had, until today."

Charlton looked chagrined at admitting this.

"Apparently," Lord Geoffrey contributed, "she learnt that skill as a child, to recover her prized possessions when your nasty piece of a brother had locked them away. I am not surprised that she has kept it secret. It's not exactly a socially approved 'suitable skill for a Lady'."

Charlton looked thoughtful, wondering just how it was that Geoffrey knew more about his sister than he did.

Setford finished his brandy and reached out to close the lids of the boxes.

"Please lock these away for tonight."

As Geoffrey did so, Setford continued.

"I'll be away tomorrow with these, and set things in motion. I will keep you apprised of the outcomes. But it may take a month before I have much news for you."

"In that case, let me invite you to partake of my hospitality again – the Hounds and their families intend to gather here for Eastertide, and we would be delighted if you would join us."

Setford stilled, and, for the first time ever, Geoffrey saw something in his pale grey eyes that looked alarmingly like uncertainty. Then he nodded, as if coming to a decision.

"I'd be delighted m'boy. Catching up with all of you at once will be a pleasure. But now, let's to our rest. I, at least, have a long day ahead of me tomorrow."

ARIETTA RICHMOND

Chapter Fifteen

To Harriet, the week after they had descended into the hidden chapel, and recovered the evidence against the traitors, passed in an odd dream like way. The whole thing, after months of searching, and the drama of her almost abduction, seemed monumentally anticlimactic. Her abraded wrists and ankles healed, but her heart ached.

She wanted to see Lord Geoffrey, missed him dreadfully, in fact, after so long seeing him almost every day. She had hoped, at first, that he might come to visit her. He did not. Charlton told her that he had been very busy with Baron Setford, seeing off the prisoners and handing over the boxes. She supposed that was reasonable – but that did not make her heart ache any less.

Lord Geoffrey, once Setford was gone, found himself at a loose end, unable to settle to anything. The funds from the sale of the first batch of paintings had been deposited to his bank, and Raphael had sent him a quick letter, telling him so, and informing him of the astounding sum involved.

Mr Featherstonehaugh, who seemed equally a little out of sorts and lost, was working at finalising the inventory and packing of the next two shipments of goods to be sold. These would not be sent to Raphael until after Easter, for Raphael had also written to advise that he would be away again for some weeks. He neglected to mention why.

Which left Lord Geoffrey with absolutely nothing to do. Except think. About Lady Harriet, to be precise. All the time. He felt like a lovesick boy. He busied himself with simple things - visits to the tenant farmers, and meetings with each and every remaining member of his staff. He wanted them to know that they were not under suspicion, that he valued their work.

Universally, they greeted that news with relief, and a cautious warming of their attitude to him. Mrs Chester even went so far as to confide that 'she'd never held with them strange types the old master went about with'. Whilst it all needed to be done, none of it really distracted him. Thoughts of Lady Harriet were ever present in the back of his mind. He wanted to see her. Truth be told, he wanted much more than to just see her. He wanted to hold her, to kiss her, to be near her every day.

But the only way he could do that would be to... he shied away from the thought. He sent no message, for he had no idea what he could say. And the longer he was away from her, the more doubts he felt. What if she hated him for having endangered her, now that she'd had time to recover and think about it? If he didn't see her, there was still hope.

So it went for a week or more, until an invitation arrived.

Lady Sylvia would be delighted if he would join them for dinner on the morrow. His heart leapt, with hope and fear at once. He would see her. But what if she did not wish to see him?

Still, cursing himself for having been a coward, when that had never been his way, he accepted the invitation. The hours until that dinner lasted longer than any other day of his life.

~~~~~

Lady Sylvia had watched her daughter with some concern. Where was her bright, volatile child? This moody drifting girl was not her Harriet! How had it come to a point where Harriet, who had determinedly pursued Lord Geoffrey's company at any opportunity, for over a year now, was limply fretting rather than acting?

In the end, with that sense of mischief which was part of her (and which she had passed on to Harriet), she could not resist interfering, just a little. She invited Lord Geoffrey to dinner, only informing Harriet, Charlton and Odette after she had sent the invitation.

Harriet's face lit up at her words, then clouded with some fretting concern. Charlton watched the emotions chase across Harriet's face, raised an enquiring eyebrow at his mother, then smiled.

"An excellent idea mother."

Lady Odette happily agreed. Odette was still adjusting to becoming mistress of a large household, and was more comfortable deferring to Lady Sylvia's judgement as yet.

Lady Sylvia went on her way to discuss menus with Cook, and Harriet, suspecting that Charlton would ask her about her expression, developed a sudden desire to go and ride Moonbeam, as she had been rather shamefully neglecting the mare of late. Charlton wisely let her go – Harriet would work out whatever was worrying her, all in good time.

~~~~~

When John led out Moonbeam for her, Harriet smiled and thanked him as he boosted her into the saddle.

"I know you'll follow me John, but please, give me at least the illusion of being alone. I need some time to think."

The groom bowed in acknowledgement.

"As you wish, my Lady."

The mare was fresh, and keen to run, so Harriet let her do so, enjoying the feel of the wind on her face, and the scent of the first spring grass as it was crushed beneath Moonbeam's hooves. When they reached the river's edge, she slowed the mare to a walk for a while, until she reached her favourite spot.

Slipping down, she tethered Moonbeam and settled on the large fallen log that afforded a view to the bend of the river. She had told the truth when she said she needed to think.

This evening, she would see Lord Geoffrey again. What would she do? How would he react?

She was quite certain that, as soon as she saw him, she would have the completely inappropriate urge to throw herself into his arms. Which she could not allow herself to do. For, before she completely embarrassed herself, she needed some indication of his feelings. Did he truly care for her? Or was she deluding herself. And how was she to discover the truth?

The afternoon flowed away with the river, and she was no closer to having answers to those questions. Soon, she would need to return, to dress for dinner, and prepare for the moment when he walked into the room. Just a few minutes more. As she stared into the distance, a sound came to her – quiet at first, then getting louder. Hoofbeats.

~~~~~

Lord Geoffrey could no longer stand the slow creep of the minutes. He had to do something to fill the hours before the dinner at Pendholm Hall. He stared out of the window at the gardens, where the approach of spring was bringing new leaves and the first buds of flowers, and decided to ride.

He could take Rajah out for a good gallop, take a turn past the furthest tenant farmers' cottages, and then make his way to the lower ford, cross, and go to Pendholm Hall along their side of the river. He was sure that Lady Sylvia would forgive his appearing for dinner in riding clothes rather than full evening attire. Decided, he called for Hurst, and went to dress.

Half an hour later, he sped across the fields, feeling freer than he had in months.

The tenant farmers were glad to see him, and he noted with pleasure that they, and their families, looked in much better health than they had when he first came to Witherwood Chase. Good shelter and enough food through the winter had made a difference. A difference that was sure to also result in better crops this summer, and in the years to follow.

The river was high with the last of the snow melt from the hills, but the ford was still easily passable. He slowed Rajah and simply soaked in the beauty of his surroundings, deeply appreciative of land not touched by war. Even after more than a year back in England, he could not forget the destruction of the land that the war had wrought, in France, and in Spain.

Coming closer to Pendholm Hall, he rounded a corner of the path and saw ahead of him a horse standing quietly, and beyond it a person, perched on a fallen log. Immediately he recognised the horse as Moonbeam, and the dappled sunlight glinting off Lady Harriet's hair made her identity unmistakable.

His mind froze. Rajah continued along the path at a steady walk, unconcerned with the turmoil of his master's mind.

What would he do? He could not give in to his first impulse, which was to rush to her, fling himself from the horse and gather her into his arms. What if she did not wish him to do so? What if she bitterly resented the danger that he had placed her in? He had no answers. Rajah reached the small clearing, and stopped, whickering a greeting to Moonbeam as he did so.

Lady Harriet turned, her green eyes wide, and a hesitant smile touched her face.

He drank in the sight of her.

Well, not hate then, if she was smiling – that was good.

Time seemed to slow, and he slid from the horse, his eyes never leaving hers. They each stepped forward, until they stood mere inches apart, neither sure what to say, how to breach the gap that had somehow appeared between them.

His voice came out a whisper.

"Harriet..."

She watched his storm grey eyes, and saw the message in them, that he struggled for words to express. She sighed, and a tightness left her posture, which she had not even realised was there. Of its own accord, her hand reached for him, as surely as her words.

"Geoffrey... I...."

He took her hand, pulling her into his arms, and swept her words away with his lips, kissing her as he had so often dreamed of doing, as she wrapped her arms around his neck and pressed herself to him. Long minutes later, they pulled away from each other a little, still unsure of what to say, but each certain of their feelings. Keeping her fingers twined in his, Geoffrey took a deep steadying breath.

Now was the time to speak, no matter how much the words were hard to find.

"Harriet... I... I have missed you abominably this past week. Can you forgive me for not calling? I am ashamed to admit that I was afraid – afraid that you would not wish to see me, that you might hate me for having put you in such danger."

Harriet put her finger to his lips, arresting his words.

"Never think such a thing! I could never hate you. You have always been a hero to me, and the events of last week have only made that more so."

He lifted her hand, and pressed a kiss to her fingers.

"Then... if you cannot hate me, can I dare to hope that you might be able to love me? For I have discovered that I love you, beyond any sense or reason. When I saw you come so close to falling from that cart, I knew that I could never live without you. Harriet, my wonderful brave and clever Harriet, will you marry me?"

His breathing stopped, and he stood, utterly still, waiting for her response. She tipped her head to one side, and her green eyes sparkled, then she laughed with delight.

"Yes, oh yes, of course I will marry you. How could you think otherwise? I have loved you from the moment I saw you!"

He swept her into his arms again, spinning her around, her feet in the air, as she laughed with joy. When he set her feet to the ground again, she clung to him, dizzy with happiness.

For some time they simply stood that way, safe in each other's' arms, until the lengthening shadows reminded them that it was time to go.

Harriet, in that moment, suddenly realised that John must have seen, from a distance, the whole thing. And he had done nothing. How wonderful! She must thank him later.

Geoffrey boosted her onto Moonbeam, then mounted Rajah, and they set off along the path to Pendholm Hall.

"As soon as we arrive, I shall speak to Charlton. Er, how do you think he will react? Will he approve? Will your mother approve?"

Harriet looked at him like he was quite mad.

"Of course they will approve. And, if they seem to have any doubts, I will convince them."

This was the Harriet he loved – strong minded, determined, bright and beautiful.

~~~~~

Charlton laughed at the worried look on Geoffrey's face.

"Of course I approve! I shall be proud to call you brother-in-law, as well as brother-in-arms. I never thought to see this day, yet I should have known. My sister has always had a knack for getting what she wants – and she made no bones about wanting you."

Geoffrey's face lit with a grin to match Charlton's.

"I thought that we might have the wedding at Witherwood Chase, at Easter, when everyone will be here. That's just more than the necessary month needed for the banns. And I doubt Harriet wants to wait longer, any more than I do."

Geoffrey actually blushed as he spoke, and Charlton laughed again, clapping him on the shoulder.

"Come then, let's go and tell mother the news. I suspect if we take any longer to come out of this room, Harriet will come bursting in, ready to force me to agree!"

Lady Sylvia embraced Geoffrey, smiling with tears in her eyes.

"At first I was not so sure that you were right for her, you know. But the more I saw you with her, the more right it seemed. I cannot imagine a better man for my wild child of a daughter!"

At that moment, Harriet burst into the room, Charlton captured her before she had taken more than two steps, and spun her around, laughing at her expression.

"Harriet, I approve, and so does mother. You've no need to demand our agreement."

She stopped, and had the grace to flush, before looking up defiantly and reaching for Geoffrey's hand.

ARIETTA RICHMOND

Their Easter gathering was full of life and happiness, of friends become family and lifelong bonds made. It was made more joyous by the occasion of Harriet and Geoffrey's wedding, the arrangements for which had been taken in hand by Lady Sylvia. Geoffrey had never realised just how much organisation went into a wedding!

Finally the day dawned.

The small village church was full, with the Hounds and their families, including Odette's aunt, Lady Farnsworth, plus Baron Setford, as well as all of the staff of both Pendholm Hall and Witherwood Chase, and most of the villagers and tenant farmers. Even Geoffrey's brother Alfred and his wife had deigned to attend. Geoffrey was darkly amused to discover that his new status as a man of wealth with substantial property appeared to have made him a more acceptable person in his brother's eyes.

As if any of those things mattered to him. Harriet was what mattered.

It was a day full of laughter and joy, with Harriet having chosen to wear a gown of spring green which set off her eyes, and Geoffrey looking elegant in simple black and white attire.

When the words had been said, and they walked from the church as man and wife, they were met with a cloud of rose petals to rival those that Geoffrey had arranged for Charlton's wedding.

There was a very happy purveyor of hothouse flowers somewhere!

The only slight sad note in the day was Raphael's absence.

It seemed that he had not yet returned from his latest travels. Geoffrey hoped that he might still arrive, before everyone departed in a week's time, as the Easter season ended.

They all returned to Witherwood Chase, to be served a sumptuous feast and dance in the newly renovated ballroom. Lady Sylvia had settled contentedly in a quiet corner, and was watching the festivities with great satisfaction.

Both of her children wed within a few months of each other, and both so happy – what more could a mother ask for?

At least Geoffrey and Harriet had not been forced to wait, as had Charlton and Odette, by the mourning period for Odette's father. She was not sure that Harriet's quicksilver temperament could have produced the patience to wait a year to wed!

She watched the people around her, noting who danced with whom (waltzes were so revealing of people's feelings…), and whose eyes followed who.

There were some interesting possibilities before her – she wouldn't be at all surprised to see more weddings in the near future.

She was particularly delighted to see Lady Farnsworth dancing with Baron Setford. She rather thought that Lady Farnsworth's acerbic wit would appeal to Setford, and Lady Farnsworth deserved some companionship.

Also pleasing was seeing Miss Carpenter dancing with Mr Featherstonehaugh, who was cheerful and dapper as usual.

Miss Carpenter had been a patiently long-suffering shadow to Harriet for so many years now that Lady Sylvia had been concerned for her future, once Harriet was wed.

Perhaps there was nothing to worry about after all.

Setford's wedding gift to Harriet and Geoffrey had been a quietly delivered missive from the Prince Regent, which thanked them both for their recent actions to protect Crown and Country, and added a further grant of lands to Geoffrey's holdings.

He had confirmed that the remaining conspirators had been found and taken, that Jobs had been transported, and that the other two were held in Newgate, awaiting the hangman's pleasure.

The waltz ended, and Geoffrey swept Harriet out onto the terrace, where the sweet smell of the herbs in the scent garden drifted on the breeze as the Eastertide brought the growth of spring to the world. They stood, watching the stars, his arm holding her close to his side.

His voice was quiet, for her ears only.

"No more missions, no more searching. We can take life as we wish, go anywhere you wish. What do you wish, my darling Harriet?"

She stayed silent, thinking, at peace with the world. When, after some time, she spoke, it was a whisper, but her words were more powerful than a shout.

"It doesn't matter where we go, or what we do, so long as I can do it with you. Whatever may come, you will always be my hero."

The End

His Majesty's Hounds – Book 11

Sweet and Clean Regency Romance

Loving the Bitter Baron

Arietta Richmond

ARIETTA RICHMOND

Chapter One

"…and then there is Saltwitch Park – the finest of my estates. It boasts the largest house in the county, and by far the best land."

"How fortunate you are, Lord Saltwitch."

"I was sure that you would be impressed, Lady Alyse."

Alyse resisted, with grim determination, the desire to kick the man in the shins, 'accidentally' as she followed the intricate steps of the dance. He was a boor - an arrogant, self-important boor, who thought that wealth and property was enough to interest any woman. Much as she loved dancing, loved beautiful dresses and the glittering gatherings of the *ton*, she was beginning to think that her sister had the right of it. There were, as Sybilla had pointed out, rather acidly, almost no gentlemen of actual intelligence to be had.

The thought of intelligent men brought one in particular to mind, a friend of her brother. A man who made a point of avoiding most of these gatherings, to her ongoing frustration.

The music ended, and Alyse escaped, with the best grace possible, back to her mother. Louisa Barrington, the Dowager Duchess of Melton, frowned at her daughter's expression. Alyse replaced her half scowl with a bright smile, and her mother's face settled back to its normal cheerfulness. Her mother was focussing all of her attention on Alyse, and her opportunities to attract a suitable husband.

Which was Sybilla's fault. How Sybilla had convinced mother to allow her to go back to Greyscar Keep, again, rather than come to town for the season, Alyse really did not know. But she had, which left mother with no-one but Alyse. Charles was off again, somewhere, dealing with the Estates, Hunter was happily married, and Sybilla was still 'finishing writing her novel'. Which, Alyse suspected, would never be finished, whilst it provided her an excuse to avoid London.

The Dowager Duchess scooped a glass of orgeat from a passing footman, and presented it to Alyse.

"Refresh yourself, Alyse, for soon you will be dancing again. It is most gratifying to see how many of these gentlemen are taken with you. Have any of them caught your fancy yet?"

"No Mother, none of them. I am finding them all rather... uninspiring – of conversation, manner, and attitude."

"You, my girl, are far too picky. You will find yourself left alone, if you continue this way. Like your sister, who I despair of. At least you are here, meeting eligible men."

"Yes mother. I promise, I will consider them all. But some have most definitely failed to meet even the least of my criteria for acceptability."

The Dowager Duchess grimaced at her words, shaking her head, turning to watch the swirl of people, and the new arrivals as they came into the ballroom. Alyse sipped her orgeat, and watched them as well.

The churn of people parted, for a moment, and a man slipped through the gap to enter the room, moving down the stairs with an even stride, looking, somehow, at once both supremely confident, and utterly uncomfortable with where he was. He was, at first glance, an unassuming gentleman – well dressed, in a quiet way, handsome, with strong cheekbones and distinctive deep blue eyes, and thick dark blonde hair which was, as it had been every time she had met him, already curling a little in escape from the structured styling that his valet had attempted to impress upon it.

Alyse remembered to breathe again, as the crowds swallowed him up. Suddenly, the evening had become far more interesting.

∿∿∿∿∿

Gerald Otford, Baron Tillingford, had now been the bearer of that title for a year and a half. It still sat heavily upon him, an awkward thing that he had not been raised to deal with. It was not that he did not appreciate the social advantages of a title, or the wealth that came with the lands and estates attached to the title – it was simply that he always felt out of place.

He could not reconcile, inside himself, the things that he had done during the war, of necessity, with the person he needed to be, now, day to day.

These people looked at him, and saw a quiet man, who cared well for his tenants, and did not push himself forward excessively. He looked at himself and saw a monster. For he alone knew what he had done, what he was capable of.

Of his close group of friends, those men with whom he had served in France and Spain, only he, Raphael and Bart remained unwed. Raphael had just announced that he and Lady Serafine would wed within the month, and, from the way he had seen Bart and Lady Sybilla looking at each other, at Geoffrey and Harriet's wedding, he suspected that soon, Bart would be wed too.

The thought was bitter. None of the others had done the things he had done. He had, by doing those things, saved them from needing to, and he knew that they were, to the depths of their being, grateful for that fact. But those actions, necessary as they had been, had changed him. He could not, ever, expect a woman to know of those things, and not recoil in horror. He never intended that any woman would hear even a whisper of those things. But it meant that he would, almost certainly, remain alone. He had been, before the war, a naturally sociable man, with an easy manner, a man that the girls in the village had found appealing, in all his lanky awkwardness. Now, it seemed, women still found him appealing, but he could not permit them to be close to him. It would have been easier to be ugly.

Yet now he held a title – one with an 800-year history of honourable service. And its preservation meant that, at some point, he should marry, and have an heir. He felt trapped by the contradiction. Socially, he was, therefore, awkward. He attended few events, even though, with a year's practice, he had become used to swimming in the pit of vipers that was the *ton*.

For, once they had recovered from his change from landed gentry to titled, he had become prey to the husband hunters.

He had come to this particular Ball, only because he wished to speak with Hunter Barrington, the Duke of Melton, who was one of his companions at war. He had reached the point, with his restoration of Tillingford Castle, where he needed assistance – with the rebuilding of the gardens, and with the next steps in modernising the farming operations. Nerissa, the Duchess of Melton, was a talented garden designer, and Charles Barrington, Viscount Wareham, Hunter's brother, was a talented estate manager with significant experience in farming methods improvement. Gerald hoped to access both of them to help.

As he stepped through the doors, he immediately wished that he had chosen any other way to speak to them. The swirl of perfumed bodies was claustrophobic, and the assessing eyes of the young women made him feel like a stallion on the sales floor at Tattersall's. Finally, he managed to make his way across the room, to where Hunter stood with his family. Including his sister, Lady Alyse.

Gerry found his eyes drawn to her, as they always were. She was slim, but not thin, and beautiful – a classic beauty of pale gold hair, porcelain skin and lips that were often as bright as cherries, for she habitually pulled them between her own teeth, before releasing them, when she was thinking. She was different from most of the young women of the *ton*, for she could converse as well on such subjects as horses and estates as she could on dresses and female fripperies.

He did not want to like her as much as he did.

"Good Evening, Your Grace, Your Grace, and Your Grace, and Lady Alyse."

He bowed over Lady Alyse's hand, and rose from it to find her eyes on him, amused.

"Now Gerry, do stop the formality. You know how silly that sounded!"

Hunter was always annoyed by the formalities. He had never expected to inherit the title, and had been, as a result, rather unprepared for it. He had done well, regardless.

"If you insist, Hunter."

"But what brings you here tonight, Gerry? I know that you are not overly fond of Balls."

"You are what brings me here. Well, actually, that is not quite correct, it is your family that are the cause of my presence."

Hunter raised an eyebrow at the remark.

"Oh, in what way?"

"I have need of assistance. With garden design," Gerry watched as Nerissa's eyes lit with delight, "And with implementing some modern farming approaches, at Tillingford Castle. It seemed sensible to come to the talented Barrington family."

"I would be delighted to help. A new project is just what I need."

Nerissa's enthusiasm was genuine, and unfeigned.

"Charles isn't here tonight, but I'll ask him. I am sure that he can spare some time to visit you, and see what can be done."

"Thank you."

His mission accomplished, Gerry felt a sudden desire to flee the ballroom. But there was no socially acceptable way to do so. Hunter was watching him, a knowing look in his eye, a half-amused smile on his lips. Obviously, there was no help to be had there. He glanced around, and his eyes met those of Lady Alyse. Unusually for a person with pale hair, her eyes were brown. A deep, warm brown with glints of gold in them. With a start, he realised that he was staring, rudely. He tore his eyes away.

"My dear Tillingford, so good to see you again. You will, of course, not leave us this evening without dancing with my daughter, will you?"

The Dowager Duchess' voice was light, pleasant and charming. It was also a command. Gerry knew when he was trapped. Hunter, again, made no move to rescue him. The orchestra were just striking up again, and Gerry, acknowledging that the Dowager had manoeuvred perfectly, pasted on his social smile, and offered his arm to Lady Alyse.

"Of course, I would be delighted, if it so please Lady Alyse?"

Alyse looked, for a moment, as if she would refuse, which he found, to his surprise, raised a pang of disappointment, almost hurt, in him. Then she smiled, that beautiful smile which transformed her face from simply pretty to spectacular, and took his proffered arm.

"It does please me, my Lord."

He led her to the floor, only realising as they reached it, that the music was a waltz. He took her into his arms, and they began to move, effortlessly finding their balance with each other. Which was fortunate, for his ability to think had departed.

She smelled divine, some soft floral fragrance, perhaps lily of the valley, he thought, a scent that suited her appearance perfectly. A scent that was, it seemed, intoxicating. His heart beat harder, his mouth was dry, and he sought, with no success, for something to say. She met his eyes, and any remaining trace of thought faded away.

"Thank you, Lord Tillingford."

He managed, a little confused, to respond.

"For…?"

"For rescuing me. From… them… the thought of a waltz with any of the hopeful men who surround me at these events is currently unappealing in the extreme. I believe that I have, in every case, already exhausted their stores of conversational topics, and discovered the extent, or lack thereof, of their dancing skills."

"Oh. Lady Alyse, are you implying, thereby, that I am both more interesting to speak to, and more talented on my feet, than every man here? I find that, forgive me, a little improbable."

She flushed, a delightfully pretty pink glow highlighting her cheeks, but she nodded.

"Yes, I believe you have the right of it. That is exactly my opinion."

He was dumbfounded. He was, currently, at his least eloquent. At least he could be sure that he danced well – something his mother had forced him to learn, all those years ago. But… he suspected he only danced so well at this moment, because of how well she danced.

"I am deeply flattered. Does this sad state of affairs mean that you are not enjoying the Season, Lady Alyse?"

Those deep brown eyes lifted to hold his, and he felt lost in them, the other dancers around them fading away, until he guided her around the floor by instinct. She pulled one lip between her teeth a moment, and heat rushed through his body.

"I have been enjoying myself. But, now that it has been some weeks, I find that simply the pretty dresses, and the glitter of everything is not enough. The attention of so many men is flattering. But only until one becomes aware of their motivations."

She sighed, falling silent as they swept around the dance floor, turning, almost floating, so in tune were they. He considered her words, and found himself sympathetic. For, as much as he was prey to the husband hunters, so was she prey to the fortune seekers, or those who simply wished an association with the family of a Duke.

"Then, if I may be so impertinent as to ask, why are you still in town, attending these events?"

She laughed, and it seemed a little shaky to his ear.

"My mother. And, I suppose, my own hopes, to some extent. Although I am becoming convinced that mother will be disappointed, and that I will, most likely, return to Meltonbrook Chase unbetrothed, and unmarried."

He felt, at her words, a surprising relief. An emotion which he did not consider too closely, for fear of what he might see. They swirled on, her delicate scent surrounding him.

"I rather think that your mother will manage to bear the disappointment. No matter how she may push, from what I have seen, the happiness of all of her children is, in the end, her primary concern."

She was silent.

Happiness, he thought – what did he know of that? He was not sure any more – he knew satisfaction, and even pride, at times, but happiness? That was something he had left behind in France, when he had made the choice to do what was necessary.

~~~~~

Alyse revelled in the delightful sensation of dancing with a man who could dance well. The fact that it was this particular man made it all the more wonderful. She suspected that, after this, no other man would ever feel good enough. In the moment, she did not care.

They spoke, and the warmth of his voice caressed her. His obvious concern for what she felt, what she wanted, enchanted her. The absolute contrast to men like Lord Saltwitch was not lost on her at all. And, with respect to her mother, she thought that he was probably right.

"Yes, that is true. My mother may have ambitions for us all, but she will not force us to anything that we truly do not wish. Perhaps my problem is simply that I do not know, myself, exactly what it is that I wish."

Liar! She thought, internally, the smile never leaving her face. *What I wish is holding me in his arms right now.*

"You are just nineteen – there is time yet to discover your true desires."

"Perhaps you are right. You seem very wise to me."

Something odd passed over his face, an expression she might have interpreted as pain. But that was silly of her. She allowed the conversation to drop, when he did not respond, and gave herself over to the joy of the dance, the feel of his arms around her, and the clean fresh scent of him, so different from the dandified fops she had danced with earlier.

The music came to an end, and she sighed, feeling suddenly lost, when he escorted her back to her mother.

He took his leave, all politeness, and her eyes followed him across the room. There was simply something about him, that eclipsed all of the other men she had met.

She turned back to find her brother watching her, his eyes alight with all too clever curiosity.

Chapter Two

Gerry woke with a start, confused for a moment, the blue painted walls around him a far cry from the broken stone of the French farmhouse that had surrounded him in the dream. His pulse settled. He was at Tillingford Castle and the, oh so vivid, events of the dream were in the past. But the dream had left him queasy, the memory one he would prefer not to relive. The man had been a traitor – what choice had there been? None. Yet he desperately wished there had been.

No matter that the man had turned, to intentionally break a man's will, with fear and physical hurt, had never been easy to accept as a necessity, and to have to do it to a man who had been one of their own had been abhorrent. Yet he had done it.

And when the man had broken, had begged for mercy, a deal had been struck – the information the man had provided had saved thousands, by allowing them to capture a ring of French infiltrators. But the deal had been less than honourable. They had agreed to pardon him – but had not told him he would be imprisoned until the war ended, as surety.

It had not sat well with Gerry, yet he'd had no choice but to follow orders. And the man had cursed him, when he was told the way of it. Had sworn that he would live to see them suffer as he had suffered, damning the aristocracy for all his woes. No matter that Gerry had not, at that point, held any title – he had been damned by association, and his actions.

It haunted him. But the war was nearly two years gone, and the man had been released, as promised, in late 1815. But every time he relived that day, in dreams, Gerry woke with a sense of doom hanging over him, and a revulsion at himself, at what he had done, at what he was capable of. It was all the reminder he ever needed that he was a monster to the core.

~~~~~

Three weeks of Balls and soirees later, Alyse's opinion of the available gentlemen of the *ton* had not changed. Lord Tillingford had not been seen at any of those Balls. And the memory of her waltz with him remained the highlight of Alyse's Season. Not that she would admit such a thing to her mother.

Alyse had been wondering how she might convince the Dowager Duchess to abandon London and return to Meltonbrook Chase, when circumstances had solved that problem for her.

For once, her sister had managed to surprise her. It seemed that not only had she actually finished writing her novel, but also that she had succeeded in becoming betrothed. Alyse approved. (And not simply because her mother's immediate excitement at having a wedding to arrange had rescued her from what had become a tedium of Balls)

She had always liked Lord Barton, as she liked most of her

brother's friends.

She stared out the carriage window at the busy streets. Her mother's voice droned on, not requiring an answer, discussing what would need to be done for Sybilla's wedding. Hunter had fallen asleep, propped into the corner of the seat, and Nerissa leant against him, held in the curve of his arm, near sleep herself. Alyse was not sorry to see the last edges of London fall away, to be replaced by the passing countryside. Meltonbrook Chase had never seemed like such an appealing prospect.

~~~~~

A week later, her opinion on that matter had changed. At that point, absolutely everyone, except Sybilla and the Dowager Duchess, would have been delighted to never hear the word 'wedding' again. To think that this would go on for months! Not only was there much planning to do, but to add to the chaos, Raphael Morton, now the Earl of Porthaven, another of Hunter's close friends, had also just announced that he was to marry, soon – before Sybilla's wedding.

It was late afternoon, and Alyse, Charles, Hunter and Nerissa were sitting in Hunter's study – a choice based on an unspoken communal intent to escape the wedding planning.

"I am sure that there must be one of the estates needing my attention. I just need to decide which one."

"Good idea, Charles. And, obviously, it's high time, that I, as Duke, visited my estate too – whichever one it is that you have in mind."

Nerissa and Alyse exchanged a look.

"Oh no you don't – not unless I can come with you!"

Nerissa's tone was sharp, although her eyes sparkled with amusement. Alyse added her own plea to the discussion.

"If you are all going to escape, I am most definitely coming with you. I refuse to be left here to bear the brunt of mother's enthusiasm – I've had enough of that this year already!"

They paused a moment and laughed, before Hunter stilled, staring out the window for a moment before he spoke.

"Actually, we have the perfect excuse to disappear for a few weeks. Given that Gerry asked for our assistance with the gardens and farms of the Tillingford estate, it's only right that we should assist him as soon as possible. We shall simply have to go and spend a week or two with him – I can't imagine us providing adequate assistance in any shorter time."

Nerissa clapped her hands together in delight.

"Brilliant! How soon can we arrange it?"

"I'll send him a message today – we'll know in a few days' time."

Alyse looked at Hunter, her brow creased with concern.

"But how will we convince mother that I should go?"

Nerissa smiled, and reached across to pat her hand.

"Well, Gerry requested my help, and Charles', and it's logical that Hunter must come, as Gerry is his friend. I will simply insist that I need your company, so that I will have another woman to talk to. Your mother will surely not deny me that support."

Alyse nodded, smiling again, and relaxed – this might actually work! The idea excited her – the very thought of spending a week or more at Lord Tillingford's home made her heart beat faster – surely, in that much time, she could manage to capture his attention, to converse with him, to make him see her as something more than just Hunter's sister. She wondered how Sybilla had managed to get Lord Barton to look at her as more than that – perhaps she should ask.

As much as being in his presence each day appealed, she was also thrilled by the prospect of the visit for another reason. Tillingford Castle was more than 800 years old – a jumble of architectural styles, in an accretion of building around the original keep of the earliest part of the Castle. She wanted to see it, wanted to draw it – not just the landscape views of the building expected of a young lady who painted or drew, but the far more interesting detail – for there were sure to be odd carvings all over the place, and points where the texture of stone met the texture of polished panelling.

She had always drawn things, since she had first grasped a pencil, and none of her mother's attempts to encourage her in the direction of ladylike watercolour painting or traditional ladies' subjects like flowers and scenery had met with success. She drew things that interested her – things with intricate detail and structure.

Her mother had sighed dramatically, and accepted that drawings of dress designs and intricate beading were as close to more 'normal' ladylike subjects as Alyse was going to get. But, after a Season in London, Alyse had drawn enough dresses to last some years. And Meltonbrook Chase was far too new to provide fascinating oddities of detail.

At less than 300 years old, it paled in comparison to a place like Tillingford Castle.

Alyse watched as Hunter wrote the letter, sanded and sealed it, and called for a footman to send it on its way. The next few days would be torture, as they waited for an answer.

~~~~~

Gerry was sitting in his study, staring rather blankly out of the window, his attention turned inward. The view was spectacular – or would be if nearly twenty years of almost neglect had not let the gardens run riot.

The structure was there, and the design led the eye past garden beds and avenues of trees to an expanse of lake in the middle distance – but everything needed trimming, and the summer blooms grew haphazardly, spilling colour in abundance with no thought to form or pattern.

He was barely aware of it. He was tired. Last night had been filled with the worst kind of dreams – the ones where he was back there, in the war, doing terrible things – and finding pleasure in it.

A pleasure he had never felt in real life, but which invaded his dreams, leaving him to wake feeling only revulsion for himself, and horror at what he was seemingly capable of.

Those nights were not restful – he might as well not have slept. Around him, the world was full of spring growth, and happy people, yet he felt more bitterly alone every day. He knew that feeling was simply an aftereffect of the dream – but knowing did not change the bitterness.

To make matters worse, in the last weeks, he had received confirmation that, within two months, both Raphael and Barton would be married. He was happy for them, knowing that all of his companions at war were good men, who deserved a good life – but he envied them, deeply. He had done what was necessary, and he did not regret doing so in defence of his country, but he did bitterly resent that war had ever come upon them, to make it necessary in the first place.

He was startled from his grim thoughts by a knock on the door. At his call, Shackleton entered, the correspondence tray proffered in front of him.

"A letter, my Lord."

Gerry looked at it, almost puzzled. It was not his mother's writing, nor anyone else in his family. Few people had reason to write to him. He picked it up, turning it to see the seal. Hunter – he should have recognised Hunter's writing – obviously, the damn dreams had left him even more disturbed than he had realised.

"Thank you, Shackleton. I will ring if I need to send a reply."

"Very good, my Lord."

Shackleton turned and left, as calm and unhurried as always. Gerry broke the seal, and unfolded the letter.

Hunter's rather scrawled writing covered the page, informal as always with his friends. But what need had Hunter to write to him?

He scanned the letter quickly, then sat back, his mouth suddenly dry, and his heart beating faster than before.

Gerry,

At the Welmanns' Ball, you requested my family's assistance with some matters. If it suits you, we are free to visit you in this next few weeks, to address the matter of the gardens and the farms.

The party will comprise myself, Nerissa, Charles and Alyse, if you can see fit to put us up for a week or two, whilst we look to your estates.

Please let me know by return if this suits, and we will arrive on your doorstep at your earliest convenience.

Hunter.

Alyse. Lady Alyse would be coming with Hunter. How would he cope?

He wanted the gardens restored – their riotous growth demonstrated how much potential they held. He wanted the farms productivity improved, for his own and his tenants' benefit. He wanted to spend time with Hunter, just to talk. But Alyse… he wanted to see her – he could not deny that. Yet it was a foolish thing to want. He could offer her nothing, beyond conversation.

No matter how much he liked her, she was not for a man like him.

He was not sure how long he sat, staring at the paper in his hands, facing the bitter truth of his isolation again. His fingers ached from the tightness of their grip on the paper. His dark blond hair fell forward over his forehead, escaping its styling as always, and he flicked it back, assailed by memory. Once, there had been laughter, once there had been a queue of young women who wanted to spend time with him, simply because they liked him. Once, he had thought that, one day, he would marry one of them, and live a happy life.

But that was before the war. He was no longer that man. He had forfeited his right to such thoughts. To spend a week or two with Lady Alyse here would be the worst kind of torture – yet he could not refuse. He needed the Barringtons' help with the estates, and, if the price of that was to spend time with Lady Alyse, whilst being distant and polite, so be it. It would be good practice for the rest of his life.

Uncurling his stiff fingers, he dropped Hunter's letter onto the desk, and drew out a sheet of paper. His reply was even less formal than Hunter's letter – a simple note bidding them come as soon as they wished. He sealed it with the Tillingford crest, still finding it odd that he possessed such a thing, and rang for Shackleton to send it forth.

The days before their arrival flew by, but left him exhausted – the dreams were still there, but tangled with dreams in which those he hurt transformed beneath his hands into those long-ago girls from his village, or Lady Alyse. From those dreams he woke retching, full of bone deep horror at the man he had become.

~~~~~

"You want to what!??"

"I want to hold the wedding at Dartworth Abbey. The newly restored ballroom is beautiful, and the whole district is full of people I want to invite. The Marquess has already said that he is happy for us to do so."

"And what is wrong with holding it here, at Meltonbrook Chase?"

255

Alyse sat quietly in the corner of the parlour, watching Sybilla and her mother progress towards a full scale argument.

"Nothing. Except that I want to hold it at Dartworth Abbey. Do stop being so negative Mother – you haven't even seen it. At least visit and look at the place before you fly into a fit about it."

"You have that stubborn look on your face. I know that look – you will simply keep saying that until I do see the place, won't you." This was accompanied by a large and dramatised sigh, as the Dowager Duchess tried to look put upon. Sybilla simply looked determined and waited. "Well, if you insist, by all means let us go there. Although… that will mean me staying at Greyscar Keep, won't it? I have always hated that place."

"Mother, you will be surprised. Greyscar Keep is much improved from when you last saw it."

"Well. If I must suffer this, I insist upon having company. You must all come with us."

The Dowager Duchess waved an arm, indicating everyone else in the room.

Hunter smiled, and Alyse took a deep breath, waiting for the inevitable reaction to the words that Hunter was about to utter.

"I am afraid, Mother, that we will not be able to accompany you. Sybilla will have to suffice, for we have all accepted an invitation to stay with Lord Tillingford for a few weeks, to discuss improvements to his estates."

The Dowager Duchess simply stared at them for a moment, her mouth open in surprise. Then she snapped it shut, and fixed her son with a steely glare.

"All of you? Why, pray tell, are you all required?"

"All of us. Nerissa to advise on the gardens, Charles to advise on the farms, myself as one of his oldest friends to assist, and Alyse so that Nerissa will have female company in a house full of men. We have already accepted his invitation – it would be unpardonably rude to cry off at this point."

"Well…" the glare now included them all, "Then I will make do. But, as you have chosen to absent yourselves from this planning, you will just have to accept whatever tasks I allocate to you, with respect to this wedding."

She huffed ostentatiously, and turned to march out of the parlour, annoyance in every stride.

They managed to remain silent until her footsteps had faded down the hallway. Then they all collapsed into laughter.

ARIETTA RICHMOND

Chapter Three

Alyse sat in the library at Meltonbrook Chase, the large blank paged journal, in which she sketched, open on her lap. On one page there was a half-finished study of a section of the bookshelf before her – the different textures and shapes of the spines of the books, the way that the shadow fell from one book to the next, the embossed gold titles on some books, the raised lines of tooled leather bindings – all faithfully reproduced. But that was not the page she was working on.

On the next page, a wholly different image was coming into being. She drew from memory, pausing every few seconds to close her eyes and study her subject in her mind's eye. The sketch was not detailed yet – it was simply roughed out, the strong shapes and distinct lines all that yet graced the page. Yet it was immediately recognisable as a portrait – a portrait of Gerald Otford, Baron Tillingford, as he had been on the night of that Ball, so many weeks ago.

These were the sketches that she did not show her family – the sketches of people, including all of them.

Capturing people was a secret delight. She might share her sketches of everything else, but not these – they were just for her. Sketching this man, now, was a way to ease her excitement. Tomorrow, she would board their family carriage, and they would travel to his home. Just the thought of standing before him, in his home, rather than at some Ball or soiree, made her breath come faster.

Every other man she had danced with, all Season, had simply made her more certain that she wanted another opportunity to dance with this particular man, to be held in his arms, to speak with a man who actually seemed to care what she thought. A man who she had wanted from the day she had first seen him, shortly after Hunter and his friends had returned from the war.

She had told herself that she was silly, and that, with a proper Season in London, she would find other men to want, would, in all probability, find a man to marry. Yet the opposite had happened. She had enjoyed the dresses, the glitter and pomp of it all – but she had not, at all, enjoyed the men, and their shallow self-interested view of the world. She was not sure what to do about it – but, given this chance to stay at the home of the only man she had ever actually wanted, she was quite sure that she would try to do something, anything, that she could, to make him really notice her.

Her mind ran around the idea, all the while that her hands drew, capturing the man onto the page, with the candle light drawing glints from his dark blond hair, and the crispness of his cravat at odds with the determined disarray of that one lock of hair. Only when she was completely happy with the sketch, did she close her book and rise, to go to her chamber and sleep.

Her sleep was deep and peaceful, her dreams of dark blue eyes.

∿∿∿∿∿

Tillingford Castle had been empty, all but a few staff to maintain it at a basic level, for more than a decade before the previous Baron's death, and the granting of the title to Gerry. The previous Baron had moved out, and gone to live at another estate with his two young daughters, soon after his wife's death, unable to bear the memories that stalked him in these halls. It had been closed up, everything covered in dust sheets, and simply left.

It was a huge place, and Shackleton had explained that much of it, even when the previous Baron had lived there, had not been used for fifty years and more – there had been no large house parties, nothing needing large numbers of guest suites, no reason to bother with unused spaces. Gerry was fascinated with the place. At first, he had simply kept to the limited number of rooms he needed, and ignored the rest, struggling to adapt to the very idea that he held a title and estates. But, over time, he had begun to explore.

Baron Setford made certain, regularly, to drag him away from the place, and into society, and there had also been occasions of his own choosing, mainly to visit the other Hounds, so he had not actually spent all that long exploring the place, from the moment that he had decided to do so. The more he explored, the more he wanted to – who knew what he might find. Lately, he had been looking into cellars – both the ones that were used, and the ones that were not.

Some days, he felt a dark and gloomy affinity with underground spaces full of cobwebs and little else – they seemed an echo of his life now.

Other days, he walked in the gardens, and found joy in discovering little clusters of determined flowers, struggling to survive amidst the overgrowth of weeds and hardier species.

This particular day, as he waited nervously for the arrival of Hunter and his family, he had turned to the cellars again. The original castle had been simple – a round tower keep surrounded by a courtyard area inside a round stone wall. Under that were many original cellar rooms, more than two layers deep. The later building had enclosed that courtyard, roofed part of it over, and swallowed it into the castle itself, with another storey above it. Outside that, over centuries, further wings of the building had been added, in different directions. Each one had a collection of cellars under it – some interconnected, some not. Gerry wondered if he would ever actually discover them all.

Under the farthest North wing, towards the back of the Castle, he discovered some stairs leading down. The space smelled musty, as only a long-abandoned place could smell, and the cellar floor was paved with old cobbles, the dirt having settled between them until the surface was almost flat. He wondered what those who had built these rooms had expected to store there – but there were no clues. All the space contained were a couple of pieces of very old furniture, with equally old paintings leaning against them. The echoing emptiness surrounded him with the sense that it was so old that even the ghosts of the occupants had faded away.

But, as he turned to leave, he noticed something.

Surrounding the door, on the inside of the room, were panels of remarkably skilled carving – as if a trellis holding a tangle of roses grew all around the door, the carving so detailed that they seemed almost alive. He stood, in awe of the skill of the unknown carver, amazed yet again at the diversity of things to be found in his home. He had been feeling rather lonely and sad again, after finding only empty rooms, but the panels of carved roses shifted his perspective, and he returned to the upper reaches of the castle cheered, thinking of the gardens, and what Nerissa might suggest for them.

And that thought inevitably brought Lady Alyse to mind. She would be here, soon, possibly as early as this very afternoon. He remembered that waltz, when her mother had so adroitly trapped him into dancing with Lady Alyse – that waltz which had been wonderful. And she had praised him – so genuinely, with an unaffected honesty that took his breath away, after all of the society misses he had met, who were only interested in his wealth.

He remembered drowning in the depths of her rich brown eyes, where flecks of gold caught the light. He remembered the scent of her, drifting around him, and how she had felt in his arms.

He ached to feel all of that again, to have a conversation which was honest, not manipulative, to hold a woman he wanted to hold. He forced the thoughts away, the bitter reality of his life crashing in on him again. He was a monster, not fit to touch a woman like her, let alone desire her. He doubted that she could even imagine the like of the terrible things that he had done – and he was glad of that – no woman should ever know such things. He would keep her at a distance, whilst she stayed in his house.

He could admire her, like a work of art, without ever touching her. For touching her would be playing with fire, tempting the madness of desire.

A desire he could never allow to grow, no matter what.

~~~~~

On the green of Little Tilling village, a group of gypsy wagons were drawn up. The villagers eyed them with both interest and suspicion. Gypsies were always viewed with suspicion, with the expectation that they would steal. But the people liked a show, were intrigued by the fortune tellers, and by the odd collection of unique trinkets that were offered for sale.

This time, a man emerged from the wagons, and walked into the village. He was not a gypsy, by his looks, yet his dress was like theirs, and his hair was long and wild. His face was pure English though. He went to each of the shopkeepers, and the Inn, arranging supply of foods and drink, and materials for repair of wagons, all to be delivered to the gypsy encampment. And he paid with good money.

They looked at him oddly, but took the coin, and settled to gossip a little. He told them of the news from the previous towns the gypsies had been to, and asked about their neighbourhood. It was more than a year since the gypsies had passed this way, and there was much to tell.

At the Rose and Wren Inn, the Innkeeper handed him a tankard of ale, and settled in to talk.

"Well then, there's a lot been happening hereabouts, since last you gypsies were here. We've a new Baron up at the Castle. Name was Otford, if I remember right, but he's Lord Tillingford now. Young, good looking. Was a soldier, so they say, and given the title for his service, when the old Baron upped and died with no heir. Keeps to himself, but the staff at the Castle say he's a good man, treats them well. And he's spending his money here, doing the Castle up again, so everyone's happy."

"Sounds like a good thing for the village then."

The man spoke casually, but his eyes had glittered with interest at the mention of the new Baron's name.

"Aye, it is a good thing. Half the girls think they're in love with him, silly widgeons, but he's never once looked at them except to be polite. Delusional, the lot of them. A man like that, he's not going to be looking at a village girl, not when he's got all of them upper class pretty bits to choose from."

"True, very true."

They drank their ale, and talked on about the growth of the village, and where to find the blacksmith, and then the man left, continuing with his errands.

Back at the gypsy encampment, he went into the wagon he had lived in for the past year, and gathered his things together, before going out again, and making his way purposefully up the hill towards the castle that loomed over the village.

A few hours watching, from a secluded spot amongst the trees nearby, and his patience was rewarded. A man came out, obviously the one in charge, talking to another.

Cunningham's gut clenched - it was him, the bastard he had been seeking for over a year. The man who had destroyed his life.

In that crumbling farmhouse in France, the choice had seemed clear – admit to what he had done, and reveal all of the details of his French co-conspirators that he could remember, or suffer pain that he knew he could not face. The deal had seemed sound – do so, and not only would he not suffer the pain which the instruments around him in the room promised, but he would be pardoned – free to return to his family.

But they had lied. They had not been willing to allow him loose on the world while the war still raged, not trusting that a man who had turned twice already would stay loyal. They had shipped him back to England and kept him imprisoned for two long years, waiting for the war to end. Only then had they done as promised, and freed him, a pardoned man.

But by then, somehow, word had leaked out of his doings, and his fellow prisoners had shown their opinion of a traitor in all manner of inventive and painful ways.

Then, when he finally reached his family, they too rejected him, having been informed, by a letter from the army, of his actions and his incarceration. In all of the time that he had been locked up, they had not seen fit to write, or to visit. His life was destroyed, utterly – and it all went back to that room, and the man he saw before him now, wealthy, and a Lord for his efforts.

Cunningham ground his teeth, restraining the urge to surge forward and fall upon Otford. That would be too quick, too kind. He wanted to make the bastard suffer as he had suffered.

Through all of this, and all the time since that fateful day, Cunningham had never once admitted to himself that perhaps the fault lay, at its root, within himself, for having turned to the French in the beginning. For he saw their cause as righteous, once he had understood it – his life before the army had been trampled beneath the heel of a cruel and uncaring Lord, who saw his tenant farmers as nothing more than a source of money – so a cause that called to throw down the nobility had spoken to him at the deepest level.

Once captured and his villainy revealed, he had needed someone to blame, for he could not accept his own culpability. Lieutenant Otford had become the focus of his blame and hate – a hate that he had nurtured into a desire for revenge over the near four years since that day.

Now the man was before him. He no longer needed the Gypsies. Now he needed a reason to stay here, to watch, and wait his chance, to inflict a slow and terrible death upon this man, to destroy his life, as Otford had destroyed his own.

Two hours later, clean shaven, hair washed and tied back in a brown ribbon, wearing clothes that might suit any farmer, Cunningham, as Mr Reaper, applied at the servants' door of Tillingford Castle, looking for work – any work they might offer.

Shackleton eyed him, but could see nothing out of order, and, as an extra hand about the place to deal with the lowest of the drudge work would be useful, gave him a position. He was given a tiny room in the servants' quarters above the stables, and settled in quickly.

Over the next week, he learnt the pattern of the place, and became adept at listening at doors, and observing detail.

Putting those skills at spying that had originally brought about his downfall to use, he discovered all that he could about his new employer.

Chapter Four

The weather was beautiful, as spring moved into summer, and the roads were in excellent condition. It was barely midday when they arrived, so fast had they been able to travel.

The first view of Tillingford Castle quite took Alyse's breath away. It was large, and looked imposing, even while it looked rather like a jumble of child's blocks, a collection of pieces stacked together to build a not entirely harmonious whole. The ancient keep tower stood up above the porticoed entryway, like a giant guardian. She wanted to draw it, even like this, from a distance – there was so much detail that it was fascinating. Charles had been staring about as they rolled between wide fields, assessing the land's potential, and Nerissa was almost hanging out of the carriage window, trying to get sight of the gardens as they approached. Hunter watched them all with some bemusement, secretly full of happiness that these people he loved had so much passion for life, each in their own way.

As they drew up in front of the imposing entry, the doors opened, and a butler came out to stand and wait.

Their footman opened the carriage door, and let down the steps, then stood by to assist if required. Alyse was stiff from two days of sitting in the carriage, and was grateful for the steadying hand. She stood on the gravel, looking up at the imposing face of the Castle. It was real! She was here! And, in a moment, she would see... him...

As if her thought had summoned him, suddenly, he was there, the sun glinting on his dark blond hair, drawing a sparkle from his eyes. Alyse found it difficult to breathe. Then he was gripping Hunter's hand in greeting, smiling at all of them, oddly seeming a little shy as he greeted her, then ushering them in through the huge doors. The butler bowed as they passed, a genuine smile on his face, and gently shut the doors behind them.

"Your Grace, your luggage will be taken to your rooms, and Mary," the butler waved in the direction of the maid standing to one side," will be waiting here to show you up when you are ready."

Hunter turned to the butler and maid, and bowed.

"Thank you."

They looked a little startled at being thanked by a Duke, then nodded as he turned and followed everyone else to the parlour.

Alyse came to an abrupt halt as they passed the bottom of the grand staircase. She reached out, her fingers tracing the complex carving of the balustrades and banisters. Her voice was barely audible.

"I have to draw these..."

Hunter smiled, but encouraged her onwards.

Tea and refreshments were served, and Alyse found herself

torn – she wanted to be in the room, in his presence, taking the chance to be part of a conversation that was not constrained by the moves of a dance. Well – if she had not found herself unable to decide what to speak of... yet she also desperately wanted her sketch journal, and to be back out in the hallway, drawing those amazing carvings.

She could see Nerissa staring out the windows at the view to the gardens – Alyse recognised that look – Nerissa wanted to get straight into the gardens as much as she wanted to get to drawing.

Finally, the formalities of welcome were done, and, as Lord Tillingford escorted Nerissa and Charles from the room, en route to the gardens, and the home farm, Alyse slipped out, collected her sketch journal, and settled by the stairs. Shackleton, observant as always, brought her a chair.

Hunter, abandoned by everyone, shook his head in amusement, and asked Shackleton for directions to the library, and a brandy. Two hours later, Gerry joined him there, having left Nerissa in consultation with the head gardener, and Charles in discussion with the farm manager and a group of farmers.

Alyse was so deeply involved in drawing that she did not notice as Gerry paused for some time, quite some distance away, and watched her, his face alive with interest, before moving on to the library, his steps almost silent on the marble floor.

~~~~~

In the library, Gerry collected a drink and settled into his favourite chair.

"Your family are all so passionate about things. I suspect that we will need to send a search party for Nerissa and Charles if we are to have them attend dinner."

Hunter laughed, nodding his agreement.

"You are probably right. Be glad of it – for it will serve your needs well. I much prefer them as they are, to the bored families I have met elsewhere. I do not understand how so many people manage to do so little with their lives."

"Neither do I. But perhaps our perspective on such things was changed by so many years of needing to act, every day, simply to stay alive?"

"True. War does rather change everything."

Gerry was quiet for a while, wishing that he had never brought the spectre of war into the conversation. Determinedly seeking something to speak of, to turn his thoughts to brighter things, the image of lady Alyse, as he had just seen her in the hallway, came to mind.

"I did not know that Lady Alyse was interested in drawing – that is what she is doing, in my hallway, is it not?"

"Yes, indeed. But you will not find the walls of Meltonbrook Chase cluttered with insipid landscapes, or lopsided studies of flowers. What Alyse draws is far more interesting."

"Oh?"

"She draws detail. Fiddly complicated things. She is currently drawing the carvings on your stairs. If she will show the result to you, you will be startled at how well she can capture light and shade, texture and complex intertwined shapes. It does not seem to matter to her whether what she is drawing is the detail of beaded decoration on a dress, or the detail of centuries old carving on stone – so long as it is detailed and complex, she will draw it."

"Then I believe that she will not lack for amusement whilst you are here. This castle is full of odd pieces of decoration from hundreds of years' worth of occupancy."

"We'll be lucky to get her to the dinner table – just like the others."

They settled into companionable silence, sipping their drinks, the need for conversation obviated by many years of friendship. Gerry, watching Hunter's face as he had spoken of his sister, had felt a wave of envy roll through him.

He did not have such a good relationship with his own family, and had never managed to live up to their expectations. Even now, with a title, his relationships there were strained. His older brothers resented the fact that he had been granted an honour they had not, and his parents cared more about making themselves vicariously important by association with him, than about what he wanted, as a person. Even as a young man, he had never quite met his family expectations. But now, he could never meet anyone's expectations. The bitter sadness engulfed him for a moment.

He drifted in it, staring blankly at the shelves of books lining the walls. The image of Lady Alyse rose in his mind, as she sat in his hallway, utterly focused on what she was doing. That singularity of purpose, that ability to care about something so much that the world fell away when you were doing it, was remarkable. It was something he had never really had. And she had looked so beautiful – graceful, unstudied, simply herself, wisps of her pale gold hair escaping the pins, curling about her face, lit by the long rays of the afternoon sun where they shone through the fanlights above the great front doors, and cast beams of light into the hallway.

The picture of something he wanted, and another thing he would never have, could never have.

He sipped the brandy, but the warmth of it sliding down his throat did nothing to warm the chill of his soul, where the darkness of his deeds had settled.

~~~~~

Despite Hunter's fears, Nerissa and Charles did manage to return in time for dinner, flushed from an afternoon spent pursuing each of their favourite activities in the world. Alyse had to be reminded of dinner, but once the spell of drawing had been broken, she stretched, and was grateful for a chance to move. As soon as she did her stomach reminded her just how long it was since she had eaten. Dinner seemed a very good idea.

She hurried to her room, to change and ready herself. As she dropped her sketch journal onto the bed, it fell open at the half-finished portrait of Lord Tillingford.

She paused and considered it. It was not quite right. There was something about him – something she had seen in his eyes today, as he greeted them, which she had not captured. She would need to study him closely, until she had it. Just thinking about him made her feel warm, and took her mind back to that waltz. She was still standing, reliving it in her mind, when the maid tapped on the door, come to help her change for dinner. Quickly, she closed the journal, and opened the door.

Half an hour later, Alyse stepped into the small dining room, and was shown to a seat. This was an informal room, the table round, and quite small – a room for dining with friends, not the huge formal dining room which was sure to exist in a castle of this age. She was glad of the intimate setting, the sense of warmth and friendliness, after the months of intense formality in London.

But... she was seated between her brother, Charles, and Lord Tillingford. So close to him. She glanced sideways, under her lashes, and watched him. His strong profile was undeniably handsome, the determined fall of that lock of hair to his brow softening it somehow. She wanted to touch it, to brush it aside, and feel its softness, to feel his skin beneath her bare fingertips. The unbidden thought made her flush, suddenly too hot, and she turned her eyes away, concentrating on her plate as the first course was served.

But her awareness of him remained, the heat of his body so close beside hers palpable, the clean fresh scent of him surrounding her, distinct, even in a room filled with the scents of food. It was almost intoxicating, dizzying, carrying with it the memory of that waltz. She wanted to capture it... but one could not draw a scent.

She was so caught in those thoughts that she barely noticed what went on around her, until she realised that Nerissa was speaking to her.

"...and Alyse, there is the most wonderful carved bench in the rose gardens, all intricately twined roses –many different varieties, carved all over it. I am sure that you will wish to draw it."

~~~~~

Gerry had been watching her, from the moment that she was seated beside him, caught, despite himself, by her beauty, and had barely turned his eyes aside in time, when she had glanced his way from under her long lashes.

He wondered what she saw, when she looked at him. He breathed, and the delicate floral scent reached him, muddling his thoughts. The curve of the table meant that their knees were close to each other, beneath the table – he could almost feel her warmth, and felt a most unseemly desire to shift his leg, to allow it to drift casually sideways until they touched.

He forced concentration, forced his attention away from the woman by his side, and focused on the conversation. Nerissa was talking about the gardens, with great enthusiasm - and telling Lady Alyse about the carved bench in the rose garden. For a moment, he was not sure that Lady Alyse had heard – curious – what was she thinking about? Then she seemed to shake herself a little, and responded.

"The carving is so detailed that you can recognise different rose varieties? How fascinating! You will have to tell me which is which, so that I can label them on the drawing."

"Of course!"

"I suspect that this entire castle contains a myriad carvings, which I will want to draw. I will have no chance to capture more than a tiny part of it in the few weeks that we will be here." She turned to face him, and the impact of her eyes directly meeting his stole his breath. "I must rely upon you to show me the most interesting pieces, my Lord."

He experienced a sudden sense of unreality, as if he were a different man, a man who was not a monster, a man who could have a family, light conversation, happiness, a man who could look a woman in the eyes, and allow himself to think of having far more than simply conversation with her. He wanted the moment to last, but he knew, instantly, that it could not, that he could not permit even the thought, even the slightest trace of that pleasant life – for, if he tasted it, the loss would be all the harder to bear, when it came. Her eyes were still on his, her expression expectant.

His voice sounded harsh to his ears as he finally spoke.

"I fear that you overestimate the charms of the Castle, Lady Alyse. Whilst I have not explored every crevice of it yet, much of it is rather dank and musty, untouched for generations in some cases, and not inspiring at all. There are some small pieces worthy of attention – the rest are likely to disappoint."

Her brightness dimmed a little, and an expression which might almost be hurt passed over her face. The sight of it brought an ache to his chest. He hardened himself against the reaction. He could not allow himself to be close to her, to care so about her feelings. Then she smiled, forcing her expression back to cheerfulness, as if that moment of hurt had never existed.

Had he imagined it? He did not think so.

"Perhaps you underestimate my ability to be fascinated by the oddest things, my Lord. I will appreciate whatever you may be able to show me."

Her voice was light, almost teasing, and the gentleness of her answer to his rather churlish words struck him deeply. He had no choice but to be minimally gracious.

"As you wish, my Lady. I only hope that you are not entirely disappointed in your expectations."

"Thank you."

She turned her attention back to her dinner, releasing him from the hold of her rich brown eyes, and he found himself able to breath properly again. This few weeks was going to be harder than he had thought.

He would simply have to be careful. He would be more than a fool to allow himself to forget, even for a moment, what he was. There would never be that warm loving family for him. Not his own birth family, nor one that he might build around him – not with what he had become.

Bitter loneliness would be far easier to live with than the horror on a woman's face, should she come to understand what he truly was.

Chapter Five

Tillingford Castle was just as fascinating as Alyse had expected. Every corridor, every room, seemed to contain some small detail to catch her eye, some detail worthy of being captured in a drawing. This was far more fun than the Season in London had been – and the company far more congenial. For part of each day, true to his rather ungraciously given word at that first dinner, Lord Tillingford escorted her about the building, to explore its detail and history. A footman accompanied them, for propriety's sake.

Soon, Alyse realised that Lord Tillingford was exploring, just as much as she was. Some parts of the Castle he had already explored, but much of it he had never looked at closely. Each day, she enjoyed his company more, even though he seemed moody, and was often terse with her. It was as if he had some reason to hold aloof, but kept forgetting to do so, only to realise again, and pull away from her, back into that sad, almost frosty demeanour.

It only made him more intriguing.

She wanted to know what went on in his thoughts, what possible reason he might have for that coldness. It did not seem natural to him, that hard surface, and the moments when she saw the warm and amusing man beneath the surface made her determined to discover more of him. His smiles were rare, but, when they came, they transformed his face. Alyse made it her intention to make him smile, at least once every day. So far, she had succeeded.

The warmth of the spring day was almost oppressive, a hint of the summer to come, so Alyse had curled herself into the windowseat of the large parlour window, allowing the gentle breeze to drift through the open window, cooling her, and bringing her the scent of roses and more from the gardens below. At first, she had watched Nerissa walking about the gardens, followed by a cluster of gardeners, as she set them to specific tasks. Already, the changes could be seen – the shape of paths becoming clear, and the weeds disappearing from the garden beds closest to the house. But, after a while, bored with watching, Alyse had opened her sketch journal, and begun to draw.

On the page, another portrait was emerging from the careful strokes of her pencil. Lord Tillingford again, as he had been the day before, when they had explored a long gallery, high in one wing, where tall windows collected the afternoon sun, and mirrors alternated with paintings on the opposite wall. The room had been filled with light, reflecting and re-reflecting, turning his dark blond hair to burnished bronze, and highlighting the strong planes of his face with lines of gold. His eyes had sparkled, and she had made him not only smile, but actually laugh.

Now, she sketched quickly, wanting to capture what she had seen, to capture the carefree man he obviously could be, not the dour and terse man he often was. So intent was she on her work, that she did not hear the door, did not realise that he had entered the room, until he was almost upon her. His footfall on the polished timber of the floor alerted her at the last minute, and she snapped the journal shut, her face flushing instantly. What if he had seen?

~~~~~

"Where might I find Lady Alyse?"

"In the parlour, my Lord."

Gerry nodded, and turned in that direction. Shackleton watched him go, his face impassive, but a speculative look in his eyes.

Gerry opened the door quietly, and stopped, his motion arrested by the sight before him. Lady Alyse was curled on the windowseat, drawing, as always. The midday light gave her pale hair a glow that made her seem somehow ethereal. She had pulled her lower lip into her mouth, and was working it between her teeth as she concentrated. The rich redness of her lips stood out against her pale skin.

His thoughts scattered, his body heating, his reaction to her beyond his conscious control. He wanted to kiss those lips, to take them gently between his own teeth, to trace their shape with his mouth.

He forced himself to breathe again, to move. She looked so right, curled there. As if this was her natural setting. A rush of longing took him, so hard that it stole his breath again.

He was not aware of moving, until he was almost upon her.

His feet moved across the rich deep carpets silently. When he reached the polished timber at the end of the rugs, the soft sound of his steps must have alerted her to his presence, and she looked up, startled. Just as he reached the point where he might have been able to see what she was drawing, she slammed the journal shut, her face flushing, the rose colour spreading across her cheeks and down her neck to disappear under the neckline of her modest gown.

His eyes followed it a moment, before he raised them to meet her brown gaze.

They stayed that way, eyes locked on each other, for some interminable time. He did not understand what passed between them – he simply knew that something did.

"Lady Alyse – are you ready for the day's explorations?"

She paused a moment, as if struggling to find words, as if the conversation of their eyes was so far removed from this one of words, that she could not reconcile the two. But when she spoke, her voice was light – perhaps he had imagined her hesitation?

"Why yes, my Lord, I most definitely am. What part of the castle do you intend to show me today?"

"As the day is so warm, I had thought to show you a remarkable piece of carving which I discovered recently, in the cellars of the North wing. The cool of the cellars should be welcome, on a day like this."

"That sounds interesting. This Castle is so full of surprises – although a cellar seems an odd place for remarkable carving."

"It does – but it's there – who are we to guess at the motivations of generations past?"

"Indeed. I find myself more interested in the motivations of the people around me now."

A moment of unease took him – could she be referring to his own motivations? If so, she would never know of them. He stiffened a little at just the thought of anyone discerning his intent in the world, or what had brought him to be the person he now was. She watched him, brown eyes wide, and sighed – as if she had seen, and understood, the tension which had taken hold in his body.

But he was being foolish – how could she have done such a thing?

"Oh?"

He could think of nothing more intelligent to say.

"Yes – people are endlessly interesting to observe, although perhaps less interesting to converse with, unless they are congenial. Whilst I found much entertainment in watching those around me during the Season, I rarely enjoyed conversing with them. I far more enjoy our conversations here, even if they are focussed on things that most might find rather dry."

He could, he thought, discuss anything with this woman, and not find it dry or boring.

Her perspectives tended to surprise him, and, despite his intention to remain aloof from her, she had a knack for drawing him out, for lightening his heart for long moments, enough that he smiled, genuinely, in her presence.

"I do not find our conversational topics dry, Lady Alyse."

"I am glad of that! But let us proceed – you have raised a great curiosity in me – I wish to see this carving that you describe as 'remarkable'."

She uncurled herself from the padded seat, untangling her skirts from under her. For a moment, her ankle was in his view, as she moved. His mouth went dry, and his thoughts became disarrayed again. She could do that to him so easily! Standing, she bent again to gather up the small bag in which she stored her pencils, and the knife with which she sharpened them. He watched, unable to think of anything but the shape of her, silhouetted against the light from the window.

"How do we reach the cellar that contains this carving, my Lord?"

He shook his thoughts back to the practical, and waved her forward.

"In the section below the North wing – it will be fastest if we cross the rear courtyard to reach it."

They left the room, and Mills, the footman who quietly followed them everywhere, for propriety's sake, fell into step behind them, carrying a lantern. They were silent as they crossed the courtyard – a comfortable silence, which did not demand filling. A startling thought came to him as they walked – apart from his fellow Hounds, Lady Alyse was the only person with whom he felt comfortable in such a silence - not even with his own family was he so at ease. He pushed the thought away, unwilling to pursue the reasons behind the fact, lest they reveal things he did not wish to admit to himself.

He spoke instead.

"I begin to think that it will take me years to find everything there is to find in Tillingford Castle. It is as if it holds its secrets close, intentionally."

She looked at him, her eyes alight with enthusiasm at the thought.

"But that is wonderful! I cannot imagine anything better, than to live somewhere that remains interesting, and provides such scope for entertainment."

His mind filled with the image of her living in Tillingford Castle, and the longing ached through him again. He pushed the idea, and his desires, aside firmly. There would be no woman for him, no company here through the years. He needed to remember just what sort of man he was. He could not allow himself to imagine things he would never have. That way lay only pain. *'But…'* a small internal voice reminded him, *'if that is the case, how will you get an heir?'*

He pushed that thought aside too – an unsolveable problem. They reached the side of the North wing, and he opened the door for her. The dimness of the corridor swallowed them, cutting off the bright light of the sun, and the heat that reflected from the paving. It seemed like his life – moments of light and warmth, quickly swallowed by cold and darkness.

They paused whilst Mills lit the lantern, then Gerry opened another door, into the servants' corridors, then another, revealing a set of steep steps, going down into darkness. The chill of the earth surrounded them as they descended. Lady Alyse stayed close against him as they moved downwards, almost touching, feeling her way in the dim light of the lantern.

He could feel her warmth, and her scent surrounded him. It would be so easy to take her arm, to reach out and touch her shoulder, all in the context of making certain that she did not miss her footing. He forced himself to do neither, to simply descend the stairs beside her.

They reached the bottom, and went through the old wooden door, the thickness of its timber the only reason that it had not rotted away decades, if not centuries, ago.

He moved to the middle of the room, and then allowed himself one touch upon her arm.

"Stop, my Lady. Mills, stand near the doorway, and hold the lantern high." She stopped, staring ahead of her in the darkness. "Lady Alyse, please turn around, and look back the way that we came."

~~~~~

The walk down the stairs into the cellars, with him so close at her side, had been a delicious torture. So very close, that she could feel his warmth, hear his breathing. Her heart beat so hard that she wondered that he could not hear it. She had been tempted, oh so tempted, to allow herself to stumble, to give him reason to touch her, to assist her. But that would be manipulative – and she could not bring herself to be that way, certainly not with this man. If he touched her, she wanted it to be by his choice. So she had breathed deeply, taking in his scent, mingled with the musty odour of long disuse in this part of the Castle, and repressed her longing.

When he stopped her, she simply stood, uncertain.

But when she turned at his urging, she nearly stumbled in truth. What met her eyes was truly remarkable.

In the wavering light of the lantern, the carved roses seemed real, as if they moved in a slight breeze. The detail with which they were carved was extraordinary. She stepped forward, pulling her journal from under her arm, fumbling for a pencil, the need to capture what was before her intense. Sketching standing was difficult, but she could manage.

Moments later, her concentration was broken by a scraping

sound beside her. Lord Tillingford had managed to produce, from somewhere, an old worn table, and a somewhat rickety looking chair. She sank onto it cautiously, dropping her journal to the tabletop. When the chair held her successfully, she went back to sketching at a feverish pace.

~~~~~

Gerry stood behind her, unable to make himself move away. He was fascinated, caught by her rapidly moving hand, as a faithful replica of the carving began to appear on the page. What must it feel like to have such skill? He shuddered – what skill had he, but that of successfully hurting people? His dreams reminded him every night of the monster he was.

Watching her reminded him what amazing capabilities people could have, it made him feel simultaneously warmed and chilled by how different he was from normal. He should step back, yet he could not force himself to – he ached to be near her, to have her delicate lily of the valley scent surround him, to have a few moments of forgetting.

There had been a message that morning, from the Dowager Duchess, about the plans for Lady Sybilla's wedding. It was full of joy, and enthusiasm for the magnificent ballroom at Dartworth Abbey. Hunter and his family were cheered by it, glad that their sister and mother had reached agreement.

Gerry found himself feeling bitterly out of sorts as a result of hearing its contents. This year had already been agonising, with Charlton's wedding, followed by Geoffrey's wedding, and the news of Raphael's and Bart's to come. Hearing about it in great detail brought home to him again what he would lose, by never marrying.

He struggled with the feeling, and had simply turned and left the room, unable to remain and be polite. Hunter had watched him leave, but said nothing.

Now, watching Lady Alyse draw, all of the bitterness, the envy and the loneliness rushed in on him again. He simply stood, wanting to touch her, torturing himself – as seemed only right – by allowing nothing but observation. For the rest of her stay, he would need to somehow avoid their daily excursions about the building – for it was harder each day to maintain any distance, when all he wanted was to feel her in his arms. Worst of all, he had begun to suspect that she wanted his company, as much as he wanted hers. He could not let her throw herself away on one as worthless as he.

For the rest of their stay, he would find excuses to stay with Charles, or Nerissa, as they established the plans that would transform his home and estate – it would be far safer that way.

He made himself step back. She glanced up at his movement, and her hand moved, as if to stop him. Then her eyes darkened, and she let her hand fall back to the page.

~~~~~

Cunningham watched, over that week, where the visitors went, and what they did, as well as what Otford did. Perhaps there was leverage here – he would know soon enough by watching. He found tasks that took him into the courtyards, and through the lower rooms of the house, and watched – everything.

Each day, Otford went about for part of the day with the young woman. She was beautiful, obviously a woman of the quality, her clothes on any one day were worth more than

Cunningham had earned in a month in the army, if not more. Another thing to resent – that Otford had access to a woman like that. Over the period of a week, watching them, Cunningham saw, in Otford's behaviour, something that made him lick his lips with anticipation.

He was quite certain that Otford desired the woman, cared about her far more than he cared for any of the other people present. For, when they were together, Otford watched her all the time – she seemed unaware of it, but to an outside observer, it was obvious. He rarely touched her, yet his hand often hovered at her elbow, ready to steady her if she stumbled. She would do nicely, as a tool to exact his revenge. And he might even enjoy himself in more than one way, with such a pretty piece in his grasp.

After four years of waiting, he was not going to make any mistakes. Revenge would be sweet. He kept watching, and began to plan, seriously.

The woman began wandering about with only a footman attending her, and Cunningham readied himself. He only hesitated because he had not yet decided where he would hold her, once he had her. Then, as he carefully began to explore parts of the cellars, in the hope of discovering a suitable spot, he heard gossip in the kitchen as he delivered more firewood – the guests were leaving in the morning.

He was not ready! He could not let her escape... yet, he could not make a mistake – he would have only one chance. He ran back to his small room above the stables, and sat, shaking with rage, wanting to dash through the Castle, find her, and drag her away screaming. Just enough rationality remained to stop him, the cold hard centre of his need for revenge telling him to wait, a better chance would come.

Once calm, he went about his duties again, his mind still working feverishly.

Chapter Six

Alyse remembered that moment in the cellars as a turning point – in the wrong direction. For after that moment, he had seemed to be avoiding her. The week went by slowly, her days somehow duller without his presence. Mills faithfully guided her about, wherever she expressed an interest in going, but Lord Tillingford had excused himself from his promise to guide her, using consulting with Charles and Nerissa as an excuse. Alyse knew that it was an excuse – she just did not know why he felt the need to avoid her, to her intense frustration.

Every time they were close to each other, he would move away. Only at dinner time was he unable to avoid her proximity. She delighted in those moments, barely noticing the food on her plate, soaking in the sensation of his presence at her side while she could. When he spoke of things he cared about, with respect to the estates and the plans that had been created, he was bright, positive, genial, his face lighting with enthusiasm to a handsomeness that stole her breath. Yet when she spoke of other possibilities in life, that changed.

It was as if the thought of any happiness, any opportunity, beyond the growth of his estates, made him surly. His face would still, his eyes shutter, and his words become dismissive, cold, and negative. The contrast was stark. It only intrigued her more. She was sure that the bright man was the real person, and the cold man a mask that he put on, for some reason she did not understand. Yet. For she was determined to discover the truth behind it.

Like all of her family, she was stubborn. If he thought to turn her attention aside by his terseness, he would fail. Perhaps she would ask Hunter – if she could raise the courage to let Hunter see how strong her interest was.

The week dragged on, and the day of their departure drew closer, with Alyse having discovered nothing further of the reasons behind his manner. On the second last day, she wandered deep into the cellars under the oldest part of the castle, greatly daring, alone, for Mills had been busy when she had come downstairs, so she had simply taken the lantern, and gone by herself. Much of the rooms under the Keep tower were bare, musty, with little carving or texture anywhere, save that of the huge blocks of stone that formed the foundations of the place.

After some time, when she was considering turning back, and seeking luncheon, she came to a room where there was, along one wall, a stack of wine barrels. They were aged, and when she tapped on them, some seemed to still have contents. She drew them, the shadows from her lantern giving them depth, emphasising their curved shapes. Then she noticed the pile of boards and wooden blocks beside them.

Intrigued, she turned to them. They seemed the sort of thing that was often used to create temporary shelves, and were a jumble against the wall. She reached out, and touched the old dry planks, wondering why anyone would simply leave them there, when they could have been used elsewhere. At her touch, the balance of the pile shifted, planks sliding down with a clatter. Alyse jumped back, startled by the noise in the close space.

The slide of timber settled, and where it had stood, the wall revealed was not even. Alyse stepped forward, holding the lantern high. There appeared to be a space, an alcove, perhaps a passageway. She reached out carefully, pulling the last of the planks away from the wall, and then eased herself into the narrow space. It did not occur to her to be afraid, she simply wanted to explore.

The alcove contained a passage off to one side, so she followed it, her lantern casting a flickering light across the uneven walls and floor, and then the ancient wooden door at the end of the passage. She pushed on the door, and it slowly opened, the rusted iron hinges creaking as it did, loud in the silence. Holding the lantern high, she moved into the room, wondering how long it had been since anyone had stepped through that door.

What greeted her brought her thoughts to a standstill, and she gasped, pulling back, the wild movement of the lantern light which resulted making the contents of the room seem to loom and reach for her. She refused to turn and run. She would not be so weak. It was just old things in a cellar! Her heart beating hard, she made herself step forward again.

Once she examined it more closely, the lantern held steady, the contents of the room became clear to her. It appeared to be a dungeon, a torture chamber, like something out of the worst kind of gothic novel.

It was, she supposed, not such an odd thing to find, under a building which had been there for more than 800 years. Long ago, people had been far more brutal in their ways, more prone to warring, she thought.

Now, standing there, still and considering, the objects ceased to be so threatening, although she was careful not to think too much upon the purposes of individual items. What she began to see was the shapes and textures, the surprising craftsmanship in how some of the objects had been made. Setting the lantern down on the old table which stood in the middle of the room, she opened her sketch journal and began to draw.

She was, in a way, intrigued by the dusty remains of past suffering. She saw it as a reminder that everything passes – no power is forever – those who tortured and those who were tortured were long gone, and the long-term impact on the world was minimal. This room had fallen to dusty disuse many generations ago, and now, it seemed probable that no one remembered the names of those who had hurt, or been hurt here. For the first time, her sketches became about capturing a message as much as simply capturing fascinating detail.

Perhaps it was morbid, and even unhealthy, to be so fascinated by this – it was not something she would mention to anyone, yet she could not help but be captured by it. It gave her faith that even the most terrible things in the world were transitory, and she sought to capture the sense of that in her drawings.

Finally, when she had drawn almost everything in the room, she gathered up the lantern, and stepped back into the passage, closing the door behind her, and went in search of the warmth and light of the open air.

As Alyse stepped out into the courtyard, brushing the dust from her skirts, she realised that she had explored but a small portion of Tillingford Castle, yet her current sketch journal was almost full.

She knew, already, that she would wish to return, to dig further into the building. And, the thought came, to spend more time in Lord Tillingford's company, no matter how distant he might be at times.

She could cope with those times, for the pleasure of the moments when he was unguarded, when she saw the light of warm interest in his eyes, before he pulled himself away again. But, beyond asking Hunter, how could she come to understand more of him, to discover the reason for that repeated distance that he enforced upon himself?

Perhaps they could find reason to come back?

~~~~~

Finally, the day of their departure arrived. Gerry was torn – he wanted Hunter, Charles and Nerissa to stay longer – that was simple – but he desperately wanted Lady Alyse to both stay and leave.

He wanted to be close to her, no matter how much that made him wish for things he could never have, yet he wanted her away, taking temptation and pain with her.

It was not his choice to make.

They stood at the foot of the front steps, taking their farewells. He felt awkward, and tried to cover it with conversation.

"I must thank you all for your company, and your excellent advice. I am quite certain that, by this time next year, Tillingford Castle will be restored to its best, and the farms will be more productive than ever before. If, at any time, you should wish to visit again, know that you will be most welcome."

Lady Alyse's eyes lit at his words, and his stomach churned – what had he done? He knew, in that instant, that she wanted to return, and that he most desperately wanted her to, no matter what her presence did to his peace of mind.

The morning sun was warm on his face, and it lit her hair to a confection of spun gold. He wanted to touch it, to touch her. Hunter's voice drew his mind back to the conversation.

"… and I am sure that another visit can be arranged. After Sybilla's wedding, perhaps, when the chaos that is causing in the family settles a little."

"Whenever is convenient for you – the place will seem empty without you, after your presence this last few weeks."

"I will make sure to send the tradesmen we discussed to speak with your blacksmith, and the farmers, as soon as possible – I am most interested to see how fast we can improve the production from those lower fields."

Charles' genuine enthusiasm for farming innovation echoed through his words.

"My thanks, again."

"I also would be happy to return – I have barely begun to discover all that there is here, which I would wish to draw. The thought of exploring further is very appealing – although I will need to bring extra journals to draw in!" Lady Alyse spoke quietly, yet firmly. She hesitated a moment, then went on. "I thank you for your company, whilst we have been here. I greatly enjoyed exploring with your guidance, and would hope that there will be a future chance for you to show me what you discover, between now and then."

A blush had risen in her cheeks as she spoke, but her eyes met his. The world around them faded away. The warmth in her eyes was unmistakable, and she nervously drew a lip between her teeth, worrying it to cherry redness. His body tightened, and his imagination ran riot for a moment, considering those lips. He forced his eyes away, to discover Hunter watching him, a half smile on his lips.

That would not do at all – Hunter was far too perceptive. Gerry pulled his scattered thoughts together, and forced words from his mouth.

"I would be honoured to assist, Lady Alyse, if you truly think the dusty corners of this ancient pile of stone worth digging into further."

She smiled, derailing his thoughts again. His heart was racing, his mouth dry.

"Thank you."

He turned to Nerissa, and spoke of the gardens, his heart returning slowly to its normal pace as he did so. A few minutes later, with polite conversation completed, their carriage drew away.

He stood on the gravel, watching it as it disappeared down the long drive, painted gold by the late morning sun. Unnoticed by Gerry, Shackleton stood at the door, patiently waiting to open it, watching Gerry watch the carriage, a small smile on his normally impassive face.

~~~~~

As Gerry watched the carriage, someone else, as well as Shackleton, was watching him. Cunningham, a hat pulled down over his face, pulled weeds from the rose beds which formed a barrier around the curve of the drive to each side of the portico.

No one noticed gardeners. He had been able to overhear the entire conversation. By the end of it, he was smiling – a grim expression, which did nothing for the appeal of his face.

He was elated – they would return. The girl had specifically asked it. And Otford most definitely cared for her, and, it seemed, she for him, if the expression on her face, and the blush on her cheeks, was anything to go by.

He could wait. Another few months might be frustrating, but would be worth it, for his revenge to be sweet. And if the two of them came to care further for each other by then, well, that would sweeten it even more.

He turned back to the weeds, and ripped them from the ground savagely, tearing each one into small pieces before dropping it into the barrow, imagining tearing something else entirely as he did so. He whistled as he worked, savouring the future for the first time in four years.

~~~~~

As if Lady Alyse's words had been a command, Gerry felt compelled to continue exploring the Castle, digging into cellars and attics, closed up rooms and cupboards, finding himself noticing far more detail than he had before, as a result of Lady

Alyse's visit. Seeing the place through her eyes had changed his perspective.

He began to take notes, capturing information about parts of the castle that he thought Lady Alyse would enjoy, would wish to draw. Her ability to see beauty in the smallest things, in the construction of the simplest items, had been somewhat of a revelation to him. His life had been very much focussed on the practical – to now see the beauty inherent in those practical things brought him some pleasure in the world – more so than anything had, since his return from the war.

In that, she had given him a great gift.

It was a gift that helped, a little, to balance the effect of the dreams. For he still dreamed, most nights – dreamed of what he had done, saw again the faces of the men he had interrogated, the men he had reduced to terrified wrecks, who gave up their secrets. The fact that those secrets allowed them to save others, sometimes whole battalions, by knowing more of the enemy's plans, did not change what he had done. The dreams cared nothing for that – they replayed the horror, reminded him how monstrous a man he was, to have been capable of such things. And, worst of all, they tempted him, showing him what it would be like to take pleasure in such things.

He was glad, in an odd way, that he always woke revolted by the idea – the dreams confirmed his monstrous nature – but they also confirmed the fact that he clung to some humanity – he might be capable of doing what was needed, but he had successfully refused to take pleasure in it.

ARIETTA RICHMOND

Chapter Seven

A short few weeks later, as they prepared for the trip to London for Raphael's wedding to Lady Serafine, Alyse found herself, as she had so often of late, thinking of Lord Tillingford. She missed him. Even though he had been so often terse and standoffish, his company had been enjoyable. He was still, of all the men she had met, by far the most interesting. He made her heart race, as no one else ever had.

She hoped, rather desperately, that he would be at Raphael's wedding – she could not imagine him missing the wedding of one of the other Hounds, although she suspected that he did not enjoy weddings, as he seemed not to enjoy Balls and other social gatherings. The puzzle of why that was so nagged at her.

Still, all she could do was hope. In the end, she had not been brave enough to ask Hunter about him, about what might lie behind his moodiness, and his rather bitter edged view of the world. She could not reveal how much she cared, lest her brother tease her forever after.

Finally the day came, and, as they stood in the church, watching Raphael and Sera wed, Alyse cast her eyes about, looking for Lord Tillingford. He was there! He had slipped in to the church late, as the ceremony began. His face was set, studiedly blank, but some deep emotion played about his eyes. She wondered what he was thinking.

After, back at Porthaven House – Raphael's new residence, as part of the estates he had received with his ennoblement to Earl – she watched him, always. He stayed close to the other Hounds, or to Baron Setford, his face only truly alive when speaking to them. When he watched Raphael with Sera, he seemed full of sadness – an odd emotion to see at a wedding. Alyse wanted to go to him, to touch him, to wipe the sadness from his face, to give him reason to feel joy. Propriety's requirement that she stay close by her mother, or Nerissa, chafed.

As the dancing began, the men came towards them, Hunter seeking Nerissa, Lord Barton seeking Sybilla. Lord Tillingford came with them, seeming as if he would far rather escape the room, but trapped by politeness. Alyse watched him as he approached, struck yet again by what a fine figure of a man he was. As Hunter led Nerissa towards the dancing, the Dowager Duchess fixed Lord Tillingford with a steely eye.

"So nice to see you again, Lord Tillingford. You seem to be lacking a partner, as is my daughter. Perhaps you can see your way clear to dance with Lady Alyse?"

Lord Tillingford looked, for a moment, as if he would flee. Alyse understood – that expression on her mother's face was prone to make people quail.

Then he drew himself up, and, presenting a perfectly acceptable polite smile, bowed over her hand.

"I would be delighted, if it suits Lady Alyse?"

She smiled, meeting his eyes, and was beyond pleased when they widened, and lit with an unmistakable warmth.

"Thank you, Lord Tillingford."

She placed her hand on his arm, delighting at the feel of strength wrapped in fine tailoring, and allowed him to lead her to the floor. The strains of a waltz began, and she smiled, well pleased as he took her into his arms. It was as that first waltz, months before – within moments, they were so well attuned that they seemed to float, effortlessly, drifting through the others on the floor, without need of thought. She inhaled the scent of him, and allowed her eyes to meet his. Deep blue drew her in and all else faded from her awareness. There was something, something about this man, that overwhelmed her senses. In the midst of all the happiness that weddings drew forth, he seemed sad. The need to know why nagged at her again, even whilst she gloried in the feel of his arms around her.

She dared not ask him. His eyes held hers, the music swept them along, and she wished to suspend time in that moment, forever.

$$\sim\sim\sim\sim$$

"Your mother would make a good General."

As he said the words, he wondered if they went too far, but she looked up at him, laughing.

"She would. Hunter has remarked on it before. When she determines to do something, swaying her from that path can be very difficult. Of us all, Sybilla has the most success."

"At least, from what I have seen, most of her decisions are sound, and well intentioned."

"That is very true. From the way that you say that, it seems you have experienced rather different intent, somewhere."

He felt himself stiffen, and forced himself to relax – she could not know anything of his life – surely Hunter had not spoken to her of his family, or of his experiences at war? With her, it was too easy to relax, to say things that led, inevitably, to questions he would rather not answer. Holding her was a delight. Dancing with her was far more pleasant than with any other woman he had ever danced with – it took no effort, it simply seemed to happen without thought required. Her lily of the valley scent wrapped around him and the warmth of her body close against his drew him, tempted him utterly.

"A little. Let me just say that my family is far less... unconstrained... with each other than yours. And I have always been the one most likely to be the point of contention."

He was, obviously, quite mad – he was actually revealing things about himself, to a woman – to this woman in particular – when he had sworn to hold aloof from her. But her deep brown eyes pulled him in, the gold flecks in their depths lit with pleasure in the moment, and the words slipped out. The room was filled with happy people, and his sense of loneliness was intensified by it.

The bitterness of his empty future threatened to swallow him, here where everything that he could not have surrounded him. Her hand on his shoulder was warm, her back beneath his hand warmer still. He felt as if she were a lifeline, the need to hold her, to converse with her, keeping him from drowning in the sea of unattainable joy.

"I am sorry to hear such a thing – my family may be, at times, infuriating, yet they are the people I love most, and always support me, even when I want to do things that they heartily disapprove of. I cannot imagine what it would be like, if that were not so."

"You are blessed."

He could hear the yearning in his own voice.

She looked at him, her head tipped slightly to the side. Unconscious of what she did, she pulled her lower lip between her teeth, worrying at it as she considered him. Heat rushed through him, and the temptation to tip his head down to hers, to kiss that lip where she worried at it.

The only thing that stopped him was the fact that they were in a crowded ballroom. And the fact that he should not begin something he could never finish. He had to remember that he could never have the love of a woman like this, could never marry.

But she tempted him almost beyond his will to resist. He pushed all thought of happiness aside, and reached for the bitterness which had sustained him these past two years. It was far safer that way. As he did so, a look of hurt appeared on her face, as if she could see the change in him.

But surely, she could not – he was adept at keeping most people unaware of his thoughts.

The dance carried them on, in silence, but their eyes clung to each other, full of things unsaid and questions unanswered.

Once Raphael's wedding was over, with barely a month until Sybilla and Bart's wedding, the Dowager Duchess swept them all back to Meltonbrook Chase, and into a maelstrom of organisation.

Alyse watched it all, wondering how a wedding could become such a mammoth enterprise. She shuddered to think what it would be like, when her turn came. That thought brought only one man to mind, and she stared out the window, tuning out her mother's listing of tasks, picturing Lord Tillingford's handsome face in her mind's eye.

She missed him. The more time she spent away from him, the more she missed him. That one waltz at Raphael's wedding had made the sensation even stronger. She did not know what made him sad, what had made him pull back into his bitter aloofness, when their conversation had seemed so innocuous to her. But whilst his conversation had ceased, and his manner had stiffened, his eyes had told a different story. She clung to the memory, determined to find a way past his reserve.

~~~~~

After the wedding, the world seemed darker than before. Gerry threw himself into exploring more of his home, not admitting to himself that he did it only with the thought of showing what he found to Lady Alyse.

Chapter Eight

The cellars of the Castle had continued to produce an odd collection of items of interest – some old furniture, paintings and decorative items worthy of restoration, some intriguing pieces of old carving on the walls and stairs below, and occasionally, the potential treasure of long stored wine, in casks or bottles. Always, he tried to see it as Lady Alyse would – as an endless supply of intriguing and delightful detail, which provided clues to the past, and to how people had lived and thought.

There came a day when he decided to look into the oldest cellars, those beneath the central Keep tower. They ran two, perhaps three layers deep, and had barely been used for decades. Shackleton informed him that, once, they had been used to store root vegetables through the winter, on racks and racks of re-arrangeable shelves, adjusted each year based on what needed to be stored. As a boy, Shackleton remembered helping the then Cook collect supplies from in the dark depths. Now, only a few large barrels of very aged port were stored there.

The sky overhead was grey, and Gerry's mood matched it. A deep dark place, full of the sad sense of ages past, seemed like an option well suited to his mood. He took the lantern, and opened the weathered door to descend into the darkness.

~~~~~

Cunningham, as always, watched Otford. Whenever he could, he arranged his tasks to allow him to hover around the edges of Otford's day. Shackleton and the other staff left him much to his own devices – so long as the wood for the kitchen fire was there, the coal scuttles filled for the upper rooms, the waste removed to the compost pits or the current midden, everyone was happy – for he did the tasks that no-one else wanted to do.

He had become accustomed to Otford's habit of exploring the cellars of the Castle, and dogging his steps suited Cunningham's purpose well – in those cellars, he hoped, eventually, to find the perfect place to exact his revenge. Somewhere deep and dark enough that a scream would go unnoticed above.

Once Otford had descended into the cellars of the old Keep, Cunningham looked around, and, satisfied that no one was in sight, he propped his broom against the wall, and followed. He needed no lantern – his night sight had developed well, from years in a darkened prison, and from nights creeping about on Gypsy business that was best left unmentioned.

The stairs were steep, and he moved cautiously, listening to the echo of steps below.

Slipping steadily down, he was pleased when Otford continued past the first doors, deeper into the cellars, and even more pleased when the stairs turned – if there was no straight path, sound would not carry so far. His mind was full of feverish images, his imagination running wild with what he would do to the girl, with how Otford's face would look, when he was forced to watch, and unable to do anything about it.

He reached the bottom, and watched from the last turn of the passage as Otford opened an old door, and stepped through, leaving it open. The light of his lantern cast huge shadows across the far wall, illuminating stacked wine casks, a scatter of fallen timbers, and a dark opening. Otford disappeared into it.

Nodding to himself, Cunningham turned and hurried back up the stairs. He would come back, and explore further – this was a most promising cellar indeed. But for now, he needed to get back to his broom, and his appearance of being an innocent, and rather slow witted, worker.

~~~~~

The chill of the deep cellars wrapped around him, the further down Gerry went. He could see why these cellars were used for the type of storage that Shackleton had spoken of. Their temperature would vary little, all year round. At the bottom of the steep stairs, the passage wound along, ending in a wooden door, banded in iron. He pushed it, and the hinges creaked a little, as it opened.

He studied the room before him.

It seemed he had found the wine casks. They loomed, huge against the wall, and he wondered how many decades the port had been maturing in them. They were, he suspected, if the wine was good, now rather valuable.

He turned his attention to the rest of the room. A scatter of planking and blocks lay tumbled to one side – the remains of the shelving that Shackleton had mentioned, he suspected. It looked, from the way that it lay, and the uneven distribution of dust, as if it had recently been disturbed – but who would have been down here?

No doubt he imagined it, deceived by the flickering lantern light. Behind the edge of the pile, an opening in the wall lay in deep shadow, seeming somehow ominous. He stepped forward, skirting the fallen planks, and held the lantern into the crevice. It was a passageway, turning, and continuing to one side. It seemed to have far rougher walls and floor than most of the cellar rooms.

Intrigued, he stepped into it, and followed the passage cautiously. After some distance, he came to an ancient iron bound door, so heavy it appeared better suited to a fortress than a cellar. When he pushed on it, it opened slowly, its weight making it ponderous. The rusted hinges squealed like tormented souls, echoing through the passage. He flinched at the sound, then stepped through the door.

Time stopped. The flickering lantern light revealed the stuff of his worst dreams. He stood in a torture chamber, equipped with a far more devilish collection of instruments than he had ever seen. It was too much to face. Retching, he spun on the spot, and ran, not stopping until he reached the empty courtyard above.

Chapter Nine

For weeks, Gerry went nowhere near the cellars. He turned his explorations to the attics, and the long unused wings of the house, doing his best to ignore what he had seen below. But it would not be expunged from his memory.

The dreams were worse, far worse – in them, he became, fully, the monster with no soul, and took pleasure in what he did to the helpless – in the dreams, everything he feared to be, he became. And the helpless, as presented by the dreams, wore the faces of everyone he cared about, especially Lady Alyse.

He did not rest, almost afraid to sleep, and feverishly engaged in working with his farmers to implement Charles' suggestions, preparing the fields for winter, with a plan for the following spring. The days blurred together, and he considered inviting Hunter and his family to return, for there were things he was unsure of, with respect to the new farming methods.

But how could he ask them? How could he let them see the wreck that he had become?

The date of Lady Sybilla's wedding to Bart fast approached, and Gerry tried to prepare himself to attend. Once this wedding was done, he would be the last of the Hounds unwed. And it would remain so. The aching void of loneliness loomed ahead of him, but he was even more certain than before that he could not marry – how could he even consider exposing a woman to the nightmare he was, to the dreams, and the monstrous truth of him? He could not. He would not. As he thought the denial, still, his mind brought back the memory of Lady Alyse in his arms, taunting him with what he could not have.

Quite how he would manage to get through another wedding celebration without snapping at everyone, he did not know. But he would. He owed it to those who cared more for him than his own family.

Cunningham, delighted when Otford stopped delving into the cellars, took the chance to extend his own explorations. When he discovered what lay beyond the room with the wine casks, he stood there and laughed – a sound of madness, which would have chilled the soul of any who heard it. But the cellars swallowed the sound into their silence, muffling it in the dust of ages.

Here. He would bring her here, once he had her. There could be no more perfect setting for the completion of his revenge. His patience had been rewarded, far better than he could ever have imagined.

~~~~~

Although he resolved not to do so, somehow, at Lady Sybilla's wedding, Gerry ended up dancing with Lady Alyse again, as a result of some careful manipulation by her family. Again, it was a waltz. He was beginning to suspect that they planned this, trapping him into these moments with intent.

As before, it was perfection. Dancing with her was like dancing with no other woman he had known. She smiled at him, even when he scowled, and spoke gently, her words sliding past his bitter coldness and somehow drawing him out.

"My Lord, those weeks at Tillingford Castle seem so long ago now! Churlish as it is of me to say so, I am most glad that my sister's wedding is now done. Perhaps Mother will settle for a while, and we may all draw breath again. But perhaps I am an optimist – it is, I expect, far more likely that she will turn her attention to me again, and push me to find a husband."

At her words, Gerry's heart clenched, an odd ache running through him at the thought of Lady Alyse with another man. It was the height of foolishness to feel so, for he could never have her – he had no right to judge what should happen in her life. Still, to think of such a thing, whilst she moved in his arms... It was almost beyond his ability to bear.

"You speak of what your mother might wish for you. But tell me, Lady Alyse – what is it that you wish?"

She met his eyes, hers full of something he did not understand, and chewed on her lip, in that way which sent heat to every part of him.

"What do I wish for myself? Certainly not what my mother wishes for me. I have found all of the men she has suggested to be utterly unsuitable – mostly boorish and boring." A sensation unaccountably like relief coursed through him as she went on.

"I believe that I would wish a man with whom I could converse honestly – as I always have with you. And a man who could accept my rather idiosyncratic interests in drawing. A man who can dance well, a man who has strength, and power, yet is not arrogant. Perhaps I will never find a man who meets my standards. Mother informs me that I am far too picky."

As she spoke, her eyes stayed locked on his, both of them dancing entirely by instinct. Her eyes said far more than her words. What her eyes said terrified him, as did his own reaction to it.

For her eyes said that the man she wanted was him. And he could not permit it. But every fibre of his soul wanted it – wanted her, as he could no longer deny having wanted her for months. He tried to speak, but the odd lump in his throat prevented it. Finally, he forced words out.

"I applaud your determination to not settle for less than what you truly want. Especially in the face of your mother's... force of personality."

She laughed, delighted by his understanding, and his wording.

"And you, Lord Tillingford – what do you wish for yourself?"

For a moment, he lost the ability to breathe. How could he answer that? What did he wish? *'My life to be different, the war never to have happened, you in my arms every day.'* He thought it all, and could not say any of it.

"I... am not sure that I know what I want, if I am completely honest." *Which you are not being, and cannot be,* said the small voice in his head. "I must, eventually, marry and produce an heir, for titles come with that responsibility. Yet I cannot imagine doing so. After the war... perhaps I am not a man well suited to marriage, anymore."

It was as close as he could drive himself towards truth, especially at such a place and time. Her voice was soft, and her fingers moved within his, gently squeezing.

"My Lord, I am quite utterly certain that you are a man well suited to marriage... to the right woman. One who accepts you for who you are, no matter what stain the war may have left upon your soul."

Her eyes spoke to him again, and he felt his heart beat erratically, his breath come short. Her words touched too closely upon the core of his problems, and what they suggested...

But he could not believe such a thing possible.

No decent woman could accept one as monstrous as he. He had no way to answer her, and simply lost himself in her eyes. She seemed not to mind his silence, and within a few minutes, the music wound to a close, rescuing him from further conversation.

He returned her to her mother, bowed himself away politely, and escaped to walk in the gardens. He had to push her away. He could not allow her to continue to grow to care for him, as she seemed to be doing – what he wanted did not matter – not tying her to a monster for life was far more important. The moon lit the garden paths to silver, making the world cold, black and white – far simpler than life.

∼∼∼∼∼

Every time she saw him, every time she danced with him, Alyse was more certain that he was the man she wanted.

It did not matter that he tried to push her away, for whatever reason, it did not matter that a darkness dwelled in him, stealing his joy in life for much of the time. He was who he was, and he affected her as no other man ever had, or, she suspected, ever could.

Dancing with him, as, all around them, people celebrated Sybilla's wedding to Lord Barton, she was struck, again, with how perfectly they fitted together, how perfectly they danced together, how perfectly, it seemed to her, they could do anything they chose together. Yet he pushed her away. She was sure of it. One moment the warmth in his eyes was undeniable, the next, he had hidden it behind a cold veil. She was not deceived, even if everyone else was. She would persist.

~~~~~

Back at Tillingford Castle, Gerry felt suspended in a waking nightmare – for nothing had changed – the dreams made good sleep impossible, and he was, finally, beginning to run out of parts of the house to explore – parts that were not cellars, at least.

The days loomed large and long ahead of him, empty of brightness, empty of meaning. Even focusing on restoring the Tillingford Castle gardens, and improving the farms could not break through his gloom. Everything seemed dull and uninspiring.

Worst of all, the room he had seen in the cellars, for those fleeting seconds before his revulsion had sent him running, haunted his daytime thoughts, as well as his dreams. In a horrifying way, it called to him. Which was the most terrifying thing of all. But it drew him, and he was tempted, every day, to return, to see in better light what he had only glimpsed. He refused to succumb to that temptation.

But he felt utterly alone, unable to confide in anyone, now separated from the other Hounds by their state of happy matrimony. A state that he would not tarnish by speaking to them of his horrors. He knew, also, that if he did speak with them, they would, eventually, ask him, probably jokingly, when he was going to find a wife. He was not sure that he could bear it.

Everywhere he went, he passed parts of the house that Lady Alyse had been captivated by, had drawn, with that absolute focus that overcame her when she had pencil in hand. The constant reminders kept her in his thoughts, his memories of their conversations, their dances, torturing him, and helping him stay sane at the same time.

He remembered his thoughts at Lady Sybilla's wedding – that he wished his life might be different, and that he might hold Lady Alyse in his arms every day. If anything, his wish was even stronger now. He could not imagine anything more wonderful than spending his life with her, which made the impossibility of that even more painful. How had he become so involved? How had he allowed his heart to become engaged – for it surely was? He did not know – all he knew was the ache of her absence – an ache that would never end.

Even if she returned here, with her family, to capture more of the Castle in drawings, he would have to stay completely aloof.

The world had become a narrow and bitter place.

Chapter Ten

The days passed, and turned into weeks, then months, and exhaustion had become the only way that Gerry slept. He ate less, and drove himself harder, seeking to escape his demons that way, yet, if anything, the dreams were worse. In the dreams, every person he had interrogated during the war paraded past him, accusing, until he was quite certain that, had he the skill, he could have drawn a faithful likeness of each of them, so clear were they in his mind, no matter how he wished he might forget.

Late in the autumn, a message came, inviting him to yet another wedding. This time, it was Charlton's mother who was marrying. Gerry, whilst tortured all over again by the thought of another wedding, was happy for her. Charlton Edgeworth, Viscount Pendholm, another of the Hounds, had come back from war to find his widowed mother distraught, and a terrible scandalous mess left to him by his now deceased older brother. The Dowager Lady Pendholm was a wonderful woman, and deserved happiness.

There was nothing for it – he would have to attend.

~~~~~

Cunningham's frustration grew, with every day that passed. He had expected that the girl and her family would have visited again, by now. His hunger for revenge grew, eating away at his sanity like a canker, and his impatience made him less careful at times, and more likely to snap at people. He was reprimanded for his attitude, twice, and it took all the control that remained to him to look repentant and to turn his behaviour back towards the invisibility he needed, until the day came.

He spent his days and nights dreaming of what he might do to her, of the look he would see on Otford's face, of how sweet that revenge would taste. The more days that passed, the more elaborate his imaginings became.

Worry also began to assail him – what if the girl did not return? How then would he have his revenge for the destruction of his life? How would he punish Otford for having the temerity to be titled and wealthy, when he, Cunningham, had nothing left? Perhaps he needed a new plan. But... the plan to use the girl was so perfect, that he did not want to give it up. He forced himself to patience.

~~~~~

Somehow, Gerry pulled himself together enough to attend and, as he had expected, the wedding of the Dowager Lady Pendholm to Julian Stafford, Duke of Windemere, was another occasion of unalloyed joy.

Gerry gritted his teeth, smiled at everyone, and tried very

hard not to snap tersely in conversation. So many weddings in the year, in combination with the dreams, had worn his façade of unconcerned content with his life very thin.

He feared it no longer convinced anyone.

As was natural, when everyone gathered at Windemere Towers for the wedding breakfast, and the long afternoon of celebration that followed, Gerry gravitated to the other Hounds, their families and friends. Far better to have company, and some conversation, than to stand alone and morose. Yet it was still difficult – they were all, universally, so very happy in their lives.

It was also difficult because, inevitably in that group of people, was Lady Alyse. He found himself looking for her when he entered the room, unable to stop himself. When he saw her, standing with Hunter and with her mother, his breath caught, and his mouth went dry.

The afternoon sun through the ballroom windows lit her soft gold hair to a glow that surrounded her like a halo, and the pale blue of her gown suited her perfectly, emphasising her unspoiled beauty, and her slim elegant shape. His desire for her, his need for her company, even if he could only allow himself one afternoon of such indulgence, struck him like the blow of a sword.

He walked towards her, lost to all other considerations.

"Good day, Lord Tillingford, such a happy occasion, is it not? Five weddings in one year! And now all of your friends are wed – will you be making it six weddings this year, perchance?"

He was pulled from his distraction when the Dowager Duchess spoke, beaming at him, her words going instantly to the heart of his personal pain.

"I expect not, Your Grace. I do not, currently, have any plans in that direction."

His voice sounded hoarse to his own ears, and, whilst he bowed over the Dowager's hand in greeting, his eyes barely left Lady Alyse. She was watching him, her brown eyes deep pools into which he could fall, and drown.

"A pity! I do so enjoy a good wedding. Well then, as an unattached man, it is obviously your duty to dance with all of the young ladies."

She waved her hand gently in the direction of Lady Alyse, who blushed prettily at her mother's outright manipulation. He was, he realised, yet again, trapped. He could not, now, be so rude as to avoid dancing with her – and if truth be told, he did not wish to. He wanted to hold her in his arms again, no matter how painful that was. He wanted to taste, for the short span of a dance, that which he could never have for longer. He bowed to her, and offered his arm, as the orchestra struck up for the next set.

As it always seemed to be for them, it was a waltz. He began to suspect Lady Alyse's mother of having some sixth sense, some intuitive knowledge of exactly when a waltz was to be played, no matter what event she was attending.

She smiled, and placed her hand on his offered arm. So brilliant was that smile that he almost stumbled as it took his breath away. Somehow, he managed to walk, to lead her to the dance floor.

She turned into his arms, and they began to move. He was, again, struck by how perfectly they flowed together, by how right it felt to hold her, how easy it was to dance with her, how different from any other woman he had ever held.

"I do apologise for my mother. I assure you, it is not just you – she does that to any gentleman she can – she is quite certain that, without her intervention, I would never dance at all."

He discovered that the very thought of Lady Alyse dancing with a plethora of other men made him angry. His arms tightened around her, and she met his eyes, a curious expression crossing her face.

"I believe that I have seen Her Grace applying her... social skills... often enough now to know when I have been subject to her favourite manoeuvre. But you need not apologise – there is no need of such manipulation to convince me to dance with you. You are, by far, my favourite person to dance with – you dance so well that it is like floating – delightful."

A madness had taken hold of him – he was allowing his feelings to show, at least a little – somehow, in her presence, no matter what he had resolved, he could not help himself. She blushed, her eyes holding his, and he swallowed, trying to remind himself that he should be aloof, that she could never be his. That damnable lock of his hair chose that moment to escape its styling, and fell, encouraged by the movement of the dance, to drop across his forehead, and almost into his eyes. Her eyes followed it, and her hand, where it rested on his shoulder, twitched, as if she wanted to reach up and brush it aside. Perhaps she did. The thought of her doing so heated him from head to toe.

Desperately, he reached for the bitterness, reminding himself of what a monster he was, forcing himself to draw back from the warmth of her gaze. Somehow, she detected the change, for she gave a little frown, a tiny shake of her head, and drew her lip between her teeth, biting at it. His head swam – how was he supposed to resist such a sight?

After a moment, she seemed to come to some decision.

"I know that something troubles you, always. Each time I see you, the black stain of that worry sits deeper in you, dimming your natural brightness. Will you not tell me about it?"

Her words were forthright, beyond what polite society would normally allow, they stripped him of any easy, casual avoidance of her question, any instant denial. Her eyes held his, waiting for his answer. The music swept them on, and he struggled, internally. With this woman, his instinct was simply to answer her – yet to do so would reveal the terrible truth, and he could not, had sworn not to. What could he say? In the end, there was only one choice.

"I fear that you have an overactive imagination, Lady Alyse. Whilst I am flattered that you perceive me to have a natural brightness, I must assert that the idea of a deep stain of darkness upon me is not at all flattering. I cannot see where you might derive that idea from at all."

He made his voice light, a little condescending, a little mocking. His heart hurt, with every word. Yet he could see that he was achieving his purpose – she drew back, a little, in his arms, obviously hurt by his rebuff, the pain clear in her eyes. His success tasted bitter - like the rest of his life.

"I see."

Her soft voice was full of sadness – he wanted to take back his words, to do anything to not have hurt her. But he could not. Far better this hurt, than to ever see horror on her face, when she understood how much of a monster he was. They danced on in silence, all of the joy of the moment gone, until the end of the music released them.

Once Lady Alyse was returned to her mother, Gerry went

seeking other conversation, which he found with Baron Setford, who looked at him with raised eyebrow, but did not ask, instead allowing him to carry on an inane conversation about Tillingford Castle and estate management.

~~~~~

Alyse had been watching Lord Tillingford all day, from the moment that she had spotted him outside the church in Bridgemere village, as they all waited for the ceremony to begin. She simply could not drag her eyes away from him. He seemed, mostly, rather withdrawn, watching the joyful events of the day with a less than joyful expression.

Whatever it was that troubled him, she saw it more clearly every time they met. He was, even whilst conversing with those around him, somehow withdrawn, holding himself back. She wished that she knew why. For the few moments that he relaxed, and allowed his natural brightness to shine, he was breath-taking – then he would shutter that brightness, and draw aloofness about him like a cloak. It made her heart ache, made her want to somehow drive that pervading darkness away. But she did not know what caused it, and, truly, she had no right to intrude.

But she wanted to. No-one else seemed to notice it, how they missed it, she was not at all sure, so obvious it was to her. When her mother, yet again, manipulated him into dancing with her, unable to politely decline, she was elated. She had dreamed, for months, of his arms around her – she would take any chance she had to feel that in real life.

He was, for once, almost relaxed, charming. Amusing to speak to.

And then, for no reason that she could discern, as they moved about the floor, he drew away again. Rashly, she had simply asked him about the darkness that dimmed him more each time she saw him. It had been beyond foolish, for he had drawn back even further, laughing off her concern with cold mocking words. She deserved it, she supposed, for intruding, beyond what politeness allowed. But it hurt, it hurt almost more than she could bear. He did not trust her, or, perhaps, did not see her as worthy of his confidences. She should have expected it, but her natural optimism had allowed her to believe, for those few moments of madness, that simply asking would be enough.

The rest of the waltz they had been silent, a stiffness of manner in both of them, as if their ability to converse had been completely stolen by her one impetuous question. Now, standing beside her mother again, she watched him hurry away, as if he could not wait to be gone from her presence. She stifled the urge to cry, forced her best false smile onto her face, and tried to add something intelligent to the general conversation.

Hunter watched her, and watched Lord Tillingford walk away, his eyes full of questions, but said nothing. She was grateful for his forbearance.

~~~~~

Gerry sat, alone, in the private parlour of the Inn in Bridgemere village. Hunter and his family had gone out to walk about the village, appreciating the morning sun. The Dowager Duchess was, he was told, still abed, and most of the others had already departed for their various homes. He sipped his coffee, idly noting how much worse it was than the coffee that Setford always seemed to have ready, and thought about the previous day.

The hurt expression on Lady Alyse's face haunted him. Yet his choice was to hurt her now, or hurt her, far more, later. Still, he wished, more than anything, that it was not necessary – that he might spend time with her, might allow himself to love her – but he could not, and wishes were pointless.

The couch he was sitting on must be old, for there was something hard digging into his lower back. He wriggled about, but it did not improve things. Sighing, he stood, and turned to rearrange the cushions, in the hope of making it more comfortable. As he lifted the first cushion, he stopped, staring at what was revealed. A book. A very specific book. Without thought of what he was doing, he reached down, lifting it gently. He recognised this book. It was Lady Alyse's sketch journal. He sat again, cradling it, staring at the cover. He should not. It was a personal thing. But… his fingers were not listening to his thoughts – they reached out, seemingly of their own accord, and opened it, gently turning the pages. He had known that she was talented, but this… this demonstrated just how talented she truly was.

There were illustrations of so many things – things that he would never have noticed as interesting – yet here, on the page, she had made them fascinating. So many pages of tiny snippets of her life. Then, as he turned the next page, his breath left him. For his own face stared back at him from the paper.

She had drawn him as he might once have been, before the war – as she had drawn it, his face looked cheerful, kind and positive. There was no hint of darkness in the man she had drawn. He did not understand how she could possibly see him like that. It simply made him more aware of how much of a monster he had become. How he wished that he could wipe out the war, wipe away every memory, and simply be that cheerful young man again, be the man she had drawn.

Looking away from the image, he turned another page. Here were images of parts of Tillingford Castle, and he leafed through them, intrigued by her perspective. He found another few pictures of himself, which he quickly turned past, and then he came to a page which almost made him fling the journal from him. He sat, and shook, his mind refusing to believe what his eyes were seeing.

But... it was real – pages of sketches, his worst nightmares (at least without the people, thank God) perfectly rendered in intricate detail. The top of the first page had an annotation 'Tillingford Castle – cellars below main keep, near wine cask room'.

She had been there! Been in that terrible room, by herself, or with only Mills (but surely, if Mills had been there, he would have mentioned it?), and she had not run screaming – she had sat down and drawn the terrible things that the room contained.

He struggled to reconcile the idea. How could she not have been utterly horrified? Most women he had met would have fainted dead away at such a sight. Yet she had simply seen it as another piece of history to document in drawings, another set of interesting shapes and complex construction to capture.

He stared at the drawings, and, slowly, fascination overcame horror – how did she see these things? What were such things, when viewed simply as shapes and textures, lines and light and shadow, with their purpose ignored? When viewed that way, they were not so terrible, they were simply things – built for a terrible purpose, admittedly, but simply things, not truly terrible until a man chose to use them.

At that thought, his revulsion at himself took hold again – for he was such a man. He might not have used things as terrible as most of these, but he had chosen to use similar things. That he had done so out of need, to discover information that had saved thousands, did not change the fact that he had made that choice.

He shut the journal with a snap, and dropped it back onto the couch, wishing that he had never looked. Looking at someone else's personal journal was never a good thing – he deserved to suffer for his intrusion into her privacy. Yet... her image of him, that first image, of him, as a man not stained by war, stood clear in his mind.

Could he ever be that man again?

At the sound of the others returning, he gulped the last of his cold coffee, and stood, hurrying from the parlour to go to his room and pack for his return to Tillingford Castle. Let Lady Alyse discover her journal without him being present.

Cowardly though it might be, he did not wish her to be aware that there was any possibility that he had seen its contents.

Chapter Eleven

Another month passed, and Tillingford Castle seemed a lonely and empty place. The dreams still troubled Gerry's sleep just as much, and thoughts of Lady Alyse filled his days, especially that look of hurt upon her face. He threw himself into the work with his farmers and estate manager, and attempted to follow the plan, but it had become obvious that he really needed to consult with both Charles and Nerissa again, if the planned works were all to be done before winter set in completely.

But... if he invited Hunter and his family back to Tillingford Castle, Lady Alyse would most likely be with them – and he had promised her, that, should she return, he would show her more of the Castle. The idea of seeing her drew him, and he knew that he should not, for that way lay only pain, yet, in the end, he could not resist. He sent a letter to Hunter, inviting all of them for another visit.

Alyse stared out the window of the carriage, watching as Tillingford Castle grew larger in her view. The landscape was gold, fading to grey, as winter approached and the autumn leaves began to fall. She was nervous, and fidgeting. She wanted to see him, but... how would he treat her? That last conversation, whilst they danced at Lady Pendholm's wedding, was much in her thoughts. The weeks since had seemed to drag, and each time she replayed the conversation in her mind, she castigated herself more for her foolishness in asking such a blunt question of him. Yet she wanted to see him again, even if he was cold and distant. She refused to give up hope. And she did still want to draw more of Tillingford Castle – she had barely begun to explore what it had to offer of interest.

At last, they turned into the long drive, the trees on each side forming an arch of reds and golds through which they travelled, as if in some magical golden hallway. The Castle seemed, somehow, even more imposing than when she had last seen it.

Shackleton opened the door, with a genuine smile of greeting, and ushered them in out of the wind. Moments later, Lord Tillingford came down the stairs, hurrying to them. She watched him, drinking him in with her eyes. He looked tired, and leaner than when she had last seen him, yet his eyes lit with pleasure as he took Hunter's hand, and bowed to Nerissa. When he turned to her, however, his eyes darkened, some deep emotion flitting across his face before it became cold, closed off. His greeting was polite, and perfunctory.

Alyse felt suddenly close to tears. It would seem that she had not been forgiven for her intrusive question. She took a deep breath, and smiled.

"It's so lovely to be here again, Lord Tillingford. I can't wait to get started drawing some more of this fascinating place."

"Feel free to draw whatever you wish."

His eyes clung to hers, full of something she did not understand, even whilst his words were simply polite and cold. She wondered what it was that she saw there, as they all moved to the parlour. Over tea and cakes, a plan for the next two weeks was concocted, to everyone's satisfaction.

"I want to look through the library here – it occurred to me that there may be drawings or other information on the original garden designs, which might help us decide what to do with those areas that just don't look right."

Nerissa was full of her usual enthusiasm, and Hunter smiled fondly at her words.

"Why did I never think of that? The library here is large, and much of what it contains is disordered, so I have not delved too deeply."

Lord Tillingford looked a little chagrined to have not considered something which seemed so obvious, now that it had been suggested. Hunter laughed.

"Everything seems obvious once it's been thought of – but it rarely is before then."

"So true! Now, Charles, let me tell you about what's been achieved with the farms – and about where I am completely unsure of what to do next."

"Please do."

As the afternoon disappeared into conversation and planning, Alyse pulled out her sketch journal and began to draw – for once, she was drawing people, rather than detail – she drew each of the people before her, trying to capture their enthusiasm, and the animation of their conversation.

But all the while, she was wondering exactly where in the Castle she might start, the next morning.

In the end, she decided to ask for assistance – if he was already being cold towards her, what difference would one more question make?

"Lord Tillingford, tomorrow, might I trouble you to show me what part of the Castle you think would be of most interest to me?"

He turned to her, his expression serious, and appeared to think before speaking. What was there to think about? Surely, he knew his own home well by now?

"My Lady, I believe I know just the thing – there are some very interesting pieces that I have discovered in the attics, which I would be delighted to point out."

He did not sound delighted, but it would be impolite to notice that fact, so Alyse simply nodded, smiled, and agreed.

"Thank you, my Lord, that sounds suitable."

By the time afternoon had become evening, and dinner had passed, Alyse felt exhausted. No matter how she tried, she simply could not achieve a real conversation. So she'd settled to listening to the others talk, and watching him, envying the more open and comfortable way that he spoke with everyone but her. Sleep was welcome – perhaps tomorrow would be better.

~~~~~

He rushed down the stairs, annoyed that he had not heard the carriage wheels on the gravel. When he turned the curve of the staircase, and saw her, standing there at the bottom, her hair and face lit by the coloured light where the sun shone through the fan light above the door, he nearly stumbled and fell, so much did her appearance affect him. Blessedly, he did not fall – what an impression that would have made, landing in a tumbled heap at her feet!

But he watched her, as long as he could before she realised that he was coming, and looked up. He looked away before their eyes could meet. By the time he arrived at the bottom of the stairs he had himself under control.

He would hold himself aloof from her, be coldly polite, and pray that she did not look too closely at his reactions, for he feared that he would not, entirely, be able to repress how he felt about her, in her presence.

The initial conversation went by in a blur, and he found himself, by early afternoon, having agreed to escort her about the house on the following day. The thought was terrifying – hours spent with her alone, during which he would need to stay as distant as possible.

By the time that dinner was done, he was exhausted, having managed, somehow, to remain distant to her, whilst actually having the conversations he wanted to have with everyone else. Both Nerissa and Charles seemed to think that the challenges which had stopped him, in their respective areas of expertise, were completely solvable – which was a great relief. He dropped into sleep, and for once, barely dreamed at all.

∿∿∿∿∿

Cunningham had heard the gossip in the kitchens – finally, the girl and her family were coming back to Tillingford Castle.

Once he knew the day, he had made sure to do tasks that took him either outside, near the front of the Castle, or in and out of the rooms off the main hallway, so that he would have the best chance possible to see the arrival, and to reconfirm his belief that Otford cared deeply about her.

The timing, in the end, was perfect. He had just filled the coal scuttle for the small downstairs parlour, and returned it to the room, when he heard the carriage wheels on the gravel outside. So he did some unnecessary tidying of the hearth, and waited. With the door open a crack, he watched the greeting in the entryway. He needed no more confirmation than watching Otford's face as he descended the stairs – there was no doubt that the man was smitten. Smiling a grim smile, he slipped from the room, and out through the servants' corridor to the courtyards.

~~~~~

The following day, true to his word, Gerry escorted Lady Alyse about the Castle, showing her the more interesting of his discoveries in the attics, and long disused rooms of the original Keep tower. He was polite, and as distant as he could be, although he wanted nothing more than to sweep her into his arms. She looked at him curiously, and he could see the questions in her eyes – but she did not ask them.

Not directly, anyway.

"Lord Tillingford, I am yet again amazed at the fascinating character of this Castle. You must enjoy living in such a remarkable place."

"It can be... intriguing... yet it is also, in some ways, overwhelming. There is so much history embedded in every room, that it weighs upon me. The responsibility of doing the right things to maintain it is large, and I was never trained to manage an estate, having never expected to own such a thing."

As always seemed to happen, as soon as he began to converse with her, he somehow said more, revealed more of his true thoughts and feelings, than he had intended. She paused at his words, lifting her deep brown eyes to his, obviously considering.

"I had not thought of it that way. You are so very perfectly the titled gentleman, that I forget that your expectations in your early life were so different. Viewed from that perspective, I can see why this would seem overwhelming. Yet you manage it so well, and your plans for improvement and restoration go far beyond what many a nobleman would do for his estates."

Her words made him flush, feeling embarrassed. How she managed to see him in such a favourable light, he did not understand. Perhaps it was simply that she had no indication of his true, horrific nature.

"I fear you flatter me, Lady Alyse, but I thank you for your kind words. Let us, today, start with the highest rooms in this tower. They have not been used for at least two generations. They contain some beautiful carvings in the stone."

They continued up the long flights of stairs, and the further above the ground they were, the better he felt, for the further they were from the cellar room that he knew lay below. No matter where he was in the Castle, now, he was aware of where he was, in relation to *that* room, which haunted his dreams. It was easier once she was drawing, absorbed in what she did. Gerry stood at the window, staring out across his lands, taking pleasure in the visible signs of change in the gardens below, and the fields in the middle distance.

Anything to distract himself from watching Lady Alyse, for she looked beautiful as always, her soft gold hair escaping its pins in fine tendrils, the morning light making it glow. He wanted to touch it, to run his fingers through the silky strands, to brush aside the curl that fell around her cheek, fluttering with her breath as she concentrated on her work.

Better not to look, not to allow himself to be tempted.

So went the rest of the day – an agony of closeness to that which he could never have, a flow of conversation where small pieces of his real thoughts and feelings slipped out, despite his best intent. By late afternoon, when they returned to the main part of the buildings, he was exhausted, mentally, if not physically.

Looking into the library, they discovered Hunter, Nerissa and Charles with a pile of very old books on one desk, and some old plans unrolled on another. It seemed that Nerissa had located the drawings from a previous garden redesign, almost two centuries before. Gerry could not help but see the resemblance in manner between Nerissa poring over the design, and Lady Alyse absorbed in drawing. He discovered that he envied them. There was nothing in his life that truly absorbed him like that.

The stack of books on the other desk were, it turned out, estate management journals and ledgers from various times in the past, which Charles and Hunter were scanning through, looking for clues to what had been most profitably done with the land in the past, and where those same things might be even better done now, with the new methods they were implementing. Gratefully, Gerry allowed himself to be drawn into their discussion.

There were a few moments, during that first day, when Alyse thought that Lord Tillingford was relaxing, just a little – when their conversation flowed, and he seemed at ease. But, each time, he drew himself up and that cold mask slipped over his face again. It was so very frustrating!

She wished that she understood why he responded like that. Sometimes, she felt as if he cared for her, as she increasingly cared for him, and then the next minute he would be completely distant. It made her doubt her own judgement, doubt what she had seen, yet... she could not make herself turn away from him. Still, no other man had ever interested her as he did.

Once they were back in the library, seeing what the others had found, she felt isolated again, almost ignored, as he threw himself into conversation with Hunter and Charles. Dinner was no better, she felt invisible at times, and eventually pleaded fatigue, and retired early. Hunter watched her go, thoughtfully, but said nothing.

The next few days, Lord Tillingford spent some time showing her parts of the house – but less and less each day, as he was drawn into the activity surrounding the gardens and farms. If she were to be uncharitable, Alyse might had thought that he was beginning to actively avoid her. She pushed the thought aside, unwilling to accept its implications.

Eventually, there came a day where he professed to be unable to accompany her at all, leaving her to Mills' assistance only, again.

~~~~~

Gerry could stand it no longer. He could not spend another day so close to her, and not touch her, not speak of how he felt.

Treating her coldly, when he wished to do the exact opposite, left him achingly miserable. They sat in the parlour, sipping an after-dinner drink. He took a deep breath, and spoke.

"Lady Alyse, I fear that I must leave you to your own devices tomorrow, with Mills' assistance, of course, so that I can focus on the work needed for the farms. Please feel free to explore wherever you wish, of course."

Her face fell at his words, and he felt a cad for speaking them. Yet what choice had he?

"Gerry, I'm sure that Charles and I can move things along – your farmers know us now – you can spare part of the day for Alyse, surely?"

Hunter spoke softly, but Gerry turned to him in surprise – why would Hunter say such a thing? This was 'help' that he did not need!

"No. I feel that I need to be there, to see their reactions, and reassure them. After all, I am the one who will have to deal with it all, once you go home."

Hunter frowned, but before he could say anything further, Lady Alyse spoke up.

"Lord Tillingford, I understand, that will be perfectly all right – I am certain that Mills can show me anything that I wish to see, he has been most helpful."

Her words were polite and calm, but her voice shook a little, and her fingers twisted together. She looked down, nibbling at her lip as she finished speaking.

"Thank you, Lady Alyse."

She looked up, meeting his eyes for a moment, and such sadness filled hers that it stole his breath. Then she hid the emotion, and forced a smile onto her face.

"I find myself fatigued after the day – I believe I will retire now, the better to feel more awake tomorrow. If you will excuse me?"

"Certainly. Good night."

Nerissa watched Lady Alyse walk from the room, then turned, her eyes meeting her husband's.

"Hunter, do you think Alyse is well? She seems very tired and out of sorts these last few days – not really herself at all."

Hunter glanced at Gerry, who looked hastily away.

"I am sure she'll be fine, Nerissa – if I know my sister, she'll worry away at whatever is disturbing her until she solves it."

Gerry wondered, at Hunter's words, what 'solving it' might look like, in this case, if what worried her was himself.

~~~~~

Cunningham, sweeping the courtyard, slowly, watched as the door opened, and the girl came out, followed by the footman, Mills. Good. Otford wasn't with them. Perhaps this was his chance. Casually, he followed them, all the while making it look like he was simply doing a job.

Chapter Twelve

"Oh! How silly of me. Mills, I wanted to go down into the cellars again today, and we haven't brought a lantern. Please, go back and fetch one. I will wait here — it's pleasant to feel a little sun on my face, even if it's quite cold today."

"Certainly, Lady Alyse. I'll be back as quickly as I can."

Mills turned and went back the way they had come, passing a servant who was sweeping the courtyard. Quite what he was sweeping, Alyse couldn't tell, for the courtyard looked scrupulously clean to her — but she supposed it only stayed that way if it was swept all the time.

She stood, turning slowly in place, studying the building yet again, her sketch journal firm in her grasp. It was a new one, for she had, just the previous day, used the final page in the previous one, which now lay beside her bed upstairs. New journals were wonderful — the paper crisp and untouched, the edges a little ragged where they had been cut, the whole thing still smelling of the binder's glue and the scent unique to paper and leather, untouched by ink.

In the sunlit silence of the courtyard, the soft swish of the broom on the cobbles came to her clearly, from behind her. Then it stopped. Almost before she had time to notice, she was grabbed, roughly, from behind. She opened her mouth to speak, to scream, to... she did not know, and, before she could, the chance was taken from her, as a large, dirty hand clamped over her mouth. A strong, sackcloth clad arm wrapped around her, pinning her arms to her sides, and hauling her back against a hard body. The smell of the man made her gag.

Then they were moving.

She squirmed, fighting against his grip, but he was far stronger than her. He made a deep growling noise, and simply kept dragging her along. They went through the door, and rapidly down the shallow stairs towards the cellars. As he turned along the passage, passing side doors, moving towards the door which led into the deepest cellars, she began to struggle again, her mind full of terrified thoughts about what he might want, what he might do to her.

He dragged her onto the steep steps going down into the darkness of the next level, and she kicked at him, twisting desperately.

"Be still, ye little baggage, or I'll drop ye, and let ye fall all the way down. There's lots o' steps, and by the time ye reach the bottom, I've no doubt ye'll be in no condition t'fight me. One way or t'other, I'll be getting ye t' the bottom."

Alyse stilled, horror at his words driving a chill through her. It would seem that he didn't care if she was hurt – and a fall like that could break bones. If she were to escape, she needed to be whole of body.

His strength was frightening. He just lifted her, with that one arm, and went down, surefooted in the darkness, holding her so that she hung limply against him. Her journal was still clutched in her hand, and her bag of pencils flapped against her, where it dangled from her wrist. It seemed nonsensical to keep hold of the journal, yet reflex made her do it.

As they descended, her eyes adapted to the darkness, and she recognised, with a start, where she was. Through another door, and she was certain – before her was the wall with the stack of wine casks, and the shoved aside pile of planks and blocks. He moved as if he knew where he was, as if it was planned. When that movement took them across to the dark opening in the wall, Alyse panicked. She knew what was in the room at the end of this passageway.

Struggling, flailing, kicking, she fought his grasp. She felt her pencil bag slip, and fall from her wrist as she struggled. He laughed in her ear, a sound which had nothing to do with happiness, and which contained the echoes of madness in its tone. He dragged her onwards, until they reached the iron bound door. Kicking it open, he pulled her through.

"Here we are. Such a nicely decorated room, isn't it, milady? I'm quite certain we'll have a lovely afternoon here. I fully intend to enjoy myself. Now, lets get you settled. Where might be best?"

The torture chamber surrounded her. Full of implements which, in the hands of a madman like this, could wreak utter destruction on a frail human body. Fear froze her in place. He dragged her forward, until they stood before a wall from which various chains and manacles protruded. He took his hand from over her mouth, and reached out to tug on one.

"Let me go! What…"

She got no further.

"Silence, woman. I'm not wantin' ye screamin'... yet"

He accompanied the angry words with a hard slap of his free hand across her face, and the world went grey and unsteady. The second slap was even harder, and the blackness closed in. She barely felt herself falling.

~~~~~

Cunningham let her drop to the floor, kicking away the damned book that fell from her hands. He unrolled the rope that was wrapped around him, beneath his tunic, and considered where best to bind her. The manacles were rusted shut, so that wouldn't work. But there was a chair in one corner – a devious thing with loops to tie things to, and which looked like it was designed for use with any number of the other things in the room. That would have to do. He picked her up, taking his time about feeling the shape of her body as he did so, and carried her over to drop her on the chair. A pity that he needed Otford as an audience, before he did anything much to her – it was a long time since he'd had anything of a woman, especially one so clean and pretty as this.

He tied her to the chair, arms and legs held in place, and some ropes about her neck and body, just to be sure. Satisfied, he went to the corner of the room, and pulled out the lantern he had stashed there weeks ago, lit it, and hung it from a hook. Studying his handiwork, he smiled, a grim smile. Now, to make sure that Otford came to find her, alone.

He might have to go out and lure the man here – but best to wait first, and see if luck was with him. While he was waiting, he might as well have a close look at the tools in the room, and decide what to use on her. Nothing too nasty – at least to start, but things that would have an impact, which would leave very visible marks. He wanted Otford to suffer, just from watching, as much as possible.

~~~~~

"Damn!"

Gerry pulled his horse to a halt, and slipped down. Lifting the horse's front foot, he confirmed his suspicion – the shoe was gone. Somewhere along the road, it had come off, and now the horse was limping.

"I'll have to walk back with him. Not only is the shoe gone, but the large stone I just pulled out has bruised him. He'll likely be lame for a week or so, even with a new shoe. You go on to the outer farms without me."

"We will, and we'll report back on all of our discussions. At least the weather's dry – not such a bad day for a walk!"

"Indeed, Hunter – and we walked through worse many times in the war – I'll not suffer much for a good walk. I will see you this evening."

Turning, Gerry set off, leading the limping horse. Half an hour later, he could see a horseman coming towards him, moving fast. He wondered who it was, and why they were in such a hurry – for this road only went to his farms – who would need to rush out here?

A terrible sense of foreboding came over him, and he watched the horse approach, wishing it faster still, so that he might know, now, what had happened to occasion such hurry. Soon, the horseman drew up beside him, the horse breathing hard.

It was Mills. Gerry looked at him with great concern – the man rarely rode – why was he here?

"Mills, what..."

"My Lord..."

They both spoke at once, then stopped. Gerry waited, waving Mills to continue.

"My Lord, I... Lady Alyse..."

"What, man? Get a coherent sentence together, and tell me."

"She's missing. I left her in the courtyard, near the door to the old Keep understorey, and went back to get a lantern, as she wanted to go into the cellars, and when I returned, she was gone. Just gone. I've searched, and I've left others searching, but we haven't found her."

Gerry felt his heart stop in his chest. Missing! But what could possibly have happened to her? He did not know, but a sense of panic seized him, a sense of certainty that something was terribly wrong.

"Here, take my horse and walk him back, he's lame. I'll take yours and ride back as fast as I can."

"Yes, my Lord, as you wish." Moments later, Gerry was galloping down the road, his mind running through a series of wild imaginings of anything and everything that could possibly have happened to Lady Alyse.

He wished, in that instant, that he did not have as good an imagination as he did.

Alyse woke to flickering lamplight, her head fuzzy and aching, the side of her face feeling oddly tender and wrong. It took a few moments for her mind to make sense of what she saw in front of her – a few moments in which she also discovered, when she went to raise a hand to feel her face, that her arms were bound to the large chair she seemed to be in. It all came rushing back, and she suppressed a scream as she realised where she was. Panic could not help her – somehow, she needed to stay calm. The light showed her, all too clearly, the room's collection of torture implements – and the man who was moving amongst them, picking things up, fiddling with them, putting them down again, and moving on to the next thing.

She did not want to consider why he was doing so.

Now that she could see him, she realised that her abductor was the servant who had been sweeping the courtyard. But why? What reason would a servant have for this? The words he had spoken came back to her - words that had implied that he planned to hurt her – and she shuddered, fear chilling her. She was bound and helpless, in a room full of devices specifically designed to hurt people, held by a madman with apparently evil intent. It was like something out of a Gothic novel, the sort of thing that Sybilla might write, except that it was real, and she supposed that it was entirely too much to hope for, to be rescued by a hero, as would happen in a novel.

At that thought, the image of Lord Tillingford rose in her mind, and she wished, desperately, for his presence – surely, he could deal with this man who held her?

But... no-one knew where she was. The servant had timed things precisely. No-one had seen her taken, and Tillingford Castle was so large – they would have no clues for where to start.

Although... Mills knew where he had left her – that was at least a beginning, something to cling to as giving some hope. She was quite certain that Mills would have raised the alarm. So perhaps it was a matter of time, perhaps she needed to concentrate on surviving, on somehow convincing this madman to not hurt her, not kill her, long enough to give them time to find her.

It was not much of a plan, but it was the only plan she had.

~~~~~

Gerry abandoned the winded horse at the stables, apologising to the groom as he ran towards the Castle. When he reached the courtyard, he stopped, observing everything before proceeding. The first thing he noticed as out of place was the broom, dropped and seemingly abandoned in the middle of the cobbled space. Very strange – his staff were normally tidy about such things.

He walked towards the door to the Keep understorey, where Mills had apparently left Lady Alyse, looking for any sign of anything unusual. Inside, his mind screamed at him to hurry – but where to? There was no point rushing if he did not know where she was.

She may have simply become impatient, and wandered inside, then become caught up in drawing. He could not discount the possibility, although it seemed unlikely, given that Mills had been unable to find her. The door was ajar, which might be significant, and might not. But when he reached it, something glinted in the sun. Looking closer, he saw a few strands of pale gold hair, caught on a splintered edge of the old door.

How long had it been there? Could it be from one of the many times she had been through that door? Or was it a sign that she had gone this way, today? Gerry paused – he needed a lantern – if there was a chance that he would need to go into the cellars, he needed light. He spun on his heel, and rushed across the open space to the kitchens, demanding a lantern from the shocked kitchen staff. With a command that they send footmen to follow him, he spun again, and ran back to the Keep door.

Once inside the Keep, he had to choose a likely direction. Down seemed best, as she had spoken of going to the cellars, so he turned onto the shallow steps that led down to the first level of cellars. Studying the steps, he saw what might have been ordinary marks, but which looked more like a new set of scuffs on the steps, and on the near side wall. Could she have slipped? Or was there a more sinister possibility. His blood ran cold in his veins at the thought. But why would anyone wish to harm her, or to take her? He could not imagine a reason.

He kept going, but there were no more signs of anything unusual. At the bottom of the steps he continued, passing through the next door. Here, the floor was earth, and here, there were signs of something odd.

Across the floor, and along the passage, to the door which led to the steep steps, which went down to the next level of the cellars, there were what looked like scuff marks, overlaying faint footprints at random intervals. Almost, he thought, as if one person were dragging another, unwilling, with them. He stood a moment, coming to terms with the terrible possibility that such an image might be exactly what had happened. Then, taking a determined breath, he pressed on. He did not want to descend those next stairs – for down on that level lay a room that he never wished to visit again, much though it haunted him.

But the trail of footprints and scuff marks led through the door, so he went. There were few marks on the stairs, but more on the floor at the bottom, and another few wisps of hair on the lower door. And then he was standing in the room with the wine casks, the room with an opening on the other side, that led to only one place. Gerry paused, shaking. He did not want to go towards that room. But he must. Slowly, he crossed the dusty floor, until he stood before the opening. That part of him that the dreams called to wanted to simply go down the corridor, to see that room again. Another part of him wanted to turn and run. But what steadied him, in the end, was remembering what he had seen in Lady Alyse's sketch journal.

She had been in that room, and had the courage to see it simply as a collection of old artefacts, much like an attic full of old furniture. If she could view it like that, surely, so could he. He stepped into the passage, and, as he did, his foot brushed against something. He stopped, and looked down. It was the bag that Lady Alyse carried her pencils in. A mixture of horror and elation filled him. She would never willingly lose that bag. But at least he now knew that she had been here.

He scooped up the bag, dropping it into his coat pocket, and then, shuttering the lantern so that only the barest sliver of light came out, he continued.

~~~~~

Alyse watched the man as he moved around the room, carefully wriggling her arms and legs to test the ropes. But the ropes were firm – there was little chance that she would be able to break free. She prayed, fervently, that Mills had reported her missing, and that, by now, someone was searching for her.

The man stopped at a table piled with strange objects, and rummaged about amongst them. After a few minutes he lifted one, peering intently at it, turning it in all directions. Then he smiled, an expression that made the fear rise in her, threatening to destroy the fragile calm that she had achieved. He turned towards her, muttering, the device still in his hand.

"This one, yes, this one. With this, I can take what she cares about, even while I destroy him…"

It was obvious that he spoke only for himself, almost as if he did not see her as real in some way, as if she could not hear him. or perhaps he did not care what she heard. He stopped in front of her, and held the thing out, showing her.

"This, pretty one. We will put your hand in this. Ye like to draw, don't ye? So, that's the first thing I'll take away. How badly – well that will depend on ye, won't it?"

Alyse did not understand what he meant, but his words terrified her, nonetheless. He set the strange box like thing down on the wide arm of the chair, next to her right hand.

"Ye see this little flap here?" he pushed one end of the box, and it opened, "Inside, ye see those nasty sharp spikes? Well, we'll push yer hand in through there, under the spikes. Goes in easy. But if'n ye pull back, them spikes'll dig in ter yer pretty hand, and make a right mess o' it. If'n ye can stay still, nuthin will happen. But I'll do me best to make yer move." He laughed, watching her. It was a high-pitched sound, hysterical, mad. She was sure that he could see the dawning horror on her face. "I'll put yer hand in, and ye can just sit – until himself arrives – he must be a looking fer ye by now. No point wastin me effort, until he's here to see, until I can begin to destroy him, as he destroyed me. It's only right that it be in a place like this."

Alyse struggled to understand what he meant – who was he waiting for? Lord Tillingford? But why? None of it made any sense. Perhaps the man was simply mad. Then, all thought of his meaning fled her mind, as he lifted her hand, and moved the terrible box towards it. She struggled, as much as she could, but he simply slapped her again, so hard that everything went grey. She clung to consciousness – she could do nothing to help herself if she was not aware.

He slipped the terrible box over her hand – she felt the spikes drag gently over her skin, not digging in because her hand was moving in the direction they were angled. But she could feel the sharpness, roughened by rust. An involuntary shudder ran through her, and even that small movement made the spikes prick at her skin. She forced herself to utter stillness.

He laughed again, watching her.

"Now we wait. Ye best hope he's quick about it. Yer wouldn't want me t' get bored, and start playin' with ye, now would yer?"

Alyse simply sat, saying nothing. The madman seemed to feel the need to fill the silence, and kept talking, rambling on at her about France, spies, torture, Newgate, Lt. Otford, being cheated, being rejected, revenge and more. At first, none of it made sense, but, after a while, she began to see what might be a distorted story in the ramblings – a story that shook her perceptions of the world. Otford was Lord Tillingford's name, was it not? Before the title was granted, he would simply have been known by that. She should not give credence to a madman's ravings, but... what if some of what he spoke of was true? Was Lord Tillingford a far different type of man than she had thought? But... if that were true, why would her brother be his friend?

There were no answers. Her arm and side began to ache,

from the effort of staying completely still. Her mother had always said she was a fidget – now, she suspected that was true – she had never imagined how hard it would be to simply stay still.

~~~~~

As Gerry approached the iron bound door, which stood a little ajar, he could hear a voice – deep, a man's voice. At first, he could not make out the words, but as he got closer it became clear. He stopped, and listened. It took but a few sentences for him to understand what was being spoken of. His skin broke out in a cold sweat, and he felt an almost uncontrollable urge to retch.

This was like one of his dreams, where those he cared for were threatened, and hurt, by him, because of him. But this was real. There was a man in that room, with Lady Alyse, who he had to assume was restrained in some way (let it not be worse than that!). A man whom he had interrogated in France, and broken in some way, a man who had come here for revenge – against him. And Lady Alyse was the innocent victim that he had chosen to use to perpetrate that revenge, it seemed.

He crept towards the door, his mind filled with horrifying images of what was in that room, what might be there that he had not seen, in that one quick glimpse he'd had, and what might be done to a beautiful woman using those tools. He needed a weapon. He was a fool to not have taken the time to collect one. He would have to make do.

He reached the door. The flicker of lantern light shone through the small gap, and he saw, lying there, just into the passage, an object. He bent and lifted it.

Lady Alyse's sketch journal. A new one, if he was not mistaken, larger and heavier than the previous one. Perhaps even that could be a weapon, or at least a distraction. He inched forward, studying what he could see of the room through the small gap. Just inside, there was a pile of what looked like, and probably were, fire pokers. They would have to do for weapons – better than nothing.

He waited, listening, sick at heart to hear his monstrousness being laid out in all its terrible detail to Lady Alyse, shaken by the tale that the man told – for it seemed that he had gone mad, and had laid all blame on Gerry for what had happened to him, rather than seeing that his own betrayal of his country at the start had brought about the whole chain of events. How many others, Gerry wondered, had he sent on a spiral into madness?

He could not touch the door, for he remembered that it creaked, abominably. He edged around, to see as much as he could through the small amount that it was open. Balanced awkwardly, craning his neck, he managed to see across the room. She was there! Lady Alyse was tied to some odd bulky chair. And... he could not see clearly, but some object appeared to be attached to her arm. Bile rose in his throat – what had the madman done to her? His vision blurred, and it was all he could do not to simply rush into the room in a murderous rage.

In that instant, his feelings for Lady Alyse became very clear to him. He could not allow her to be hurt, could not imagine never seeing her again. His desire to defend her warred with his need to approach cautiously – for the mad were unpredictable, and the wrong choice on his part could have disastrous consequences. He clutched her journal so hard that his knuckles were white. Then, as he went to move back from his awkward position, and consider his next move, he teetered, unbalanced for a second, and bumped the door.

It creaked – loudly. He froze in place.

"Oho! We have a visitor. Who lurks at the door? Do come in, I've been waiting for you."

The voice was rough, full of a kind of insane glee that chilled Gerry to the bone. As he heard it, he also heard a stifled cry from Lady Alyse – a sound of pain, rapidly repressed. He knew what pain sounded like, in its many guises – there was no doubt in his mind that she was in pain. He had lost the chance for complete surprise – but perhaps he could still do the unexpected. From the sound of the voice, it was not far from where he had seen Lady Alyse. He would have to be very fast, if this was to work.

He clutched her journal, praying that she would forgive him for what he was about to do with it, took a deep breath, and slammed the door open. The man stepped to stand beside Lady Alyse, his hand tangling in her hair. She drew in a sharp breath, but stayed absolutely still, her eyes finding his, full of hope and fear. It nearly undid him.

"Ah, it's you, Lt. Otford. So unpleasant to see you again. Yer just in time fer the show. Don't do anything rash now, or I'll make sure she pays fer yer attitude."

Gerry stopped, dragged his eyes from Lady Alyse's, and took in the situation. Her right hand was enclosed in a metal box. A wave of nausea struck him as he realised just what it was. That was why she was so still, when the madman's grasp on her hair had to be hurting her. He could not act yet – not while the fellow held her, for any action that moved him, would move her, with horrific consequences. A memory stirred, as his mind put together the fragments of ramblings that he had heard through the door.

"Cunningham, isn't it?"

"That was quick, yer high and mighty Lordship. Ye always were a clever one. Seems I'm strong in yer memory like ye are in mine. I wasn't ever fergettin the man who destroyed me life, but I'm surprised ye remember me. Wasn't I just one amongst the many ye destroyed?"

"You're the one who destroyed your life, Cunningham – you would never have been delivered to me for attention if you hadn't turned traitor in the first place."

Gerry spoke calmly, but inside, that voice in his mind screamed at him – *'Monster!'*.

"Attention – is that what ye call it? I called it torture, meself. But yer too high and mighty fer words like that now, I s'pose."

Gerry watched Lady Alyse's face. Her eyes held uncertainty, confusion, even doubt, but not outright condemnation. That was better than he had any right to hope for.

"Cunningham – what do you want? Why are you holding Lady Alyse – she was never in France, has nothing to do with what happened to your life."

If only he could get the madman to take his hands off Lady Alyse!

"What do I want? I want ye to suffer, t' pay for every beating I took in Newgate, every moment o' life with me family ye stole from me. I want to destroy ye utterly, to take from ye everything ye care most about. So, I thought I'd start with her. I've seen the way ye look at her, I know ye want her – so I'll make sure ye never have her. This place was such a find. What better way to do it, than make ye watch. Man like ye, ye might even get something out of it, before ye suffer too." Gerry flinched at the words, at the echo of his dreams, at the proof that he was not the only one in the world who understood how monstrous he was. His face must have paled, and he found himself helplessly shaking his head in denial. Cunningham watched him, then laughed. "Squeamish now, are ye? Developed some fine feelings along with that fine title? Funny, I was sure that ye were a man who enjoyed yer work, back then...."

"Never! I acted from necessity, not pleasure."

"So ye say now – be that just fer her benefit? Well, let's see how ye cope with bein' the helpless one."

Cunningham twisted his hand in Lady Alyse's hair, and bent down, tipping her head back as if to kiss her. She tried to squirm away, then squeaked in pain, and stilled again.

Her eyes went to Gerry, full of despair. Cunningham grinned.

"Darlin', I'm just getting started. If'n that makes ye squeak, then ye'll be wailin' soon enough."

Gerry ground his teeth together, desperate to get the man away from her, so that he could act. Almost as if his fervent prayers had been answered, Cunningham released her hair.

"Just have a little rest darlin', while I choose me next toy ter play wit' ye with. And ye can stay right there, Otford – if'n ye move one bit, I'll make sure she's screamin' proper."

Gerry stayed where he was, near the door, watching carefully. Cunningham moved a few feet away from Lady Alyse – not far enough – it needed to be too far for him to grab her again quickly. Gerry watched as Cunningham drifted further, looking at the implements around him, flicking his eyes back to Gerry regularly. Finally, he stopped, at a table laden with knives and spikes. Gerry refused to think about the man's intent – to even consider it would distract him from his immediate need to act.

As Cunningham bent to examine the items, Gerry flung Lady Alyse's journal at him, aiming for his head, and dropped to the side, grabbing up two of the long pokers from the floor, before launching towards the man. The journal flew true, and struck Cunningham on the side of the temple. He staggered, half falling against the table.

As Gerry reached him, he pulled himself upright again, shaking his head, and roaring with inchoate anger, a long rusty knife in his fist. There followed the strangest fight that Gerry had ever fought, with the two fire pokers used as sword and shield, to deflect the rusty knife from finding its mark.

Cunningham was far stronger than Gerry had expected, the unnatural strength of the mad, who care not for their own safety, only for achieving their aim. Minutes passed, as they circled each other, neither gaining a true advantage. If this went on for too long, Gerry would tire, and the madman's strength would prevail. Dramatic action was needed.

Gerry waited until Cunningham was far away from Lady Alyse, and as close as he could push him to the wall, then struck at him with one poker, as a distraction, before throwing the other poker, as hard as he could, at the man's head. Cunningham grunted, and staggered, his head slamming back against the wall, and the rusty knife dropping from his hand, as he tried and failed to avoid the thrown iron. Gerry snatched up a knife from the table – a wicked long stiletto style dagger – and leapt forward, bringing it to Cunningham's throat.

Cunningham's roar cut off mid sound, as the blade went into his skin with his movement. Gerry, seizing the chance, dropped the other poker, and smashed his fist into Cunningham's face, slamming his head against the wall again. The madman fell, unconscious, at his feet. Gerry tore off his cravat, and immediately bound Cunningham's hands behind him. He kicked the dropped knife well away, then looked around for something to bind his feet.

"The rope around my body – it will be quickest to use."

Lady Alyse's voice shook, but her suggestion was sensible. He was grateful that she had not fainted, or panicked.

Quickly, he untied some of the ropes that bound her, and tied Cunningham's feet, making sure that there was nothing in range of him that he might use to worry at the ropes. Leaving the unconscious man lie, he turned back to Lady Alyse.

"Let me untie the rest of the ropes, and then we will see about freeing you from that device."

"There are spikes… they have scratched me, dug in a little, but I have mostly managed to hold still. I do not believe that I have ever been still for this long in my entire life before."

Her words came with a small brittle laugh.

"I know that there are spikes." He worked at the ropes around her ankles, gently pulling them away from her abraded skin, where her stockings had been no match for the roughness, wishing that he might be touching her ankles in a very different circumstance, and then berating himself for the very thought. He admired her strength, her courage – that she had managed to stay calm, was still calm, albeit shaky, astounded him. When all of the ropes were removed, he stood, preparing himself for what he had to do. "To get this off you, I will have to move it, and your hand – we will need to be very careful, and it may dig in, a little, but there is no other way."

Her eyes met his, full of trust, and she nodded. He did not deserve her trust. He placed his hands on each side of the box.

"I need to lift it. Let your hand be lifted with it, without any other movement." She nodded again, and he lifted, carefully, curling his fingers under the bottom edges, to find the two secret catches that should be there. "Are the spikes into your flesh at all?"

"No. When they dug in, I pushed my hand forward again, as much as I could. They are touching me, but not caught in the cuts – at least I think they are not."

"Good. Push your hand down, flat – now."

He pushed the catches up, and slid them, as she pushed down. For a moment, he was afraid that the mechanism was rusted, and would not work, but then, suddenly, with a loud click, it let go, and the whole top part of the box, including the spikes, lifted up off the base.

The pressure of her hand slammed the base down onto the chair arm, leaving him standing, holding the rest of the device. He released the breath he had not realised he was holding.

Lady Alyse stared at her hand, as if she had expected never to see it again. A ragged sob escaped her. Gerry cast aside the remains of the box, and carefully lifted her hand, feeling each part of it with gentle fingers, to assure himself that nothing was broken.

"No bones have been broken, and the cuts are small, thanks to your good sense and courage. Had you panicked, you would likely have mangled your hand completely. The cuts will need to be washed, and we must pray that they do not become infected, but, barring that, they should heal well, although you may have some small scars."

She nodded, her eyes brimming with tears that she refused to shed. He saw the way she looked at him, her eyes saying so

362

much, and all of his feelings for her rushed through him. He had come so close to losing her! And that was an unbearable thought. Life without her was an unbearable thought. Despite all his best intent, he had to face the fact that he had come to care very deeply for her. He did not know what to do with that fact.

"How... how did you know how to open that... thing...?"

Immediately, all thought of softer emotions left him. He was a fool. She had just been told exactly what sort of a monster he was. He had just proved it to her, unequivocally – not just in what he had said to Cunningham, but by being able to open that damned box. No normal man would know such a thing. He drew the bitterness about him, and made his face expressionless and his words cold. Better to not hope, for surely she would turn from him in horror, once she'd had time to consider what she had seen and heard.

"I... I have seen such a thing before... during the war. It is knowledge I never thought to need again."

~~~~~

Alyse watched the mask come over his face again. Moments before, he had been looking at her as she had dreamed of him doing, with warmth and something more, now, he was cold and distant again. All, it seemed, because she had asked about how he had known how to save her hand. She did not understand the reaction.

He had saved her. She had wished for a hero, imagining it to be him, and he had come. If she had been half in love with him before, she was more so now.

The way that he had fought that madman, with such skill, with no proper weapons, fascinated her – such skill, and she had not known that of him. It did not matter why he chose to be distant to her – he was a hero, and she would cling to that, to the moment when he had looked at her as if she were precious to him.

Perhaps, one day, she truly would be.

"I am not sure if I can stand – I feel rather shaky, and I ache all over, from staying completely still for so long."

He held out his hand, and she took it, the warmth welcome.

"I will help you. Let me get you back up out of the cellars – we can send some of the larger grooms and footmen to haul that madman up and keep him in custody until he can be dealt with."

He pulled her to her feet, and she wobbled, her breath catching as pain shot through her legs with returning sensation. He slipped his arm around her waist, taking her weight against him. She leant into him, enjoying the sensation of strength, of hard muscle against her. His immaculate clothes were in disarray, his cravat gone and a delicious triangle of skin visible at his throat, yet he felt perfect to her, in that moment. Her mind replayed the way that she had seen those muscles move as he fought for her safety, and heat flushed through her body.

How different this was, being held against this man, compared to the horror of being clutched by that madman. Leaning into him, she tentatively took a step.

"I believe that I can walk now, with your assistance. But... was that my journal that you threw at him? Can we retrieve it?"

"Indeed it was. And an excellent emergency weapon it

turned out to be. Come to the door – you can hold on to that for a moment whilst I collect the journal, then we can tackle the stairs."

He helped her across the floor, and she stood, watching, as he bent to pick up the journal. His dark blond hair fell over his forehead, in complete disarray, and he flicked it aside unconsciously as he stood again. She was filled with the desire to touch it. Once he returned to her, he handed her the journal, and slipped his arm about her again.

"It is well made – it was not damaged at all by its fall, save for a slight nick in the leather binding. Oh, and I have your bag of pencils too – I found them on the stairs as I came down."

"Thank you. Every time I draw in this, I will thank you. He told me, the madman, that he had chosen to start with my right hand, so that he could take from me something I cared about, whilst also hurting you. And truly, I do not know what I would do, if I could not draw. Perhaps I would learn, as some people do, to use my other hand? I am glad that I need not find out."

They fell into silence, going slowly up the stairs. The further they went, the better she felt, as the movement warmed her muscles and the feeling of the man at her side warmed her heart. Finally, they reached the courtyard, almost colliding with Mills as he ran towards the door. Alyse laughed at the expression on his face.

"Mills, thank you. As you can see, I have been found, although I am a little the worse for wear."

"My Lady, I'm so sorry – I should never have left you alone, not for a minute."

"Balderdash, Mills. You had no reason to know that I was anything but perfectly safe. Do not blame yourself."

"But I do, my Lady. What happened?"

As he spoke, Hunter and Charles came rushing across the courtyard, having just arrived back, and been informed by the grooms of all the dramatic comings and goings.

"Yes, what has happened. Alyse – I've never seen you look so shaken. And your hand... is that blood?"

Lord Tillingford spoke firmly, in the face of Hunter's question.

"I'd suggest that we get Lady Alyse into the parlour, with a brandy and some tea, and get these cuts cleaned. Everything can be explained then, with everyone present. Mills, down in the deepest cellar below here, you will find a room full of very nasty old items, and one bound villain. He is a madman, and dangerous. Please take four strong men down there, and carry him up, and lock him away somewhere safe, until the magistrate can be called."

"As you wish, my Lord, I'll summon the grooms at once."

Alyse discovered that her legs were not very stable again, at the mention of the madman, and she leant into Lord Tillingford, wavering on her feet.

She could see Hunter observing her, and the fact that she was held in Lord Tillingford's arm, but he said nothing about it.

There were times when she truly appreciated her brother.

Chapter Thirteen

Once inside, and settled on a couch, Lady Alyse allowed everyone to fuss over her. Gerry had felt a sense of loss when he had finally released her from his hold, and lowered her to the seat. He had not wanted to let her go, had wanted to hold her tight to him, reassuring himself that she was safe, allowing himself the pleasure of her touch. But he had released her, as was proper. He had no right to more, now that she was safely able to sit somewhere comfortable.

As the housekeeper was tutting over her hand, washing it, covering it with healing salve and binding it up, Nerissa came rushing in, having just returned from the groundskeeper's cottage, where she had been laying out the final plans for the garden to the gardening staff, and a new flurry of questions occurred.

Gerry spoke up, once Nerissa slowed down.

"Nerissa, please, let Mrs Pitt finish first – there are still the abrasions on Lady Alyse's ankles to deal with. Then the story can be told to everyone at once."

Alyse was flushed, obviously embarrassed, but had allowed Mrs Pitt to lift her hems and fuss over her ankles. It no doubt felt most improper to have her lower legs exposed like that, in a room full of men, yet she looked grateful for the soothing water and salve on the torn skin.

He sat in his favourite chair, watching her, watching them all, waiting for the moment when the story would need to be told. He dreaded it – for he would need to speak of his history, of his work during the war, in more detail than he ever had – there would be no avoiding it. Yet… in a way, it was a relief to know that he could speak of it.

He might lose his friends, might lose everything he cared for, yet he would also lose the weight of the unspoken, which he had carried for so long. It was ironic that, potentially, Cunningham would achieve what he had wanted – his actions might yet destroy Gerry, if indirectly – for, if he lost everyone he cared for, if they all turned away in horror, he would have little left in his life.

Finally, Mrs Pitt was finished, and gathered up the bowl of water, the cloths and the salves, and left the room. Nerissa poured the tea that the maid had brought, and all eyes turned to Gerry and Lady Alyse. Suddenly, everything seemed to still. Gerry felt calm, almost detached from the situation, the world crystal clear around him.

"I believe that the beginning of this tale is yours to tell, Lady Alyse."

At his words, she nodded, and then sat a moment, her eyes cast down, her hands twisting in her lap, composing herself. He ached to touch her, to ease her tension – had he been sitting beside her, he was not sure that he could have resisted the temptation.

When she finally lifted her gaze and spoke, her voice was steady.

"When I had gathered up my journal and pencils, I set off to explore. I had decided to venture into the cellars again, but, when I reached the courtyard door into the Keep understorey, I realised that I had been silly enough to forget the need for a lantern. So I asked Mills to go back and get one, while I waited near the door, enjoying what little sunshine there was. I looked about me, as I always do, appreciating the quiet and the sun – for the only noise was the broom of the servant who was sweeping the cobbles – and I was studying the shape of the old iron latch on the door, when I was grabbed from behind."

She paused, and sipped her tea, whilst everyone waited, watching her.

"The sound of the broom had stopped, moments before, so I have to suspect that the man who grabbed me was the one who appeared to be a servant. But I am not certain. I did not even have the chance to scream, for he clamped his hand over my mouth. He was big, and strong, and had wrapped an arm around me, trapping my arms against my sides. He half lifted, half dragged me into the building, and down the stairs. When I struggled, he threatened to push me down the stairs, so that the hurt I suffered in the fall would make me easier for him to handle."

Gerry ground his teeth together, filled with rage yet again, at how Cunningham had treated Lady Alyse. Hunter and Charles exchanged a look which said that their rage was no less. How would they react, Gerry wondered, when the tale of what had happened in that torture chamber was told?

Alyse continued, her hands twisting in her lap as she spoke, her face pale.

"When we got to the bottom of the stairs, I recognised the room we were in, for I had found it once before. When he began to drag me across that room, to the opening on the other side, I panicked. For that opening led to a passage, which went to only one place – a room that I had seen once before, and drawn the contents of. I struggled frantically, and somewhere in that, my pencil bag dropped from my wrist. The man didn't care, he just laughed at me, and dragged me onwards. I could barely see, for he had no lantern, but my eyes had adjusted to the darkness somewhat, as his had, obviously. He dragged me along the passage, and into the room at the end."

"But – what was in the room, that the memory of it had made you panic?"

Nerissa's question dropped into the room like a bomb into Gerry's life.

Here was the moment when the difficult explanations would start.

"It was a torture chamber, no doubt centuries old, and centuries unused, from the amount of dust and rust to be seen there. I had found it before, and seen it as simply a collection of strange objects from a time long past, things which I would not expect to be used in this more enlightened age. It was, in a sense, rather validating of the concept that all things, no matter how bad, eventually pass and crumble to dust. But it was not a place I wanted to be, in the hold of a madman who apparently wished to do me harm."

Hunter's eyes met Gerry's and the sense of approaching doom intensified.

"What happened once you were in that room?"

Hunter's voice was low, but held a lethal edge in its tone.

"He dragged me to the wall, and uncovered my mouth to reach up and see if he could open manacles that hung there. They looked rusted shut. I attempted to speak, and he cursed at me, threatened me, then simply hit me, twice, so hard that I fell into blackness. I think that I dropped my journal then, or perhaps earlier – I am not sure. When I came to, I was sitting, tied into a huge chair of some kind, and he had lit a lantern. Its flickering light made the contents of the room all too horribly visible. He was raving about revenge, and hurting me, so that he could hurt Lord Tillingford. It made little sense to me. He walked about the room, picking up and discarding devices, until he finally chose one – 'to play with me' in his words. It was a box, a devilish design that allowed a hand to be pushed into it, but not pulled out again without being ripped to pieces. He chose my right hand, so that, if I could not stay still, and moved my hand, I would lose my ability to draw. Then he told me that he intended to make sure that, in the end, I moved, and screamed."

Lady Alyse stopped, her voice having become unsteady, and sipped at her tea. After a moment of shocked silence, the room erupted into discussion.

"He what! Where is this reprobate? I have a sudden personal desire to see to his disposal."

"I believe my wishes align with yours, Hunter. But, as the man is bound and locked away, if I heard things aright in the courtyard, perhaps we should hear the rest of the story first."

Hunter looked, at first, as if he would disagree with Charles, then nodded curtly, and turned back towards Lady Alyse.

Nerissa had risen, and gone to Lady Alyse, wrapping her into a comforting hug. It was, Gerry thought, the point at which he should take over the tale.

"I believe that the next part of the story is mine. Nerissa, Lady Alyse, you know that I left here with Hunter and Charles – but halfway out to the furthest farms, my horse lost a shoe, and picked up a bad stone bruise. I decided to walk him back, whilst Hunter and Charles went on. When I was halfway back to here, I saw a horseman, coming towards me, fast. It was Mills, bearing the news that Lady Alyse was missing, and that they had not been able to find her. A terrible sense of foreboding overcame me, and I left Mills to walk my horse back, and took his, to ride here as fast as I could. When I reached the courtyard, there was no sign of disturbance, beyond an abandoned broom on the cobbles. But on the edge of the door to the understorey, there were a few strands of pale gold hair – so I made the assumption that Lady Alyse had been taken through that door. For by then I was convinced that someone must have taken her – I could not imagine her not being true to her word, to wait for Mills."

"Thank you for your faith in me."

Gerry's eyes met Lady Alyse's for a moment, and he drew strength from the warmth with which she regarded him.

"I felt like simply rushing in, but I had at least enough presence of mind to go back and get a lantern. Then, I went into the understorey of the Keep – by such small things as scuff marks on the stairs, I tracked the path that he had taken her, praying all the while that I was not reading too much into the small signs I found. But, when I found Lady Alyse's pencil bag on the passage floor, I knew that I was going the right way."

"If that was what led you to me, then I am so very glad that it fell."

"As am I. I picked it up, and went carefully further down the passage. I, by then, recognised where I was, for I too had once before found that room. It was a room that I never wanted to return to."

Hunter looked sharply at him, but said nothing. Gerry was grateful, and went on, feeling the inevitable moment approaching.

"I shuttered my lantern, and crept down the passage, for I could hear the rumble of a voice. The words did not come clear until I was almost at the door to the room. The door was ajar – perhaps one third open. I stopped and listened, moving carefully and peering through the gap to see what was happening in the room. I almost fell over Lady Alyse's journal, which lay on the floor just outside the door. It was then that I realised how unthinking I had been, in my haste to find her. I had not brought a weapon. I looked and saw, just inside the door, a pile of fire pokers – which would have to do for weapons. Through the gap, I could see Lady Alyse, bound in a chair, her hand in a device which rested on one arm of it. A device I am afraid to say that I recognised. It was all I could do to stop myself from simply rushing blindly in, so great was my rage. But I managed to stop, and listen to what the man was saying. He was, as Lady Alyse commented, raving – rambling on about the war, his life, getting revenge, destroying the man who had destroyed him. But... I understood it all, I knew what he spoke of, and why. For I am the one he wished to destroy. All of this is my fault. My unforgivable fault."

"What do you mean? I cannot imagine you destroying someone's life, Gerry."

"My thanks for your good opinion, Nerissa, but I fear that, in a way, the madman is right."

"Why would you believe that?"

Hunter looked at him, puzzled.

Gerry almost laughed – if even the man who had been his commanding officer, who had directed the need for his actions, in that crumbling farmhouse in France, did not see it, what hope did he have for understanding, once he explained the bald and terrible truth of it? Probably none. But there was no other option. He had to finish what he had begun.

"Because of what I did to him, in France. For, you see, I waited, and watched, hoping that I might be able to surprise him, when he was not near Lady Alyse, enough to overcome him somehow. But the position I was in was awkward, to see the right part of the room, and, in the end, I slipped, and bumped the door – which creaked, very badly. When he knew someone was there, he called out, calling me in. I slammed the door back, still hoping for surprise, but he was faster, and moved to her side, gripping her hair, and forcing her to move. Her cry of pain as her hand was cut stopped me in my tracks. But, standing there, I recognised him. Truth to tell, I remember all of their faces, all of the ones that I broke. But his – his I remember most of all, because he was one of ours that had turned."

"Ah. I see. I never asked, in France, exactly what you did to them. I was just grateful for the results that you produced, and that I did not have to interrogate them. Personally, I would have wanted to kill them, and I was glad that you managed not to."

Gerry forced himself not to gape at Hunter. He had understood that the others had appreciated not having to do what he did, but it had never occurred to him that their reasons might be a perception that they would be more destructive, more merciless, than he. Lady Alyse was watching him, her brow furrowed.

"I am afraid that I still do not really understand."

"Let us finish telling the tale of what happened in the cellar, and then I will explain, as best I may."

He was caught, again, by Lady Alyse's eyes, which still met his with warmth – a warmth that would surely disappear when he did explain.

"Yes, I do want to know exactly how you overcame the man, and released Alyse, given that you had no weapon. Do continue."

Nerissa's voice brought him back to the moment, and he tore his eyes from Lady Alyse, and continued with the story.

"I stood there, just inside the door, and he gloated at me, about me now being the helpless one, about the fact that he intended to hurt Lady Alyse in front of me, because I care for her, so that would hurt me, and then intending to do physical damage to me, as the final part of his revenge. I had no doubt, at that point, that he intended to kill us both, slowly and painfully." Nerissa gasped in horror. "He told me to stand where I was, and not move, or he would hurt her more. So I waited, and when he moved about the room, choosing what terrible instrument of torture he would next use, I chose my moment. When he was some distance from her, I flung her journal, which I had picked up at the door, as hard as I could, at his head."

"And it hit him, very solidly, on the side of the temple. Never have I been so glad to see a book of mine mistreated."

"I took the opportunity that gave me to grab up two of the pokers, and leap at him. He, in turn, shook off the effects of the blow, and rounded on me, with a long rusty knife in hand. We fought, and truly, I do not remember much of it. He was strong, in that way that madmen are, where they care nothing for themselves, only for achieving their aim. I knew that, if I let the fight continue for too long, he would wear me down. So I conceived a plan to get the advantage."

"And very successfully. I sat there, unable to move, my hand hurting from the damage already inflicted, and the sharp spikes pricking at my skin, praying as I watched. Lord Tillingford's actions were heroic, and I was amazed at his skill, holding off the man with only improvised weapons, but I could see that the madman's size and strength were a problem. Then, without warning, Lord Tillingford flung one of the pokers, which he was using as swords, right at the madman's head. The man was close to the wall of the room, and his flinch away crashed his head into the wall, causing him to drop the knife he held, as the poker hit him."

"When I threw the poker, I was beside the table full of knives, so I snatched up a stiletto dagger, and threw myself upon him, holding it to his throat, before he had recovered from the blow. He stilled when the rusty blade cut his skin, and I took the chance to apply my fist to his head with enough force to snap his head back into the wall again, and fell him. Between my cravat, and the rope he had used on Lady Alyse, there was enough to bind him securely, and I left him lying with nothing too close to him, which he might later abrade the rope upon."

"Cleverly done! But how did you release Lady Alyse's hand from the device?"

Nerissa's eyes glowed with curiosity. Now came the part where his explanations would begin, where the truth of his monstrous nature would be laid out before them.

He took a rather large swallow of the tea which had been sitting on the table beside him, and went on.

"Somehow, he knew exactly how to open the device, without hurting me."

The pressure of everyone's eyes was a heavy thing, as they

waited for him to explain.

"I mentioned France before. I have never spoken of it, but… my role, in our team during the war, was that of interrogator. It was my job to convince the French spies and soldiers that we captured to tell us what they knew of the French army's plans, so that we might gain the advantage, and prevent our forces from being caught in any traps. And so that we might find other infiltrators amongst us, and remove them."

"And by doing so, he can be said to have saved many thousands of British lives."

"Thank you, Hunter, I pray that is true, for I never saw the impact of what I did, directly. But to the point in question – I knew how to open that device, because I had seen one like it before – I had seen many things like the items in that room in the cellars before. The 'interrogation kit' which I inherited from the previous interrogator for the regiment, contained many such items. I did my best not to use such things, to obtain information more by creating fear, than directly by pain."

Hunter watched him, the light of understanding dawning in his eyes. Gerry wondered what reaction might follow the understanding. Part of him simply wished to disappear, another part awaited Hunter's next words with hope, no matter how foolish such hope might be.

"But sometimes, you did use such things, when there was no other way. And to be able to do that, you had to learn the purpose and operation of all of them, even if, in the end, you were never to use them." Gerry nodded. "And ever since, you blame yourself for using them, for not finding another way to cause those enemies of our country to break their silence, and give us the information we needed."

"Yes, exactly. What kind of man am I, that I could visit such brutality upon another man? In the end, is that not worse than what that man had done, by being an enemy? I do not know. But this man – his name is Cunningham, although I do not know what name he may be going by now – this man was one who took some application of such tools – not much, but still... he was British, but had been seduced to the French cause, had turned traitor, and it took strong persuasion to convince him to turn back to us, including the offer of a pardon if he did. But... a man who had turned twice – we could not leave him free while the war still raged, so he was sent back here, and held in Newgate until the war ended, at which point he was pardoned and released, as had been promised."

"Then why is he so bent on revenge? I do not understand."

"Because, my Lady, those well above myself, and Hunter, chose not to mention that little condition of 'not until the war is over' when a pardon was offered. So he considered that a betrayal."

"I see. That makes some sense of his ravings, but still – there was more, something about his family, about everything having been taken away from him."

"I do not know – to understand that, we will have to ask the man himself, and see if sense can be gained from him. And I do not want to be the one asking him those questions. Let the magistrate do so, and welcome to it. I may never be able to undo what I have done, no matter how necessary it seemed at the time, may never be able to forget their faces, or forget what it taught me about myself. I may be a monster at the core, but I can, at least, refuse to allow myself to ever do such things again."

~~~~~

Alyse stared at Lord Tillingford, absorbing the words he had just uttered. He believed himself a monster? Because he had done the job assigned to him, during the war? A job which had saved many more lives than it had damaged? It seemed remarkable to her that he could see it that way. Was this why he had so often been distant, been cold to her? If that was the case, then suddenly, it all made sense.

But... was there any truth to his belief?

Had the madman been right, when he had suggested that, during the war, Lord Tillingford had 'enjoyed his work'?

That thought terrified her. She could not believe that of the man she knew, the man who had just spoken so strongly of regret and uncertainty. But... what if some element of it was true? She would need to think about this deeply. For now, she could, at least, speak of what she saw, when she looked at him.

"I... I struggle to see you as anything like a monster, Lord Tillingford. A hero, after your actions today, most definitely. But a monster? No. I respect your courage, in doing what had to be done, during the war – many men did things they would never have done by choice, but which needed to be done."

"I must agree with Lady Alyse – whilst the very idea of what you were required to do horrifies me, it does so as much for your sake, as for the unfortunates who were subject to interrogation. I cannot see that your actions make you anything other than a loyal soldier."

Nerissa's words were firm, and her expression kind.

"I also agree – you have my eternal gratitude for being able to do what you did, and I do not see that it reflects in any way into your life, now – beyond this unfortunate madman's crusade for revenge. I believe that we should go and see the man, as soon as the magistrate arrives, and hear his story. I would like to better understand what happened to him, after he was shipped back to England, which created this insanity."

Hunter looked to Lord Tillingford, who swallowed, visibly gathering his thoughts.

"I do not look forward to it, but I believe that we must."

"I, however, wish never to see him again, if that is possible. The scars on my hand will remind me always. So I believe that I will stay here, while you deal with that. Although I would like to know, afterwards, what you discover."

In the end, Nerissa stayed with Alyse, and the others went with the magistrate, who had just arrived, to deal with the man.

As Alyse sat, sipping tea, she went over, in her mind, the things that Lord Tillingford had said. He had said, quite clearly, she realised, 'because I care for her' when speaking of the madman's intent to hurt her, to hurt him.

Turning that over in her mind, a glow of warmth filled her. He had not said 'because he believed I cared for her', which would have implied that the madman was mistaken. No, he had simply said 'because I care for her'.

Was it true? Did he care for her, truly? She clung to the hope that the words gave her, even whilst the niggling doubt that his other words had caused remained.

Before the others returned, she had dropped into exhausted sleep, right there on the couch.

~~~~~

When the men returned, Nerissa gestured for them to be quiet, pointing to where Lady Alyse lay, asleep. Without discussion, barely without thought, Gerry simply stepped forward, and lifted her gently into his arms. She curled against him, and sighed, all without waking. Nerissa smiled, and stood, leading the way upstairs to Lady Alyse's room, and opening the door so that he might deposit her on her bed.

Only once he had released her from his arms did any thought of the impropriety of it enter Gerry's mind, and he quickly looked to Hunter, embarrassed. Hunter simply smiled, and waved for him to leave the room. They retired to the library, and much needed brandy, without a word said. For Gerry, the world had become impossible to comprehend.

He had spoken of it all, admitted the worst, and none of them had rejected him outright.

He did not, he discovered, know how to deal with that fact.

Over the next few days, the world settled back into a sense of balance. Cunningham was shipped off to prison again, and would likely never be released, and Gerry moved through his days in a daze.

Soon, everything that needed to be done, for the farms and the gardens (at least until spring) had been done, and Hunter spoke of returning to Meltonbrook Chase. Lady Alyse had recovered from her ordeal, somewhat, but seemed reticent to speak to him, and subdued, simply sitting and reading, rather than drawing, although her sketch journal was never far from her hand.

He did not know how to speak to her, beyond the basic courtesies – he could not bear to mention the cellars, or to touch on the dramatic events. For the first time, he found conversation impossible – when she had always been a person he could converse with.

Her eyes would meet his, and they were full of confusion, or pain, and sometimes something more – but no words seemed possible between them. He drew back, unwilling to intrude on her, and resorted to the isolation and coldness that he knew so well. Hunter watched both of them, he knew, and seemed annoyed for some reason – but, as usual, said nothing. When they departed, it was almost a relief, he was ashamed to admit.

~~~~~

Back at Meltonbrook Chase, Alyse found her thoughts trapped in a cycle of uncertainty, with Lord Tillingford never far from her mind. She drew obsessively, and ignored everything else, to her mother's despair.

Chapter Fourteen

At Tillingford Castle, the days passed slowly, the world seeming dreary and grey to Gerry. With the last of the work done to prepare the gardens and the farms for winter, there was nothing for him to distract himself with. After weeks with others in the house, he discovered that he was lonely, more conscious of the emptiness around him than ever before. And his thoughts never strayed far from Lady Alyse, and the dramatic events in the cellars.

He could not go past the fact that his actions during the war, his ability to take on the monstrous role that he had, were what had brought into being the situation which had put Lady Alyse at such risk. Whilst she had not said so, he was sure that she must blame him – and rightly so – and that her reticence after those terrible events was due to that. Any sensible woman would feel the same, and step back from contact with a man such as he. He should stop thinking about her. Should step back from any association, and simply allow their separate lives to move forward. But his mind refused to obey that intent.

For he had discovered, in that cellar, that his feelings for her went far beyond the care of a friend. He had no right to hope for love, and was a fool to allow himself to feel it, yet he did. And he had not been able to remove that feeling, no matter how he tried.

Christmas approached, and the prospect was empty of cheer. He could not face going to his parents and siblings – for, though they would welcome him, they would want to poke into his life, to attempt to make him be as they wished, rather than as he wished for himself. And, worst of all, they would attempt to matchmake, inviting an endless stream of the daughters and sisters of their friends, all good young women, who would be delighted to marry a title. The thought made him queasy. It was not that he disliked the women – it was, he was forced to acknowledge, that none of them compared to Lady Alyse, who had become, somehow, the standard by which he judged all women.

So his Christmas would, perforce, be spent alone at Tillingford Castle. The dreams still haunted his rest, more confused than ever. Now, at times, he relived the scene in the cellar – sometimes as it had happened, sometimes, most horribly, where he had hurt, rather than helped her, where the monster had risen in him, and nothing else had mattered. From those dreams, he woke in a tangle of bedclothes, soaked in sour sweat, and with a pounding headache.

After a particularly bad night, he rose from his bed, rang for Briggs, and allowed the valet to shave him and dress him without complaint – no matter how he felt, it was best to present to the world as a gentleman. The remnants of the dream stayed with him, souring the day.

He broke his fast, eating slowly, thinking about the dreams, and all that had happened. It still seemed incomprehensible to him, that when he had spoken of his actions in France, no-one present had turned away, no-one had rejected him. How could they see it differently? And yet he thought that their reactions and words were honest – they were people he trusted above all others. Did that mean that he, himself, saw things differently from others?

He realised, as he stared blankly at the coffeepot before him, that the dreams were what kept it so real for him. His memories could not fade, for they were reinforced in horrific detail most nights. But... the dreams often showed him things that had not happened, things that were extreme versions of what might have happened, if he had chosen to act differently.

Could it be that his view of everything had become distorted, as a result?

How could he find the truth of it? The torture chamber in the cellars came instantly to his mind, and he flinched away from the thought. He considered his reaction. It was just a room, full of old, if unpleasant things, as Lady Alyse had said. So – why could he not bear the thought of going there?

The only possible conclusion, was that he was being a coward.

He sat with that thought, his coffee cooling and his food already cold on the plate, forgotten. He had never been a coward – sensibly cautious, yes, but a true coward, no. So why now? It was time to change things – he could not let dreams and fears rule his life forever. If Lady Alyse could walk into such a room, and not flee, he should be able to do the same.

Admittedly, she had done so before the madman had taken her there, but still... he turned to where the footman stood quietly to one side.

"Mills."

"Yes, my Lord?"

"Bring me two lanterns."

"Yes, my Lord."

He would do this, before he could reconsider, now, whilst the thoughts were fresh in his mind.

~~~~~

Every step he took down into the cellars was a reminder of what had happened, and yet... the cellars were empty, quiet, even his footfalls absorbed by the dust, the only sign of recent movement the patches of floor where the dust had been disturbed. There was an odd peace to it.

With some apprehension, he pushed open the ancient iron bound door, the creak of its hinges loud in the silence. The lantern light barely reached the far corners of the room. Quickly, he fully unshuttered both lanterns, allowing as much light as possible into the room, then placed the lanterns at opposite ends of the space. He stood in the middle, and allowed himself to look, truly look, at everything that surrounded him.

The things around him were many centuries old, from an era far harsher than this. Never, in everything that he had done to interrogate the enemies of Britain, had he used such cruel and destructive tools.

Some had been available to him, true, but he had always stayed with the least cruel options he had. The age of these things was a reminder that men have always been cruel to their fellow men, when faced with a need to defend what is dear to them. What he had done was, by comparison to what some nameless man had done, in this very room, centuries before, far less cruel – and far less cruel than what the madman had intended to do to Lady Alyse.

Knowing that did not make him regret, any less, what he had needed to do in the war, but it did allow him to see it with a new perspective. He could have been, so easily, far worse a monster than he was. Could he, ever, he wondered, forgive himself? After all, whilst his actions had, in part, created the madman, they had also given him the knowledge to save Lady Alyse from terrible harm when she was trapped.

The dusty remnants of past brutality lay around him, silent witness to the madness that men could perpetrate, but also, witness to how futile such things were – all fell into dust in the end. The only thing that went on was life – through children, and what they were taught – perhaps, one day, men would no longer teach each other how to do terrible things. He was not sure why, but his burden of guilt felt lightened by the understanding he had reached.

If Lady Alyse could face this, could see it simply as a testament to the foolishness of the past, and still speak of it that way, even after having been held here by the madman, surely he could do no less? He was decided – he would push the dreams aside, would not allow their terrible false message to hold him trapped in the war. He did not quite know how to make that change yet, but he was determined that he would.

He gathered up the lanterns, and left the room, firmly shutting the ancient door behind him. He would arrange for a lock to be fitted on it, so that no-one else could misuse its contents. In the courtyard above, the pale winter sun warmed him, and the world seemed a better place.

~~~~~

"Will you come to dinner at Lord Chester's? I am sure that Lord Kevin would be pleased to see you."

The Dowager Duchess persisted in sounding hopeful, in the face of Alyse's total disinterest in anything social.

"No thank you Mother, I will just stay here and draw. I really have no interest in conversation at present."

"Perhaps you would if you tried it again! You have been a figure of gloom ever since you came back from Tillingford Castle. Your hand is healed – why do you persist in this rejection of everything?"

Alyse sighed, and closed her journal, looking up at her mother.

"Because I want to. Because I am just not interested in any of the people we commonly socialise with. Because I am tired of you thrusting eligible men at me."

"I don't 'thrust' them! I simply introduce you, in the hope that one of them captures your interest. Is that too much to hope for?"

"At present, yes. I feel a megrim coming on. I am going to lie down and rest."

With that, Alyse stood, and left the room, conscious that she was being rude and abrupt, and that her mother was actually being quite reasonable – but she could not stand to have that conversation, again. Once behind the locked door of her rooms, she settled into her favourite chair in her sitting room, and opened her sketch journal again. Flipping through the pages, she looked at what she had drawn, since that terrible day in the cellars of Tillingford Castle.

Every second page, in that journal which he had used to such good effect as a weapon, was a sketch of Lord Tillingford. The journal seemed to her now, somehow, bound to him, infused with something of him, from the time that it had spent in his hands. Some sketches showed him as he had been, fighting for both their lives in the cellar, some as he had been in the days afterwards – withdrawn, apparently inward looking, and so distant that she had not known where to start, to attempt to reach him.

So she had taken the coward's path, and not tried.

She was, if she were truthful with herself, also still unsure about what kind of man he really was. She could not imagine that her perception of him had been completely wrong, yet the madman's words still echoed in her mind, suggesting that Lord Tillingford was a man who could enjoy hurting others. And when he insisted, himself, that he was a monster of some kind... what was she supposed to think?

It was as if she sought her answer in drawing him. As if her fingers might capture some essential truth about him, which her mind had not discerned.

So she drew.

He was a wonderful subject, well-shaped, with a strong face and hair that caught the light, eyes that spoke to her, and a mouth which quirked with dry humour, when he thought no-one was watching. She picked up her pencils, and began another sketch of him, as he had been, standing in the doorway of that torture chamber, watching her, waiting his chance to intervene, and save her.

Perhaps this one would reveal the truth.

~~~~~

Hunter Barrington, Duke of Melton, was worried about his sister. She was normally bright, fairly cheerful, and happy to socialise. Yet the weeks since her ordeal beneath Tillingford Castle had seen her changed.

She moped about the house, staring off into the distance, or drawing obsessively, but showing no-one her sketches, or she walked in the gardens and nearby edge of the forest, drifting as if in a dream.

He had some suspicions about why she was being so uncharacteristically glum – suspicions he would not attempt to discuss with her, for the almost certainty that she would denounce him for a meddling nuisance and storm off in a huff.

He had watched her, at Tillingford, and watched Gerry too, and some things seemed very obvious to him.

Of a certainty, they cared for each other – which was a concept to delight Hunter.

The idea of having yet another of his closest friends become a brother by marriage was wonderful – if it could be brought to happen.

But both Gerry and Alyse were stubborn, and not good at talking of their deepest concerns. He had watched, with growing frustration, in the days after their ordeal in the cellars, as they became distant and unsure, drawing away from each other.

He had hoped, when Gerry had so instinctively gathered her up and carried her upstairs in her exhausted sleep, that they might allow each other close, after their shared experience. But it had not happened. And no direct interference of his could do anything but harm. If he wanted to influence this, he would need to be subtle.

Truly subtle, not his mother's idea of subtle, he thought, with a wry smile.

Perhaps the first step would be simply to get them in the same place again, for more than a few hours. An inspiration struck. He knew that Gerry would avoid going to his own family for Christmas, but... if Hunter invited him to Meltonbrook Chase, perhaps he would come, for he generally found Hunter's family congenial, when the Dowager Duchess wasn't trying to manipulate him, along with everyone else.

He would have to phrase the invitation carefully, to make it seem the most natural thing in the world that Gerry should accept, perhaps playing on the fact that Bart and Sybilla would be there too, and that they would have a chance to simply relax together, and enjoy the season. He would most definitely *not* be mentioning Alyse!

Hunter went to his study, and sat, drawing out a sheet of paper to write to Gerry, inviting him.

Chapter Fifteen

From the day that he had gone back down into the deep cellars, and faced his fears about the room, and himself, Gerry began to feel different. Slowly, with some days far more positive than others, he began to believe that, perhaps, he could come to forgive himself, in time. The dreams persisted, but they had less hold on him, and, more and more, he dreamed of Lady Alyse – not just as she had been, trapped in that room below, but as she had been, in his arms, dancing, light and happy, a joy to be with. And sometimes, in those dreams, he was not a monster.

On the bad days, he took the key, and went down into the cellars, to stand in that room, and remind himself that he had never been anything like the worst he could have been, that all things fade away with time, and perspective. Each time, he renewed his determination to change, to let go of his sense of guilt, and allow himself the possibility of something else in his life but memories.

To his surprise, he found himself smiling more often.

Then, one morning, he woke slowly, feeling warm and happy, drifting gently out of a dream where he danced with Lady Alyse, and she laughed in his arms, simply for the joy of being there. He lay abed for a while, savouring the sensation of a pleasant awakening, before rising to get on with the day. As he sat in the breakfast room, Shackleton came in, bringing a letter.

"Thank you, Shackleton."

"My Lord. It came by messenger. I have sent the lad to the kitchens for some food. He was told to wait for your reply, but not to be in a hurry about it, so I will send him to rest once he's eaten. This afternoon will be soon enough for him to set off again, if your reply is ready by then."

"Thank you. Let the boy rest. I'll read it, and consider the reply, once I've finished here."

Gerry turned it over in his hands – Hunter's seal. He put it to the side, idly wondering what it might be about, as he finished eating. Half an hour later, he sat in his study, reading Hunter's letter.

It was an invitation.

To spend Christmas at Meltonbrook Chase. His initial reaction was to shy away from the idea, to stay in his safe isolation. But... it tempted him, and, he realised, if he were to be true to his determination to change, to approach the world differently, then he would need to step outside that isolation soon. What better way to do so, than with his closest friends? To spend the holiday season with people who would not parade every eligible woman in the district in front of him, people who already knew much about the worst of him, and had not immediately turned away?

Not giving himself the chance to hesitate, he went to his desk, and wrote an acceptance of the invitation. As he sealed it, all he could think of was that he would see Lady Alyse again. The thought left him almost giddy with anticipation, as if he were sixteen again, and discovering girls for the first time.

~~~~~

The Christmas season arrived, with steady snowfall, and Gerry was glad that he had reached Meltonbrook Chase a few days before Christmas Day. To be inside, in a warm room, with pleasant friends, whilst the snow piled up outside, created a sense of wellbeing, more so than he had felt for some years. His first sight of Lady Alyse, upon his arrival, had taken his breath away. She was, if anything, more beautiful than ever, and he had almost stammered like a schoolboy when greeting her. She had been gracious, but distant – which had left him feeling lost, and questioning all of his thoughts.

Was he deluding himself, to think that she might care for him, might have the ability to look beyond the horror of his past? He should not expect anything, yet he could not stop himself from hoping. Now, as Christmas afternoon moved towards evening, he was no further ahead in knowing what she thought. She had, in the intervening few days since his arrival, mostly avoided him, although they had spoken a few times, of inconsequential things.

He wanted, desperately, to find a chance to speak to her in private, however inappropriate such a wish might be. He wished to ask after her state of mind, to assure himself that she was truly recovered from her traumatic experience.

He had no idea how he would achieve such a conversation.

He sipped his drink, listening to the conversation around him, occasionally contributing to it, thinking.

"Now that we have finished splitting much of the enclosed lands into separate pastures, we've been able to increase the number of good mares to breed. Next year, we'll have many new foals on the ground, and the year or two after, the investment in both Gallowbridge House and the changes on Greyscar Keep and Dartworth Abbey lands will begin to repay handsomely."

Bart's enthusiasm came through clearly as he spoke, and Sybilla reached out and took his hand, smiling as she confirmed his words.

"I am quite certain that we will do far better than we had ever imagined. The quality of the stallion we have obtained is remarkable, and the mares are all beautiful – of temperament, as well as appearance!"

Gerry asked the question he had been holding for some time.

"And will the progeny of these paragons of horseflesh be for sale to your friends, or only to the wealthy of the racing community? I must confess to a desire to own one of these horses for myself."

"Of course we will sell one to you!"

"Excellent! So – how many mares do you have now?"

The conversation rolled on, all centred around horses, for some time, until the Dowager Duchess finally spoke.

"Could we, perhaps, manage to talk of something other than horses? I, for one, have had quite enough of the topic for now! We could, instead, speak of our plans for the coming year, in other areas – such as the Season, and when we will all go up to London. For we must plan ahead – perhaps Alyse will find a man to please her, this Season."

She sighed dramatically, her eyes on Lady Alyse, who looked, for a moment, as if she might explode into an angry retort. But then her face stilled, and she looked down. Her voice, when she spoke, was calm, but a little shaky.

"Must I go to London, mother? I find that my interest in another round of Balls and soirees, full of dandified fops who only care for my dowry, does not appeal to me at all."

"Of course you must my girl – how else will you find a husband?"

Lady Alyse chewed on her lip, in that way that affected Gerry so strongly, and sighed. He watched her, discovering that the thought of her marrying, the thought even of her dancing, with any other man, made him feel most irritated. He forced his eyes away from her, disturbed by his own thoughts, and discovered that Hunter was watching him. What, he wondered, did Hunter see – what was that half smile on his face for? He looked back to Lady Alyse, unable to prevent himself from doing so.

"Mother, I am not certain that I have any interest in finding a husband, if the men I met in London are all that I have to choose from!"

The fingers of her left hand rubbed on the back of her right hand, as if she would rub away the scars there.

He doubted she was aware of her actions.

"And where else, pray tell, might you meet a suitable man?"

"I don't know, mother. But there are certainly none in London."

The Dowager Duchess sighed theatrically, and let the subject drop. A silence descended on the room. After some minutes, Charles asked Gerry about his hopes for the Tillingford estate lands, come spring, and conversation began again. Lady Alyse was silent, looking unhappy. Gerry, caught in the conversation, glanced at her, worried by her quiet and seeming disinterest. Her eyes met his, and, for a moment, it was as if nothing else existed. He lost track of the conversation, until Charles' words pulled him back to it.

Some time later, the click of the closing door caught his attention. She was gone from the room – without a word said. What was wrong? He forced himself to sit, to continue as if nothing had changed, all the while wishing nothing more than to leap to his feet and pursue her from the room.

~~~~~

Alyse was acutely aware of where Lord Tillingford was, every moment from when he alighted from his carriage at the door. She could not stop herself from watching him, wondering about what he was truly like. None of her sketches had left her feeling any closer to the truth of the man. He seemed so distant, still, and she was afraid to try to break through his reserve – what if he simply did not want anything to do with her? Yet when she met his eyes, it was as if no-one else existed.

As if his eyes spoke to her, of things far more than cold politeness. But perhaps that was just her wishful thinking.

It was painful, sitting in the same rooms, attempting to converse cheerfully, when he was so close. She wanted, somehow, to find the chance to speak to him alone, to discover what he thought and felt – no matter how inappropriate that would be. But finding such an opportunity seemed unlikely in the extreme.

And now, here it was, Christmas Day, and all her mother could find to talk about was the coming Season, and finding her a husband. She could cope with conversation about estates, and horses, but not about who she should marry. Not when the man she was almost certain she wanted was right there, in the room. But... what if she was wrong about him? It was an impossible situation!

It was a relief when her mother finally, grudgingly, let the subject drop, and the conversation moved back to safer topics. But then she felt unnecessary, with nothing to contribute to a discussion of estates and their management. She studied Lord Tillingford, seeing how much more open he seemed when he spoke of such things, and wishing that he would speak with her in such a friendly manner. Then, without warning, he turned, and caught her staring at him. She flushed, her whole body feeling warm, but their eyes met, and for a moment, everything else ceased to matter.

But he turned away, his face hardening, and she felt as if all warmth had been stolen from the room. She could not bear it. She stood, and simply walked out. She would go to the library and read, or draw – surely no-one could object to that.

The library was peaceful, and, much though she loved her family, being alone seemed preferable in that moment. She opened her sketch journal, and looked, yet again, at all of the images she had drawn of Lord Tillingford, seeking the truth of the man. When none of them spoke to her, she selected a pencil, and began to draw again.

Gerry found himself unable to settle, unable to focus on the conversation, for wondering where Lady Alyse had gone, wondering what he had seen in her eyes, in that moment of connection. He was, more and more, acutely aware of how lucky his friends were, in having found wives who so suited them. Just seeing Nerissa and Hunter, Sybilla and Bart, together, he could not doubt their happiness, their ease with each other. Even Charles, it seemed, had found someone, although he did not speak of it much, as she was a widow, he believed, waiting out her mourning. He envied them all.

But, instead of simply sliding back into the bitterness which had been his refuge for so long, he found himself feeling, just a little, hopeful. It was a new sensation, but one that had been slowly growing, ever since he had decided to try to change his view of the world. But… his hope was focussed on Lady Alyse, and she seemed to have drawn away from him, more and more, since the cellars. He was discovering that hope was just as much a painful thing to live with as bitterness was.

A little while later, as the conversation slowed, the Dowager Duchess spoke up again, looking up from the embroidery she had been working on.

"I believe that it is time for us all to go and freshen up, and change for dinner. We have a large Christmas meal ahead of us, after all. Please reassemble here in two hours' time."

There was general agreement, and everyone left the parlour to go their separate ways. The thought of two hours sitting in his chamber, no matter how elegant the Meltonbrook Chase guest suites were, did not appeal, so Gerry decided to spend some time in the library, before going up to change.

He stepped into the room, feeling welcomed by the distinct scent of well cared for books, and closed the door behind him.

For a moment, he simply stood, allowing some of the tension to leave him. Only when he stepped forward towards the armchairs and couches arrayed before the fireplace, did he realise that one of them was occupied. Lady Alyse sat on a couch, her legs curled under her, her sketch journal on her lap, utterly focused on drawing. She had not noticed his arrival in the room, so focused was she on her work. He could not resist – he moved forward, his feet soundless on the thick carpet, until he could see what she was drawing. What was on the page shocked him into a gasp – for it was an image of him, as he had been that afternoon – animated, talking. He did not know that he looked so! At the sound of his indrawn breath, she looked up, startled, then smiled, a little uncertainly, and closed the journal.

"Lady Alyse…"

"Lord Tillingford…"

The both spoke at the same moment, and stopped, unsure how to go on. He swallowed, and tried again.

"Lady Alyse, might I speak with you?"

Chance had provided him the opportunity he had hoped for, and he would be a fool to cast it aside. She looked at him, glanced at the closed door, and seemed to come to a decision.

"Yes, my Lord, let us speak, for I wish to converse with you, also. Please, do take a seat."

She waved to the couch beside her, and his heart beat faster, a flutter of ridiculous hope moving in him. he moved forward and sat – so close was she that he could easily reach out and touch her. Her lily of the valley scent surrounded him, and, for a moment, he imagined a world in which he might have the pleasure of simply sitting with her, every day.

He was not in any way certain how to begin this conversation, now that he had the opportunity. But the silence was stretching too long – she seemed equally uncertain. So he simply leapt in.

"Lady Alyse, I wanted to apologise."

"Apologise, Lord Tillingford? For what?"

"For my manner towards you, in the days after that most regrettable incident in the cellars of Tillingford Castle. I realise that I must have seemed most abrupt and aloof – which was rude of me, in the extreme."

She considered him, her deep brown eyes wide, her fingers tracing the scars on her hand, her lip pulled between her teeth. Suddenly, the room felt too warm.

"Thank you. But – I fear I must join you in apology, for my manner to you was equally distant – which was unforgiveable, after you saved me so heroically."

"Shall we, then, begin again, as if those days of aloofness had never happened?"

He felt himself smiling, and suspected that his hopes were writ large on his face. He waited for her answer, his heart beating far faster than was comfortable.

"Yes, I believe that would be for the best. I... I wanted a chance to explain. I am glad that you chanced upon me now."

"My Lady, I do not see that you have anything to explain. But I am happy to hear whatever you may wish to say to me."

"Thank you. From the moment that I was safely out of the cellars, I found myself more and more confused and disturbed by that madman's words. The things he said about you..."

Her words brought back every doubt he had ever felt about himself, and made his faint hopefulness seem deeply foolish. He swallowed hard before speaking.

"Ah. As I explained in the conversation immediately after we had come out of the cellars, there is much in what I did during the war that I deeply wish I had not done. Whilst his words may have been distorted by his madness, I fear that, in some ways he was correct." She looked at him, her eyes wide, and inhaled sharply, as if his words hurt her. He deserved no less. "I have spent much time thinking since that day, and I will understand if you wish to have nothing to do with me, now that you know what I have done, what I am capable of."

"I... I think that I would like to understand more. For I am not clear about one thing, at least. That madman suggested, if I understood the intent of his words, that you had not only tortured people, as part of your work, but that you had enjoyed doing so."

Her voice shook as she laid forth her concern.

"He did, indeed, suggest exactly that. One thing that I can assure you of, is that I never took pleasure in my work. Was it torture? That would, I expect, depends on one's definition of the word. It was certainly interrogation, and the methods could be unpleasant, but I took great pains to avoid outright torture, even though others suggested that I should use those methods. For a man in pain will confess to anything, simply to make it stop. Far more effective is the fear of what might be done to him – for then, he has a chance to consider his options with a clear mind. But... the very idea that, if I have the capability to apply the techniques that break a man's resistance, then I might also have the capability to, in some way, come to enjoy doing so, haunts me. That I might be capable of becoming that much a monster terrifies me."

He sat a moment, his words hanging between them, a shape of horror in a place of peace. Her eyes drew him in, as always, and he waited for her reaction.

"I do not believe that the man I know you to be could do such a thing, and take pleasure in it. His words disturbed me, and made me wonder if I had misjudged you, but now that I see you before me, as you speak of it as something you fear so much, I see the sincerity in you, and I see that I was foolish to ever countenance the idea that the madman's words might hold truth."

The breath he had been holding, all unawares, left him in a great sigh.

"I have not spoken of this to anyone before – not even to the other Hounds. I apologise for laying so unpleasant a topic before you. I am honoured that you have such faith in me. You have far more than I have in myself!"

"Why should I not have faith in you? I was a fool to even consider otherwise for a moment. I am in awe of your courage, and your dedication to king and country, that you took on such a terrible task during the war, because it needed to be done. And then, in the cellar, you demonstrated your courage again, defeating that madman with only improvised weapons. I am beyond grateful that those terrible war time tasks gave you the knowledge to save me from that device the madman trapped me with."

"It has, truly, never occurred to me that someone might see my actions in such light. I have been so full of revulsion for myself that I have not considered that I could be seen any other way. You have given me a great gift with your words, as well as with your actions."

"My actions? I do not understand."

He flushed, suddenly embarrassed, realising that the only way to explain his words was to admit to looking through her journal, in the parlour of the Inn in Bridgemere.

There was nothing for it but to tell her – he owed her honesty in all things, after her ordeal and her courtesy to him.

"To explain, I must apologise again, and make an admission. Let me start with that. After Lady Sylvia's wedding, there was a morning when I was alone in the private parlour at the Inn in Bridgemere. I discovered, by accident, your journal, slipped down between the cushions of the couch. I am ashamed to admit that, wrong though it was of me, I could not resist, and I opened it, and looked at your work."

She blushed, her mouth opening in a small 'O', as she considered what he might have seen.

"But… what has that to do with my actions?"

"I saw the drawings of the things in that room of the cellars, so I knew that you had been there. It shocked me, that you had drawn such things. That you had not fainted on the spot, or run away screaming, as I suspect most young women would, when confronted with such a chamber of horrors, but had stopped and looked at all of those terrible things, simply as things – as objects and shapes and textures, which were interesting enough to draw. It made me realise how differently others might view things. For, when I had found that room myself, it had brought forth the worst of my nightmares, reinforcing my horror at myself. I spent weeks from then trying to understand how it seemed to you."

"Oh!"

"And then, after we had returned from the cellars, even whilst you were hurt and exhausted, you spoke of how you saw it – as the dusty remnants of something of the past, with no relevance to today, as a symbol of the fact that all things fall to dust in the end. That perspective was a great gift to me."

"And... have you come to see it differently, as a result?"

"Slowly, yes, although I still dream, and I still wonder if I can trust myself not to be the monster that I imagine I could be."

Gerry felt oddly light, as if he had shed an enormous weight – simply to speak of these things was freeing. Her deep brown eyes regarded him with a warmth that he had hoped for, longed for, for months. As if unaware of her actions, she reached out and placed her hand on his, her fingers curling around his gently. Heat infused him from her hand, spreading everywhere.

"I do not believe you a monster, nor capable of becoming one. I... have always admired you, and found you far more interesting than other gentlemen of my acquaintance."

She flushed charmingly as she spoke, and the hope bubbled up inside him again, a far headier sensation than any other he had felt.

"I am flattered indeed. But, if I may be truly impertinent, there is one other thing I would ask you, for there is another way in which seeing your drawings affected me. I saw, as I believe you have surmised, drawings that you had made, of me. They shocked me almost as much as the other drawings. For the man you had drawn was not anything like the man I feel myself to be. You drew a man with no darkness in him, a man who could be happy, a man who could laugh. It was like looking at an image of my younger self, before war tarnished everything about me. So I ask – why did you draw me? And why that way?"

Her fingers tightened on his, and she looked away, biting at her lip, as if embarrassed. When she spoke, her voice was soft, hesitant.

"I draw people to understand them. Sometimes, what I draw is a clearer truth of the person than what I perceive by simply looking at them. I draw you because I want to understand you. I have seen, for so long now, that there was a darkness in you – although you denied it when I was fool enough to ask directly." He was the one to flush with embarrassment now, remembering his boorish response to her question at the time, "and I could not fathom it. So I draw you. My drawings show me many things – but your words today have shown me more."

"And what is this truth that you have seen in me, in my words?"

"That you are that man I drew, the one who was happy, and caring. That the darkness is a temporary thing, a thing that you can be free from, in time. That I am right to care for you as I do."

He reached out, greatly daring, stroking his finger gently across her cheek, and used it to turn her face up to him. His breath caught at the look in her eyes. He did not deserve what he saw there, but he wanted it, more than anything he had ever wanted before.

"If that is what you see, then I will do my best to be true to your vision of me, to force the darkness to release me. To be worthy of your care."

Her lips opened on a shallow breath, her pulse beat in her throat, she nibbled at her lip, and he could resist no longer. His head came down to hers, slowly, a movement which seemed inevitable, yet earthshakingly important. Their lips touched, and she sighed against him.

His tongue traced her lower lip, and she released it from her teeth. He deepened the kiss, and a little moan escaped her. Her hand tightened on his, and her other hand came up to cup the back of his head, holding him to her.

He slipped his hand from under her chin to cradle her face, and his other arm slid around her waist, drawing her closer to him. She came into his arms willingly, fitting there as if it was simply where she belonged. He did not think, he was aware of nothing but her soft body against his, her tentative exploration of the kiss.

The reality was far more wonderful than his dreams of her.

Time passed, in which her journal slipped to the floor, unnoticed, and nothing existed for either of them but touch. They might, he suspected, have stayed in that blissful state for hours, had not the mantle clock chimed loudly. They started apart, brought back to the mundane reality of the day.

'Oh, I...''

Her confusion made her prettier, and he found himself smiling.

"Say nothing more, for no words are needed after that. But – I forgot to tell you – we are all summoned to be dressed for dinner and back in the parlour, a little over half an hour from now. We had best hurry if we are to be ready for the Christmas dinner, or your mother will be most displeased."

She laughed, a wonderful sound.

"Displeasing my mother is not something I like doing – the result is simply too irritating for everyone. I had best hurry." She looked around, puzzled. "Where is my... oh."

Her journal lay on the floor where it had fallen, open to the most recent pages. His face looked back at him. She had captured him, animatedly talking. His eyes were laughing, and he looked relaxed. He looked at it in wonder, and with growing hope and determination. He would become the man she saw, because she wished it.

~~~~~

Alyse slipped from the library, and almost ran up the stairs to her chambers, her journal clutched to her, her heart singing.

He had kissed her!

She did not know what would happen now, if he might not yet retreat into his darkness and aloofness, but, at least this once, she had spoken with him honestly. She was sure of her own heart, and could but hope that he might care as much for her, as she did for him. Surely, he would not have kissed her like that, if he did not truly care?

Throughout the dinner, their eyes met, again and again, and she felt overheated, the memory of the kiss ever present. The next few days, until the snows slowed, and he eventually departed for Tillingford Castle, were little different – they had no further chance to be alone, but their eyes followed each other, and just his presence in the room was enough to leave Alyse feeling giddy and happy, full of hope for the future.

She was determined to write to him, to not lose the chance to build on the connection they had. All she needed now, was an excuse to see him again soon. Surely there would be one... or, perhaps, Hunter might help?

ARIETTA RICHMOND

Chapter Sixteen

Only a few weeks later, another wedding invitation was delivered to Tillingford Castle. This time, it was Raphael's sister, Miss Isabella Morton, who was marrying. And marrying a Duke – that would set the *ton* on its ear, yet again – the daughter of a merchant, marrying a Duke! He sat with the invitation in hand, examining his feelings. Unlike the last few wedding invitations, his first reaction had not been a rejection of the whole idea. As with the other weddings of the past 12 months, he was glad for those who were to marry. But this time, their happiness did not eat at him like gall.

This time, he was, almost, enthusiastic about the idea of going. It was an odd sensation. The sense that he might never have that happiness for himself was still strong, but hope now battled with bitterness in his thoughts, and the possibility of marriage was now something he could at least think about. But the first thought he'd had, on reading the invitation, was that, if he attended, he would almost certainly see Lady Alyse again. His mouth went dry at just the thought of it.

That kiss was branded on his memory.

She had written, once, since then, with news of her family, and enquiries after his health, and the state of Tillingford Castle. It was an ordinary letter – but it was a letter to him, just for the sake of it – that alone was something to treasure. It gave him no real clues as to her feelings, no hint of whether the words she had spoken in the library at Meltonbrook Chase, of caring for him, had truly meant anything – yet it gave him hope that they did, by its very existence.

Buoyed by thoughts of Lady Alyse, he wrote and sent his acceptance of the invitation. Shackleton, handed the letter to send, considered his master's smiling face with interest, and wondered what had happened, to finally make the man look happy.

~~~~~

The wedding was spectacular, an absolute crush, with the huge ballroom of Hartswood House filled by people of all stations, celebrating Bella's wedding. As Gerry walked into the room, his eyes scanned the crowd for Lady Alyse. At the church, she had looked, to him, more beautiful than the bride, her soft gold hair lit by the wintry sun, and her gown the perfect colour for her. He had not been able to speak to her then, so crowded was the space, but he had simply watched her, glad to be near her.

Now, in this crowded ballroom, he wondered if he would have any chance to speak to her at all. He was determined to achieve that, somehow. And, if he could, to dance with her – what had once been something to avoid had become something to desire.

He made his way through the crowd, greeting people as he went, looking for the Dowager Duchess – she was sure to be somewhere near Lady Alyse, much of the time, and was also, he suspected, quite certain to manoeuvre him into dancing with her. This time, he would be happy to be manipulated.

~~~~~

Alyse was standing with Nerissa, Sybilla, and the other Hounds' wives and friends, who were excitedly discovering that they were all increasing – at the same time. They were so happy, and it left Alyse feeling a little out of sorts. She wanted the kind of happiness they had. Whilst she listened to them talk, she scanned the room, looking for Lord Tillingford. He had not written, not even in response to her own letter, since leaving Meltonbrook Chase just after Christmas. Which left her feeling most unsure of his feelings.

At the church, he had instantly caught her eye, handsome as always, but something about him had changed. He looked, she thought, almost happy – which was startling, after so long seeing him always looking sad and withdrawn. It made him even more attractive. There had, however, been no possible way for her to speak to him there. She'd had to be content with looking. Now, she was awaiting his arrival eagerly. Surely, here, she would have the excuse to speak to him, perhaps even to dance with him. The memory of their other dances rose in her mind, bittersweet, each having been both wonderful and difficult.

Bella came and joined the conversation for a short while, and Alyse, watching her glowing joy, felt a deep stab of envy – to be so sure of someone's love!

413

She glanced around the room again, just in time to see Lord Tillingford arrive. Her eyes followed him across the room, wondering where he was going, with such apparent purpose. Oddly, it looked as if he was going towards her mother. Well, that was somewhere she could go, and be totally unexceptional. Without questioning the convenience of the opportunity, she slipped away from the conversation, and went to join her mother.

She reached the Dowager Duchess shortly before Lord Tillingford did, as his passage across the room had been delayed by his need to greet various friends and acquaintances.

"Ah, there you are, Alyse. There will be dancing soon. You must take this opportunity to dance with as many of the eligible men as possible. Surely, soon, a man will appeal to you!"

"Of course I will dance, mother. But I make you no promises beyond that!"

Her mother sighed, theatrically as usual, but accepted what she had begun to see as the inevitable. At that moment, two things coincided. The orchestra began to play, and Lord Tillingford arrived beside them.

"Good afternoon, Your Grace, Lady Alyse. I hope that you are enjoying yourselves."

"Lord Tillingford. I am having a most interesting day. I have met some remarkable people, from all walks of life. The Mortons have such an eclectic circle of acquaintance!"

"They do – it's part of why Raphael is so successful."

"Good day, Lord Tillingford."

Alyse was annoyed to discover that her voice shook.

But really – standing so close to him, she found herself

strongly affected. She remembered his arms about her, his lips on hers, and she felt the flush rise into her cheeks. She fanned herself, attempting to look calm, and unconcerned. Did he want to see her as much as she wanted to see him? Her mother, oblivious to her state of distraction, was talking.

"Ah, the music has begun – your timing is perfect, Lord Tillingford – I am certain that you will dance with my daughter, won't you?"

Alyse, expecting him to look pained at her mother's blatant manipulation, was shocked, and instantly delighted, when he simply smiled, and turned to her, offering his arm. His eyes upon her were warm, full of something very far from objection to the idea of dancing. She dropped a little curtsey, and placed her hand on his arm, smiling broadly, despite her best efforts to look dignified.

They reached the area of the room set aside for dancing, and she realised that, yet again, it was a waltz. She went into his arms gladly, feeling, as before, the wondrous moment when their bodies aligned, and the dancing became a thing of no effort, a miraculous floating, where all she was aware of was the heat of his body close to hers, the feel of his hand on her back, and the strength where his fingers held hers. She lifted her eyes to his, not attempting to hide her happiness at being in his arms.

Their eyes met, and, for some time, no words seemed necessary.

~~~~~

Gerry had almost laughed – the Dowager Duchess had looked surprised, and almost suspicious, when he had immediately acquiesced to dancing with Lady Alyse, with no flicker of objection.

But then his eyes had met Lady Alyse's deep brown ones, and thought of everything else had left him. As he swept her into his arms to waltz, it was as if an empty space had been filled, as if an ache which had been with him since he had last seen her had been soothed.

She did not seem to require conversation, and he was happy simply to hold her, to allow the dance to carry them. But his mind was working. This was how he wanted to feel, every day. Complete, warm from the regard, perhaps even the love, of a woman – one who could accept him for himself. In that instant it became clear to him that he did not want 'a' woman, he wanted 'this' woman, specifically. The thought of letting her go, of simply walking away at the end of the dance, of never knowing when he would see her again, was intolerable.

Somehow, against all of his intent, against all of his belief about what he should do, he had managed to fall in love with her. There was no doubt in his mind, now. The intensity of the emotion was almost frightening, but it was the most wonderful thing that he had ever felt, all at the same time. He wanted the right to hold her close every day, for the rest of his life. His hands tightened on her, as he reached that momentous conclusion, and she looked up at him, smiling, almost as if she understood his thoughts. The music slowed – he could not bear to simply stop, so, as they neared the doors onto the terrace, he swung them off the floor, and quickly opened the door, twirling her out into the crisp afternoon air. The door shut behind them, and the noise fell away.

They spun to a stop, and he did not release her, nor did she pull away. The cold air made their heated breath mist around them, and the gardens below the terrace lay still, faint shoots of green just showing above the melting snow. No one else was in sight. He released her right hand, and it fell, so naturally, to his shoulder, as his hand moved to cup her face. There was no hesitation in either of them as their lips met, only a sense of rightness, of the filling of an undeniable need.

His heart pounded, so loudly that he wondered if she could hear it. The intensity of the kiss made him more certain than ever that he wanted to spend his life with this woman. Dare he ask her to marry him?

If he had been asked, two hours before, when he would consider marriage, he would have said that he did not know, but that it would not be for some time. Now, the answer was different – now, he was not only considering it, but looking for the courage to propose. After some time, they drew apart, both short of breath, flushed, and a little shaky, she smiled at him, her arms still around his neck, and he pulled her close against him, just holding her, wondering at how good it felt to do so. Her head rested against his shoulder, her arms tightened, and they clung to each other, as if each afraid the other would disappear.

He should speak, but fear suddenly assailed him – what if she rejected him? What if she was still unsure, in some way. He cleared his throat, and she moved back a little, looking up at him.

"Lady Alyse, I…"

The sound of one of the terrace doors opening stopped him, and they snapped apart, turning to stand, side by side, looking out over the gardens. At the other end of the terrace, two people emerged, but only stayed a moment. A voice drifted to them.

"James, it is far too cold to be out here, without a wrap or cloak. No matter how much I wanted fresh air, I can't be this cold. Let's go back in."

The door creaked, and clicked closed again.

Gerry looked at Lady Alyse, discovering that the words had abandoned him. She shivered, as if just becoming aware of the chill. The moment was lost. But he would ask her soon, somehow. He was staying at Barrington House, with Hunter's family, for the next week, at least. There would be a better opportunity.

"You're shivering. We should go back inside. I apologise – it was inconsiderate of me to bring you out here in the cold. No matter how pleasant the last few minutes have been."

She looked up at him again, eyes wide, then, slowly, a smile lit her face, and she rose on her toes to bring her lips softly to his for a moment, before settling back down.

"Pleasant indeed, thank you. Do not apologise. But yes, it is cold, and we should go inside."

He offered her his arm, and they slipped back into the ballroom, the picture of propriety.

~~~~

Hunter, aware of the people he cared about, as always, had seen Gerry and Alyse slip out onto the terrace. He was pleased.

He knew that Gerry could be trusted with his sister, and he hoped that they were getting close to admitting to each other how they felt. For how they felt about each other was very obvious to Hunter and Nerissa, even if the Dowager Duchess appeared to be completely blind to it. Perhaps progress was being made.

When they reappeared not too long after, both a little

flushed looking, Hunter and Nerissa glanced at each other, and nodded, before joining the next set to dance.

~~~~~

Alyse floated in a cloud of happiness for the rest of the afternoon and evening. He had kissed her, and held her, as if he did not wish to let her go. She was sure that he had been about to say something important, when they were interrupted. It did not matter. Whatever he was going to say, he would say soon, she was now certain of it. His kiss had said everything that words had not, and the expression on his face, as he had started to speak... She hugged the memory to her, now as confident of his feelings as she was of her own.

He would be staying with them for the next week, at least. Plenty of time... she would be patient – although that would be hard, for she already ached to feel his arms around her again.

~~~~~

The next morning, Gerry rose early, and went out to ride, letting the crisp morning air refresh him.

The previous afternoon on the terrace played over and over in his mind, and the more he thought of it, the more certain he was of his decision. He wanted to marry Lady Alyse. But how could he ask her? How could he create a suitable moment? As he turned back across the park, intending to return to Barrington House, an idea came to him – an idea so simple, and yet so perfect that he laughed aloud for the joy of it.

He turned his horse towards Porthaven House instead. He needed to visit Raphael and Sera.

~~~~~

The week passed quickly, and Hunter watched Gerry and Alyse, torn between amusement and frustration. When they were near each other, the intensity of their attraction was obvious – one could almost see sparks flying between them. They gravitated to each other, in every conversation, sat close, but never touching, as if 'by accident' each day, and went out – riding, or driving in the open carriage, a number of times.

Yet still, nothing had been said, nothing admitted.

He was amazed that Alyse was being so quiet – he might, knowing his younger sister, have expected her to have dragged an admission of his feelings out of Gerry by now. But perhaps she was, wonder of wonders, being shy about admitting her own feelings? Soon, Gerry would be going back to Tillingford Castle, he could only hope that, before then, he would get up the courage to speak!

Chapter Seventeen

Alyse, whilst extraordinarily happy, was also worried. Lord Tillingford had still said nothing directly of his feelings. Everything he did spoke of his love for her, and she felt more alive than she had for a long time, simply for his presence. But he had not spoken.

The next day was Saint Valentine's Day, and Alyse was feeling a little melancholy as a result. Even the servants were whispering of Saint Valentine's favours and gifts for wives and sweethearts, and she was facing the concept that Lord Tillingford might not speak, that he might go back to Tillingford Castle, leaving her alone again.

It was a depressing prospect. She had been sitting in the parlour, staring out the window, watching passers-by on the street, but turned back to her sketch journal. On her page was yet another portrait of Lord Tillingford – she was trying, and failing, to capture how he had looked, immediately after he had kissed her. She wanted to save that expression, that look in his eyes, forever.

A knock came, at the front door. She heard Selwood open it, and the sound of a short conversation, before the door closed again. Curious, she stood, and went into the hallway.

"What is it, Selwood?"

"A parcel, for Lord Tillingford, my Lady. I believe he is out with His Grace, so I will leave it here until his return."

"Thank you."

Selwood placed the package on the side table, beside the mail tray, and went about his business. Alyse stared at it, wondering what it was. It was not large – what could Lord Tillingford be receiving? She would, she supposed, likely never know. For she had no right to ask.

Disgruntled, she turned away, and went back to drawing.

~~~~~

Saint Valentine's Day dawned crisp and clear, with enough sun that it felt like a hint of the spring approaching. Gerry rose early, and paced about the room a little. He was nervous, wondering if his brilliant idea was as good as he had thought it.

Still, Sera had done a wonderful job. The parcel had arrived yesterday, and he had opened it late last night, wondering what he would see. Inside the plain packaging lay the most amazing piece of work he had ever seen. It was a Saint Valentine's Day favour. Sera and Raphael owned a business that made them, based on Sera's designs. They supplied the Prince Regent, and most of the *ton*.

But this – this was exquisite – the best piece he had seen.

The favour was quite large, made with the highest quality of paper, but embellished with beads and tiny, sparkling gems. The gems were laid down, in shades from diamond to jet, to look like a pencil, drawing an intricate decorated heart – which was not quite finished. The unfinished section created the illusion that the gem encrusted pencil really was drawing the heart, scattering gemstones onto the paper.

His first sight of it had stolen his breath. It was a folded sheet, so that it could be opened, and a message written inside. He had agonised over what to write, for half the night, and had, in the end, settled for heartfelt simplicity. Once the ink had dried, he had carefully closed the favour, and slipped it into the pages of a book.

Now, the day had arrived, and although the rest of the household would barely be stirring, he felt as if he should rush downstairs immediately, with the book in hand. Which would be pointless, as Lady Alyse would not be anywhere to be seen, yet.

He made himself leave the book on his dresser, and went down to break his fast. He surprised himself by eating heartily, and began, a little, to relax. Hunter and Nerissa declared their intention to go for a ride in Hyde Park for the morning, and Charles had departed for Meltonbrook Chase on the previous day, citing estate business. Gerry had wondered, from Charles' manner as he spoke of it, if his business might be more of the heart than the ledgers, but had not asked.

As Hunter and Nerissa finished eating, and left the room, Lady Alyse arrived, still yawning a little, somehow managing to look even more beautiful than usual.

"Good morning, Lord Tillingford."

Her smile dazzled him, and his heart beat faster, his nerves returning on the instant.

"Good morning, Lady Alyse. If you will excuse me?"

Her face fell at his words, but she simply nodded politely, and focused her attention on her food, as he left the room. He would allow half an hour, then bring the book down to the parlour, where he expected she would be found, drawing.

~~~~~

Alyse finished eating, alone in the breakfast room, feeling disconsolate. She might almost think that he was avoiding her, so fast had he left the room when she had arrived. She sighed heavily, and went to the parlour. She was attempting to improve her ability to draw from memory, and had decided to draw things she had seen at Tillingford Castle, then compare the drawings to those she had made whilst there.

Not long after she had settled into her favourite chair, Lord Tillingford came into the room and simply nodded in greeting, chose a chair, and began to read the book he had brought with him. The light from the window, and the light from the fire, highlighted his face, drawing out the strong shape, and the curve of his cheek. Alyse found herself staring at him, and, after a moment, turned to a new page in her journal, and began to draw him. Perhaps she could capture that light... As always, drawing absorbed her, and she forgot, for a little, her despondency at the fact that he had not spoken of his feelings.

For some reason, he kept adjusting his position. The movements, and the small sounds that went with them, broke her concentration, and she glanced up to find him watching her, as if fascinated by her work. She felt her face flush red with embarrassment at being caught surreptitiously drawing him, again. Their eyes met, and something, some hesitation, in his manner was replaced by what seemed a moment of decision.

He stood, drawing something from between the pages of his book, then dropping the book to the chair. Carefully holding whatever it was in his hands, he took the few steps to stand before her. Alyse snapped her journal shut, her flush rising even more. She looked up at him, and, he went as if to speak, then stopped. She waited.

Finally, without a word, he extended his hand, offering her the item he had carried so carefully. She took it, her nerves afire where his fingers brushed hers as she did. Looking down at what she held, she gasped, in awe of the workmanship of the favour she held.

"This… this is beyond beautiful, my Lord."

"Please – open it."

At his words, she realised that the favour was one of those folded, so that it could be opened, and the message written inside discovered. With great care, she slid her fingers between the edges, and unfolded it.

Her breath stopped, her heart ceased to beat for a moment. There was no pretty poem inside. The words on the page were few, although written in a beautiful hand, but they were the most treasured words she had ever read.

My darling Alyse,

Marry me? For I love you more than life

Yours Always

Gerry

Her eyes filled with tears of happiness, and all of her uncertainty and irritation of the recent days fell away. He stood there, his heart on his face, and she could see that, still, he feared rejection. Surely, by now, he realised how much she loved him?

She laid the favour, and her journal, carefully aside, and stood, smiling. Then, unable to restrain herself any longer, she flung her arms around his neck.

"Yes, oh yes. I was afraid that you did not, that you would not…"

"Never doubt my love for you. And your love for me finally gave me the courage to believe that I might have happiness – I simply took time to be brave enough to ask."

"I am so glad you did – you are the only man I have ever wanted, from the first day that I met you."

He laughed, full of joy and relief.

"Then I have been doubly a fool, to have taken so long to understand what I felt."

He swept her up into his arms, and spun her around, only stopping so that he might kiss her without them both collapsing from dizziness. As they deepened the kiss, the door opened.

"Well! Does this mean that you have something to tell me?"

The Dowager Duchess stood in the doorway, attempting to look her sternest, but Alyse could see the half smile that she was repressing. She turned, keeping a firm grip on Lord Till… on Gerry's hand, and smiled brightly at her mother.

"Yes, mother, we do. I am afraid that I must inform you that you have the onerous task of arranging another wedding, for Lord Tillingford has just asked me to marry him, and I have accepted."

The smile escaped her mother's control completely, and the Dowager Duchess beamed at them.

"Well, this is a little irregular, young man – after all, you are supposed to ask the head of the family for leave to court her. But I can't imagine that he'll be at all distressed by this. None of my children do things the way that polite society expects. Well, I'll leave you two to… talk. I have plans to set in motion. Am I correct in my assumption that you will wish to marry as soon as can practically be arranged?"

"Err, yes, Your Grace, I believe that speed would appeal to both of us. And may I say now, that I am happy to leave all of the arrangements in your capable hands."

"Wonderful. I had best get started. Do provide me your family's direction, and some information about them – I don't believe we've ever met."

Alyse watched what could only be seen as a grimace pass over Gerry's face, before he replied.

"I will do so. I think that you'll find my parents most accommodating. They are, not to put too fine a point on it, fond of being associated with titles and people of importance."

"Ah, I see. Have no fear, I'll manage to deal with them… appropriately. Leave it to me."

She swept from the room, leaving Gerry looking rather overwhelmed, and Alyse on the verge of laughter. Laughter which never quite happened, because Gerry swept her up, and spun her around again.

"I believe we were busy when we were interrupted. I find I'd like to resume from that point."

His lips met hers again, and everything else ceased to matter at all.

Epilogue

Five short weeks later, they stood in the church at Meltonbrook village, surrounded by family and friends. The church was beautiful, quite old, and had been the location of many weddings in the Barrington family in the last few centuries. Alyse was filled with joy as she walked down the aisle to join him, her hand shaking a little where it rested on Hunter's arm.

Gerry's eyes were upon her, shining with love, and she was filled with a sudden impulse to cast aside all dignity and run to him. She did not. She would not risk catching the hem of her beautiful dress, which Madame Beaumarais had graciously made for her, even though it had now been revealed that Madame was actually the Marquise de Beaumarais. That would be unforgivable, when the lady in question was amongst the guests!

So she walked, outwardly calm, her heart beating faster than it ever had before, until she stood beside him.

The ceremony seemed a blur – she had eyes for nothing and no-one but Gerry, and she repeated the words as required, in a daze, until, at last, it was done. Stepping out into the early spring sunshine, her hand in Gerry's, she breathed in the scent of roses as the, now expected, storm of rose petals hit them. She had dreamed of this day for so long, she could scarce believe it was real – but it was.

It was a short carriage ride back to Meltonbrook Chase, and she curled against Gerry, his arm around her, glorying in the fact that she could, now, be in his arms every day. If she'd had the choice, she would have ignored the wedding breakfast and all the celebrating, and snuck away with Gerry to somewhere quiet. But she knew that her mother would never let that happen. Still, it was only a few hours to put up with.

They were long hours, filled with talking, and dancing, and being congratulated, over and over again. Late in the evening, they settled together on a couch in one corner of the ballroom, simply watching others dance, content to simply be with each other. Alyse noticed, amongst the dancers, Charles, dancing with Maria, Countess of Granville, who was Nerissa's sister. Maria's story was sad, for she had married with great celebration, only to lose her husband, within a year, to a terrible accident. She was only recently out of mourning. Alyse had rather thought that her brother was taken with Maria, but he had never said anything of it. Perhaps this was a sign. She would be interested to see what happened there.

Gerry slid his arm around her, pulling her against him, and she let her head fall to his shoulder, as the reality of it sank in. She was married, to the man she had always wanted.

She was not sure that it was possible to be happier than she was at that moment. Gerry brushed a kiss onto her brow, then whispered in her ear.

"Shall we slip away, and leave your mother, Hunter and Nerissa to deal with the departing guests?"

"Oh, yes please. I want nothing more than to be alone with you."

"Nothing more? Are you sure?"

"Well... perhaps a little more..."

He turned her face to his and kissed her gently, savouring the moment, then stood, drawing her up with him.

"Then come, my darling Alyse, and let us discover more of happiness together."

No one but Hunter noticed them go, and he simply smiled, and said nothing, overjoyed that his sister, and his friend, had found what they needed in each other.

The End

His Majesty's Hounds – Book 12

Sweet and Clean Regency Romance

Falling for the Earl

Arietta Richmond

ARIETTA RICHMOND

Chapter One

Late March 1818

A scatter of flower petals and pollen, bounced up by the force of her landing, fell across Jane's face, causing her to sneeze. She looked up past the hedge above her to the blue sky of early spring, and laughed, suddenly feeling as if she were a young girl again.

She lay there, her skirts undoubtedly the worse for the sudden contact with the grass and flowers of the verge of the lane, and allowed herself to enjoy the moment.

"I do apologise! May I help you up?"

The voice was rich and warm, resonant. A voice for speaking lovers' words, or praise, not for complaint. A large hand, obviously belonging to the gentleman whose voice she had just heard, appeared in her view. Suddenly, she felt rather silly, lying in the grass and laughing. She turned her head, and smiled at the owner of the extended hand, then raised her own hand, and allowed him to pull her to her feet.

"Thank you."

As she had no idea who he was, she did not risk any specific form of address – although his clothes spoke of wealth.

"It's the least I could do, given it was my fault that you landed in the grass in the first place. If I hadn't been in such a hurry, you would not have needed to leap out of my path to avoid being trampled."

The horse under whose hooves she had barely avoided being trampled snorted quietly, continuing to eat the spring grass where his rider had abandoned him to come to her aid. Jane looked down at her skirts, and smoothed the crumpled folds. There were definitely grass stains, which might never come out. She found that she did not care. For the first time in many years, money was not an issue – if the dress was not saveable, she could easily afford another.

"True. But you could not have expected to find someone walking along an isolated country lane in the middle of the morning. And I have come to no harm."

He looked at her, seemingly surprised at her calm acceptance of the situation. She suspected that he had expected to be berated for his actions. She could not find it in her to do so. The day was far too pleasant for being irritable. He was far too pleasant, for that matter.

Whoever he was, he was a well put together man, not in the first flush of youth, but fit and healthy regardless. Unlike her late husband, this man had not allowed himself to run to fat. His hair was dark, beginning to silver at the temples, and his eyes were a soft green, matching the spring grass that surrounded them.

"I thank you for your kind forbearance. May I assist you in any way?"

"That is not needed. I will simply continue on my way, and leave you to continue on yours, although perhaps at a less precipitate pace?"

"Indeed, that is probably wise."

He looked a little chagrined at having his foolishness pointed out, but took it in good part.

"Then I bid you good day."

"And I you. Let us hope that, should we meet again, it will be in a less dramatic fashion."

So saying, he bowed to her, with the elegance of a man long used to courtly behaviour and, smiling, turned to disrupt the horse's grazing. Soon, he had disappeared from sight around the next bend in the lane. Jane stood for some minutes, feeling the warm sun on her face, smelling the crushed grass and flowers, listening to the birds and the small animals in the hedgerow.

It was a truly beautiful day. She had not, she realised, been paying attention to that fact at all, until the unknown gentleman had caused her to fling herself into the grass. She was grateful to him, for such a day should be appreciated. Smiling, she started walking again – it was not far to the village, and she had things to do, and people to see.

It was still strange to her that she, Jane Canfield, who had eked out a poor living in Bridgemere Village for years, now lived in the Dower House of Windemere Towers, where her daughter now lived, a Countess, with her grandson, who was now an Earl, and heir to a Duke.

Mostly, she felt more at home with the villagers than with her new extended family, even though Julian, the Duke of Windemere, had been her childhood friend.

Perhaps, one day, she would get used to it all.

~~~~~

Nicholas Belmont, the Earl of Amberhithe, was not used to making a fool of himself. But he rather thought he just had. His heart had nearly failed when he had rounded the corner in the lane, riding like a madman, letting out all of his frustrations in the wild ride, and discovered a woman immediately in his path.

That she had the agility, and the presence of mind, to fling herself to the side, he was eternally grateful for. And when he had turned back to ascertain her wellbeing, she had been lying there like a young girl, laughing in the spring grass, flower petals scattered through her hair. He had been instantly charmed.

Once he had helped her to her feet, he had seen that she was not so young. She was, most likely, of an age with him. But she was beautiful, in an unaffected way, completely unlike the women of the *ton*. He had been so struck by her presence that he had not even introduced himself and, as he looked back on it, it was clear that his conversation had been inane. Still she had apparently forgiven him, for both nearly trampling her, and for his conversation – or lack thereof.

A most unusual woman, indeed. He rode along the lane, rather more slowly than before, and wondered, as Windemere Towers came into sight, who she was, and if he would ever see her again.

Chapter Two

More than a year earlier – late January 1817

Nicholas could feel the pressure rising in him as he glared at his son before him. He gritted his teeth, and restrained his anger. His voice was scathing, as he spoke.

"Do you do nothing but waste my money on gambling? Once, I thought you a reasonable man, but now, I have come to doubt that there will be anything left for you to inherit, given the rate at which you have been spending!"

Gervaise simply leant back in his chair, the very picture of negligent ease. For a moment, there was a flash of something in his eyes, but it was rapidly replaced by the casual air that was so fashionable amongst the young men of the *ton*.

"What else would you have me do? There is nothing to fill my days. I have put in the time to learn about our estates, yet you leave nothing in my control! A man must do something with his time, or go mad."

Nicholas considered him, thinking.

There was, he had to admit, an element of truth in those words. Yet what was he to do? He could not trust the wellbeing of his estates and tenants to Gervaise – not when he was as likely to be out, drinking, gambling, and indulging in heaven knew what other vices, until the early hours of every morning, and then not awake and sensible until evening.

Since Clara's death, Gervaise had become impossible. He understood that the boy grieved his mother – but no more than Nicholas grieved the loss of his wife. He had been lucky, to have had a marriage full of love – yet that just made it all the harder to deal with the loss. And his burden was doubled by Gervaise's attitude – for he had, in a sense, now lost his son as well.

"Perhaps if you were not so busy drinking yourself to oblivion, you might be in a state where I would trust you with more responsibility. But this last two years you have shown no sign of caring enough to change. Well, I have had enough. I will no longer supply you with funds on this scale, nor will I pay your debts. Your monthly allowance will be reduced to one quarter of its current amount, as of next week. It's up to you to get yourself out of the difficulties you may have sunk yourself into."

Gervaise stared at him a moment, shocked, then a hard expression crossed his face, some tangle of bitterness, hurt, anger and resentment.

"I had not thought you that cruel. But so be it. You will see, in the end, that I am far more than you believe. I must, I suppose, be thankful that you have not cast me from the house. Do not expect to see me often, however, Father, for I find my appetite for your company rather reduced."

Gervaise stood, and, with a mocking bow, left the room.

Nicholas sighed, and let his head fall into his hands. He no longer had the least idea how to deal with his son – Gervaise seemed not even the same person that he had been, before Clara's death. He prayed that, somehow, Gervaise would come to his senses, but he no longer held much hope of that happening any time soon.

~~~~~

Gervaise Belmont, Viscount Woodridge, forced himself to walk calmly through the house. It was only once he was behind the closed door of his rooms that he allowed himself to express his anger. He snatched up the small bowl from his desk, and flung it across the room, watching it smash into his fireplace with some satisfaction.

His father would see. He would prove that he was not as useless as his father thought. But he would say nothing yet. Nothing until the ship came in, which could be a year. A year in which he would have to survive on far reduced funds, and still pay out the rest of his debts. Suddenly depressed at the thought of the year ahead, he sank into the armchair under the window, and stared out across the London rooftops.

He was not, now, so certain that he had made the right decision. When he had won, and won an astounding amount of money, he had not paid out all of his gambling debts. He had put most of the money into an investment – an investment in a well renowned shipping company – Morton Empire Imports – who were adding a new ship to their fleet, and establishing a more regular trade with India and beyond.

If the venture succeeded, it would repay him ten times his investment, or more.

The company did not normally take on investors – they had enough funds of their own to not need to do so – but he had been introduced by his great aunt, Lady Farnsworth – who seemed to know everyone – and that had opened doors for him. He was grateful for the opportunity.

He just had to survive until the ship returned – and pray that no ill befell it on its journey. Now, given his father's restriction of his funds, he wished that he had not put quite so much of the money into the investment. Those he still owed debts to were not very forgiving. Still – he had won before – won well enough to make the investment. Perhaps the only way to survive until the ship returned was to keep gambling – surely he could win again.

$$\sim\sim\sim\sim\sim$$

January 1818

The damned ship had not yet returned. Any time now, they said – there was word of her having reached Spain, but she had not yet reached London. And he no longer had any choice. Every last penny of his funds was gone, but the few pounds in his pocket. He had been a fool. He had kept gambling, but there had not been another big win. And now the threats had become serious.

Gervaise had seen what the moneylender's thugs did to men who couldn't pay – and he had no intention of being around for them to find. He'd left instructions with Mr Pensworth, his man of business – detailed instructions on who to pay, how much, and what receipts were required, if the ship arrived.

He'd sent a letter to Morton Empire Imports, instructing that his funds were to be paid via Mr Pensworth.

And now he was running. He'd sent his carriage off with Hattam, and a reasonable amount of luggage, to Percy's country estate. Percy Charlesworth, Viscount Northdown, had been his friend since they were both new boys at school, and always told him to 'visit whenever he liked' – so he planned to. Eventually. He'd allow Hattam to get there, and give it a week, just in case the thugs followed the carriage. He didn't expect them to leave London... but best to be sure. Gervaise would ride, with minimum luggage, and stay in some out of the way Inns for the few days, until he felt sure he was safe. He had no idea when he would return to London – best give it a few months, in case the ship was further delayed. He refused to consider the possibility of the ship never returning.

The cold of late January was bracing, and the first two days passed without incident. Gervaise took a meandering route, far from the direct way to Percy's, and spent time going cross country, as much as on the roads, to ensure that he was not followed. By the third day, he was feeling freer and safer than he had for months. A kind of wildness took him, and he rode fast through the icy woods, exhilarated by the rush of the wind.

The woods he was in were obviously tended – he passed through a number of clearings, with signs of old woodcutter's cottages, and long unused charcoal burner's kilns, yet he saw no people. The empty clearings flew past, as did the ice laden branches. He felt alive, in a way that he never did in London.

Then, suddenly, the trail turned and, as the light of another clearing opened up before him, the horse twisted, skidding on the ice, and launched into a jump. He saw, as he began to fall, the dark bulk of a huge log across the trail below him. Desperately, Gervaise clung to the horse, but the twist before the take-off had shifted his balance too far.

Time seemed to slow as he fell, the air crisp and cold on his face, the entirety of his vision filled by the enormous log below him. Then he crashed into it, there was a sickening crack, pain overwhelmed him and he felt his leg twist into an impossible position as he slid down the side of the log. By the time he landed in the snow, he was unconscious.

Chapter Three

Late March 1818

Jane reached the village, still wondering about the man who had almost run her down. Who was he? He had not introduced himself, and she had not asked – nor had she introduced herself, for that matter. He was obviously wealthy, but that could mean anything, as far as his station in life. She supposed it didn't matter – she was unlikely to ever see him again.

At that thought, there was a pang of almost disappointment. She pushed the silly reaction aside – what did it matter if she ever saw him again? He probably thought her some kind of fluff brained silly goose – she had not exactly delivered sparkling conversation, after all – and she had been lying in the spring grass, laughing like a mad thing. She pushed all thought of him aside, and decided to deal with her appearance first. Mrs Tanner was the village seamstress, so she had a mirror – a very large mirror, which she was inordinately proud of. Jane turned her steps that way, intending to discover just how bad the grass stains on her skirts were.

Mrs Tanner fussed over her, because Jane claimed to have simply tripped and fallen onto the verge. She was really not interested in starting off a chain of speculative gossip about that man. For some reason, which she did not examine too closely, she wanted to keep his existence, and their meeting, all to herself.

Half an hour later, Jane emerged, wearing a new dress, carrying the old one in a parcel, and with the flower petals all combed out of her hair. Mrs Tanner was happy, having made a sale, and Jane had been regaled with the village gossip from the last week. Truth to tell, Jane had stopped listening after a while – Mrs Tanner required no answers, and simply droned on.

A few words here and there had interrupted her thoughts, which had, mostly, drifted back to remembering exactly how pleasant that man had been – both to look upon, and to listen to. Mrs Tanner had been rambling on about the woodcutters, and something about invalids, and gypsies in the next town. Jane assumed that she would hear it all again from others in the village, and that it would eventually make sense.

But by the end of her visit, after some tea and cakes in the new little tea house, and some more shopping – mainly for new toys for Daniel, she was no wiser. Perhaps Mrs Tanner had been imagining things. She set off back to the Dower House, well pleased with her day.

~~~~~

Nicholas found that his need to rush had disappeared. Something about seeing a grown woman allow herself to laugh with genuine pleasure in the day had changed things.

Her soft brown hair had looked beautiful, full of flower

petals. It was that odd mid brown colour which allowed grey hairs to fade into it – so he was not sure of her age. To him, she had simply looked beautiful, her eyes alight with pleasure in the day, and her manner unaffected. He had not thought of a woman as attractive for a long time – not since Clara's death, if he were honest with himself. Yet the woman on the road had most definitely seemed attractive to him.

He found himself hoping that he would see her again. The thought made him feel guilty, disloyal to Clara. Yet that was an irrational way to feel. Clara was gone. And she would not wish him miserable and alone for the rest of his life. He knew that for a certainty – she had told him so, in those last dark days before the illness had taken her life. Yet still, he felt guilty.

He turned his thoughts away from women, and back to his purpose. Windemere Towers was now before him. He had not been here for many years, yet it was clear in his memory. He had first met Julian when they were both at Oxford – they had both been far more likely to spend time in the library than out on the town with a raucous crowd of their peers. They had become fast friends, and he had spent a few term breaks at Windemere Towers.

Last he had seen it, it was mostly closed up, and somehow sad and worn. Antonia had never liked the place, and Julian had not been here often while she was alive. Today, it seemed different – brighter, the gardens well-tended, the new spring flowers lending colour everywhere. He was glad. Julian deserved a far happier life than he'd had with Antonia.

He swung off his horse in front of the imposing portico, to be greeted by a waiting footman. As the man took his horse, assuring him that it would be taken to the stables immediately, the front door opened, and Felton, his valet, came rushing down the steps.

"My Lord! I was beginning to worry..."

"Nonsense Felton, nothing to worry about. I've no intention of disappearing..."

He paused, his jaw clenched. He could not say the words, could not finish the sentence - *'like Gervaise'* his mind finished it for him, internally. The silence extended a moment, then Felton spoke again.

"I've everything arranged in your rooms, my Lord. The Duke has provided a delightful suite. Perhaps you'd like to freshen up before greeting him?"

"A good idea. Lead on."

It was strange to step through the doors of Windemere Towers again, after so long. Part of him still expected the old Duke to be there, for everything to be as it had been, thirty years before. He shook off the odd sensation, admiring the gleaming floors and furniture, and the new, lighter coloured drapes and wallpaper. The place looked good, and, somehow, it felt cheerful, happy.

The valet led him up two floors, and along a hallway, where the portraits of Julian's ancestors glared down at him from gilded frames. That much had not changed at all. The guest suite was large, with a parlour, a large bedroom, a dressing room, and two small rooms off that for servants. Hattam, Gervaise's valet, waited nervously for his arrival. Nicholas shook his head sadly in answer to the unspoken question, when Hattam's eyes met his.

The man turned away, and busied himself with the provision of a bath in the dressing room, as Felton helped Nicholas shed his dusty clothes. A perfectly prepared set of clothes lay waiting for him on the bed. Nicholas sighed – if not for the reason for his visit, this would be a most pleasant day.

He allowed himself to be cleaned and tidied, and dressed to perfection, then went downstairs to greet Julian, and his new wife. And to meet Julian's daughter-in-law, and his grandson — that was a story he wanted to hear more of, indeed.

~~~~~

Jane heard Barnes' deep voice, quickly followed by Daniel's bright child's tones, then the closing of the front door. Moments later, the parlour door opened, and a high speed small child flung himself across the room to land on her lap.

"Hello Daniel! Could you perhaps not squash me?"

Jane hugged the child, before gently pushing him off her, so that she could breathe. He stopped, looking at her, his head tilted to one side, his eyes bright.

"You don't look squashed Gramma."

"I'm not – quite – I caught you in time!"

He laughed, and Jane looked up to the doorway, where Marion watched them, her face alight with amusement.

"He's getting rather heavy, isn't he?"

Daniel looked at his mother, attempting to look offended at her words, then spoiled the effect completely by giggling.

"You can't deny that you're growing, Daniel. I think you've grown a foot taller in this last year. But... I think you still like toys just as much as you did when you were smaller – don't you?"

The boy's eyes lit with interest, and the acquisitive curiosity common to all children.

"Toys?"

"Yes, toys. If you look in that box over on the chair…"

Jane did not need to say anything further. Within seconds he had reached the box, pulled it open, and tipped out the new toys she had brought back from the village the previous day.

Marion joined Jane on the couch, and Jane rang for tea and cakes. Marion watched Daniel for a while, then turned to Jane.

"That should keep him occupied for a while, at least. You seem to have an instinct for exactly the sort of toys that will most engage him."

"I simply asked Mr Joiner what he thought a young boy would like, and let him make what he thought best – I can't claim any credit for cleverness."

"Then I must thank him, next time I go to the village. But I came to see you today to tell you about the latest things to happen up at the Towers. You so rarely come to me, mother."

Marion sighed, and Jane looked a little guilty at her words. She could not explain it to Marion – she still felt so out of place in the Duke's home, no matter that she had run wild in its hallways as a child. But it was Marion's home now, and Jane supposed that she would get more used to it with time. She was certainly grateful for the Dower House, and having a home of her own.

"I will come more often, perhaps one evening next week, for dinner?"

"That would be wonderful! Our guest will likely still be with us then, too."

"Guest?"

"He arrived yesterday. The Earl of Amberhithe. He is an old friend of the Duke's, from their school days. They seem very alike, in some ways, for the Earl is a kind man, from what I have seen, and not prone to excess."

"It is good then – for it seemed to me that Julian has been very lonely for many years – a visit from an old friend must be good for him."

"Yes. But the Earl's reason for visiting is a sad one. His only son, Viscount Woodridge, is missing – has been missing since late January, and he is deeply worried. He has come to seek the Duke's aid in searching for the Viscount."

Jane looked at Marion a moment, then spoke gently.

"That must be hard for him – and hard for Julian, and for you – for surely it is a terrible reminder of Martin's loss. Julian will do everything in his power to help, I know, for he could not bear to see a friend suffer the loss of a son, as he has done."

Marion nodded and, fleetingly, her eyes clouded with grief – a grief that nearly five years had done nothing to diminish. She shook it off, smiling wanly at her mother.

"Yes, that is true. I hope that they find him, but the Earl has already searched extensively, and I fear that he despairs. His wife has been gone these two years now, and the loss of his son would break him, I think."

Jane nodded, saddened at the thought.

With unspoken consent, they turned the conversation to lighter topics – to the gossip from the servants' hall, and from the village, to the changes in the lives of the people they had lived amongst for so long, as commoners like them. There was a measure of joy in simply seeing the lives of those they knew go on, knowing that Julian's return to live at Windemere Towers, and Marion's rise in status, had given the village new energy and purpose.

Daniel, once thought an illegitimate nothing, now the Earl of Scartwick, and heir to a Dukedom, played on, scattering blocks and carved animals about the floor in front of them, blissfully oblivious to the concerns of adults.

Chapter Four

Jane, as was her habit most days, went walking through the extensive gardens that ran from the back of the Dower House down towards the stream. It was peaceful, and beautiful.

She was particularly fond of the artfully constructed folly near the stream – it looked like an old wall, with wrought iron 'window' traceries set into it, and covered in vines and flowers.

Somehow, outside, with spring flowers surrounding her, it was easier not to think about how empty the Dower House seemed, when she, with a few servants, was the only occupant. After years of living with first, her late husband, then with her mother as she cared for her, and then with Marion and Daniel, being alone was a strange experience. At first, it was pleasant, especially with the space that the Dower House gave her, but soon, she began to crave more company.

She was not comfortable imposing herself upon Julian, especially as he was only recently remarried, and her visits to the village did not really fill the emptiness.

She was, in a way, ashamed of feeling that way for, after all, she was now better off than she had ever expected to be – to complain seemed ungrateful in the worst way.

Yet the loneliness remained, and became worse with each passing week.

The day after Marion's visit, she had taken a book with her, and sat on the stone bench by the folly, not really reading – simply staring out across the stream, thinking, twirling a flower in her fingers. She concluded that she needed a purpose, and needed new acquaintances. Not that there was anything wrong with her current acquaintances, but... they were all either of the nobility, or very thoroughly common, from the lower orders of society in country villages and amongst the servants.

Jane seemed, to herself at least, to be stuck between the two extremes. She got on with people from both levels of society, but did not really belong in either. She wondered, in truth, if there were others as suspended between as she was, or if she was alone in that state. Her musings were interrupted by the sudden cessation of birdsong, followed by the clatter of a pebble on the rocks of the stream edge. The sound came from behind her.

"Ah, we meet again. Still amongst the flowers, but at least you have a seat this time."

The resonant voice slid through her, warm and rich, making her think of the heated drink she had tasted, made of chocolate and an extravagant amount of sugar and cream. It seemed to vibrate to her very bones, drawing forth an involuntary shiver of pleasure at the sensation.

She turned, shading her eyes against the sun.

It was the man who had so nearly run her down a few days

before. He smiled – a smile that filled his eyes, and made his face seem even more handsome than before. That smile was quite breath-taking. Jane found herself lost for words, struggling to find a polite reply, in the face of the impact of his presence. She forced words out.

"Yes. It is a rather more comfortable place to appreciate the day than the grass of the verge."

"Indeed. Might I join you?" She nodded, tucking her skirts out of the way, and waving him to the seat beside her. "Thank you. This is a beautiful spot."

"It is. I come here often, just to immerse myself in the peace of it. Everything else seems less urgent, less stressful, once I have sat here for a while. Here, I can think, without interruption or distraction."

As she said it, she realised that, perhaps, her words could be interpreted as somewhat rude, as implying that she resented his intrusion. She flushed, embarrassed. What was it about this man that somehow discommoded her, threw her off balance so?

"Ah. Perhaps I am an unwanted distraction, then?"

"No, no. I must apologise. I did not mean to imply so. In truth, I find your company restful, for you have been everything that is polite and kind to me, with no expectation of any specific response on my part. It is refreshing to have a conversation outside the settings of polite society, and the inherent expectations and constraints that such settings bring."

She felt her heart beating harder as he looked at her.

She wondered what he saw. As she had spoken, she had realised the deep truth of her words.

Here was a conversation in that liminal place she had been considering – for she did not know who he was, had no idea of his status in society, beyond that his clothes spoke of wealth, and he did not seem to feel the need to impose that status upon their interaction.

In this small piece of time, she simply was, not trying to be either commoner or quality, but simply Jane, talking to a man who was being simply himself. Had she been young, it would have been scandalous, this meeting alone, yet as she was a widow, she suspected no one would care.

His considering gaze slid over her, gently, not carrying any judgement that she could detect. Then he smiled again, and the air left her lungs. His warm voice caressed her ears again.

"You are right. It is rare to have the chance to converse in a context where there are no subtle agendas and undertones. And yes, this place, and this situation is peaceful. I confess, I have been in need of peace, lately."

"Then let us treasure this. Let us not contaminate it with any other part of life, from outside this place. My name is Jane – let us leave it at that – simply a name, with no other attachments."

"I believe that you are wise indeed. The concept appeals to me greatly. My name is Nicholas. It is many years since I have been simply that – and now, speaking as such, choosing to be nothing but that, I feel a great weight lift from me. Perhaps it is the freight of others' expectations that I cast away, at least for this little while."

"Nicholas. A good name. it suits you."

Jane had no idea why she felt that, but she did.

"Thank you. Names are strange things – we somehow gain

impressions of them, as if a name might determine a person. Yet how can it? But it does. Jane is also a good name. I have never met a Jane I did not like."

She flushed again, looking away a moment, embarrassed by the implied compliment, then turned back, mischief lighting her eyes.

"Then I shall try not to disappoint you. I would not wish to be the first to create a bad impression."

"My dear Jane, I cannot imagine you doing so. For I know, already, that you are a woman of uncommon wisdom and good sense. A woman who is forgiving, and thinks things through. A woman who had the forbearance not to berate me for unconscionably bad behaviour on our first meeting. How could you, from an impression like that, fail to continue to delight?"

Was he... was he flirting? Jane was not sure, for it was many years since she had indulged in anything like that. Yet... it felt as if he was, gently, yet with honest intent. She was, she decided, pleased. There was a warmth in her, a feeling of being seen, of being appreciated, in a way that had not happened for a very long time. She savoured it – for who knew when she might feel that way again?

"You describe me as a paragon, and set me a high standard to hold to. I am flattered, but, perhaps, a little daunted."

"Do not be – I truly have the feeling that, should you set your mind to something, you will achieve it, despite any obstacles you may encounter."

Well, that was true. So far in her life, Jane had not let anything stop her. Survival had depended on that stubbornness for far too long.

"Thank you, Nicholas."

They sat and talked, neither paying attention to the passing of time, speaking of simple things, like the book she was reading, and what else each liked to read. She decided that she liked living in this liminal space, where social status did not exist, and common consent let them speak of nothing which might introduce it. Eventually, though, the lowering of the sun cast long shadows from the folly across them, as the afternoon closed in. Even as Nicholas started, looking up and noticing the lateness of the hour, Jane wished desperately to hold back time. She did not wish the afternoon to end. Yet it must.

"Dear Jane, I fear that we have become so absorbed in this delightful conversation that we have lost track of time. I must return to that world where others hold expectations of me, and where I have cares and woes to deal with. Thank you for this respite from all of that. Perhaps I will see you here, another day?"

"Yes, Nicholas, I would like that. Should you happen to pass when I am here, let us step again into a suspension of expectations, and enjoy the moment. May whatever challenges you face be easily overcome."

"Thank you again. For now, farewell."

He bowed over her hand, suddenly the consummate courtier, then turned, and walked away, back along the stream. She did not watch him go. She did not want to know where he went, for that would spoil the magic of the afternoon.

~~~~~

When Nicholas had left Windemere Towers, he'd had no

idea where he would go – he simply needed to walk, and let the sensation of movement convince him, for a little while at least, that he was doing something. That it was possible to do something, anything, which might bring him closer to finding Gervaise.

His son had been missing for six weeks now, and, whilst Nicholas clung to the belief that Gervaise still lived, that he would find him, it was becoming harder every day to sustain that belief. Julian was most sympathetic to his plight, having lost his own son five years earlier, to a pointless duel. For four long years, Julian had not known of his daughter-in-law or his grandson, and, once his wife had died, had felt alone in the world. Now, with a new wife and the heir he had not ever expected to have, he wished such joy for everyone. He had set things in motion to search for Gervaise, even more than Nicholas had already done.

The problem, Nicholas had come to realise, was that they had absolutely no idea where Gervaise had gone. No hints, beyond what he had told Hattam when he left London. He had planned to stay at Inns along the way, under an assumed name, and to take a winding route to his destination, to ensure that the moneylender's thugs could not easily find him.

So the search was spreading, in an ever widening pattern, to either side of the most direct road from London to Percy Charlesworth's home. And part of that search area extended in this direction.

He clung to his hope, and distracted himself with riding, and walking, whilst more and more men searched the countryside, looking for Gervaise. His only consolation was the thought that, if he couldn't find Gervaise, then most likely neither could the moneylender's thugs.

All of this was running through his mind as he walked, a never-ending cycle of regrets and self-recrimination. He felt that he had failed. He had been so deep in his own grief when Clara died, that he had not understood how deep Gervaise's grief was, and how dark a path it had led him down.

The day was bright, and gently warm with the soft spring sun. The countryside was pretty, the estate well-tended and pleasant. He walked through the gardens, and discovered a stream, so he followed it, with no intent to go anywhere in particular – it was as good a path to follow as any, for a man who simply needed to move, to avoid sitting and thinking. When he rounded a bend in the stream, coming out from a copse of trees into a more open, meadowlike area, he was surprised to see, ahead of him, what looked like a folly of some sort. On closer inspection, it was situated at the bottom of a long stretch of well-crafted gardens, which extended from a house which he could just see one corner of, past the trees at some distance. He had not expected another house, here.

Moving forward, he reached the point where he could see past the edge of the folly wall. The path was narrow here, and the pebbles skittered away from his feet, clicking on the larger rocks, and splashing into the fast running stream. The sound broke the silence, and interrupted the birdsong which had been an ever-present background to his walk.

He stopped, staring. Beyond the folly wall, in the curve of its artfully constructed 'ruined' walls, was a stone bench, surrounded by flowers and vines which trailed over the wall and across the ground nearby.

And on that bench sat a woman. Not just any woman, but the exact woman whom he had nearly trampled on the lane on his way to Windemere Towers. The woman who had so disconcerted him that he had made somewhat of a fool of himself. The woman who he had not been able to get out of his thoughts ever since.

The early afternoon sun lit her face, and drew glints of gold and silver from her hair. She stared into the distance, as if deep in thought, a book lying forgotten in her lap. Her dress was a shade of pinkish peach, which made her seem all warmth amongst the old stones. The red petals of the flower in her fingers stood out starkly against the softness of the colour of her dress.

Coherent thought deserted him. There was a beauty to her that was far more than the surface appearance. Yet... he felt that she seemed a little disconsolate – he wondered why. He could not stand there, just staring at her. He stepped forward again, kicking pebbles as he did, and spoke, so as not to come upon her entirely unawares. Even as he did, he cursed himself for the inelegance of his words.

"Ah, we meet again. Still amongst the flowers, but at least you have a seat this time."

She seemed, as before, to be unperturbed by that fact. She turned slowly, and raised her hand to shade her eyes. He felt her regard as if she had touched him. Her eyes were a rich goldish brown, like dark honey. Somehow, he managed to converse, and soon found himself invited to sit beside her.

There followed the most remarkable conversation of his life. At first, he thought that he had interrupted her solitude in a way that was not appreciated, but soon, she disabused him of that notion. She claimed that he, through his attitude, added to her peace. He was astounded, for somehow, he became a bumbling fool in her presence. It seemed that she did not perceive it that way.

They agreed to disregard convention, and societal requirements, and to converse for that moment in time, as if none of that existed. To do so was remarkably freeing. He was flattered to be asked to call her by her forename, to address her simply as Jane. And he discovered that the sensation of being simply Nicholas, with no title, no family name, and no social position attached, was rather delightful. It was something he had not been since he was a small child. Just Nicholas.

He did not know who she was, and she did not know who he was – not in the sense that most of the world cared about, anyway. But Just Jane, and Just Nicholas had a most wonderful and peaceful afternoon, speaking of everything and nothing – everything except the constraints of society and others expectations, that is.

So lost did they become in conversation, that he did not notice that the afternoon was gone, until the shadows closed in with the fading of the day, stealing the colour from the flowers, and rendering everything into graduated shades of mournful grey.

Reluctantly, he tore himself away, knowing that he must return to the world where Gervaise was still missing, and where his life was a shattered and empty thing.

Rashly, he asked if, perchance, he might see her there again, some day. Instantly, he was filled with the fear that she would say no, and deny him the chance of such respite from the world, again.

But she said yes, and her eyes lit with what seemed genuine pleasure at the suggestion. He had released the breath he had not known he was holding, and smiling, taken his leave. After the afternoon in her company, his world seemed brighter, and his hope for discovering Gervaise, alive, was renewed.

∿∿∿∿∿

The following day, Jane walked to the village again. She had no real need to go there, for her servants would purchase anything she needed, and run any errands required, but she chose to go. She chose to keep up the friendships she had made, in many years of living in the village, as one of them. She liked to hear the tales of their lives, and, when she could, to help those who needed help. After all, every single one of them had helped her, at some point in the past. Now that she had wealth, it seemed only the right thing to do, to help when she could.

As she walked along the lane, she took note of the spot where she had landed on the verge, and paused a moment, sending up silent thanks for that unexpected meeting, for now she had a new acquaintance, and a wholly different outlook on the world.

She picked a flower from the grass, and twirled it in her fingers as she walked on. In her mind's eye, she saw Nicholas again, looking at her with that appreciative, open, respectful warmth and, even just in memory, it heated her through, and brought a flush to her cheeks.

In the village, she visited most of the shops, not so much to buy things as to chat to the shop owners and the patrons. They were happy to regale her with the latest gossip, and she soon knew who was courting who, who had done something scandalous (at least by village standards) and who had new babies. All of that was ordinary, and to be expected.

What was not ordinary caught her attention. She was sitting at a table in the new tea shop, talking to Mary, the baker's wife, when she overheard part of the conversation at the next table.

It was Mrs Tanner speaking, and what caught Jane's attention was the mention of 'the Woodcutter's invalid' – a term she remembered from Mrs Tanner's rambling just the other day. She sipped her tea, waiting for Mary to finish what she was saying, then spoke quietly.

"Mary, what's that Mrs Tanner's talking about? Something about an invalid? I'm sure she said something of the like to me, the other day when I was in her shop, but I was distracted and I'm ashamed to admit that I let her words roll right over me."

Mary stifled an inelegant snort of amusement.

"Wouldn't be hard to have her words roll over you – there's enough of them!"

Jane repressed her own laughter, nodding. It took her a moment to regain enough composure to speak again.

"Yes… but what is she talking about?"

"Oh. Seems the Woodcutter and his wife have taken in some man they found injured in the forest. It's a bit of a mystery. He refuses to tell them who he is. Says it's better that way. They found him in a terrible state, just near one of the clearings. Broken his leg, he had. Must have fallen from a horse and landed hard on one of those big logs that Joe hadn't finished cutting up yet. No-one's found the horse."

"When did this happen?"

"Some weeks ago. We only heard about it here when Joe came into town to get supplies – and he only does that every month or so. They're very self-sufficient out there."

"That sounds very odd. Why on earth wouldn't he tell them who he is?"

"Who knows? Perhaps the fall gave him a knock on the head,

464

and knocked the sense out of him. But Jess has a soft heart, and so does Joe, really. They couldn't leave him there, so Joe pulled his leg back into place and bound it up with some timber for supports, then carried him back to the cottage. He's lucky it was Joe who found him – not so many hereabouts know how to put a leg back in place like that. He'll likely walk again without much of a limp, but he'll be some weeks more before he can even think about trying it."

"He's lucky indeed. Do they have enough? Enough to deal with another mouth to feed like that, so close after winter?"

"Just, I think – I gave them some extra bread, but Joe's proud – he wouldn't tell me, even if they did need more."

"Perhaps I should go out for a visit, and see if they need anything. I could take Potts with me, so there would be another pair of hands."

"That's very kind of you to think of. I do worry about them, but I suppose the stranger can't do much harm if he can't even walk."

"I'll see if I can organise that soon, then. For today, though, I'd best be getting back."

Jane took her leave of her friends and, gathering up her parcels, set off back to the Dower House.

Chapter Five

Over the next two weeks, Jane saw Nicholas again, every few days, as she sat near the stream, or as she walked along its banks. Each time, they stopped, and sat and talked, careful to never enquire into their separate lives outside the peaceful moments of conversation.

Each time, she found herself more drawn to him, more comfortable in his presence. And each time, it became harder for her to deny the fact that she found him immensely attractive. She had not considered a man that way for a very long time. Whilst Peter had been dead for more than five years, she had never considered looking for another man, another marriage. Many thought that odd of her, but she had treasured her independence. And, truthfully, she had not met any man who interested her in the slightest, that way.

Until Nicholas. The sensation of finding a man attractive was confusing – at her age, with a daughter of 25, and a grandchild, she had never expected to feel such a thing again. But she did.

She was grateful for their agreement to not speak of the rest of their lives – it made things simpler, and allowed her to still enjoy their conversations, without needing to deal with her feelings.

One afternoon, as they finished a conversation, sitting on the bench at the folly, she found herself disturbed – for Nicholas had seemed sad for the entire afternoon and, whilst he did not speak of it, it was obvious to her that his heart was heavy. Yet she could not ask him about it – and he would not speak of it, for whatever brought the sadness to his eyes was part of the outside world – part of the things that they had banned from these conversations.

They parted as the light faded from the sky, and she took herself back to the Dower House feeling far less cheerful than she usually did after speaking to him. She settled into the parlour to read, feeling lonely – the house seemed so big around her and, after an afternoon of conversation, the silence wrapped around her, emphasising that emptiness. There was a tap at the door, and Potts came in, bearing the silver correspondence tray. Jane thought the correspondence tray a rather pretentious thing, for one such as her, but her staff insisted.

"A message, Mrs Canfield."

He proffered the tray. Jane picked up the message. Julian's seal. She broke it open. It was a simple invitation to dinner, the following day. Would she ever get used to the formal way that those born into titles did things? Probably not. She went to the small desk, and penned a note of acceptance, handing it to Potts to deliver.

Nicholas paused as he reached the bend in the stream, and looked back, watching as Jane stood, and shook out her skirts, before turning away from the stream, and walking up the hill through the gardens. He wondered where she went, where she lived, then pushed those thoughts from his mind. Their agreement left no space for such wonderings.

Still, his eyes clung to her slim figure until she passed out of his sight. She was undeniably beautiful, in a completely natural and unaffected way. Each time he saw her, he found her more attractive, and each time he thought of her that way, he was overcome with confusion, with a sense of guilt, of disloyalty to Clara. He had never expected to be attracted to a woman again, for he had loved Clara deeply, and her death had been a terrible blow. He was sure that he could never love like that again, nor did he want to, for with such love came eventual pain, inescapably.

So why did he find himself wanting to spend more and more time with Jane? Confusion filled him, as did the aching sadness caused by the fact that they seemed no closer to discovering Gervaise's fate than they had been when he had arrived here. He shook his head, and turned away, walking into the gathering darkness, back towards Windemere Towers.

~~~~~

The following evening, Julian sent his carriage down to collect Jane. She thought it silly, but did not argue.

After all, Windemere Towers was only a ten-minute walk up the hill from the Dower House. But... ladies were not supposed to get dust on the hems of their evening dresses, and evening slippers were not designed for walking outside.

So she sat in the carriage, feeling rather overdressed and out of place, as it travelled the short distance.

Minutes later, as the butler opened the main doors for her, she still felt utterly out of place. If it were not for the fact that she knew Julian so well, and that she absolutely loved his new Duchess, she would have considered turning and simply going back home. The formality, and the scale of the house, still overwhelmed her.

All thought of formality was immediately dashed aside when Daniel came rushing out of the parlour door, to hug her around the knees.

"Hello Daniel! Could you perhaps let me go, so that you do not completely crush my dress? Then I can see how handsome you look tonight."

At 5 years old, Daniel was beginning to care about how people perceived him, so this tactic worked well, and Jane found herself able to move. Taking her grandson's hand in hers, she allowed him to lead her into the parlour.

Julian came forward to greet her, embracing her as an old friend. She smiled, glad to see him, and beginning to forget all about formality. Then, as he released her, she looked past his shoulder. Her breath caught, and she felt, for a moment, as if her heart had stopped beating.

There, on the other side of the room, was Nicholas, talking to Marion. Julian, unaware of her shock, turned, and led her forward, following Daniel, who had dropped her hand and run to his mother's side.

"Jane, let me introduce you to my guest." At Julian's words, Nicholas turned, and Jane saw the same shock written on his face, as his eyes met hers. Their spring green drew her in, and everything else seemed to fade away. "Mrs Jane Canfield, may I present Nicholas Belmont, the Earl of Amberhithe. Lord Amberhithe is staying with us, whilst we assist him in a most distressing matter."

Somehow, Nicholas overcame the shock enough to bow elegantly over her hand.

"Delighted, Mrs Canfield. Your daughter has told me much about you."

His warm rich voice flowed over her, heating her blood, and resonating in her bones, as it always did. She found words, a little shakily, desperately trying to maintain the formal politeness which one might expect in people who had never met before, tempered by the private situation in which they had been introduced.

"My Lord. I am not certain how I feel about that! I can only hope that she has been kind."

He laughed, a delightful sound, and smiled again. He had not yet released her hand, and she glanced down, unsure what to do. He noticed her glance, and uncurled his fingers, a slight flush colouring his cheeks.

"I cannot imagine the Countess being anything other than kind."

"I am relieved to hear you say so."

Conversation flowed, and Jane slowly regained her equilibrium. But her eyes followed Nicholas, and their eyes often met. It was hard to concentrate on the conversation, with him in the room. An Earl! She had not suspected. Their friendship had been so completely based on a separation from the day to day world, that she had held no concept of his status.

Now, she found herself shy in his company, unsure how to go on, with a man far beyond her social status. And yet... he was still Nicholas.

A nursery maid came to take Daniel off to his supper and bed, and shortly thereafter, a footman announced that dinner was ready. Julian led the way to the dining room, and Jane found herself beside Nicholas. He offered his arm, and she took it, nervous as he led her to her place at the table. They settled into their seats, and Jane found herself still deeply distracted – Nicholas' presence at her side was somehow far different here, than when they sat companionably on the bench at the folly.

The warmth of him beside her was palpable – seeming to heat her body in turn. She was grateful when food was placed before her, and she could concentrate on simply eating – or at least trying to, for her appetite was reduced by her nervousness. Once the first course was done, conversation resumed, and Julian chose to explain to Jane the sad circumstances which had brought Nicholas to stay at Windemere Towers.

"I am not sure if Marion has told you anything of Lord Amberhithe's sad story, Jane?"

"Only a little."

"Ah, well, let me tell you a little more – and, of course, you should correct me if I have any of this wrong, Nicholas."

Nicholas nodded in Julian's direction.

"Please. I am happy for you to tell the tale. I confess that I am most heartily sick of needing to repeat it, when it hurts me so much to even think about the situation."

Jane glanced to her side, watching Nicholas' face as he spoke – some deep sadness was visible in his expression. She remembered that Marion had spoken of his son being missing, but it seemed there was more to the story than Marion had mentioned. She felt a sudden desire to reach out, to take his hand, to offer, in some way, some comfort. Instead, she turned her attention back to Julian, feeling flushed, and uncertain.

"Lord Amberhithe lost his wife some three years ago now, and his only son and heir, Viscount Woodridge, in dealing with his grief, allowed himself to be drawn far too deeply into gambling and other undesirable pursuits. This brought him into conflict with his father, much to Nicholas' distress. It seems that the gambling debts were out of control, far more than anyone realised. Nearly two months ago, Viscount Woodridge disappeared. He had intended to visit a friend's estate in the country, and sent his valet on ahead with the carriage, choosing to ride, by a roundabout route, to avoid being followed by enforcers sent by the moneylender. He never arrived at his friend's estate."

At these words, Jane gasped, looking to Nicholas again. Nicholas simply stared, unseeing, at his wine glass, his pain at the situation obvious. Again, she wanted to reach out to him. But it was not her place to do so. She turned back to Julian.

"That is terrible indeed!"

"When he did not arrive, the valet searched, and eventually came to Nicholas to tell him the sorry tale. Since then, Nicholas has searched widely, ever further afield from the direct route from London to the Viscount's friend's estate, but has not found him. So he came to me, in the hope that I could assist. Sadly, although I have called on everyone I know, so far, I have had no more success than Nicholas. His son is still missing. It distresses me that I have not been able to help – for I know far too well the pain of losing a son. I pray that we will find him yet."

After a moment, Nicholas spoke, his voice far rougher than normal.

"I blame myself, in a way. I was so caught in my own grief, I did not realise the path that Gervaise's grief had led him down, until far too late. And then, I took the approach of cutting back his allowance, in the hope of reducing the gambling. If only I had understood! I would happily have paid his debts, rather than lose my son, no matter what the cost."

"You must not lose faith, Lord Amberhithe. Surely, if anyone can discover a way to find him, it will be Julian."

Nicholas turned to Jane as she spoke and nodded slowly.

"You are right, Mrs Canfield. I must not lose hope."

The next course was served, and everyone ate in rather sombre silence, considering the potentially dire fate of Lord Amberhithe's son. Soon, Julian determinedly turned the conversation to lighter topics and, in the end, the evening passed most pleasantly. But the shadow of sadness was never far from Nicholas' eyes.

~~~~~

Nicholas was finding it harder and harder to maintain his hope. And every day, when he spoke to Marion, and saw young Daniel, it reminded him of the daughter-in-law he might never have, of the grandchild he might never have, if they did not find Gervaise.

He stood in the parlour, talking to Marion about the events of the day, while young Daniel played at her feet. There was the sound of the front door being opened, and Daniel leapt to his feet and sped from the room. Ah the vagaries of children!

He continued his conversation, vaguely aware of someone entering the room, until Julian's voice drew his attention.

"Jane, let me introduce you to my guest."

Nicholas turned, wondering who this might be, and stilled, shocked. For there, being brought across the room by Julian, was *his* Jane. The Jane with whom he shared those wonderful conversations by the stream, those conversations during which he could forget, for a little while at least, that Gervaise was missing.

Somehow, he staggered through the introductions, his mind reeling with the fact that Jane was Marion's mother, and had known Julian even longer than he had. Tonight, dressed formally for dinner, she was even more beautiful. The silk of her dress was an echo of her eyes – a rich honey colour, with a shimmering finish. The necklace and hairpins of amber set in silver added to the warm impression. He realised that he was staring, unable to drag his eyes away, and flushed.

The evening progressed, with him ever aware of her presence by his side even in those moments when Julian spoke of their fruitless search for Gervaise, and he was quite certain that he was a poor companion, so distracted was he by her proximity. How would he ever speak with her the same way again?

~~~~

As Jane drifted off to sleep that night, her mind kept replaying random pieces of the last few weeks, in the half dream state before true sleep. Much of what went through her mind was Nicholas – both during their conversations near the folly, and at dinner. But she also saw snippets of her conversations in the village, and other moments.

The juxtaposition of the two things – the image of Nicholas' sorrowful face, when speaking of his missing son, and the image of Mary's face as she described the gossip about the woodcutter's discovery of a man in the woods – made her wonder – was there any connection? She pushed the fanciful thought aside. His son had been far from this area when he disappeared, as far as anyone knew, and the chance of any connection was vanishingly slim.

Sleep claimed her, and her dreams were full of spring green eyes and a voice like warm honey.

In the morning, however, that strange thought of connection stayed with her.

Chapter Six

The image of Jane as she had walked into the parlour at Windemere Towers, all golden and beautiful, stayed with Nicholas, haunting his thoughts and his dreams. Whilst he was still utterly uncertain about how to go on, now that they knew each other's identity, and the perfect isolation of their conversations could never be the same, he still found himself wanting to see her.

After another depressing report back from the search parties, he took himself out for a walk, and soon his feet followed the familiar path towards the folly. There was no reason to expect her to be there, that particular day, yet he was full of hope – and nervous apprehension. Could they still converse as they had?

He turned the corner of the stream, and released the breath he had not been aware of holding. She was there. She looked up, as he approached, and smiled, her honey brown eyes warm, yet her smile a little hesitant. He understood – he felt a little hesitant too.

"Good day to you Jane. Do you, perchance, have time to sit and talk awhile?"

She looked away, shyly, so different from her previous demeanour, as if the knowledge of his title had somehow made him a different person. It saddened him – for the time here, without bearing the weight of the title, had been most precious to him. He would have to, somehow, convince her that nothing should change. After a moment, she looked up, the uncertainty still in her eyes.

"Of course, Nicholas."

A little of the fear left him – she would at least try to go on as before.

"Thank you. I..."

"Yes?"

"I believe it best to go on as we did before – to be completely frank with one another, and to, in most cases, leave the world, outside these moments, out of our conversation. But... I can see, in your eyes, a hesitation that was not there before. Is that borne of knowing who I am, in the world at large? For if it is, I would most strongly wish that we had never been formally introduced, so much do I value our private conversations."

She watched him, eyes wide, and said nothing, her fingers playing with a flower she had picked. He waited. He realised, as he did, just how much he had come to value his time with this woman, to value her, for her unaffected honesty and beauty of spirit. Waiting for her to speak was torture, but he could do nothing else. Finally, her smile grew larger, and she nodded, as if coming to a decision.

"I also would prefer to go on as we did before. But can we?

I admit that your station in life makes me uncertain. Such knowledge is impossible to unknow, once known. Yet I too value our conversations, and would not wish to lose them."

"Then let us pretend that our introduction never happened – at least whilst we are here, away from everyone else."

"As you wish Nicholas. What shall we talk of today?"

He paused, suddenly unsure, for all of the rest of the world seemed now available for discussion, and pushed itself forward in his thoughts. He pushed it away, unwilling to begin any discussion which could only end with mention of Gervaise.

"I have most often seen you here – but, do you often walk far afield?"

"I do. I like to walk, to appreciate the beauty of the countryside around me. I walk into the village regularly, as well as simply wandering in the grounds of the estate, and sometimes further. Most of my life, I had little choice but to walk, if I wished to go somewhere, and it has become habit."

"Then... shall we walk? You can show me the places you like, and I can learn more of the countryside."

'Yes. That would be most pleasant, Nicholas."

He stood, and offered her his hand, gently assisting her to rise, then proffered his arm. She placed her hand upon it, and warmth spread into him from the contact. She was such an attractive woman, not simply externally, but in all ways. He was, he discovered, glad of the excuse to have her touching him.

They set off, much of the time in companionable silence. He had not craved any woman's company like this, not since Clara's death. That he did so now left him confused, and feeling guilty again. He should not feel so, he knew, yet he did.

And he was almost afraid. Did he wish to feel something for this woman? But love led to inevitable pain. Yet it felt right, walking like this, her hand on his arm, her warmth beside him.

Even knowing, now, who she was, he did not really know how to treat her. For she was a commoner, and, as such, theoretically completely below his station, not a woman to be associated with. Yet... her daughter was a Countess, her grandson was an Earl, and would be, in due course, a Duke. He did not know what that meant, as far as any association between them.

It struck him then, that he did not care. Somewhere, in these last two terrible months, he had ceased to care what society thought – of him, of Gervaise, of anyone he cared for. Let him only have his son back, alive, and well, and he would bear any gossip cast against him, or against those around him.

They walked on, and Nicholas allowed his mind to wander, turning his thoughts to the world around them, to anything and everything but his feelings – for feelings led to pain. After some time, she began to speak, telling him about his surroundings – what grew in the fields, what lived in the forest, how the land changed with the seasons. Things he had never considered in such detail before. The depth of her knowledge of such things surprised him – the women of his acquaintance knew nothing of the natural world.

As she spoke, she became more animated, her face alight with enthusiasm, and his heart lifted. Somehow, despite himself, she filled him with joy in the day.

They stopped, eventually, as the sun grew lower on the horizon, and the rich light of late afternoon cloaked the trees in a golden haze. They stood in a copse of trees, on the bank of another stream.

She looked up at him, and, as his eyes met hers, everything else faded away. The gold haze somehow surrounded them. His heart skipped a beat, and, as she licked her lips, moving as if uncertain, his eyes were drawn to her mouth. He wanted, in that instant, to trace his tongue over the path that hers had just taken. The desire was so strong that he did not think, he simply acted. Slowly, as if in a dream, he bent his head to hers, brought his lips to hers, and allowed himself to do as he had imagined.

As his lips touched hers, she stilled, then, as his tongue began to trace the outline of her upper lip, she sighed, and softened, her lips parting slightly. He pulled her to him, and her hands slid over his shoulders. His heart was racing, and a wild joy ran through him when her lips moved against his in response.

The kiss seemed to last forever, and no time at all. When it ended, they drew apart, both looking flustered and confused, overwhelmed by the intensity of it. The cool afternoon breeze touched his fevered skin, and reality came crashing back down upon him. What was he doing? He could not risk love! He could not risk the friendship, the peace he had found in Jane's company. Yet he had done just that. She would be well within her rights to slap him for his presumption, to turn away from him.

Desperately, he hoped that she would not turn away. After all… for those glorious moments – she had not pushed him away – far from it, she had kissed him back.

He looked at her – she stood, breathing hard, her hands fallen by her side, staring across the stream. He wanted to reach out and touch her. He wanted to step back, and never touch her again. He wanted… he did not know what he wanted – only that she should stay in his life, somehow.

Slowly, she turned back towards him.

"Nicholas. I..."

She blushed, her cheeks stained a delightful pink. Her eyes met his, and for a moment, he thought he saw some strong emotion there. Then she looked away again. He spoke, suddenly needing to break the silence.

"Jane, I apologise. I had no right to presume, to take advantage..."

"Nicholas, I am not some green girl with no experience of life. I am as complicit as you in that moment. I am not sure that it should have happened, but I cannot regret that it did."

He felt dizzy – with relief that she was not rejecting his presence completely, and with fear – for what happened next, in a situation like this? She smiled, meeting his eyes again, and reached for his hand, twining her fingers with his.

"Jane..."

"Shhh. There will be time for us to talk of this later. I think that we both need time to adjust, to consider what we wish to do. For now, let us simply walk. It is past time that we turned back – it will be close to dark by the time we reach the folly again."

They turned, together, and began to retrace their steps. She did not release his hand, and warmth filled him at that fact.

They did not speak again until they reached the folly, and he bid her good evening, but they were both acutely aware of the other, every step of the way. He watched her walk up through the gardens, until she faded from his sight in the deepening dusk, then turned back towards Windemere Towers, his mind in turmoil.

~~~~~

For all that she had put an effort into appearing calm as they walked back towards the folly, Jane was shaking inside. As Nicholas bid her farewell for the evening, she had a moment where she wanted nothing more than to fling herself into his arms, to revisit the heady delight of his kiss.

She did nothing of the sort, firmly remonstrating with herself for the thought. Instead, she bid him good evening with a smile, and went on her way up through the gardens. She forced herself not to look back, but she had the feeling that he was watching her. Chiding herself for thinking like a foolish girl, she went into the house and settled to some sewing until dinner. There was nothing like simple practical work to takes one's mind off flights of fancy. At least that's what she told herself. Her mind, it seemed, did not listen.

Her thoughts went round and round, circling back to the moment when Nicholas had kissed her. She had not expected it. But she had, undoubtedly, wanted it when it happened. He was an Earl! She was a commoner. Nothing could come of it, and she was foolish to even consider the possibility. *But*, said the still small voice in her thoughts, *he is different, he does not treat you like most of the ton do.*

She did not know what to think. And the turmoil in her thoughts was not good for her sewing – she looked at the uneven stitches with disgust, and put her work away. Perhaps reading would be a more efficient distraction.

It was not. And by the time that Jane went to bed that night, her thoughts were no clearer. But her dreams were full of kisses that left her heated and still tired come morning.

Chapter Seven

For the next few days, Nicholas did not go walking. The pull was there, the insistent feeling, nagging away at him, that he wanted to go and see Jane. He determinedly ignored it. The more he considered things, the more he berated himself for the worst kind of fool. He should never have spoiled their beautiful friendship by kissing her, especially at the point when it was already a fragile thing, as a result of their formal introduction.

What would she want with a man like him – still broken from the loss of his first wife, and afraid to ever love again, for that way lay pain. He could not offer her what a man should offer a woman, so he should not touch her at all. He should stay away for some time, allow the moment to fade in her memory (although he was not sure that it could ever fade in his), and try to go back to the way they had been before.

The hunt for Gervaise had achieved nothing more. There had been a moment of hope, when they had identified an Inn he had stayed at, a few nights into his journey, but the trail had gone cold from there.

Nicholas refused to give up hope, yet he had to admit that, with every day that passed, the chances of finding Gervaise alive, or finding him at all, reduced. Without the relief of his conversations with Jane, his state of mind verged ever more towards the blue-devilled state where nothing seemed good in the world.

~~~~~

Jane went walking through the gardens as usual, and spent time sitting at the folly, but Nicholas did not come to talk. That fact left her feeling out of sorts, and unable to settle to anything. The weight of loneliness, which had been lifted for a while by Nicholas' presence, came crashing back down upon her.

After three days, Jane decided to go into the village, simply for company. As she walked down the lane, surrounded by spring flowers, now in full bloom everywhere, she thought about the changes that the last month had brought. All good, except for the fact that Nicholas' son had not yet been found, and for the fact that she had not seen Nicholas for days.

In that strange way that thoughts have, of making connections from seemingly unrelated things, Jane remembered the village gossip about the injured man taken in by the woodcutters, and how, in her half-asleep state, many days ago, she had wondered if there was any connection to Nicholas' missing son. The idea seemed far-fetched – after all, Lord Woodridge had been travelling a path far from Bridgemere.

Yet the thought nagged at her. There was only one way to find out.

She had told Mary that she might go and visit the woodcutters, just to see if they had enough, with the extra mouth to feed, after all. Jane flushed in sudden embarrassment – she had completely forgotten her words until now, and yet, what if they were in need? It was not like her to forget about a charitable need – especially one created by the charitable actions of the people in need themselves. She resolved to go to see them the following day, taking gifts of practical things. Potts could go with her.

In the village, Mary was happy to describe exactly where the woodcutter's cottage was in the woods, whilst filling Jane up with freshly baked tea cakes to go with the gossip of the day. That, and a visit to Mr Joiner to collect the latest toys she had commissioned for Daniel, left her feeling much happier with the world than when she had departed the Dower House that morning.

She spent the walk back planning her trip into the forest, and working out what to take with her. It served as a reasonably effective distraction from thinking about Nicholas, and *that kiss* – until she passed the spot where she had first met him. She stopped, and stared at the verge, where the grasses and flowers had completely recovered from her crushing them, springing up stronger than before. For one mad moment, she was tempted to fling herself down, to lie amongst the flowers and imagine him appearing to help her up.

She shook off the whimsy, and resolutely turned back to the lane, forcing her thoughts back to the forest, and what she could gift the woodcutters, which they might not be too proud to accept.

When Jane set out the next morning, both she and Potts were laden down with baskets of food. She had, after due thought, concluded that food was the safest thing to take – for with an extra mouth to feed, it would undoubtedly be useful, no matter what. Any other need they might have, she could assess on this visit, and deal with later.

The day was warm and still – a perfect spring day, and Jane enjoyed the long walk – although she wasn't certain that Potts took as much pleasure in it as she did. The forest was beautiful – full of small flowers, new green leaves, and birdsong, with nothing else to disturb its peacefulness. At least, that is, until they were close to where Mary had said the woodcutter's cottage was. As they got closer, the sound of an axe ringing, as it met with wood, echoed through the trees.

The path was blocked by a rather large log, at the entry to a clearing quite close to the cottage, and a little scrambling through the trees was needed – but Jane managed to navigate it without damage to her skirts. Soon, they reached the clearing in which the cottage stood, a thin plume of smoke drifting up from its chimney. To one side of the clearing huge stacks of cut wood were piled, ready to be delivered wherever they were needed. Behind the cottage, a small kitchen garden was bursting with growth, and chickens pecked through the soil. Two goats were tethered just out of reach of the garden.

A sleepy dog looked up from where it slept in the sun before the door, obviously trying to decide if they were worth barking at. It sniffed the air as they approached and, scenting the food they carried, chose to wag its tail hopefully. Jane smiled at the dog, watching it watching the basket she carried, and rapped on the door. Moments later, it creaked open, to reveal a woman with reddish brown hair escaping its braids.

"Can I help you?"

"Mrs Carver? I'm sorry to simply appear on your doorstep, when I don't think we've seen each other for a year or more. Very remiss of me. When I was caring for my mother, before she passed away, and we had so little, your husband brought me wood to get us through winter, and would take nothing for it. I've never forgotten. When I heard it mentioned in the village that you'd taken in an injured man, I thought perhaps that I could return your kindness in some way, now that I am so much better off than I was."

The woman looked at her, flustered, taking in her quality clothing, and the footman standing behind her, as well as their load of baskets. After a moment she spoke, standing aside to let them enter.

"Mrs Canfield, isn't it? I heard your life had taken a turn for the better, with your little grandson an Earl now! Come in, come in, and set your burdens down. And please, call me Jess - no need to be all formal." They deposited the baskets on the worn oak table, letting the door fall closed behind them, much to the disappointment of the dog. A man looked up from a chair near the fire, his expression uncertain. "Mrs Canfield, this is our guest. I can only introduce him as James, which is what we've called him, seeing as he wouldn't give us a name to use. Please excuse him from standing, for his leg's not quite healed yet, and getting up and down is still difficult for him."

The man nodded, almost bowing in place.

"I'm pleased to meet you, Mrs Canfield."

His words were pleasant, but he looked uncertain, a little nervous, and Jane wondered why. She pushed the thought aside – there would be time to explore the reasons for that, later.

He was a well-made man, young – early twenties if she had it right – and his clothes, though having seen hard use of late, were obviously of fine quality originally.

As he looked up at her, the door opened again, as Mr Carver came into the house. The sunlight streamed in through the door, a beam of light across the room, and fell full across the man's face. Jane almost gasped aloud. For the face thus revealed clearly was like a younger echo of Nicholas, and the eyes that met hers were the same brilliant spring green.

In that instant, she had no doubt at all that she beheld Nicholas' missing son. She steadied herself, and turned back to the Carvers, unpacking the baskets, and pulling out the food she'd brought. Joe Carver watched with wide eyes, then spoke.

"Mrs Canfield, there was no need. We have enough."

"Ah, but Mr Carver, there is a difference between just enough, and a true sufficiency. When I had need, you helped me – and now I saw a chance to help you, when you are already helping someone else in need. Please accept this as a small recompense for the generosity that you always show."

Joe looked a little abashed, and shuffled his feet on the spot.

"Well, if you put it that way…"

"I do. Now, where can we put all of this away?"

Jess came forward, and the abundant food soon disappeared into storage boxes and cupboards, all but some bread and cheese, and a large crock of ale, which was left out for everyone to partake in. By the time it was done, and everyone settled onto the few chairs or the bench beside the table, formality had been completely forgone. Jane found it a relief, to be simply an ordinary person – for she was still not at all used to being treated as if she was somehow above others.

Jess, it turned out, made beautiful blankets from the wool of the two goats, dyed with dyes made from the plants in the forest and her garden – the blanket over 'James' legs was duly admired, and he relaxed enough to comment on how warm it was, and how much he had appreciated it, as his leg slowly healed. Jane, listening to him, could hear the echo of Nicholas in his tone and attitude. She smiled, thinking of it.

But, if she were to discover the truth of why he was hiding here, not admitting to his identity, she would need a chance to speak to him alone – how on earth was she to arrange that?

As it happened, circumstances conspired to provide the chance she needed. Joe asked Potts to assist with moving a log, which, whilst he could cut it in place, was awkward. It was a two-man job to move, but once moved would be far easier to cut. As Joe and Potts left the cottage, Jane and Jess were speaking of Daniel, and his insatiable desire for new and interesting toys.

"Mine are grown and gone to live in the big towns, but I remember that stage well. I've still got boxes full of the wooden toys Joe made for them, stored away in the little shed!"

"I think all children are similar at that age."

"Oh yes, definitely. If Daniel is like that, would you like me to dig out those boxes, and see if there's something he'd like?"

"That would be wonderful!"

"I won't be long, I'll just go and find them."

And suddenly, Jane found herself alone with 'James'. She turned to him, choosing her words carefully.

"Now that we are alone, I must ask you a question. I'll do it now, in private, for I suspect you won't want to answer."

"A question?"

He kept his voice light, but his whole body had tensed at her words.

"I believe that I know your true identity. I believe that you are Gervaise Belmont, Viscount Woodridge – is that correct? I know that you have refused to tell the Carvers your identity, and I must assume that you have good reason for that, but I have good reason to need to know the truth."

He took a deep breath, glancing around the quiet room. She wondered if he would answer, but simply waited.

"I... yes, that is my name. But please, I beg you, do not reveal it to anyone. I must stay hidden, or my life is in danger. I am grateful to these people, for without them I would most likely have ended my life lying on the forest path, and I would not bring those who hunt me down upon them. But... what reason have you to need to know?"

She nodded at his words, for they confirmed everything.

"Your father has been searching for you, for the many weeks since you disappeared. He is staying at Windemere Towers, not far from here, and his old friend, the Duke of Windemere, is assisting in his search for you. Your father is distraught, and I think that he has come to believe that you are dead, that he will never see you again. It is destroying him. Surely he could protect you from whoever hunts you?"

Gervaise laughed, a sharp, brittle sound, and shook his head.

"I am a fool, three times over. I have gambled myself so deep that unless a miracle comes about, there is no escape. And whilst there is a possible miracle in my future, if a ship manages to find its way back whole, from India, the moneylenders have lost all patience with me. And the men they send to punish those who do not pay are not kind. They will happily kill me, or close to. And I cannot pay. Nor will I ask that of my father – he was right when he called me a fool, but my stubbornness made me defy him. I must face the fate I created for myself. But I will delay the inevitable as long as possible. I beg you, do not tell him that I am here, promise me that!"

"If you are quite certain... then yes, I promise. But it will be very hard for me to see your father's despair, and not tell him. You place me in a most cruel position."

"I regret the need to do so, and I am more grateful than you can imagine for your forbearance. Perhaps, if my planned miracle does occur, it will be some recompense for him, even if I am, by then, truly gone."

"Do not speak so! Surely, there will be a way to evade such a fate, once you are whole again."

"I pray that is so. But I am not hopeful."

They fell silent as the door opened, and Jess carried in a large box of toys – all hand carved, and where needed, dressed in garments made from the beautiful wool she spun. Jane allowed herself to be drawn into sorting through them, but the despairing tone of Gervaise's words stayed with her. In that moment, she pitied him, trapped in a chair, barely able to stand or walk, hunted, and forced to be away from those who cared for him. He was extraordinarily lucky that Joe Carver had found him, or he might, indeed, have been dead – but was this hidden life much better?

Later that afternoon, as they walked back through the forest, Potts now laden down with baskets full of children's toys, Jane pondered the situation. How could she not tell Nicholas?

Yet how could she tell him, and break her promise to Gervaise? There was no good answer. She would simply have to see what happened, to look for ways to help. Perhaps, if she could get Nicholas to tell her more about Gervaise, she might be able to assess whether the threat to his life was as great as he seemed to believe.

Of course, getting Nicholas to talk to her required seeing Nicholas. Which had not happened since *that kiss*. Well, the toys gave her an excuse to go up to the Towers, where she would surely meet him. It was not a very good plan, but it would have to do for now.

Chapter Eight

The next day, Jane found herself still unsure. She had left the toys with Mrs Barnes, the housekeeper, to have the dust of years of storage cleaned off them, before they were given to Daniel. So, pending her excuse to visit the Towers being ready, she went walking down through the gardens, to sit at the folly and read, ostensibly to keep herself busy, and avoid the loneliness that was so much more noticeable in the house, but actually, if she was honest, in the hope of seeing Nicholas.

Perhaps that hope was foolish, but she could not shake it, any more than she could make herself actually read, rather than sit dreaming of Nicholas' kiss. Nothing could wipe that from her memory, or change the fact that she wanted to experience it again.

She picked flowers, and spun them in her fingers, she wove them into chains, and cast them into the stream with wishes, just as small children did, and, all the while, she watched, hoping. Eventually, past all expectation, her hope was rewarded.

Nicholas came walking along the path by the stream, tossing pebbles into the water, just like small boys did. Jane could not help but smile at the sight. His eyes met hers when he was still quite some distance away, and everything else seemed to fade away around her. Now that she saw him again, the resemblance between Gervaise and his father was strikingly obvious – especially the eyes.

How could she not tell him? But, how could she? She did not know.

He stopped in front of her, looking down, and she drank in his presence, acutely aware of how much she had missed him, in their few days apart. Neither of them spoke, for words seemed unnecessary, when their eyes said so much. Finally, she dragged her eyes from his, gathering her skirts to one side, and waving him to the seat beside her.

Time passed, in which she was acutely aware of his warmth beside her, of the sound of the stream, of the singing of the birds, and of the soft breeze in the trees. The world seemed drawn sharper and brighter than ever before. After some time, he spoke, his voice low and soft, but, as always, rich and resonant, vibrating in her bones, in her soul.

"Jane... can you forgive me? I have no excuse for stepping beyond the bounds of our agreement. I will understand if you do not wish to continue our... conversations, after what I did..."

She turned to him, astounded. Why did he think that his kiss was something potentially unforgiveable? What should she do? Did he expect her to react like some highborn lady, and be offended by his actions? She did not know how to act like a highborn lady...

And... why would a man do such a thing, kiss a woman, if he

was not serious about his intent, and at a point where he expected her to respond favourably? She felt her cheeks flush with embarrassed confusion. Was he, then, not serious, if he could so easily suggest that she might refuse to speak to him?

Was her attraction to him not returned as strongly as she had thought that kiss indicated? Perhaps it was best that she made herself clear, without openly declaring how engaged her feelings had become.

"Nicholas, I am not a highborn lady with fine sensibilities, nor am I a green girl. I do not see your actions as something so terrible that they require forgiveness. And our agreement… to my memory, it had nothing in it about the expression of affection, only a constraint on bringing the strains of the outside world into our space. I see no reason not to continue with our conversations."

That was as direct as she could be, without exposing herself to the risk of rejection. She watched him, waiting for his response, deeply uncertain. His hands lay on his knees, his fists clenched, as if he fought some internal fight, his eyes held hers, and a cascade of emotions flitted across his face. She did not understand what she saw, what struggle he fought internally. But she could not simply let him suffer so. She reached out, taking his hand in hers, gently uncurling his fist, and twining her fingers through his.

He released a sigh, tension suddenly leaving him, as if he had given in to something, had simply stopped fighting. His other hand came up, to brush her hair aside from her brow, and to slip down to cup her cheek.

Her breath caught, and her heart beat far faster than it should. He drew her to him, and she went, willingly, suddenly desperate in her desire for the touch of his lips.

The kiss began butterfly soft, and deepened into something far more, with an intensity that stole her breath completely. Warmth spread through her, and desire rose – a desire she had not felt, nor even considered, since some time before her husband's death.

When they finally drew apart, his hand still held her cheek, and he smiled, his spring green eyes holding hers.

"And am I still forgiven, now that I have doubly stepped beyond the bounds of normally acceptable behaviour?"

She laughed, suddenly carefree, giddy, and happy.

"Of course, you are. I believe that behaviour beyond the normally acceptable has much to recommend it."

He laughed in turn, and they sat in companionable silence, watching the stream flow past, their fingers still entwined, and a vast scope of possibility unspoken between them.

Jane ached to tell him about Gervaise, but her promise not to stopped her. Let that wait, let there be a time, soon, when she could convince Gervaise to change his mind. For now, this wonderful moment was enough, just as it was.

~~~~~

Nicholas sat, his body warm, and Jane's fingers soft in his, whilst his mind whirled with uncertainty. He still felt disloyal to Clara, and he still feared the pain that any association could lead to. But he wanted to kiss Jane again, and again.

Chapter Nine

"Mr Pensworth?"

"Yes, how may I help you?"

"Good day to you. My name is Manning. I deal with the accounting for Morton Empire Imports. I believe that you are man of business for one of our investors, Viscount Woodridge?"

"I am, indeed. The Viscount is out of town, but left me instructions, for when this day arrived. At least… you are here because the ship has returned, are you not?"

"Yes, that is correct. The ship has returned, with an excellent cargo, which has sold for a better than expected profit. I hope that Viscount Woodridge will be pleased - he is receiving fifteen times return on what he put in."

"That is excellent news! I have his detailed instructions on the disbursement of funds – do, please take a seat, and let us arrange things. I'll send my clerk for some refreshments."

"Thank you."

Manning settled into the seat, and things were soon arranged – some funds to be delivered to Mr Pensworth in cash, and most to be deposited to Viscount Woodridge's bankers.

~~~~~

The following day Mr Pensworth began a series of calls to the less salubrious parts of London, accompanied in each case by three hired guards – large men, and men he knew he could trust, from past experience. Each time, he carried only the necessary sum of money to address the particular debt.

The moneylenders were not happy about the guards, but soon calmed upon seeing cash in hand. In some cases, it took the application of threats to get them to write out the required receipts, and the declarations that Viscount Woodridge's debts were completely cleared. Mr Pensworth stood firm, and the guards' looming presence convinced the moneylenders that attempts to extort more than was owed were not viable. The receipts and statements were written, cash was delivered, and Mr Pensworth returned to his rooms, with one more thing crossed off his list of instructions.

When all of the debts were paid, the amounts remaining in Viscount Woodridge's bank were substantial, and Pensworth was happy in the satisfactory performance of his duty. Happy all but for one thing. He did not, at present, know Viscount Woodridge's direction. Last he had heard, the Viscount had intended to visit his friend, Lord Northdown, but Pensworth had expected him returned by now.

It was essential that he inform Lord Woodridge of the completion of the assigned tasks – but how?

The only option seemed to be a letter, sent via Lord

Northdown, in the hope that Viscount Woodridge was still visiting him, or that he knew Viscount Woodridge's current location, and could send it on.

Pensworth settled to his desk, and wrote a long account of his actions, and of the funds now available to Viscount Woodridge, and the fact that the receipts and statements from the moneylenders were now locked away in his safe, to ensure their availability if needed. Once the ink was dry on that, he folded and sealed it, then wrote a letter to Lord Northdown, asking that he pass on the enclosed missive to Lord Woodridge as a matter of urgency.

Two of the guards were then engaged to travel to Northdown Park, to deliver the letter directly into the hands of Lord Northdown. And, should he need to then send it on further, to carry it then wherever it needed to go.

Satisfied that he had done all he could, Mr Pensworth closed up his office for the day and went home.

~~~~~

Lord Northdown was startled when two large and somewhat rough-looking men arrived on his doorstep, asking after Viscount Woodridge. Once they explained their mission, and he had read the letter from Mr Pensworth, he looked at them with a worried frown.

"Gentlemen, Lord Woodridge never reached here. His valet, who had come on ahead, was rather distraught, and, after some days, went to Lord Amberhithe with his concerns."

The two men looked at each other, brows furrowed.

"Then we had best go to Lord Amberhithe with this too."

"I believe that would be best. Try his country estate — Amberton Grange — it is but two or three days ride from here. But first, let me offer you food and drink, and a place to stay — for it is too late in the day to travel on."

"Thank you, my Lord."

Three days later, the Butler at Amberton Grange looked at them with equal uncertainty, until they explained their mission. He too shook his head sadly.

"Lord Amberhithe is not in residence, gentlemen. He has expanded his search for his son, who is missing, and has gone to stay with the Duke of Windemere, whilst he does so. Perhaps you could seek him out there?"

"If you can give us the direction, we will do so."

The Butler was happy to provide details, and the two men set off again, beginning to be utterly wearied of this chase after a Lord who seemed not to exist, anywhere. And... the butler had said something about the Earl's son being missing — was there another son? Or had their task just become harder?

They would not know for a week, for the directions provided by the Butler would take them a long way from Amberton Grange. All this for a letter! They hoped that its contents were worth all this fuss. Still — they were being very well paid, in the end, it made no difference to them. They rode on.

Jane sat in the parlour at Windemere Towers, watching as Daniel played on the priceless rug at her feet. The first of the toys from the woodcutters were scattered everywhere, and he was thrilled with each and every one of them. Marion made sure that the toys stayed at least vaguely constrained, so that no-one fell over them. The Duchess, Sylvia, formerly the Viscountess Pendholm, was sitting on the floor with Daniel, helping him play. She was a most unusual woman, whom Jane had become fast friends with almost on first meeting.

Julian and Nicholas were discussing the ongoing search for Nicholas' son. It seemed that nothing further of use had been achieved, since the discovery of the Inn he had stayed at one night. Jane could see the pain in Nicholas' eyes, as he discussed where they might look next, spreading the area of search ever wider. He sounded dispirited, and almost beyond hope, kept going only by Julian's determination that they would succeed.

Jane's mind was in turmoil. She longed to leap up and rush to Nicholas, to tell him that she knew where Gervaise was, but she did not. She had given her word that she would not. How much longer she would be able to be true to her word, she was not sure, given how much it distressed her to see Nicholas so distraught.

A knock sounded on the front door, echoing in the marble hall of the entryway, and everyone looked up, startled – no-one was expected – who could it be? The Butler's footsteps tapped across the marble, and the slight creak of the opening door followed.

Moments later, the sound of more footsteps was followed by the closing of the door, and a tap on the parlour door.

"Your Grace, there are two... gentlemen here, with a letter which they insist on handing to Lord Amberhithe, in person."

"Show them in, Fordham."

The two men shown in were large, and somewhat rough looking, showing signs of the dust of long travel.

Julian waved them to a seat, and sent for refreshments.

"Gentlemen," he waved towards Nicholas, "Here is Lord Amberhithe. You may deliver your letter directly to his hands."

"My thanks, Your Grace," the larger of the two men spoke, in surprisingly educated tones, then turned to address Nicholas, "My Lord, the letter we bear is for your son, from his man of business, Mr Pensworth. As Mr Pensworth did not know Lord Woodridge's current direction, he sent it, originally, with an explanatory note, to Lord Northdown, who he believed Lord Woodridge had intended to visit. Lord Northdown advised us to seek you out, as Lord Woodridge had never reached Northdown Park. We went first to Amberton Grange, where we were told that you were here."

The covering letter, and the letter addressed to Gervaise, were passed to Nicholas, whose hands shook a little as he took them.

There was silence as he opened the covering letter first.

After a moment, he looked up, and addressed everyone.

"Apparently the letter to Gervaise is with respect to the satisfactory completion of some tasks which he had directed Mr Pensworth to complete – tasks related to funds. Mr Pensworth believes it critical that Gervaise hear of this immediately."

Nicholas weighed the other letter in his hands, as if unsure whether to open it.

Julian spoke gently.

"Gentlemen, Lord Woodridge is, at present, missing. Amberhithe, my friend, whilst this is addressed to Woodridge, I feel that you must open it, for there is the possibility that its contents have bearing on your son's disappearance. You cannot afford to leave any possibility for information untouched."

Nicholas nodded, and lifted the letter, breaking the seal and unfolding it carefully. The clicking of wooden blocks against each other as Daniel played was the only sound to disturb the expectant silence in the room.

Nicholas paused, giving a little gasp, then turned to the next page of the letter, and continued reading. Finally he looked up, the glitter of unshed tears in his eyes.

"Gentlemen, you have done me, and I must hope, my son, a great service in bringing this to me. Please, accept the hospitality of this house for the night. I will pen you a response to go to Mr Pensworth, so that you may depart tomorrow."

The men were shown from the room by the butler. The door closed, and Nicholas looked at the expectant faces surrounding him, and took a very deep breath.

"It seems that I have grossly misjudged my son. After my wife's death, he did not cope well. He assuaged his grief with drink and gambling, and I thought him hopelessly mired in that. We argued, and I cut off most of his funds, in the hope that he might change. But it seems that he was far more sensible than I believed – just too proud to tell me what he had done."

"What had he done?"

Julian's voice was soft, encouraging his old friend. Nicholas stared blankly at the paper in his hands, his voice a little shaky as he continued.

"He had actually won a large sum, and rather than pay off all of his debts, he invested it. He was trying to survive until the investment paid off – and I cut off his funds for survival – I feel such terrible remorse, now. I suspect that is why he went back to gambling, and why he ended up disappearing. I know that the moneylenders were trying to collect on his debts – that is what Gervaise told Hattam. I must pray that he has hidden himself somewhere, rather than that those thugs have found him, and done him harm. For, what this letter from Pensworth tells me, is that Gervaise's investment has, indeed, given a good return, and handsomely so. Pensworth has done as instructed by Gervaise, and paid off all of those debts, using the funds from the investment. And he has obtained signed receipts and statements of debt clearance from every lender. Gervaise is safe from pursuit, and a rather wealthy man. If we could but find him…"

Jane stifled a gasp at his words – surely, now, she could convince Nicholas' son to come forward, to come out of hiding? Or would Gervaise's pride hold him back in some way? She did not know, but she had to convince him to come away from the woodcutter's cottage, to reveal himself to his father. Nicholas continued speaking, unaware of Jane's reaction.

"If Gervaise is hiding, it is critical that we find him, so that he may know that he is safe – but how will we do that, if in near three months of searching, we have failed? We cannot give up – either he must know that he is safe, or I must know, for certain, if I have lost him forever."

Chapter Ten

By the next morning, Jane was sure of what she needed to do. She began her day with that purpose in mind, and, by late morning, she was on her way.

Carrying a basket of her cook's best pies, she made her way through the forest towards the woodcutter's cottage. All around her, the bright evidence of spring made the landscape beautiful, and there was birdsong everywhere, the birds seemingly unconcerned by her presence. She picked flowers as she went, laying them in the basket, that Jess might have something beautiful to brighten her home.

Now that she knew the path, it seemed much shorter than it had before and, soon, she was approaching their door. As she did, a wave of doubt assailed her. What if Gervaise would not listen? What if he did not believe her? What would she do?

She paused, thinking, and then, chiding herself for worrying about things that might never happen, she pushed herself into movement again.

As she reached the stoop, the same dog came trotting around the side of the cottage, tail wagging, as it watched the basket she carried with hopeful eyes.

She shook her head at it, amused, and reached out to knock on the door.

Moments later, it opened, and Jess looked at her, startled.

"Good morning Jess. I've come to thank you again for the toys – Daniel is obsessed with them – and I have only given him less than half of them so far! I've some flowers and some of cook's pies for you too."

"Why thank you! Please, come in."

Jess stepped back, and Jane entered the dimly lit cottage, where the only light came from one dusty curtained window. She was pleased to see Gervaise, just lowering himself into his chair by the hearth. That he was moving, however small a distance, by himself, removed a load of worry from Jane's heart. He turned those green eyes, so like his father's, towards her and frowned.

"Mrs Canfield, delightful to see you again."

His tone carried more of doubt and concern than delight, but Jane understood that. She smiled at him with as much cheerfulness as she could express. Placing the basket on the table, she settled onto the wooden bench.

"It is good to see that your leg is improving, James. Seeing you able to move by yourself is wonderful."

He grimaced, shifting in his seat.

"True, it is good, but I am still most limited in my movements – more than a tiny distance is painful, and my leg is so weak!"

She nodded, sympathetic.

"It will improve with time. You are lucky that Mr Carver is a man skilled in many things – if someone less skilled had moved your leg, you might be far worse off."

"Indeed, and I am most grateful to him."

Jess had been busily removing the pies from the basket, to store them away, and had fetched a small pottery vase for the flowers.

Once she had settled onto the other bench, Jane took a deep breath – there was no point putting off the difficult conversation.

"Jess, I must ask you to forgive me in advance – for what I am about to say will seem, I suspect, like the veriest nonsense to you, at least at first." Jess looked puzzled, but nodded to her to continue. Jane turned towards Gervaise. "James, I have also come here today to tell you something. You will remember our conversation on my last visit."

Gervaise looked worried, his eyes wide with fear.

"I do."

"I have been true to what you asked of me then. But I have news for you which I hope will cause you to change your mind."

He had relaxed at little at her first words, but now tensed again.

"I see. And what news might that be?"

"The Earl of Amberhithe received a letter yesterday. From a Mr Pensworth. A letter detailing the return of a ship from India, and the disbursement of substantial funds, according to instructions."

Jess was staring at them as if they were both mad, wondering, indeed, what any of this had to do with her guest. Gervaise had gasped at Pensworth's name, and released a great sigh when she spoke of the funds.

Now, he looked almost eager.

"A ship? Substantial funds? Enough to...?"

"Yes, and far more than that. It seems that a certain investment was far more profitable than even the greatest expectations. And that Mr Pensworth is a treasure, who has carried out his instructions to the letter, and more. The Earl is delighted – and heartbroken again. For he still does not know the current direction of the Viscount Woodridge, to inform him of this change in his fortunes."

Gervaise sagged back in the chair, his face white, almost with shock, and dropped his head into his hands.

Jane went on, her voice gentle.

"The Earl is distraught, more and more blue-devilled each day that passes. For he has no way to inform the Viscount that he is safe, and wealthy, no way to know if he will ever see him again. After the loss of his wife a short few years ago, the thought that he may truly have lost his son is leaving him a broken man."

Gervaise looked up, his face paling further at her words.

"Is it truly that bad?"

"Yes, it is, despite everyone around him trying to keep his spirits up. Will you not, having now heard this, change your mind? For if I understand it aright, this means that your reason for asking that of me is no longer valid, no longer necessary."

Jess looked back and forth between them, deeply confused.

Gervaise sat, deep in thought, obviously debating his next words. For this moment might change the path of his life.

Eventually, he looked to Jane again.

"If it is as you say, and I have no reason to mistrust your word, then it is time for me to swallow my foolish pride, and step back into my life. There are some things I will never do again – and I will tell my father so, much though it will gall me to admit that he was so very right."

"I am so glad that is your decision. It has been hard, these past days, watching him suffer, whilst I could not speak. But before anything else, I think that, now that it is safe to do so, you owe the Carvers an explanation."

"I do." Gervaise turned to Jess, who was, Jane thought, beginning to understand what was happening. "Mrs Carver, Jess – I will be forever grateful for your care, and your hospitality. Without that, I would, most certainly, be dead. You know that I have never given you my true identity, and, again, I am overwhelmingly grateful that you chose to still care for me, when I would give you no information with which to judge what kind of man I am. But I refused you that information for good reason. I was, when you found me, a man pursued. Pursued by men whose only task was to take whatever I had, to beat me for my inability to pay more, and to leave me dead, or almost so. If you did not know who I was, you could not suffer by association, if they came to this village, seeking me."

Jess gasped, her eyes round.

'Who would do such a thing? And why? You are, to my experience, a kind and well-behaved man."

Gervaise smiled a bitter smile.

"Now, that is true, but for some years I was wild and foolish, drowning my grief at my mother's death in gambling and drink, until my debts grew out of control, and I could not pay. I took steps then, towards a day when I would be able to pay – but when it took too long to reach that day, their patience wore thin. I ran, to hide myself away, and whilst running, fell – which is where you found me. Where my horse ended up, I have no idea – probably with gypsies far from here by now."

"But… what has that to do with what Mrs Canfield has told you? I admit to still being very confused."

"Jess, it is time that I told you who I am. My name is Gervaise Belmont, Viscount Woodridge. I am the Earl of Amberhithe's son. Forgive me for keeping it from you so long – I did it for fear that the moneylenders' thugs would hurt you for helping me, at a time when I was helpless to defend myself, let alone you."

"Oh my… what must you think of us! And you a Lord, living here in our tiny cottage!"

"I think that you are the most generous and kind-hearted people I have ever met. You have restored my faith in people, and given me some hope that the world is worth living in – hope that I have been sadly lacking in, since my mother's death."

Jess, lost for words, simply stared at him. Jane took the chance to broach her next request.

"My Lord, will you allow me to arrange for you to be transported to Windemere Towers, to see your father, and let him know that you live?"

"Yes. I doubt that I could walk that far, even in a week, and the track the log cart travels is blocked in two places, Joe tells me. So I will need to be carried, like some Maharajah on a sedan chair. I believe that I will feel utterly ridiculous – but, if that is what it takes to move me, let it be done."

"Good, then I will leave you to ready yourself. I expect to return in a few hours, to carry you away."

"Mrs Canfield... thank you – for being true to your word, and for your care for my future."

Jane blushed at his words, nodded, and went, in a hurry to be back, with men, and whatever litter they could arrange to carry him.

~~~~~

Three hours later, as the afternoon sun began to turn to that golden tone which bespoke the lateness of the hour, Jane led an odd procession out of the woods and onto the lane leading to Windemere Towers. She had returned to the woodcutter's cottage with Potts, Barnes and three of the men from the village, who were agog to see what had been hiding so close all the time.

Leaving Jess and Joe with more gifts of food, and a promise to visit soon, they arranged Gervaise as comfortably as possible upon the hastily constructed platform, and lifted it carefully. At times, they had to stop, and ask Gervaise to hobble a few steps with his makeshift cane, where the path was too narrow, or obstructed. Finally, they came forth from the woods, and he was able to simply lie there, exhausted, while they carried him.

As she walked along the lane beside the litter, passing the spot where she had first met Nicholas, Jane thought upon the rather momentous changes she had seen, since that fateful day. She regretted none of it, but, as she walked, it occurred to her that she had not thought beyond this moment.

For, once Nicholas and Gervaise were reunited, there was no reason for Nicholas to stay here. He would leave, going back to his life in London, or at Amberton Grange, and she would not see him again. Their conversations by the stream would become a memory to treasure, but no more than that. A terrible sadness assailed her at the thought. She pushed it aside, and focussed on the moment – on the joy that finding Gervaise alive would bring to Nicholas.

That she had allowed herself to become emotionally engaged with Nicholas was her own fault – she had always known that anything between them was impossible – she had just allowed a few kisses to distract her from the truth.

~~~~~

Nicholas, as usual, went out to walk along the stream, mid-afternoon. That Gervaise was now safe from all threat was wonderful, but knowing that made it weigh all the more heavily on his heart that he did not know if Gervaise still lived. Even if he was alive, which Nicholas devoutly hoped he was, where was he? Sadness ached within him, and he found himself looking forward to the moment when he would see Jane, to the time he would spend with her, forgetting everything else. To the kiss or kisses he might steal, while in that strange space they shared, where he could almost believe in love again. Almost.

He followed the now familiar path, and rounded the bend of the stream, looking towards the folly, fully expecting to find Jane there. But the stone bench was empty, the mass of flowers surrounding it somehow less bright without her presence. He stopped, and stood idly kicking pebbles into the stream, disconsolate. Perhaps, if he waited here for some time, she might come?

He felt, in that instant, like a foolish boy, attending his first Balls, hopelessly enamoured of one young lady or another, and always desperately waiting upon her appearance. He did not like the feeling. He hated seeming foolish. He was far too old for such behaviour.

Shaking his head, he forced himself to turn away, and walk further along the stream, towards the place where they had kissed that first time. Movement helped his state of mind, yet every step reminded him of Jane.

He missed her presence. When he reached the spot where they had kissed, he stood, watching fallen blossoms float on the water. It was beautiful, and peaceful, but it was not the same without Jane.

Sighing, he turned back, hoping that when he reached the folly, she would be there. She was not, and the gloomy reality of not having found Gervaise closed in on him again, moreso with every step he took back towards the Towers.

He found himself walking slower, and slower, the further he went. His life stretched out before him, seeming bleak. Without Clara, things had been difficult, if Gervaise was truly lost to him too, what was there left for him to care about in life?

All that he had worked for would end up going to his cousin, and all trace of Nicholas would have faded from the world.

He forced the thoughts aside, and made himself keep walking.

Chapter Eleven

Those carrying the litter bearing Gervaise were very glad to see Windemere Towers before them, now only a short distance further, along the gravelled drive, between the hedges of the formal gardens that spread to each side. Gervaise raised his head to see it, the whole situation obviously still seeming unreal to him, after months of living in the little cottage in the woods. Jane watched him, a smile on her face.

"It will seem strange at first, after so long hiding, but I assure you that you are safe, and that you will be made as comfortable as possible. I know that your father will be beyond happy to see you."

"It will most definitely be strange. This may sound most self-centred of me, but, whilst seeing my father again fills me with some trepidation, the thought of a warm bath was the thing uppermost in my mind, when I first caught sight of the house ahead of us."

Jane laughed, delighted that he was bearing up well, and that his sense of humour remained intact.

They passed the gates through the hedge to the garden which led down towards the stream, and Jane imagined all of the days that Nicholas had gone through that gate, on his way to meet her. Her sadness rushed back, but she pushed it aside, forcing her thoughts back to the moment.

They approached the front steps and a footman rushed out, calling back to another inside to arrange assistance. The crunching of many footsteps on gravel surrounded her, and at first Jane did not hear the voice.

~~~~~

Nicholas wound his way up through the gardens towards the gate which let onto the drive, near the front of the house. The fact that the day was fading from golden afternoon into grey evening seemed appropriate – his mood faded with it. The gardens were undeniably beautiful, but he struggled to appreciate them. He sighed, reaching out to open the gate, and stepped through. Shutting that gate felt somehow like shutting the door on a stage of his life.

In his slow trudge up the hill, he had come to accept that he might never see Gervaise again, and, quite possibly, Jane might not wish to see him. He did not know. Everything seemed dark and pointless. He set his feet on the gravel of the drive, and turned towards the house.

Looking up, the building was still lit by the last afternoon light, burnished gold, the old stone almost glowing with it, and the windows reflecting as if dipped in gold. The glare was blinding for a moment. He blinked. What was that ahead of him?

On the drive, not far away, between Nicholas and the entry

stairs, was a strange collection of people, close together, and apparently carrying something. Puzzled, and pulled out of his sad thoughts by the surprise of it, he hurried forward, keen to assuage his curiosity.

He reached them just as the door opened and a footman rushed out. There were five men, and they were carefully lowering something to the ground. They stepped aside, and he saw that it was a makeshift litter, and that a man lay upon it. Beside the litter stood Jane. His heart missed a beat, and his mouth went dry. Hope rushed through him in a cascade of sensation.

His eyes locked on the man on the litter, whose attention was towards the house. Could it be? But why on a litter? Nicholas was still moving forward, unaware of his own steps. He pushed through the men, until he stood beside the litter, immediately behind Jane. Jane spoke – but he did not hear the words, for the man on the litter turned at her voice, and Nicholas saw his face.

It was Gervaise. Rough, unshaven, dirty, and with his leg strapped up, and a cane beside him. But alive. Which was all that mattered. He had not known that he was going to speak, until he heard his own voice, rough with emotion.

"Gervaise…? Is it really you? Where have you…? What…?"

He fell silent, overwhelmed. Jane turned to him, and took his hand.

~~~~~

Nicholas' voice. Jane knew it instantly, even roughened with emotion.

As always, its warmth resonated through her, deep into her bones, her very soul. His voice stopped, sliding into shocked silence. She turned, to see him staring at Gervaise, who was returning the stare, equally struck dumb by the moment.

Unthinking, instinctively, Jane reached out and took Nicholas' hand, drawing him gently forward as the men assisted Gervaise to stand, leaning shakily on his cane. Jane spoke, quietly, whispering to Nicholas.

"I have told him of the letter, the money. He knows that he is safe. He will tell you his story. All that can wait, simply be glad for now, that you have your son back."

Nicholas nodded, only registering the words enough to comprehend the basics. Reaching Gervaise, Nicholas pulled him into a careful embrace. Gervaise's voice, against his shoulder, shook with exhaustion, and the release of months of fear.

"Father... I... I was a fool, twice over. Forgive me."

Nicholas pulled back, his eyes shining with barely contained tears.

"None of it matters to me – what matters is that you are here, alive. But for now, let us get you inside, with a bath, food, and a doctor, soon."

At that Nicholas, having seen how weak Gervaise truly was, simply scooped him into his arms, as if he were still a child, not a man grown, and carried him towards the house. A hovering footman gathered up the makeshift cane as it fell, and followed them.

Jane stood, watching them, until they entered the house.

It seemed final, the closing of that door, as if shutting her out of Nicholas life.

She swallowed the threatening tears, and turned to the men, instructing that the makeshift litter be taken to the stables, where it would, most likely, be broken up for firewood. Potts and Barnes set off to deal with that, and she thanked the village men, sending them towards home with the assurance that Lord Amberhithe would most likely wish to thank them himself, on the morrow.

Once they were gone, rapidly retreating from sight down the drive, Jane found herself alone. Silence surrounded her. She hesitated, but then turned, her steps slow as she walked back to the Dower House. By the time she reached her door, the last of the light had faded from the sky. She let herself in, as Potts and Barnes had not yet returned, and stood in the entryway. The emptiness of the house around her seemed a tangible thing, a reminder of the fact that she was alone.

Everyone she cared for had others, closer to them, to care for, and be cared for by. The life ahead of her felt like a gilded cage – available wealth and comfort, yet always separated from the real world in a sense, looking out at others' happiness. She went to the kitchen, and Cook took one worried look at her, then spoke.

"You just be sittin' down there at the table Mrs Canfield and I'll get you a warm cup of tea and a nice fresh pie. You look all done in. I hope that means that you brought the young man back as planned?"

Jane dropped onto the old kitchen chair, the wood polished by decades of use, and leant on the table.

"Yes, he's up at the Towers now, with his father."

"Good. But... I thought you would have stayed up there, Mrs Canfield, seeing as it's all your doing he's found."

"I..." Jane hesitated, trying to find the best way to say things. "Mrs Dobbins, I just felt like I would be intruding. Lord Amberhithe needed some time alone with his son, after so long fearing him dead. And, once it was done, I just felt so tired – I don't think I'm in any state for making polite conversation."

"Well then, you'd best just have your tea and pie, and have an early night. Sleep always helps."

Mrs Dobbins put the pot of tea, Jane's favourite cup, and a plate with one of her excellent pies, in front of Jane, and left her to it, busying herself about the kitchen, without talking. Jane was grateful, for conversation truly was the last thing she wanted, but the company was welcome, before she took herself back into the loneliness of the main part of the house.

Soon, she finished her meal, and took herself off to bed, as suggested. But sleep was elusive, no matter her tiredness. In her mind's eye, she saw Nicholas' face when he had first seen Gervaise – such love had shone in his eyes. In that moment, she had envied Gervaise. She was foolish to do so, for she had no right to Nicholas' attention, and to hope for it was an activity she should never have indulged in.

She had not wanted to intrude on their reunion, and, if she were honest with herself, she had not been able to bear the thought of being that close to Nicholas, and virtually unnoticed. She had become used to having his full attention when in his presence. Chiding herself for being a silly goose, she finally drifted off to sleep. But her dreams were full of spring green eyes and kisses in the gold of afternoon.

Chapter Twelve

Nicholas carried Gervaise straight to a bedchamber, which a maid was hastily preparing. He lowered Gervaise into the armchair near the window, and sent the footman, who had brought his cane, to fetch food and water. He sent another to summon Hattam and Felton, who, upon arriving, expressed horror at Lord Woodridge's state, whilst being overjoyed at him having been found. They immediately set to arranging a bath, and clean clothes.

Gervaise sat in the midst of it, looking somewhat dazed. Nicholas simply sat with him, unable to find a place to start with any conversation, just drinking in the fact that his son was right there, beside him. Another footman had been sent to fetch the local doctor – the one that Julian had, upon Jane's advice, decided to trust.

Three hours later, Gervaise was fed, washed, clothed in nightclothes suited to his status, and settled into a most comfortable feather bed. The doctor had been, and pronounced him likely to heal completely, perhaps with a slight limp.

The fire in the hearth was keeping the room at a pleasant temperature – warm enough that Gervaise was almost asleep. Nicholas looked at him, his heart full of gratitude and joy at his return.

"Gervaise…"

Gervaise stirred, and opened his eyes again, smiling.

"Yes, Father?"

"The bulk of the tale can wait for tomorrow, for its obvious that you are badly in need of sleep, but… can you tell me how it was that you came to be carried to the door this afternoon?"

Gervaise laughed softly.

"For that, Father, you can thank one stubborn woman, who cares very much for your feelings and your health."

"What do you mean?"

Nicholas had a suspicion that he knew, but he needed to hear the words – for in that instant, it came back to him that it had been Jane standing beside the litter that afternoon.

"Mrs Canfield. She had obviously heard something from the villagers of my existence, although I had never given my name to those who had saved me from dying alone in the forest, and saved my leg too. She is astute – I believe that she suspected who I was, from what you had said. She came to visit my saviours, and took the chance to speak to me alone. She rightly identified me, and I did not deny it. But I refused to allow her to tell you – for I still feared that the moneylenders' thugs would find me, and, given my weakened state, would not only hurt or kill me, but most likely those who cared for me, too."

"But surely, I could have protected you?"

"Perhaps – I can admit that now. But at the time I left London I was still too proud and foolish to tell you all. And I was not sure – I did not want them to find me, and hurt you too. But Mrs Canfield is stubborn. She gave me her word not to reveal me, although it hurt her to do so, for it was obvious that she truly cared for you, and did not wish to see you dismayed. And she kept her word. But as soon as the letter from Pensworth arrived here, she made the first excuse possible to visit me in the woods again, and tell me about it. But, even then, she did not directly reveal me, even though she spoke in front of my hostess – she allowed me the dignity of doing so myself, once I understood that the danger was gone. She again begged me to allow her to arrange for my removal to this house, for your sake, far more than for mine. Knowing I was safe, and therefore so were those around me, I agreed."

Nicholas sat for a moment, overwhelmed by what he had just heard.

Jane. He had Jane, and only Jane, to thank for the return of his son.

"You are telling me that, without Mrs Canfield, you would still be in a cottage in the woods, perhaps never venturing out?"

"Yes, that exactly. And I must tell you, though it shames me to admit it, it took hearing her description of how distraught you had been at my disappearance, and how desperately you had been searching for me, for me to see how foolishly proud and stubborn I had been, for all of the time since mother's death. I am sorry – sorry for all of the pain that I have caused you."

The sincerity of his words was obvious to Nicholas, and his heart swelled with pride, that his son was man enough to admit his failings.

"A year ago, I might have railed at you, for all of it. But this last few months of living without knowing if you lived or died have given me ample time for reflection. I was as proud as you, and just as unable to cope with your mother's death. I think it best that we leave all of that behind us. Although, I would like to hear the tale in full tomorrow, just so that I understand it all. For now, thank you – for what you have said, for being here, alive. For being you. Know that I am proud of you, Gervaise. Now sleep, for I can see that you struggle to stay awake."

Gervaise smiled at Nicholas, allowing himself to relax, fully, for the first time since well before he had left London. As his father turned to leave the room, he spoke again, wishing to say the words in private, knowing that his father needed to hear them.

"Father. I do not know what converse has been between you and Mrs Canfield, but I know that she is a good woman, who cares deeply about you. If you care for her at all, do not waste this chance. Mother would not have wished you to live the rest of your life alone and miserable. I would not wish that for you either."

Nicholas stopped, his hand on the door. He did not turn, he simply stood, allowing the depth of meaning in his son's words to settle in his mind. Then he nodded.

"Thank you."

He opened the door, and left the room. Gervaise smiled as sleep took him.

~~~~~

As Nicholas left the room, it struck him that he had not seen or heard Jane since that moment outside, when she had taken his hand, and drawn him forward to Gervaise. He had assumed, in that moment, to the extent that he was thinking at all, that she would follow into the house, that she would be there... later.

But she was not. Had not been. Where had she gone?

Gervaise's words had unlocked something in him, some tight and painful place he had kept hold of since Clara's death. In the light of the last few hours, his thoughts of the last few months seemed foolish, and excessive. He had not, in the end, lost Gervaise. Those dark thoughts, where he feared all love, assuming that it would end in pain, now seemed overly dramatised and unreasonable. But the way he had felt, when with Jane – that, when he looked back, was the only time that he had been rational.

The feelings he had for Jane were far deeper than he had admitted to himself. And Gervaise was right – he should not waste such a chance. Clara's last words to him, exhorting him to find love again, to honour her by being happy for the rest of his life, came back to him now, as if she whispered in his ear. He could almost imagine her telling him to stop being a fool. He straightened his shoulders, and strode down the hallway, to seek out the footman who had opened the door for them, and ask where Jane had gone.

"Mrs Canfield, my Lord? She did not come into the house. She saw the men who carried your son on their way, and then I believe she returned to the Dower House."

"Thank you."

Tomorrow. He would go to her tomorrow. He would not disturb her rest now, for it was late, but tomorrow, he would see her and, somehow, he would tell her how he felt.

He would risk being rejected – for he was not, entirely, certain of how she felt towards him - but he was full of hope. She had, after all, not rejected his kisses, and she had, most cleverly, discovered his son's hiding place, when all else had failed. And Gervaise said she had done so for him – did she truly care as much as Gervaise thought? Nicholas certainly hoped so.

Once he had eaten, and spent some time with Julian over a glass of port, Nicholas took himself to bed, suddenly feeling the tiredness borne of months of fear roll over him like a tidal wave.

~~~~~

The following morning, Nicholas rose, dressed with unusual care, and went first to see Gervaise, who looked much improved for a good night's sleep on a soft bed, in a warm room. Once he was assured that Hattam had settled into the adjoining valet's room, attached to the dressing room, and that Gervaise was receiving all the care he should be, Nicholas went to break his own fast.

He was nervous, he realised. It reduced his appetite, and made him disinclined to conversation. If he had seen another man reacting as he was, he would have been amused – now that it was himself, he found it rather more difficult to laugh. He could not, in good conscience, go to see Jane too early. That would be impolite in the extreme. But all he wanted to do was rush out the door.

He forced himself to wait, to settle and read until a suitable hour. Julian and Sylvia regarded him with an almost indulgent air, sharing a smile between them as they left him to the quiet of the library. One would almost think that they knew of his intentions. Perhaps they did.

The thought was not reassuring – was he so obvious?

Once the hour finally crept past midday, Nicholas rose, gathered up his hat and coat, and set off down the drive towards the lane to the Dower House. It felt odd to be seeking Jane that way, rather than through the gardens and along the stream. But for this day, some formality seemed called for.

As he traversed the path that led to the front door of the Dower House, he looked at the beautiful gardens surrounding it from a wholly new angle. They did not disappoint. Whoever had designed these gardens was skilled, and the current gardeners maintained them perfectly. He looked over the hedge to his right, and saw Jane, some distance away, surrounded by roses and trailing flowering vines, which had been trained over a shaded pathway, beside which a bed of mixed coloured flowers lay.

He paused, caught by how beautiful she looked, as vibrant as the flowers that surrounded her. He continued, and discovered a small gate, set into the hedge. All thought of formality fled – his only thought was Jane. He opened the gate, and stepped through onto the rich green grass of the gardens.

His steps were silent on the grass, and she was not aware of his presence until he was almost upon her. She looked pensive, a flower in her hand, which she twirled idly, as she had the red flower on the first day he had seen her at the folly.

He stopped, simply watching her for a moment, his heart swelling with the intensity of his feelings for her. He stepped onto the finely gravelled path, and she turned suddenly, startled by the sound so close. Her hand went to her breast, and the flower fell from her fingers. Nicholas bent, and retrieved it, offering it solemnly to her with a bow.

She smiled, laughing, and took it, returning him a curtsey.

"Nicholas, you startled me so! I did not expect you..." she waved her hand around, indicating the direction he had approached from, "here."

"I do apologise for surprising you. I wanted to see you, to be sure of seeing you. I thought... I thought that approaching from the front of the house was, perhaps, a more certain way to do so."

She laughed again, shaking her head.

"I am sure that, if you wanted to find me, you would, regardless. For we seem to have strayed ever farther from our agreement to keep the rest of life apart."

"Does that distress you, Jane?"

"Only a little. For I find that I am happy to see you, no matter the context."

At her words, his heart beat faster, and he felt flushed, suddenly terribly nervous again.

He stepped forward, until he stood very close to her, reaching out to take her hands in his. He took the flower, and slipped in into her hair, before returning his grasp to her hand. She looked at him, wide eyed, uncertain. He smiled, lifting her hands to his lips, to kiss them gently.

Her breathing was uneven, and a flush rose to her cheeks.

He thought it made her even more beautiful.

"Jane..."

"Yes, Nicholas?"

Her voice was soft, breathy. He swallowed, then plunged on.

This was not a time to hesitate.

"Jane, I want to thank you – for giving me back my son, more, for giving me back my life, for helping me to see that the world is not a dark and lonely place, unless I make it so. Thank you for simply being you – for you are a more wonderful woman than I ever deserved to meet. I have realised that I have come to care for you deeply, far more deeply than I ever expected, far more deeply than I ever admitted to myself – until last night. I can lie to myself no longer – I would be more than a fool to do so. I love you, Jane. I never thought to love again, but I do – I cannot help myself, even if I wanted to – which I don't. Could you... could you ever come to care for me Jane, as more than a friend, more than someone to share a stolen kiss with, in a time outside of real life?"

She stared at him, her mouth a little open in a silent 'oh!', her eyes wide. Her hands shook in his. He waited, almost shaking himself, his future now cast into her command. He was afraid, terribly afraid, and yet he could not, truly, imagine a world in which she was not his.

"Nicholas... I... it is not a matter of coming to care for you that much. For I already do. I love you, Nicholas, and I think that, in some way, I have done so from that first moment that you lifted me up from a bed of grass and flowers."

He discovered that he could breathe again. She had said... she had said that she loved him! The world seemed to spin around him and he was filled with a kind of delirious joy.

"Then... Jane... will you marry me? I cannot imagine living without you..."

She gave a strange gasp, on the edge of laughter, and nodded, the flower in her hair shedding petals as she did.

531

"Yes, oh yes, Nicholas! People will talk, for I am so far below your station in life... but... if you are willing to face that, then I will proudly be your wife."

"I care not for the approval or disapproval of the *ton* – all I care for is you, and making you happy."

He pulled her into a close embrace, and her hands naturally slipped around his neck, as his slid around her waist. His lips came down upon hers, and the kiss was filled with far more intensity and passion than any kiss before it. She surrendered to it, melting against him, her mouth on his as hungry as his on hers. He tightened his arms around her, lifting her off her feet and spinning around, allowing his joy to drive the movement. In moments he was giddy, but he did not care – he had not felt so free or happy for many years – not since before Clara's illness began.

She clung to him, and their lips parted a moment, as they both succumbed to joyous laughter. He spun, and the giddiness intensified, until his foot caught on the edge of the flower bed, and they tumbled, laughing harder, to land amongst the flowers.

He looked at her, and saw her, again, as he had that first day. There were flower petals in her hair, and scattered on her dress – she looked, as she had then, like a young girl, who knew the joy of spring but had yet to discover the pains of the world. He bent to kiss her again, as they lay there, gently, slowly, savouring every second of it. When they broke apart this time, he smiled, a lazy smile full of happiness. He could not resist.

"I think that you will always look best amongst flowers – preferably with flower petals in your hair."

Jane laughed at his words. She seemed to be doing very little but laugh, and kiss Nicholas, but that seemed, in that instant, the best possible combination of things to be doing. She felt as if she was 17 and discovering love for the first time. This was so different from the love she had shared with Peter – perhaps age allowed one to appreciate things more.

She had been shocked when he appeared in the garden, and, despite her certainty that he would leave soon, now that Gervaise had been found, she could do nothing but smile at him. When with Nicholas, it seemed, it was impossible for her to retain any sense, or any doubt. And then... then he had shocked her to the core, by saying that he loved her! She had hoped, but... to have it confirmed was beyond wonderful. When he had been so honest about his feelings, she could do no less – she was far too old for blushing dissembling – and had hoped for those words for far too long to hesitate.

Now, as she lay amongst the flowers, she felt dizzy – and not just from being spun around in his arms, but from joy.

This feeling was utterly intoxicating. They lay there amongst the flowers for some time, allowing the truth of it to settle around them, like the scattered petals. They would have time – the rest of their lives. Neither would have to be alone and lonely. She could imagine nothing more perfect than life with Nicholas.

Eventually, though, her practical nature asserted itself.

"Perhaps we should rise. Our clothes will have suffered, and I suspect that your valet may never forgive you. The gardener will certainly not forgive us! And... I think that I want to rush up to the Towers and tell everyone our news. Is that silly of me, to want to behave like a green girl?"

Nicholas laughed again, easing himself out of the flowers, and offering his hand.

"Not silly at all. I find myself in complete accord with that plan."

Epilogue

The news had been received with enthusiasm by everyone, and, when the banns were called in the Bridgemere Village church, all of the villagers were agog at the news that another 'one of their own' was to become a Countess.

Jane still walked to the village, and insisted that they all still call her Jane, for, she reminded them, she was still the same person they had known for so many years.

At the end of the month, as spring moved towards summer, the church was crowded with family and friends, and the residents of the entire district.

There were flowers everywhere, a kaleidoscope of colour.

In contrast, Jane wore a dress of a simple dark cream shade, which made her stand out dramatically against the vibrant tones of the flowers. Everyone agreed that it was the most beautiful wedding they had ever seen, with much sighing over how obviously in love the bride and groom were.

When it was done, as they left the church together, Nicholas pulled a few bright red flowers from the arrangements they passed, and tucked them gently into Jane's hair. They shared a secret smile between them, only they knowing why he had done so. As they stepped out of the door, Gervaise stood to one side, carefully supporting himself with his new, and far more impressive cane, whilst Hattam hovered nearby, in case he was needed.

Gervaise stepped forward.

"Father, I am so pleased to see you happy – and you also, Jane. May your days be filled with joy from now on."

Nicholas and Jane both embraced him, and Jane's eyes filled with tears. They turned, and a cloud of thrown flower petals greeted them, from the townspeople. Laughing, they went to the carriage, which would take them to Windemere Towers for the wedding breakfast. Jane made no attempt to brush the petals from her hair or dress.

Gervaise watched them as they stepped up into the carriage, and felt an odd sense of relief – until that moment, he had not realised how much he had struggled with the change in his father, after his mother's death. Now, seeing his father again the happy, caring man he had been, Gervaise found his own peace with the world. His mother was gone, but Jane was a woman that Clara would have loved, a woman worthy of his father. If only he might, himself, one day be blessed with the kind of love that his father had found.

THE END

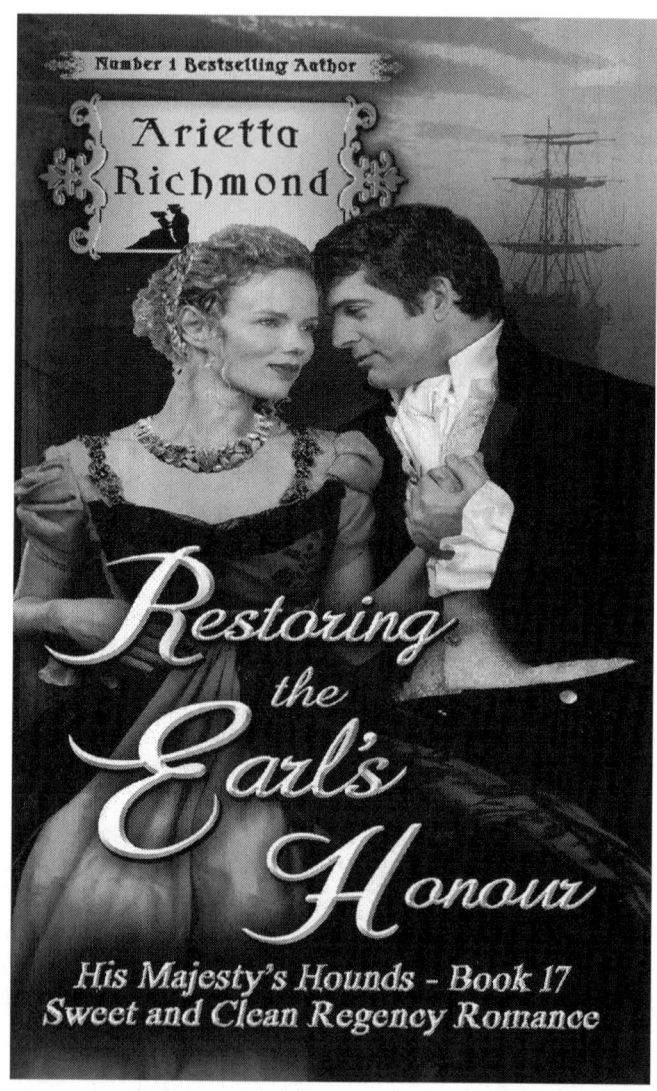

Number 1 Bestselling Author

Arietta Richmond

Restoring the Earl's Honour

His Majesty's Hounds - Book 17
Sweet and Clean Regency Romance

His Majesty's Hounds - Book 17

Sweet and Clean Regency Romance

Restoring the Earl's Honour

Arietta Richmond

ARIETTA RICHMOND

Chapter One

Drummond St. John had been called many things in his life, in recent years mostly 'Drumm' or 'Sin' – a name that came from the way people often said St. John – as if it was 'sinjun'. But the name he carried now was one he had never expected to bear. The Earl of Hungerwood.

The wind blew his dark hair about, despite the black ribbon that tied it, and the sail bellied out above him as the ship ran before the wind, carrying him back to England, to the home he had never expected to see again. That both his father and brother were dead still seemed improbable – he had seen death, more than enough for a lifetime, this past few years, yet somehow it still felt like something that touched others, not those of his blood. But the letter which had reached him in Georgetown, rather battered after months in transit, had been quite clear. Unbeknownst to him, his father had died, of an apoplexy, three years gone. His brother Hugh had become the Earl, stepping into the role he had been trained for. But now, near nine months ago, Hugh had found death too - yet another duel.

It was, Sin thought to himself, perhaps something he should have expected. Hugh had always been fiery, and fast to call a man out for small offences, or to stand second for others. Truly, it had been, in some ways, only a matter of time before he met his death. But Sin had hoped... hoped that Hugh might calm as the years passed, that Sin's sacrifice for him, for the family name, might prove worthwhile.

It seemed not. And now, it all fell to Sin, a heavy weight to bear – not only the dishonour he had shouldered near six years before, to allow Hugh to remain acceptable in the eyes of society, but this new dishonour to the name – the dishonour brought about by the fact that Hugh's death had been in a most illegal duel, a duel not about any high minded or important matter. No, the duel that had taken his brother's life had been tawdry – a duel about nothing more than the favours of an opera singer, an actress of little renown.

Bitterness soured his pleasure in the wind, in the sea. What he had thought would be his life had now been stolen from him, yet again, by his feckless brother's actions. All he had now was a name and a title stained with dishonour, estates likely groaning under debt, and all of the responsibility that came with it. It seemed likely that, once they docked in England, he might never set foot on a ship's deck again.

~~~~~

"Daniel is five now Marion – it is time that he met other boys of his station, that Society was made most clearly aware of his status as my heir. I do not want any of the gossip to survive long enough to taint his experience of life."

Marion Stafford, Countess of Scartwick, looked at her father-in-law sadly. She had known that this day was coming, that she could not hide at Windemere Towers forever. She no longer feared appearing in society, but she did not, in any way, enjoy it.

"Must we go to London for this Season? Can we not wait another year?"

The Duke shook his head – his expression was gentle – he fully understood Marion's hesitation, for her experience of society had not been kind. She had not been born to it, and, whilst his son had loved her unstintingly, the very fact of their different stations in life had made her every day difficult. In the end, that difference had brought about the duel in which Martin had been killed, not long after his clandestine wedding to Marion.

"I believe that we must. Whilst I would never seek to dim his childish enthusiasm for the world, he must begin to learn to deal with the *ton*, he must begin to make friends who will support him, towards the day when he is no longer the Earl of Scartwick, when, upon my death, he becomes the Duke of Windemere."

"Please, do not speak of your death! I pray that you have many more years with us to enjoy, that such a burden does not fall upon Daniel's shoulders before he is ready."

"I fully intend to be here for many more years. But that does not change my desire to see him well prepared."

Marion sighed. "If we must. I admit that my hesitation is for myself, more than for Daniel – there are those amongst the *ton* I still do not wish to ever see again."

"I assure you, my dear girl, that I will not allow them to disparage you in any way. It is time that you began to have a life for yourself again, not overshadowed by grief and fear, and not only dedicated to your son."

Marion shivered a little at his words, the memory of fear rising in her. But he was, she had to admit, correct. She should not let the actions of young fools, near six years past, rule her life forever, should not let it steal joy and peace from her heart.

"I am not sure that I know how to do that, how to let go of the past that much. But I will try, because you are right."

"Thank you, Marion. I am sure that you will not regret this. I would hope that you will find love again in your life, and the happiness it brings. My own experience proves to me that it is more than possible."

Marion nodded, knowing that he spoke the truth – for his second marriage had brought him much joy, as had her own mother's second marriage. If she found half so much happiness again in her life, she would count herself beyond lucky. But to find such happiness would mean meeting men, would mean courting. And of that, she was afraid. For, when going about in society, she would inevitably meet those who had made her life a misery before. And now that she was acknowledged the Countess, now that she had wealth and position, some might say influence and power, some of those same men might seek her hand. If they did, she would deny them.

She pushed her thoughts away from the past, and allowed the conversation to move on to other things, simple things, like new toys for Daniel, and new clothes – for, like most children, his ability to destroy clothing was extreme.

But she would, she knew, need to think about it all again, would need to prepare herself for what she would face in London, so that she could carry herself with grace and dignity, no matter what happened. At least she could be sure that she would not ever have to face the man whose blade had taken Martin's life, or the man who had stood second to him, for the former had fled the country, taking up a commission, and been killed at Waterloo, and the latter had also gone, to the Americas she believed. But the others... those, she would have to be polite to, no matter what she wished to do, in her heart.

~~~~

When Sin stepped onto the Portsmouth docks, it was a chill grey day in January 1819, with a light snow drifting from the sky, driven into muddied drifts by a sharp wind. The contrast to the West Indies was stark, and he shivered, long unused to the English chill. The world rolled beneath his feet, as his mind caught up with the fact that he was on land again.

Before they had docked, he had cleaned up, as best he could with the last of the fresh water on board, and tidied himself into a state where he had some hope of being treated as a nobleman. It was a poor echo of how he should appear, but it was enough to allow the quality choice, the Wind's Rest Inn, to rent him a small suite of rooms – or perhaps it was simply the gold in his hand that made that happen.

But once he had luxuriated in a warm bath, shaved, tied back his now clean hair, and then spent yet more of his gold on clothes of good quality and current fashion, the Innkeeper became most obsequious. He found it bitterly, darkly amusing that appearance mattered so much. Surely, honour and integrity should mean more – but no, his brother had proved that untrue, over and over.

He stayed there another day, quietly discovering the gossip from London, and attempting to find his bearings in the complex tangle of society's activities, after so many years away – he did not wish to step into the bear-pit that was the *ton* without at least some idea of who currently held power!

The bitter thought rose in him, that perhaps it would not matter – if they all gave him the cut direct, then dealing with society would not, at least at first, be required.

The next day, in a hired carriage with his meagre trunk of possessions, he set off for London. He assumed that his mother and sister would be there, at the townhouse, but, if they were not, then he would see the family bankers and man of business, then travel on to Hungerwood Chase. He was not, truth to tell, looking forward to seeing his remaining family at all. His mother, most likely, would immediately inform him that he should marry, and get an heir, for the sake of his duty to the title – an idea which left him utterly cold. The women of the *ton* were not his picture of a woman he would want to spend his life with – once, he might have seen them so, but no more. He did not want to deal with any of it.

But he no longer had a choice.

Chapter Two

When Sin finally arrived outside Saint House, he was relieved to see that the knocker was on the door. It seemed that his family were in residence. A street urchin rushed up to hold the horses, while the coachman set about unloading Sin's meagre possessions, and Sin flipped the boy a coin for his trouble.

As he stood at the top of the front steps, staring at the door before him, he felt a moment of fear greater than any he had felt in his years as a privateer. He pushed it aside – there was no room in his life for fear, if he was to restore the family honour. He lifted the knocker, and let it fall. The sound echoed through the marble entrance hall so strongly that, even through the closed door, he could hear it. That did not bode well – the more empty a space, the more it echoed. The sound suggested a lack of furniture, which, itself, suggested straightened funds.

Footsteps added to the echoes, then the door creaked open. Grey-green eyes, in a lined and aged face, considered him – blankly for a moment, then with dawning recognition. Sin allowed himself to smile.

"M… my Lord?"

"Yes, Foster, it's me. The letter eventually found me, and I have returned. Is my mother in?"

"Yes, my Lord, and most glad she will be to see you, if I may say so."

The aging butler stepped back to allow Sin to enter the house, a smile now wreathing his face, and waved a footman past him to collect the luggage which had been piled at the bottom of the steps.

"One moment – now that I know the family is in residence, I must pay off the coachman."

The waiting coachman grinned when Sin reached the bottom of the stairs, and dropped more than the agreed price into his hand.

"Thank ye, milord."

He sketched an awkward bow, and turned back to his carriage. Sin smiled again – one small thing at a time, he would make certain that his reputation was no further tarnished.

Once inside, he was shown to the small family parlour, where, he was informed, his mother spent much of her time. He studied the house around him – somehow it seemed smaller than it had been in his memory, and more wear was obvious. There was, indeed, less furniture than there had been when he had left, and fewer paintings on the walls. He wondered how deep the hole in the family finances was – for he had returned with a sizeable fortune, garnered from his share of the privateer's plunder – but would it be enough?

He pushed that worry aside, for now.

Foster tapped on the parlour door, and his mother's voice

called for him to enter. She sounded almost frail, and that shocked Sin – in his imagination, his mother had not aged – now he realised that, of course, she would have done so, and also most likely suffered from the stress of his father's and brother's deaths.

Foster opened the door, and announced, in his most imposing voice, "Lord Hungerwood!"

As Sin stepped past him into the room, there was a startled gasp, and a most unladylike squeal – which emanated from his sister, who was seated beside his mother on the couch. Faith lost no time in leaping to her feet and rushing to fling her arms around him. It was abundantly clear that she was no longer a gangly thirteen-year-old.

"Drummond! I was beginning to wonder if you would ever return!"

As he untangled himself from Faith's enthusiastic greeting, his mother's voice came to him – shaky, and almost uncertain.

"And I was beginning to wonder if you were still alive, or if I had lost another son. You did not write. But I am beyond glad to see you here, alive, and apparently well. Could you not have sent a note warning us, once your ship docked? The shock when Foster announced you quite gave me palpitations!"

Sin went to his mother, and dropped to sit beside her, taking her hands in his. She seemed far older than he might have expected, even had he thought about it – her once dark hair was greying to an elegant steely shade, and her face was lined with the evidence of worry. But her eyes were bright still, and glittered with unshed tears.

Ever so gently, he drew her into his arms, and held her, trying to say with his actions everything for which he had, as yet, no words. She stiffened a moment, then sighed, and relaxed.

They stayed that way for minutes, and Faith had the sense to say nothing. Eventually, Lady Hungerwood lifted her head, and sat back from him. Sin released her, and watched as silent tears slipped down her cheeks. He drew forth his handkerchief, and offered it to her. She took it with a grateful nod.

"Oh my! I did not intend to be such a watering pot!" She wiped the tears away, and smiled. "Faith, do ring for some tea – and perhaps some brandy."

"Yes Mama."

He found that he did not know what to say. For nigh on seven years, he had thought of his family, regretting that he would most likely never see his mother and sister again, and now that he was here, he found himself struck silent, the tumble of years' worth of tales to tell making it near impossible to start. Faith, having spoken to the footman who had answered the bell, returned to them, and settled into a nearby chair. He cleared his throat, and forced words to come.

"I... I don't know where to start. When I left England, I expected to never return, yet here I am. I expected never to bear the title, yet now I do – and I suspect that there is much work to do, to overcome my brother's actions, and his rather scandalous death – am I correct?"

His mother glanced at Faith, then met his eyes. He inferred from that glance that there were likely some things that Faith was unaware of.

"You are correct. We are... less well-off... than we used to be, I am afraid – not disastrously so, I believe, but still... I am glad that you are here, for I have not found it easy to deal with any of it. Two deaths in three years takes a heavy toll. But at least we are near done with mourning – for your brother died at the end of

January, so but weeks remain in which we must wear mourning colours. Whilst I would honour my dead, I cannot but admit that I am heartily sick of black, and grey, and dark depressing colours. And your sister is long overdue for a Season – she is nearing twenty, and will soon start to be looked at as a spinster!"

Sin looked at Faith – he could not imagine anything less spinster-like in appearance than his sister. She smiled at him, a mischievous smile that was still exactly as it had been when she was a child. Her voice was light and melodious when she spoke.

"Mother! I do not think my circumstance quite so dire. But I will admit to looking forward to the Season, and to wearing colours again. Drummond, I am so glad that you are here – I have missed you terribly. You seem... so very... serious? Imposing? I am not sure – but far more grown up and important than you seemed before."

Sin laughed, shaking his head.

"Seven years will change a person, as will privateering. You, my dear sister, have also grown up – rather a lot! You are, I must say, a beauty, and very different from the awkward child I said goodbye to. But... how have the *ton* treated you, given the manner of my brother's death?"

Both women frowned, and hesitated before speaking. That was all the confirmation that Sin needed.

Bitter regret twisted through him – that his brother's actions, be it the dishonour that Sin had shouldered for him, or the further dishonour that he had created in the manner of his death, should taint Faith's chances for a good Season, for a good match. And now that he was the Earl, would that be made worse, simply because he was himself – a dishonoured man? His mother spoke, softly, slowly.

"They are... less welcoming... shall we say, than they once were. But they have not turned aside from us entirely. I think that most are eager to see you return, if only to see what manner of man you are, and if the rumours of your adventures are true."

"Rumours?"

"Yes, rumours. When various of His Majesty's ships have come into port, there have been tales of the doings of many of the privateers, and your name has been mentioned. You have, by rumour, the type of dashing and dangerous reputation that makes foolish young women swoon."

Sin winced at his mother's words. That was something he had never considered – he had hoped to be quietly almost anonymous. "Oh." He could hear the shock in his own voice. "I expect that will complicate my life even further. I will just have to weather it."

His mother laughed.

"It will, at least, make it easier for you to find a wife – for, now that you are the Earl, you will need an heir – soon."

He winced again – there it was, the conversation that he had dreaded.

She went on, "But I will not press you on that matter so soon – there will be time enough, once mourning is done, and you have come to grips with the condition of our estates, and your new status."

"Thank you! I cannot say that the idea of finding a wife is appealing – I am sure that, in time..."

His mother nodded, and Faith did not speak, but her lips twisted with amusement.

The tea tray arrived, and Sin allowed the simple ritual of taking tea and biscuits to ground him back in this reality. Before he did anything else, he needed to arrange a suitable wardrobe for himself, and to make a chance to speak with his mother without Faith present, to discover the truth of the situation before he saw the family man of business. He would not speak yet of the funds that he had, of the fortune that he had amassed – he wanted to know how badly off they were, before he said anything of that at all.

~~~~~

Sin had slept deeply, the bed the most luxurious he had rested in since he had left England, all those years before. But the morning brought nothing but a sense of the weight of all that he now had to deal with. He dressed slowly, realising that, if he was to look as he needed to for the *ton* to accept him, then the first thing that he required was a valet. Rapidly followed by new clothes.

He went down to breakfast, his mind spinning with the list of things which he needed to do.

The breakfast room was warm, the fire in the grate burning brightly, but the only person present was his mother – not even a footman or maid. He frowned, and his mother noticed it.

"Faith is still abed – she would sleep half the day, given the chance! And…" she hesitated, flushing a little, as if embarrassed by what she was about to say, "we have few servants left – the cost, you know – so I am afraid that we serve ourselves at breakfast these days."

Sin nodded, unhappy to hear it, but not surprised.

"Then I will fill myself a plate. Truth to tell, after more than six years as a privateer, I am more used to serving myself anyway."

"That may be. But... it should not have to be. I am sorry – your father was never the best of men, when it came to money, but he was not the worst. Your brother, however, had a talent for spending which far outran his ability to ensure that we had income."

"I cannot say that I am surprised, Mother. Tell me truly, how bad is it?"

"I am not completely sure... I have tried to ascertain the depth of it, but Mr Wilton passed away not long after your brother, and we were left without a man of business for a time. A Mr Swithin took on Mr Wilton's clients, and I have found him to be exemplary in his attention to detail. But he is still sorting it out – he has been most kind, but it seems that, in his later years, Mr Wilton's... efficiency... suffered. You will need to consult with Mr Swithin. But there is debt, even after we sold off some furniture and paintings – thousands of pounds of debt – but not, I believe, tens of thousands."

Sin considered her words, taking the time to set food upon his plate, and coffee into a cup.

Once he had settled at the table, the food before him, he spoke again.

"Am I correct in my assumption that Faith is not aware of any depth of detail about this?"

"Yes. I could not bear to tell her how fragile our existence might become – I have been waiting for Mr Swithin to untangle the mess – I wanted to give her the truth of it, when I finally told her."

He nodded, his mouth full of food at that moment – food that he appreciated, after the simple and mostly unappetising fare that was the standard on a ship. Swallowing, he reached for the coffee. He would need to see this Mr Swithin today, but, before that, he could at least reassure his mother a little.

"I believe that to be a sensible approach. I will see Mr Swithin today, if you will provide me with his direction. But there is something you must know – the situation is now nowhere near as dire. Because, in my years as a privateer, I have amassed a substantial sum – and, unlike many of the men I sailed with, I did not spend it on pointless indulgence. If the sum required to clear the debts my brother has left us is as you suggest, then I have more than enough to deal with that, and still have funds for some time to come, whilst we ensure that the estates are productive. Some I carry with me, in gems and the like, but much is held on account with my bankers."

His mother almost sagged in her seat, the relief evident on her face.

"I had not dared to hope… I was afraid that we might not be able to afford to give Faith her Season…"

"She shall have her Season. And we will employ more staff again. Furniture – well, that is up to you – what do we need, and what do you want?"

"I… I don't honestly know – it will take time for me to adjust to this – but Drummond, I am so glad… I wondered what sort of man you would be, with all that was in the past, and with your years on the sea… but it seems that my fears were unfounded."

Sin smiled at her, although his heart was filled, again, with the bitterness of how futile his own acceptance of dishonour had been, when his brother had wasted that sacrifice.

He would, he knew, need to be exemplary in everything he did from now on, if he was to have any hope of restoring his own and his family's honour in the eyes of the *ton*.

"Thank you, Mother. I will try not to disappoint you."

The conversation lapsed as he ate, both of them deep in thought. As he finished his food, Faith appeared, still looking rather sleepy. He greeted her fondly, then took his leave, to set about the tasks of his day.

Chapter Three

Marion started awake, her heart pounding.

The stillness of the room surrounded her, moonlit where the curtains had fallen a little open, empty of everything but her – and her memories, transformed into dreams – dreams which had felt so real.

She shivered, even though the room was quite warm, the banked fire still giving off heat. The closer they came to the day when they would leave for London, the more frequent the dreams became. In those dreams, she relived the terrible days after Martin's death – the days when that crowd of arrogant young men he had thought friends had pursued her. Young men who did not believe that he had married her, who thought her a fancy piece, and called her that and worse, even while they demanded that she grant them her favours. She had been terrified, lost, unable to convince them of the truth. In the end, she had run – had, from their point of view, simply disappeared. But soon, she would see them again, would need to face them, and be polite.

For Daniel's sake, she would try, but she was not at all sure that she could do so with equanimity. Part of her was quite certain that, when confronted with one of those men, all of the years in between would fall away, and she would become again, in an instant, that frightened girl.

Sighing, she forced her mind to more happy thoughts, and snuggled deep in the covers. Sleep was slow to return.

~~~~~

"You look just the ticket, my Lord."

Sin looked at Carlton, his new valet, and took in his words. He considered himself in the large mirror which stood in his dressing room. The stark black and white of his mourning clothes suited him, he thought. Wryly, he concluded that it also made him look all the more dark and brooding – piratical, in fact, in a rather stylish way. His mother was right – young women were like to swoon at the whole effect. Perhaps, once the next week or so was done, and mourning was no longer required, he would continue to dress in this manner anyway, because it was simple, had a certain elegance, and he liked the effect.

"Thank you, Carlton. You are a deft hand with a cravat."

Carlton gave a slight bow, and turned back to tidying away the rest of Sin's new wardrobe. Sin left the room, and descended to meet his mother and sister in the entrance hall. Outwardly, he presented an appearance of calm. Inwardly, he was quivering with anticipatory nerves – it was the same sensation that he had felt, just before the privateer had closed with a prize – the expectation of battle, and of personal risk.

"Drummond! I must say, you look very dashing."

His mother's words were warm with approval.

"I give all credit to my tailor, and to my new valet. It appears that Carlton is talented with hair and cravats."

"Nonsense! No amount of good tailoring can disguise a poorly shaped man."

Faith's voice rang with the utter conviction of a young woman sure of her own judgement. He almost laughed – so, she had begun to study the shape of men, had she?

"Shall we go? The carriage is waiting, and Lady Templeton's musicale will be beginning soon – we must not be too late through her door!"

Lady Hungerwood's words caused Sin to quiver anew with that sense of battle being imminent – he supposed that his first exposure to the *ton* since his arrival could be considered a battle of sorts. Taking a deep breath, he ignored that thought, and offered his mother his arm, to lead her out to the carriage.

They passed quickly through the streets, their destination not too distant, and Sin could not help but watch the people and carriages around them as they went. His mind still half expected the raw new cities of the Americas, or the brightly coloured houses of the West Indies – London felt like a thing from his past, not his present. He would, he assumed, adapt in time, but for now, after years away, London was intriguing in its diversity.

Lady Templeton's residence was elegant – a tall townhouse with glittering light showing through every window, and a queue of carriages in the street, waiting their turn to let their passengers down at the door. When their turn came, Sin stepped down, turned to assist his mother and sister, then squared his shoulders and drew himself up. Now he would see. Would some of them give him the cut direct?

Or would the fact that he now held the title be enough to ensure that they simply treated him with frosty disdain?

The stairs seemed impossibly tall, and the queue of guests impossibly slow – he wanted this done with, wanted to know where he stood. For he knew, of a certainty, that beneath the veneer of politeness, the *ton* was a viper pit of gossip and secrets.

Finally, they reached the top of the steps, moved through the door, and were greeted by their hostess.

Lady Templeton welcomed him politely, if rather distantly, but her eyes upon him were curious, and he felt examined, as if he were some insect pinned to a board by a collector.

"Lord Hungerwood. So good of you to come. I believe that you are only recently returned from the... Americas?"

The slight hesitation made it quite clear that she well knew he'd been a privateer, and would soak up whatever tales he might tell – but was far too refined to ask. He barely prevented himself from sighing.

"Indeed, that is the case, Lady Templeton, I have been six years in those parts, and the news of my father's and brother's deaths was long in reaching me. I am... adjusting... to going about in society again."

"Then this evening is an excellent opportunity for you to reacquaint yourself with everyone of... influence..."

"Yes, my Lady, that is my intent – to renew my acquaintance with those who matter – like yourself."

Lady Templeton blushed slightly, obviously pleased by his words, and they moved on into the main parlour, as she turned to greet the next guests.

"That was well done, Drummond. Lady Templeton's opinion carries weight."

His mother's words were quiet, but reassuring – especially as a number of the people in the room had stilled, then ostentatiously turned away, when the footman at the door had announced them. But as many as there were who turned away, there were equally many who gazed at him with open curiosity – especially the young ladies present.

It did, indeed, feel like being in a battle – the uncertainty of whether each person before him was friend or enemy, and the feeling that he might be set upon at any moment, left his senses pitched to high awareness.

Faith made a little noise beside him, then linked her arm with his.

"Come, Drummond, you must meet some friends of mine."

She led him across the room to where a cluster of young women stood, whispering behind fans, the pale pastel tones of their gowns making them seem like a bouquet of faded flowers. He went, steeling himself to face their reactions.

"Lady Anne Sheldon, Lady Julia Westcott, Lady Margaret Thompson, Lady Phoebe Aldwood, may I present my brother, Lord Hungerwood."

Sin bowed to them, a little exaggeratedly.

"I am delighted to meet you, ladies."

The fans fluttered, and they simpered at him.

He could find no other word for it. Beside him, Faith stifled a giggle, damn her! One of the young women. Lady Phoebe, he thought, spoke, her voice soft and breathy.

"My Lord, forgive me for asking, but I simply must know the truth of the matter. It has been said that you were a… privateer… is… is that true?"

Sin was rather shocked at her forwardness in asking, but he supposed it was best to get this sort of the thing out of the way early – let the rumours be fed by his own words, not someone else's lurid imaginings. The other young women fluttered their fans, watching him wide-eyed, waiting for his answer.

"Yes, my Lady, it is the truth. For the last six years, that has been my life. It is not, I assure you, a life that I would recommend to anyone."

"But… my Lord, was it not exciting, dangerous and thrilling?"

Sin fixed her with a stern glare, feeling his lip curl in a bitter-edged sardonic smile. "Dangerous, perhaps – but exciting, thrilling? No, none of that – poor food, a hard bed, salt encrusted clothing, long months at sea, the risk of death – that is not my idea of a pleasant or exciting life." The girl looked fit to swoon with something which seemed part horror at his words, and part foolish admiration for a man who had survived such privations. He was, he supposed, being harsh – and, he realised, not entirely truthful – there was one part of it he had found worthwhile. "Although…" her wide eyes watched him, expectantly, waiting for his words, "I will admit to having developed a liking for the sea – the wide blue before me, the wind in the ship's sails – that creates a sense of freedom not found anywhere else."

She blinked at him, seemingly lost for words. One of the others – Lady Anne? – became brave enough to speak.

"But… is that freedom worth the privations you described?"

"Perhaps not, my Lady, yet it might well have been the

whole of my life."

"Then... regardless of the circumstance that has brought you back to Society, my Lord, I cannot but think that your life will be better for no longer being a privateer."

Sin gave the tiniest snort of self-deprecating laughter.

"I have not yet come to a conclusion on that matter, my Lady. Only time will tell."

Faith, finally realising that he wanted to escape, slipped her arm through his again, and smiled at the girls.

"My dear friends, I simply cannot let you monopolise my brother's time any longer – there are so many people I must introduce him to, so many he has not seen for many years. If you will excuse us?"

Giving them no time to reply, she turned him away, and led him across the room, towards a group of older people who stood talking quietly. He whispered to her, as they went.

"If everyone is like that, I think I shall go mad."

"Endure, brother dear, endure. If we are to be treated well by society, if they are to forget Hugh's bad behaviour, then you must deal with it all. You may scream and rant about it after we get home."

"Screaming and ranting is rather unlikely. But multiple glasses of brandy are a distinct possibility."

Faith gave a small laugh, and kept walking. He was, he realised, impressed with her wisdom – he did need to be unfazed by the *ton*, no matter what they said or did. Rumours about himself, he could accept, but if those touched on his mother and sister in any negative way, he would not be so tolerant.

They reached the group of older people, Faith provided introductions, and he was treated to frosty disdain by most of them – obviously, these people were of an age where they well remembered the scandal around his leaving the country. But they did not give him the cut direct, and they were, on the whole, pleasant to his sister. It was better than it might have been.

And so the evening went – a round of introductions, where he was greeted by either frosty politeness or thrill seeking curiosity, over and over again. Then a pause in that, while they all filed into the room where the musical performance was to occur, and sat through a lacklustre series of pieces. He took the respite from conversation willingly, even if the music was terrible. Then back to conversation and introductions.

By the end of the evening, his head was whirling – full of names and faces that he needed to remember – and aching from the effort of having maintained a calm and smiling façade, no matter what impertinent questions he had been asked, no matter what foolish young women had attempted to flirt with him. The carriage ride back to Saint House was broken only by one tiny piece of conversation.

"That went far, far better than it might have, Drummond. I can see that the years have granted you more wisdom than you had when you left."

The tone of his mother's voice suggested relief – had she truly thought him likely to still be a young fool? He simply nodded, and rested his aching head back against the padded wall of the carriage.

In another carriage, making its way home from Lady Templeton's musical soiree, Cecil Carlisle, Baron Setford, was quietly discussing the evening with his wife.

"So, my dear Anna, did you learn anything of use to us tonight?"

Anna looked at him, her lips curving gently into a wry smile.

"Not really. For once, there seemed to be none of those we are currently watching, with relation to any of your current 'cases', present. But... did you notice Lord Hungerwood, and the stir that his presence caused?"

"I did indeed my dear. I have been wondering when he might start to go about in Society. And how they might treat him."

"Oh? Why? What did you expect to happen? I noted that his past as a privateer, combined with his dark good looks and manner, seems to have the young women all swooning after him, but I admit that I found the rather frosty reception that he received from most of the older people puzzling."

"Ah. So you know nothing of the family, of the history?"

"Nothing. Should I?"

Cecil considered a moment – she might not like his answer, but he would tell her anyway. From Anna, he held no secrets.

"There was no reason, at the time, for you to know. Even though it touches on events you were close to. Hungerwood was a second son, and never expected to inherit. He left the country six years or more ago, under a cloud of disgrace."

"Disgrace? For what?"

"Everyone believes him to have been Second to Lord Jasper Sinclair, in the duel that took Martin Stafford's life, and to have pretty much incited Sinclair to call the duel."

Anna gasped, shocked – for she knew those involved with the consequences of that duel very well. Then Cecil's words echoed through her mind again.

"Believes...?"

"Yes. The truth of it is, it was the older brother, Hugh, who was the Second. Drummond, the now Lord Hungerwood, allowed everyone to think it was he who had been Second – both brothers were there at the time, and apparently Drummond took on the dishonour, to spare his family name. He left the country, and I suspect he had never intended to return. Hugh, his fool of a brother who was a rash hothead of a man, then went on to waste that sacrifice, by continuing to duel, and then getting himself killed – all over a tawdry actress, just a year gone next week. Drummond has a job ahead of him – the *ton* have not cut him completely, but that family's honour hangs by a bare thread. But from the look of tonight, I think he is solid and honourable enough to win out."

"I agree... but... Marion – does she believe he was the Second? And if so, what will happen, when they inevitably meet?"

"Yes, she does. And that is exactly my worry."

Chapter Four

The carriages were loaded, and all was in readiness. The early morning sun cast a soft gold glow through the mist that rose from the gardens and fields around them, and gilded the beginning leaf buds on the trees that lined the drive of Windemere Towers. It was a beautiful scene, but Marion found herself completely unable to appreciate it. Instead she felt sick in her stomach, almost shivering with dread.

Daniel was oblivious to his mother's mood, too full of excitement to think of anyone else too closely. He tugged at Marion's hand, with all the force that a five-year-old boy could bring to bear, attempting to drag her the last steps to the carriage.

"Hurry, mama, I want to go now! I want to see London again, I want to ride in the carriage. Now, please mama."

Marion took a deep steadying breath, and forced herself to calm. Regardless of her fears, she was going anyway, for Daniel's sake. At that moment, the Duke and Duchess arrived beside her, both smiling at Daniel's enthusiasm.

"Now grandson, you must have some patience. We will go in but a few minutes. Please do not drag on your mother like that!"

Daniel looked at his grandfather, his brow creasing.

"I don't like patience."

His voice was a little sulky, but he did as asked, and stopped pulling at Marion. She breathed a sigh of relief, casting a thankful glance at the Duke. Her father-in-law was the kindest man she had ever known, and doted on her son. Moments later, the last bag had been loaded, and the footman let down the carriage steps and opened the door. The four of them settled inside, the luxurious leather and velvet interior wrapping them in comfort.

All through the morning's travel, Marion stared out of the window, watching the early spring countryside pass. But all she could think of was what, and who, might await her in London. She had only spent a brief few months in London, since that terrible time after Martin's death – a few months in which she had mostly been hidden away, and had not needed to deal with the *ton*. This time, it would be different. This time, she could not hide.

Soon, the swaying of the carriage lulled the Duke to sleep, his Duchess also sleeping, held steady in the curve of his arm. Daniel slept too, his head on Marion's lap, and the carriage blanket wrapping him in warmth. The quiet was undisturbed, beyond the steady rumbling sounds of the carriage wheels on the earth of the road, and the occasional drift of birdsong, as spring led birds towards nestmaking. It brought no peace to Marion's thoughts. Over and over, the past replayed itself in her mind, especially those moments which had been full of fear.

Their faces were all clear in her memory, as they had been

then, laughing and leering at her, so full of their own arrogance and what she could only call greed. Would they look the same now? Would she recognise them instantly? Or might they have changed – might their weakness of character and unmannerliness be hidden beneath a veneer of civilized behaviour. She shuddered. It was as if she was back there, being grabbed at, and demanded of.

She remembered quite clearly the day that two of them had come to the house, and accosted her. If Perryman, her footman, had not been present, they would likely have had their way with her, no matter what she had said, for they were far stronger than her. Perryman had saved her – with the aid of a large marble vase, and a punch which would not have been out of place at Gentleman Jackson's. He had then unceremoniously dumped the young men in the street, and locked the doors against them.

What if they were still like that? What if they were at a Ball or Soiree, and got her alone somewhere? Her thoughts were not rational, she knew – for now she was the Countess of Scartwick, acknowledged and supported by many people of high rank in society – the chance of her suffering such a fate was slim – but the fear resisted logic, and she shivered as she sat there.

There was no choice. She would face her fear, and do as she must. She would be well supported, and, she hoped that, with time, the fear would fade. At least she could be certain of not having to ever see Martin's killer, who was himself now dead, or his Second, who was gone from the country. The others, she would find the courage to deal with, somehow. Finally, exhausted from the churn of fear, she also slipped into sleep.

The first week in London had passed quietly, with no attempt made to attend society functions. They had focused on getting Daniel settled, and quietly introducing him to some other families with children of a similar age. A pattern had been set, where, each morning, well before most of the *ton* were up and about, Marion, with the Duke and Duchess, and the assistance of a maid and the Nanny, would take Daniel to Hyde Park. There, whilst the adults, with whatever friends might be there that day, settled on blankets with some picnic food, Daniel, and any other children present would run wildly about, burning off that excess of energy which all children seemed to have.

Marion found it peaceful, Daniel was making new friends, and London was beginning to seem not so threatening after all. This particular morning, Marion allowed Nanny to run about, keeping the children in sight, whilst she watched the world around her, especially the others who had ventured into the Park early. The *ton*, she had discovered, made endlessly fascinating watching – their dress, their manner, the beautiful horses many rode, all were intriguing to watch from afar, even if, close up, Marion still felt completely out of place.

In the distance, she saw a man riding – he caught her eye, simply because he was not bright, unlike most of the dandies she saw about. This man wore stark black, relieved only by the white of his cravat, and rode a horse as black as his clothes. He moved with a spare elegance which was in keeping with his appearance, and the horse was of a quality rarely seen, with perfect gaits and a shining coat that spoke of much care.

He looked quite sure of himself, and yet, in so many ways, he did not fit in with what she was used to seeing. She wondered idly who he was, before turning her gaze back to where Daniel tumbled over the grass, laughing as he chased a ball. She rose, and went to him, scooping the ball from his grasp, and throwing it, to set him running happily again.

The man in black, on the glossy black horse, slipped from her mind completely.

~~~~~

Faith was just coming out of the breakfast room when Sin returned to the house from his ride. He had taken to riding every day, the need to be out and moving, doing something, driving him. At first, he had felt it keenly, his muscles long unused to any amount of riding after years at sea, but now, his body was remembering the way of it, settling into patterns created when he was a boy. He rode well, and was pleased with the horse he had obtained. Early in the day, the Park was at its quietest, and he revelled in the sense of peace it brought him.

"Drummond! I don't know how you can rise so early."

"Habit. And I appreciate the quiet. Especially when my day is like to be as busy as today. I must spend the day with Mr Swithin, sorting out the last of the tangle of papers that Hugh and Mr Wilton created between them."

Faith frowned a little.

"It... it will be all right, won't it, Drummond? There is enough money to deal with it? I... I can still have a Season, can't I? Oh dear, that sounds so selfish!"

Sin laughed, taking her hand, and squeezing it reassuringly.

"Yes Faith, there is enough. Had I not come home with funds of my own, it might have been rather difficult, but now, there are no major problems. You will have your Season, and the room full of gowns that no doubt entails."

She released a very large sigh.

"I am so glad! I was quite sure that things were worse than Mother was telling me."

"Well, you can stop worrying about that now. Now we just have to convince the *ton* that I am not a dishonourable reprobate."

He heard the touch of bitterness in his own words, and regretted it, as Faith tilted her head slightly to consider him. She spoke softly, carefully, as if he might object to her words.

"I never believed that you were, Sin. I worked out, long ago, that whatever had happened, whatever made you leave, could not actually have been of your doing. It was Hugh, wasn't it? You let them blame you for something he did, for the sake of all of us, didn't you? He was my brother, but I cannot say that I ever liked his behaviour – and I know that I probably didn't ever see anything like the worst of it."

Sin was struck, again, by just how wise his little sister had become. He swallowed, unsure of what to tell her, and settled on the bare minimum.

"Thank you for your belief in me, Faith. I won't speak of it in detail – it's the past, and cannot be changed. But yes, you are right – I chose to take the blame for something Hugh did – the actions of a second son are not regarded so much, after all."

She nodded, twisting her lips a little, thinking.

"But… now that you are the Earl, it is regarded seriously, and it's a problem? Is that why so many people treat you… coldly?"

"Sometimes, little sister, you are far too astute. Perhaps, one day, I will explain. But for now, it is best that you know nothing of it, that you act as you always have done, being open and friendly with the *ton*, as if there could be nothing ever, which they might be concerned by. The more truly you present that, the more strongly they will believe it, and the more hope I have of the past being forgotten."

Faith regarded him with some annoyance, then shook her head, as if shaking the feeling off.

"As you wish, although the curious part of me finds that deeply frustrating! You have always been honourable to a fault, Drummond. I really fail to see how anyone can miss it."

That did draw bitter laughter from him, and Faith raised an eyebrow at his reaction.

"That is funny – in the darkest possible way, my dear sister. But I thank you for your assertion of my character."

"Well! I only say what seems obvious to me! Will you be attending the Chesterton Ball this evening?"

"I think not. I can only stand so many events in a week, before I risk snapping impolitely at some simpering maiden. I don't know how you stand their company – they seem all rather insipid and, dare I say it, a little stupid."

Faith sighed.

"But you will come to the Norwood's event, in two days' time?"

Sin drew in a breath – he would have to attend, even though he wished not to – it was a fine balance between his sanity, and being seen and acknowledged by enough people of importance to improve the family standing.

"I will, although I do not look forward to it."

"Good."

That said, Faith took herself off to spend the afternoon preparing, and Sin went in search of some food, his ride having raised his appetite.

~~~~~

Nervous apprehension filled Marion, leaving her feeling decidedly queasy as she entered Chesterton House beside the Duke and Duchess. Sylvia, the Duchess, gently put her hand on Marion's arm, and whispered to her.

"Don't be afraid – we will be right beside you. The past is gone, this is now."

Marion knew that she was right, but it did not calm her fears – perhaps nothing ever would. Still, there was no option but to go on. Soon, they reached the head of the line. Lady Chesterton greeted them, all effusive welcome, and then they moved on into the ballroom, being announced by the footman stationed at the door.

"The Duke and Duchess of Windemere, and the Countess of Scartwick."

A few heads turned towards them, curiously, for Marion had not been about in society much.

She lifted her chin, forced her face to steady calm, and stepped into the room, as if she had always belonged in such a place. But in that instant, she longed for her mother. But her mother was still in the country, with her new husband, and would not be here in London for a month or more. The footman announced the next arrivals, and attention moved away from Marion. She breathed a sigh of relief, and allowed the Duke to lead them to a group of people on the other side of the room.

From there, the evening became a whirl of introductions, as the Duke and Duchess made certain that she became known to those of influence, and reacquainted with those she had met before. She was glad to find that Lady Setford, who she had known before when she was still Lady Farnsworth, was present, and greeted her with genuine affection. As the evening wound on, Marion began, a little, to relax. So far, she had not seen even one of the faces she dreaded, and people, if curious, had been kind and courteous. Somehow, she found herself amongst a group of younger women, not so far in age from herself. Their conversation seemed innocuous, mostly about fashion, and the most favoured gentlemen of the Season. She allowed herself simply to listen, to learn what she could of what went on in society now.

She noticed that the young woman beside her rarely spoke, but mostly listened, and watched the others, often with a slightly amused look on her face. She wondered why. As that thought passed through her mind, the woman turned to her.

"I have just realised that I have been remiss. No-one introduced us, and I have not told you who I am. I believe that I heard you announced as the Countess of Scartwick? I am Lady Faith St. John. I am happy to make your acquaintance."

"Yes, I am Marion Stafford, Countess of Scartwick. I am pleased to meet you."

It still felt wrong to call herself Countess, even after this long. But she would not avoid it – to do so would be to dishonour Martin's memory. She had a sense of familiarity with the woman's name – St. John – where had she heard it? She did not know, and pushed the thought aside for consideration later.

"You seem as disinclined to wax lyrical about fashion as I am, if I may be so impertinent as to say so."

Marion laughed, the girl's forthright manner was charming.

"Indeed, you have the right of it. I am, to some extent, interested in the chatter about people – for I have been long away from London, and must catch up on who is in favour, and what scandal has most recently caught the interest of the *ton*. But fashion – I find that I do not really care, shocking as that may seem."

For a moment, as Marion mentioned scandal, a frown creased Lady Faith's brow, but it was gone as soon as it came, and Marion wondered if, indeed, she had imagined its existence in the first place.

"Well then, let me tell you what I know of those present – where shall we start?"

From there, Marion found herself drawn into a long and enjoyable conversation, full of laughter and astute observations, which far enhanced her understanding of the current favourites and fads. She was grateful for the information, and even more grateful for the kind and unquestioning company.

Chapter Five

Sin stared across the ballroom, glaring at the man who stood so nonchalantly against a pillar. Lord Alfred Bernwelt had been amongst the crowd that Martin had run with, the crowd that Sin had been led into by Hugh. He had not matured all that well, Sin thought. He'd run into the man in the street, a few days back, and been greeted like a long-lost friend. And greeted as Sin. Whilst he thought of himself that way, as he'd been called it by many of his acquaintances, since Eton, it was still a shock to hear it here.

At sea, he'd chosen that appellation, feeling it appropriate, given his dishonoured state – Sin the sinner, the seamen had joked, and he had accepted it. But obviously Bernwelt had been talking, for the whispers behind fans now seemed to encompass that name, as well as all of the other salacious rubbish they whispered about him.

He turned away, wishing that he need not attend such events as this. But he had no choice, if he was to restore his honour, his family's honour.

The Norwood Ball was a crush, and the swirl of colour was almost dizzying, the stench of over-used perfume sickening.

Perhaps respite might be found on the terrace, at least for a while. He slipped across the room, followed, as always, by a wave of whispered gossip. As he did, he scanned the room around him, habit making him assess those present. Most were faces that he now recognised, but, at the far side of the room, a woman stood with an older couple. He had never seen them before, at any event he had attended.

Something about her drew his eye. She was of middle height, with soft pale brown hair, not quite blonde, and a face which was not classically beautiful, yet was striking. Her gown was magnificent in its simplicity, and suited her perfectly. She was a few years older than most of the young women present – not too far from his own age, he would guess.

He wondered who she was, for there was something about her which seemed somehow familiar, as if he had once known who she was, and could not quite bring the name to mind. He shook the thought aside - he had not been amongst these people for nearing seven years, before this last few weeks – why would anyone be familiar? Finally, he pushed through the last of the crowd to reach the terrace doors and stepped out through them, gratefully.

The air was cool, crisp, with just the faintest hint of the spring to come. Sin leant on the balustrade, looking out at the gardens below, the sense of the familiarity of the woman still with him. He did not like it when he could not be sure of something like that – for too long, his safety had depended on knowing all he could about those around him – it still did, he supposed.

He stayed there, staring up as the moon rose in a sky far

clearer than usual in London, for as long as he considered possible, before steeling himself to face the ballroom again.

Once back inside, he dutifully sought out the ladies whose families held most influence, and begged the favour of a dance. They grated on him, but it was necessary – the more people he could convince that he was a respectable man, who had grown beyond his 'dishonourable past', who would not repeat his brother's excesses, the better. The women were flattered, simpering and flirting, more enamoured of the rumours about him, than of he himself, but their good opinion was a path to conversation with their fathers and brothers, which might lead to a better situation for his family.

They were a far more certain path than the card room, for when he had ventured there, the response from most men had been barely civil. So he danced, and flattered, and even flirted a little. As the dances took him about the room, and he turned, following the intricate patterns of the country dances, he found his eyes, repeatedly, falling upon the woman he had noticed earlier. The more he noted her, the more she intrigued him, for she seemed nothing like most of the women present – she appeared quite reserved, yet also not shy, and she did not seem to be seeking the attention of the gentlemen present.

When each dance set ended, he delivered his partner back to her mother or chaperone, and moved on, unwilling to be caught in deep conversation with any of them. Finally, supper was announced, and relief slipped through him as he went in search of his mother and sister. Supper was a reprieve from dancing, from the need to be socially engaged with those around him. When he reached them, Faith was chattering away about who she had danced with, and what she thought of various gentlemen – her remarks were astringent, and not entirely kind.

But they were accurate enough that Sin was hard put to avoid laughing. Faith sipped at her glass of orgeat, whilst considering her dance card.

"Oh dear! Lord Fotheringham. I fear that I feel the most dreadful megrim coming on... so dreadful that we will just have to leave early, so that I can go home to recover. So sad, for I will therefore not be able to dance with Lord Fotheringham."

Both Sin and his mother considered Faith carefully, as she dramatically wilted in her seat, putting a hand to her brow. Again, Sin was hard put to prevent himself from laughing. But she had a point – he would be happy to leave early, using his sister as an excuse.

"Why of course Faith, I find myself able to put aside my disappointment at the need to leave early, for surely Lady Phoebe will understand when I renege on the dance which I had promised her, for the sake of your health."

It was Faith's turn to repress the urge to laugh – for she knew that her brother found Lady Phoebe quite the dullest of her friends. Lady Hungerwood waited until she was sure that Faith had managed to avoid laughing, then spoke.

"My poor dear – of course I will sacrifice another hour or two of Lady Templeton's gossi... errr... insights on society, for the sake of your health. Do let us gather our things and depart immediately."

Faith half choked, and quickly sipped her orgeat again, while Sin turned and looked away, quite certain that he would laugh if he continued to watch his sister. The first person his eyes fell upon was the mystery woman – again. He would have to ask if Faith knew who she was, he simply had to know.

They gathered their things, bid farewell to their hostess, and moved to the door. As they did, Sin leaned in close to Faith, and whispered to her.

"The woman near the potted palms – the one with light brown hair, wearing a blue gown – do you know who she is? I have never seen her before tonight, I believe."

Faith lifted her head from her 'half-fainting' impression just long enough to look, then nodded. They stepped through the door, into the refreshing night air, and nothing more was said until they had settled in the carriage. As they bumped over the cobbles towards Saint House, Faith turned to Sin.

"The woman you asked about – she is Marion Stafford, the Countess of Scartwick. I like her – we spoke at the Chesterton Ball."

The name sank into Sin like a knife to the heart. His face must have shown his shock, for Faith raised her eyebrows.

"Drummond, are you well? You look quite as pale as I was supposed to be from my 'megrim'."

He swallowed hard. His mother met his eyes, and shook her head gently. Faith had no idea, it seemed. He would need to speak with his mother later. For now, his world spun madly as all of what he had thought to be truth was turned on its head in an instant, and the bitterness rose within him, again, for wrongs done which could not be undone, and the recognition that the dishonour he had taken on was far deeper than he had ever imagined it could be.

So – Martin really had married her. It was clear in that instant, that he might never restore his honour.

Faith went to bed, genuinely tired. Lady Hungerwood turned to Sin, her face sad.

"Let us settle in your study, with some brandy. It is clear that we need to talk, for I gather from your reaction that you did not know."

"I did not."

They did not say anything further, until they were sitting in the armchairs either side of the fire, in his study, with brandy glasses in hand. The warmth of the liquor was welcome, as it slipped down his throat – for at that moment, everything else seemed bitter, cold, and terrible.

"I will tell you what I know of it, although some is only informed by gossip, so may not be entirely true."

"Whatever you know..."

"After his son died, the Duke of Windemere became quite reclusive, then more so after his wife died. I will be uncharitable here, and say that she was no loss to society, or to him, I suspect – she had always been a rather nasty woman. A year after her death, he came out of his isolation somewhat, and began to help two society ladies with a charitable project. Through that, somehow, a chain of events was set in motion, the details of which I do not know, which led to him discovering that, before his death, his son had actually married, at Gretna Green, a young woman. At that time, her whereabouts were not known."

"Then how...?"

"It seemed that the son had, as he lay dying, given the proof of the marriage into the hands of a friend, charging him with taking care of his wife. But she had fled London, for whatever reason, and hidden herself in the country. She was, at the time, increasing."

"Increasing? There is a child?"

"Yes. The Duke has acknowledged him as his heir, and Earl of Scartwick, and his mother as Countess. The marriage and the birth have all been entered into the records. There is no question of the validity, although at first many of the *ton* were doubtful about accepting it."

Sin dropped his head into his hands. No wonder the *ton* were so cold to him. This was far worse than simply having been thought to have incited Sinclair to challenging Martin Stafford to the duel – it was all clear now – they thought Sin a man who had incited a man to a completely wrongful duel, a duel which had not only cost a man his life, but a woman her husband and a child his father, in circumstances so bad that she had felt the need to flee and hide. It was a miracle that anyone spoke to him at all!

In that moment, he hated his older brother, was glad that he was gone, wished him to hell, in fact, that he might pay for his sins.

The desire rose in him to do something, anything, which might, in the smallest way, give reparation to Martin's widow. His honour demanded it – even if no one but his family believed him an honourable man.

"How will I ever…"

Sin had not realised that he had spoken aloud, until his mother replied.

"I do not know. But I believe that you will do your best. As you did then, when you need not have taken such a weight upon yourself. Yes, I know that it was Hugh, being Second at that duel, and that you took the blame, to preserve our reputation. That sort of behaviour was always more in Hugh's personality than yours. Perhaps I should not have let you do what you did, but…."

Again, Sin felt his world twisting. He had believed that no-one knew, save Hugh and himself. Even the others present at the duel did not know, for he and Hugh had looked quite alike, back then, and in the drama of the moment, it had been easy to convince them that they had mistaken the brothers.

"I hope that you understood then, why I chose to do what I did. I deeply regretted not having the chance to truly bid you goodbye, and my greatest sadness was that I might never see you, or Faith, again. Although... now I feel rather a fool, for it seems that my sacrifice was utterly in vain, that my brother had no appreciation for it, whatsoever. Or surely, he would not have continued as he did, have died as he did."

"I did. For I could not countenance that you would have done such a thing – that you had taken the blame for Hugh's actions seemed the only possible explanation. I know my children's characters – I could not believe such a terrible thing of you – but I could believe that you would do anything to maintain our honour."

"Does... does Faith know any of this? I had the impression that she surely could not know, for if she had, she would have understood my reaction in the carriage."

"No. she knows nothing of the detail. That you did something bad, and that the only option was to leave the country, that she knows, but no more."

Sin laughed, a shaky sound in the quiet confines of the room.

"Then, Mother dear, your knowledge of your children's characters has failed on one point. She may not know what it was that 'I' was supposed to have done, but she does know that it wasn't me – that I took the blame for something that Hugh had done. For she told me so, but a few days past. I confirmed that she was correct, but refused to tell her anything more."

Lady Hungerwood gaped at him, shocked.

"Faith has always been observant, and far too astute for her own good at times. And you were always her favourite brother. I suppose that I should not be surprised. I suspect that my desperate desire that she never need know the sordid details blinded me to the fact that she was working things out."

"That is most likely the truth. I think it better that Faith continue in ignorance of all the details, for now at least. Let her enjoy this Season as best she can, even under the shadow of my dishonour."

"For now, I agree – although I begin to wonder if we will be able to keep it from her for much longer. Drummond... what will you do, when you come face to face with the Countess? For I cannot imagine that such an event can be avoided forever."

Sin took a large swallow of his brandy, suddenly feeling ice cold at the very idea of it. His mother said nothing, leaving him the space to consider the idea. There was, in the end, only one possible answer.

"I will be as polite as it is possible to be, praying that she does not give me the cut direct – but if she does, so be it. When I first saw her, she seemed somehow familiar, but I could not imagine why. Now that I know – yes, I can see her in my memory. She was less confident then, unsure of how to go on, but the face... it is the same. I saw her with Martin, more than once. I was a fool, I let the others convince me that he was lying, that he could not have married her, yet... her father was in trade, and it seemed so unlikely. I must, somehow, do whatever I can to compensate for my error, for Hugh's blindly arrogant foolishness. But, as yet, I have no idea what that might be."

"It will come to you. I believe in you Drummond, I believe that you will find a way to untangle the mess that your brother left us all, to let the world see the truth of your honourable nature."

Sin wished that he believed in himself as much as his mother did. He finished the brandy, and retired, but sleep was elusive until after dawn, when exhaustion finally took him.

Chapter Six

Marion stood in the ballroom, a polite smile positively glued in place on her face. She wished that she could be anywhere but there, that she could be back in the Park in the morning, where everything was as simple as playing with Daniel. But she had no choice. If Daniel was to have the life he was born for, she needed to be here, making connections, becoming more accepted, becoming truly part of the *ton*. She still felt like an imposter.

Idly, she watched the door, studying the new arrivals, in part because they fascinated her, in their overdone fashion and with all of the tangled gossip of their lives, and in part hoping to see someone arrive, with whom she might converse comfortably. There were few people that she felt comfortable with, and she still watched, all the time, for the faces of those who had tormented her at the time of Martin's death.

She had seen one or two of them, and fear had frozen her to the spot at the time, but they had made no move to approach her. She dreaded the day when one of them might do so. She was pulled away from that thought by some new arrivals.

Lady Faith St. John, a woman who Marion was beginning to think could be a true friend, had just appeared at the door. Her mother stood beside her – at least Marion thought it was her mother, for Lady Faith had not actually introduced her, and beside them was a gentleman. She had missed, with the amount of noise in the room, the announcement of their names.

Who might the gentleman be? He was tall, lean, and almost hard looking, compared to the fops and the dissipated older men around him. His clothes were stark – black and white, unrelieved by colour, his hair longer than the fashion, and tied back by a black ribbon. He was undeniably attractive, yet she felt herself shiver a little at the sight of him, as if he brought the cold brush of danger with him. She was, she could tell, not the only one to judge him attractive – half the women in the room had turned to watch him, and a susurrus of whispers ran around the room, hidden behind fluttering fans. She wondered what they said – from what little she could discern of the voices closest to her, the word 'sin' seemed to be prominent.

She turned her gaze away from him, shivering again. A curl of fear ran through her, as if he had brought threat with him. She pushed that fanciful thought aside, and concentrated on the dancing, allowing her eyes to follow the couples as they moved through the pattern of the dance. Even that did not settle her, for there, amongst the dancers, was another dreaded face. A face she remembered with great clarity – the face of the man who had most tormented her, back then, the one that Perryman had felled with the marble vase. She discovered that she was shaking.

At that moment, Lady Faith appeared by her side, smiling and cheerful as always.

"Lady Scartwick! It is wonderful to see you again. I had

hoped that you would be here, that I might have the certainty of tolerable conversation."

Marion turned to her, beyond grateful for the distraction.

"Lady Faith, I also am glad to see you, for I fear that the evening was becoming surpassingly dull. It seems that, even with all of the gossip that circulates, truly, nothing of interest actually happens."

Lady Faith laughed at her words, nodding agreement.

"That is a most accurate assessment, my Lady. Even scandal palls rapidly, when discussed every day. And so rarely is there a new face to see – I do believe that I know everyone, and they are all uninspiring. I despair of ever meeting a man interesting enough for me to consider marrying him."

"Speaking of new faces... is that your mother, who arrived with you? I believe I have seen her with you before? And the gentleman who arrived at the same time – I do not believe that I have ever seen him before – can you tell me who he is? Eventually, I will get everyone straight, and cease to embarrass myself by forgetting people whom I have been introduced to before!"

Marion felt that shiver run through her again, even as she asked, almost as if she dreaded the answer. Her eyes followed him, where he spoke to a young woman on the other side of the room, then she dragged her gaze back to Lady Faith.

Faith laughed lightly.

"If you forget, then simply 'my Lord' or 'my Lady' is always a safe address – you have a very high chance of being correct."

Marion smiled in response. "Well yes, I have used that ploy at times, but I would feel so much better if I could remember."

"True, it is more comfortable to be sure. And yes, that is my mother, and the gentleman is my brother, now the Earl of Hungerwood, since my father and my older brother died. He was in the Americas when that happened, and only arrived back here in January to take up the title. Our mourning ended at the end of January, but he took a liking to the stark simplicity of black and white, and has not changed his style of attire. It does rather suit him, doesn't it?"

Marion nearly collapsed where she stood. No wonder Lady Faith's surname had seemed familiar! She forced herself to stay standing, to smile and nod at Lady Faith, to even agree with what she had said.

"It does indeed suit him, and the young ladies appear to believe that too."

Marion felt physically ill, chilled and overheated at once, as if she were feverish. There stood the man who had stood Second to the one who killed Martin in that terrible duel, the man reported to have incited his killer to provoke him in the first place – a man she had believed she would never have to meet, yet there he was, and brother to a woman she had rapidly come to like. Of all those she had cause to despise, he was the foremost, yet what could she do? She wished to simply flee, to run from the room, disregarding the impropriety of it, and to never return to a society event again.

She wished that she had never left Windemere Towers. But she would not show weakness – she was no longer that scared young woman, alone in the world.

Somehow, she managed to go on, to continue to converse with Lady Faith – although she had no memory, later, of what they had discussed. Not long after that, a gentleman approached her, and requested her hand for the next dance set.

He was an older gentleman, a friend of the Duke's and a man she trusted. She accepted, grateful for the distraction. He did not expect conversation, letting her stay in her thoughts, and she found, after a while, that the structured movements of the dance were soothing, that her heart had slowed to normal, and that she could face, just, the rest of the evening. Lady Faith had been swept away by one of her gentleman admirers, and Marion smiled as they passed in the dance – she could not find it in herself to dislike Lady Faith, no matter who her brother was.

The set ended, and her partner offered to fetch her a drink, which offer she gladly accepted. She stood alone, waiting for him to return, and concentrating on remaining calm – she need only avoid *that man*, for the next few hours, and she could go home. Surely she could do that.

Even as that thought passed through her mind, another gentleman appeared before her. In an instant, fear filled her. It was the man she had glimpsed earlier, the one that Perryman had floored with the vase, all those years past.

"Good evening my... Lady... I am quite sure that you remember me, we are old, old acquaintances, after all. I am Lord Frederick Cardston, heir to the Marquess of Waterhampton." His eyes ran over her body, pausing at her breasts, and he licked his lips. "You are, my dear, even more... attractive... than you were then. A woman like you must be... lonely... for I hear that you have not... taken up... with anyone since the unfortunate death of your... husband?"

And there was the insinuation – that he still did not really believe she had been Martin's wife, that he thought her a woman of low morals, who would be easy pickings for a man of wealth and appearance. Her stomach rolled, and a wave of illness went through her.

This was the man who had called her a lightskirt, who had tried to drag her from her home, to take her against her will. He smiled at her again, as if she should find his presence acceptable. Desperately, she hoped for the return of the gentleman with her drink, but he did not appear.

Cardston gave a small laugh, as if enjoying her discomfiture.

"My lady, it seems only appropriate that you grant an... old friend... a dance, does it not?" He offered his arm, and Marion stood, trapped. She could not simply refuse, not after dancing with another gentleman, not without a good excuse, not without causing a scene. And causing a scene was not something which would benefit Daniel. She took a deep breath – for Daniel's sake, she would do this – what could he do, on a dance floor, surrounded by other couples? She placed her hand on his arm. "Excellent, my Lady – I knew that you would see the sense in accommodating me."

He led her to where the couples were forming up for the next set, and she forced herself to move smoothly, to not flinch from him. The dance was a slower one, with more time when the couples were together, and he took full advantage of that to speak to her, there where he knew that she was trapped, and would be forced to hear him. Marion knew it, but could see no way to escape. He began the conversation simply enough, with a seemingly ordinary enquiry about how she was finding the Season, but the way he looked at her as he spoke made her feel soiled, and his hands pressed hers harder than necessary.

When she murmured an inconsequential response, he gave that slight mocking laugh again.

"Surely, my Lady, you seek a man? After so long alone – or have you been alone? Widows so often carry out affairs... the Season seems an appropriate place to seek company. Someone to warm your bed. You were easy enough with your favours with Stafford, no matter how prim you tried to be to the rest of us, back then – but surely now, there is a need... to satisfy certain desires? Yet you are alone, with none courting you – has your reputation preceded you? Perhaps you are too tarnished for many of the *ton*?"

The dance spun them apart for a moment, and Marion fought the urge to cast up her accounts on the floor. His insinuations revolted her, yet he seemed to think them perfectly acceptable. The dance brought them back together, and he smiled again, a wolfish expression which was not in the least pleasant.

"I believe that I have a solution for your dilemma, my Lady. Quite simply, I think that you should marry me. I am gentleman enough to offer marriage, not just take you as a mistress, for, I admit, I find a bit of... tarnish... enticing in a woman. I am sure that you understand my meaning."

Marion eyed him, shocked to her core, and completely repelled. She drew herself up, and when she spoke, her voice was as icy as she could make it.

"Lord Frederick, I do not know what response you expected to that impertinent set of suggestions, but I have only one. What you suggest will never happen, I have no need to marry, and I certainly would not choose you, if I did wish to marry."

He glared at her, as if shocked at her rejection of him, his eyes glittering with anger.

"We will see, my Lady. You will find that I can be most... persuasive."

Fortuitously, the set came to an end, and Marion fled the man. He let her go, a mocking smile upon his face.

She went straight to the ladies retiring room, to compose herself. She was shaking, whether from fear, or anger, or both, she could not tell. She needed to find someone, someone to speak to, to stay near, to help her avoid Cardston for the rest of the evening. Once the shaking stopped, at least mostly, she slipped back out to the ballroom, hoping to hide in an alcove or otherwise keep out of sight, but the first person she met was Lady Faith, who took one look at her, and reached out a hand to steady her, leading her to a chair behind a cluster of huge vases and potted palms.

"My dear Lady Scartwick, whatever has happened? You look so white that one might imagine you had seen a ghost. And you are shaking."

Marion was torn – she could not help but like Lady Faith, but her brother... how could she continue the friendship? But right at that instant, she needed support, and Lady Faith's calm caring expression pushed aside her hesitation. The tale of Lord Frederick's appalling treatment of her came flowing out. She managed to avoid explaining exactly the circumstances in which he had been so terrible in the past, simply concentrating on his behaviour during the dance.

"No wonder you are shaking! I have never heard of anything so uncouth! He is certainly no gentleman at all, if he has said half of what you report."

Marion gave a shaky half laugh.

"He was never a true gentleman, and I believe that he has only become worse over time. I wish that I had never come to London!"

"Don't say that! Had you not come, I would never have met you, and I would thereby have lost a friend – for I would like to call you a friend."

"Thank you, I am glad of that friendship, especially right now."

At that moment, a deep voice interrupted them. A voice that somehow sent shivers through Marion, deep into her bones – not unpleasant shivers, but more like the resonance one feels from a finely tuned musical instrument. She looked up, startled.

"There you are Faith. We wondered where you had disappeared to. Oh... my apologies for interrupting."

Lady Faith turned, smiling at her brother, and her mother, who stood just behind him.

"Ah - Drummond, Mother. I was on my way to you, after the last dance set, when I literally ran into Lady Scartwick, who was in need of aid. Lady Scartwick, may I present my brother, Drummond St. John, Earl of Hungerwood, and my Mother, Lady Hungerwood. Drummond, Mother, this is Marion Stafford, Countess of Scartwick."

Marion knew, in that instant, that this was the worst night of her life, only save the night that Martin had died. Her eyes met his, this man who had been instrumental in the circumstances that had taken her beloved from her, and she allowed all of her anger and despair to be seen.

Time stilled, and it was as if she could see the intensity of her feelings slam into him, like the blow of a knife. He swayed slightly, then swallowed, giving her an infinitesimal nod. A nod which clearly said that he understood. Then he took her hand and bowed – elegantly, respectfully. He lifted from the bow, and spoke, that voice resonating to her very core again.

"I am pleased to meet you, my Lady. I hope that my sister has been able to provide whatever aid you needed?"

Marion's world spun about her, the dizziness a result of over stressed nerves and an evening which had brought back all the worst parts of her life. His deep blue eyes watched her, seemingly filled with genuine concern, and an urge to laugh hysterically rose in her. He seemed so honest, so honourable, especially compared to Cardston – the contrast was stark. Yet she knew he was nothing of the sort, for he was, from what she had been told, the voice which drove Sinclair to the point where he provoked Martin to the duel. The fact that he had left the country, and run to the Americas was, in itself, damning. She could not let herself be deceived. She straightened.

"Yes my Lord, Lady Faith has been most helpful. I do feel restored enough to seek my father-in-law, and beg that we depart, before my incipient megrim becomes impossible."

"Might I escort..."

"There is no need – they are just over there."

She waved a hand as she spoke, her voice even icier than before, and, again, he gave that tiny inclination of his head, and a bow. Marion stood, and fled, with barely a nod to Lady Faith or Lady Hungerwood.

Chapter Seven

"I do hope that she will be all right. She looks so very pale."

Sin barely heard Faith's words. He felt physically ill – more so than he had since his first weeks at sea, adapting to the roll of the ocean. His eyes followed Lady Scartwick across the floor – he could not help himself. In that instant when her eyes had met his, when Faith had performed the introductions, everything had slowed – as it did in battle, when every tiny move mattered. She had not needed words. Her eyes had conveyed everything that she felt, everything required for him to understand that she knew exactly who he was – or at least, who he was reputed to be. She was magnificent in her anger, in the cold and dignified way in which she faced him, not pretending that there was no issue between them, but not making a scene in any way.

If only circumstances had been different… if only there were not so many lies and deceptions forming a barrier between them. In that moment, he hated his deceased brother, hated himself for being honourable.

It had been easy to shoulder his brother's dishonour when he had expected never to be seen in England again. It was not easy now, when he had to face them all. But facing this one woman was harder than facing the rest of the *ton* combined.

The worst of it was that, despite whatever he might have been told about her, back then, whatever Hugh and all of his cronies might have believed, he knew now, in that first moment of seeing her, that it had all been a lie. He could see, as if a veil had been drawn away, the essence of her.

She was beautiful, vibrant, strong, self-possessed, even in distressing situations. He understood then why Martin might have loved her, why he had risked society's disapproval, and, in the end, his own life, to marry this woman, to defend her honour, even though she was born of common stock.

He did not want to like her, but he did. The desire hit him then, as she walked away, to tell her the whole truth. For surely she, of all people, deserved to know the truth of the night of her husband's death? And he wanted, more desperately than he had ever wanted it before, to clear his name, to let his brother's dishonour go to the grave with him, and not tarnish their lives – his, Faith's, his mother's, and, in truth, Lady Scartwick's.

But it was almost certainly too late for the truth.

Yet... Lady Scartwick was obviously a woman of good character, and far kinder than he had any right to hope for. She had, after all, knowing who he was, not given him the cut direct, nor had she been unpleasant to his sister – that spoke of a just and honest character, of a woman who did not blame others for the actions of people close to them.

Somehow, he promised himself, he would find a way to convey the truth to her, even if no one else.

It would be giving her the chance to destroy what last shreds of his family honour remained, yet he could not, as an honourable man at heart, do anything else but seek to grant her the gift of the truth – even if it did destroy him. He had at least to try to tell her. There was but one problem with that conclusion – if she would not speak to him, would not stay in his presence more than moments, how would he ever speak to her of it, privately?

His eyes still followed her, until she left the room at the Duke of Windemere's side, and he ached to call her back. The spell was only broken when she disappeared from sight.

"Drummond? Drummond, what is it? You look as if your thoughts are miles away."

Sin turned back to Faith and his mother, giving his head a tiny shake. His mother's eyes were full of concern.

"Do not worry, I am all right. A little distracted, and, truth to tell, somewhat blue-devilled. Cold politeness is deeply wearing, especially when I cannot find a way to change that reaction. It is as if every event like this is simply some hours of punishment, with no hope of forgiveness. Even the young women who seek me out do not care for genuine conversation – they simply want the thrill of being near the dangerous and dishonourable Earl."

Faith rested her hand on his arm a moment.

"I am sure that, eventually, they will see you for who you are, not simply as a set of stories."

"I hope that also," Lady Hungerwood spoke softly, "but if it wearies you so much, let us depart for the evening. There will be many more Balls for Faith to enjoy, all through the Season."

"Thank you."

In the carriage on the way home, Sin closed his eyes, but the image of Lady Scartwick's beautiful face, her eyes full of anger and bitterness, rose before him in his mind. He suspected that image of her would haunt him forever.

~~~~~

Marion sat on the blanket in the Park, watching Daniel run and play, trying her hardest to find the peace that usually came to her in that place. The effort was futile. She was tired, for the last few nights, since that dreadful Ball, she had slept poorly, the dreams worse than ever, and now populated by Lord Hungerwood, and Cardston, as well as those others she remembered from the past. Lord Hungerwood's face, as their eyes had met, had stayed with her, haunting her.

The starkness of his pain – for she could call it nothing else – when her gaze had met his, had shocked her. The honourable manner of his behaviour, so soon after Cardston's caddishness had shattered her certainty about what sort of man he must be. She felt all at sea, finding that nothing about him aligned with what she had expected. And what would she do, next time they met, as they were sure to do?

She turned her thoughts away from it all, forcing herself to watch Daniel, to talk to her friends – for this day they had been joined by Baron Setford and his wife.

Lady Setford had been one of the first to help Marion when she had returned to London, even before the Duke knew of her whereabouts, and had become a very dear friend.

"My dear Marion, you look quite pale – is London not agreeing with you? Or is it something more than that?"

Anna was very astute, and Marion winced a little at her words – she was not ready to speak of any of it yet, not to anyone – her feelings were far too tangled.

"I... still struggle with the echoes of the past. And dealing with the *ton* is such an effort, for I was not born to it. But yes, I would rather be at Windemere Towers. Spring is so beautiful there, and the air is so much cleaner."

"It would not be difficult for the air to be cleaner than it is here in London! But do not worry about the *ton* – you are doing very well, and they have taken to you – I have heard nothing disparaging said, anywhere."

Marion was glad of that reassurance, for there was virtually nothing which happened in London that Baron Setford did not hear of, given his role as the King's spymaster. And his wife, she had come to understand, was privy to all that he knew.

She turned back to watching the children playing, glad that Daniel had friends of similar age, and glad that the relationships of children were so much simpler than those of adults.

~~~~~

As the day warmed, Sin eased his horse back to a walk, after some time of moving faster through the long paths of Hyde Park. The Park was busier now, and more care was required. He turned from the gravelled paths, and rode in under the trees, enjoying the dappling of sun and shade, idly watching the people around him.

There, ahead of him, on the grass between the trees and the Serpentine, some children played, running endlessly after a ball, their high-pitched cries and laughter drifting on the gentle breeze.

He turned a corner on the path, and saw past them, to where adults sat on blankets, with a picnic basket beside them.

He stopped, not even conscious of having done so. The horse, glad to rest after a morning's exercise, simply accepted the halt, and waited. There, on that blanket, was Lady Scartwick. She was, if anything, even more beautiful when seen in this unstudied simplicity. As he watched, one small boy ran up to her, and flopped down into her lap. Her arms curled around him, and she pressed a kiss to the top of his head.

The boy looked up to her, and the bright morning sun limned his face, the profile clear, even from the distance. Sin had no doubt – that boy was Martin's son. The lines of his face were the same, and Sin knew then that the boy would look very like Martin when he grew. A deep sadness filled him. There, before him, was the picture of happiness and love that Martin would never see. That Hugh's actions had stolen from him, by inciting the duel that had cost him his life. Actions that everyone believed to have been Sin's actions.

The child displayed such simple happiness, he was glad that the Duke had found him, had acknowledged him as heir. The happiness of a well-loved and cared for child was a thing to be treasured. Such happiness was something Sin would never feel again, himself. So be it, that was the choice he had made, on that fateful night so long ago.

He watched a little longer, seeing in her unaffected manner the true beauty of the woman, and the quality of her character. Eventually, he forced himself to turn away.

Watching only made his guilt greater, and the emptiness inside him more noticeable. He had not understood, when he had taken up the burden of Hugh's dishonour, just how much he was giving away.

~~~~~

Not all that far from where Sin sat on his horse amongst the trees, another man stood, leaning against the bole of a tree, also watching the picnic party on the grass. His face was twisted into a sneer.

"Such disgusting domesticity!"

Lord Frederick Cardston could not see the pleasure in such entertainment – sitting on a rough blanket on the grass and watching children did not at all appeal to him. But watching Lady Scartwick did. He would prefer to be watching her naked in his bed, but that would require further work to achieve. He had not expected her to reject his proposition so resoundingly – for, after all, she was a common trollop that Martin Stafford had taken up with.

The fact that Stafford had actually married her was amusing, but also annoying. It seemed that the status it had brought her had given her airs and pretensions above her station. Still, he was sure that there was a way to get what he wanted – which was marriage to her, so that he had not only her rather delectable body, but her money – for he knew that the Duke had settled a dowry upon her, to help her find another husband. That money was the only reason he was offering marriage. Otherwise, he would simply have coerced her into his bed as a mistress.

It was most fortuitous that he had noticed the Duke's carriage drawn up nearby, and decided to investigate. For, watching her with the child, he began to have an idea of how he might achieve his aims. Her obvious affection for the child made it clear – the boy could be used as leverage. Now all he need do was work out just exactly how that was to be arranged.

He would continue to observe her, and the boy, whenever he could, until the right opportunity presented itself.

Chapter Eight

Carlton set the last precise crease in place in his cravat, and placed the large sapphire pin for best effect. Sin stared at himself in the mirror, amazed yet again at the effect which could be created by a skilled valet.

Not that the elegance of dress and appearance made any difference to how the *ton* treated him. He felt that he was making no progress at all – the women still viewed him as a titillating adventure, the men as a dishonourable scoundrel not to be trusted. They were coldly polite to his face, did not welcome him to the card rooms, and generally made quite certain that he realised he was only tolerated because of his position, and because many of them held his mother in high esteem.

But he would continue to attend Balls, and subject himself to their disdain, for his sister's sake. Faith now had a number of admirers, and he held out hope that she might find a man she cared for, soon. But she watched him, and watched how the *ton* treated him – he saw her frown and glance at him often.

He had the dreadful feeling that, eventually, she was going to ask him to explain, in detail, exactly what had caused them to treat him so. He did not look forward to that moment.

After a last check that he was as well presented as he should be, he went downstairs to await Faith and his mother. Tonight was yet another Ball. They all seemed to blend into one another, an endless round of gossip and whispers, only enlivened by dancing, and the occasional genuine conversation. He wondered if his quest to restore his honour, his family's honour, was doomed to fail – if he would remain barely tolerated forever.

The depressing thought was pushed aside by Faith's arrival in the parlour. She looked truly beautiful, her gown a shimmer of lace over a soft pale blue, which caught the colour of her eyes. Her dark hair was intricately piled on top of her head, and threaded through with tiny silver chains. It was no wonder that men had begun to take notice of her. Soon, his mother joined them, and they departed for the home of Lady Templeton, where the Ball was to be held.

The journey was short, but the queue of carriages waiting to set down their passengers was long, and the spring twilight was long descended into the deep blue purple of night by the time they entered the building. The ballroom glittered with the light of hundreds of candles, and the swirl of people was almost dizzying.

Sin tried to see it as others did, who were warmly accepted, but could not – it seemed something apart from him, something artificial and almost cruel. He sighed, and led Faith through the crush to some seats near a tall vase in one corner. His mother settled onto one, but Faith simply stood, scanning the room, seeing who was present.

Across the room, a movement caught his eye – a woman, in a gown of the clearest, brightest blue that he had ever seen – a colour which reminded him of the plumage of the birds of the West Indies. His eyes were drawn to her, and with a shock, he realised that it was Lady Scartwick.

The more he saw her, the more he was forced to acknowledge her beauty. But appreciating her appearance was not for him to do. He was the last man in the world that she would wish to be admired by. As he thought that, she turned where she stood, and for a long moment, their eyes met across the width of the room.

Her face tightened, and she stilled. The moment stretched. Then she gave the tiniest inclination of her head, and turned away, breaking the eye contact. The meaning was obvious – it was not the cut direct, but it was close – and she wanted him to be very aware of that fact, of the courtesy she did him, by not ostentatiously cutting him. He turned away, to find his mother's eyes upon him, and Faith's – had they seen what had passed?

He did not wish to know, did not wish to speak of it, or even think of it. Instead, as Lord Haleford came to his sister, seeking a dance, he moved away from his family, and sought a young lady to dance with. Any young lady would do, he simply required an acceptable distraction, otherwise he would be left standing in obvious isolation. Lady Phoebe simpered at him when he asked her for the dance, and she happily followed him to the floor where the set was forming up. Her conversation was insipid, but he smiled at her nonetheless – anything to keep himself occupied.

And so went the evening – one dull dance after another, one almost cut direct after another, and barely any conversation worth having.

Even those who had once been his supposed friends, who had been there that fateful night, treated him with coldness, obviously glad that he was the one to bear society's disapprobation, rather than them. After the supper, he settled on a chair, feeling weary – his mother was elsewhere, talking with old friends, and Faith was at the other side of the room, talking to Lady Scartwick. Sin's heart constricted at the sight.

He was glad that Lady Scartwick did not condemn his sister for her brother's actions, that they were it seemed, friends, but the sight hurt, yet again reminding him of his responsibility to Lady Scartwick. The desire to tell her the truth – all of it – became stronger each time he saw her, yet her coldness to him did not abate in the slightest. He closed his eyes for a moment, the sight suddenly too much to bear.

"Drummond! Are you truly so tired that you are falling asleep on a chair in a noisy ballroom? I own that so much socialising can be tiring, but still!"

Sin's eyes snapped open. Faith stood beside him, an amused look on her face – but her eyes were clouded with concern.

"Not quite asleep, dear sister."

"But close. Drummond, might I pull you away to somewhere quieter – there is something I wish to speak of, privately."

Sin swallowed. Was this the conversation he had been dreading? Or something else altogether?

"If you wish. I believe there is a library just down the hall. That should hopefully be private enough."

He rose, and offered Faith his arm, and they left the ballroom.

Marion was uncomfortable. Cardston had been painfully attentive all evening, without ever actually crossing the line of acceptable behaviour. But being near him made her feel queasy. She had been happy to talk with Lady Faith, for it had provided a guaranteed reprieve from the man's attentions. But now that Lady Faith had returned to her brother's side, and the current set was coming to an end, she needed to escape – for Cardston would, of a certainty, come to her once he released his current dance partner.

Quickly, she rose, and slipped through the nearest exit from the room, hoping that Cardston had not seen her go. She hurried down the hallway, until, through a part open door, she glimpsed tall shelves of books. A Library! That should be a quiet spot to hide, for it was not the sort of place that most attendees at the Ball would seek out. She entered the room, putting the door back to its almost closed state, and cautiously went forward.

There was no sign of anyone else, and blessed quiet surrounded her. To be better certain of Cardston not finding her, she went to the furthest corner of the room between two tall sets of shelves, where there was a single chair deep in shadow. She sank down into it gratefully.

Oh, how she wished that Lady Faith was from any other family. Lady Faith was the first woman of the *ton*, of anywhere near Marion's own age, that she had met, who she thought could truly be a long-term friend. But how could Marion allow that, when her brother was who he was? Each time she saw Lord Hungerwood, it all came rushing back to her, all of the emotions of that dreadful night, even though it was years ago now. Yet… each time she saw him, she could not help but note, again, how honourable his behaviour was, or, for that matter, how attractive a man he was.

How could a man who looked like that, who behaved like that, have done something as terrible as he had? It all left her feeling deeply confused. As she sat in the armchair, her mind whirling pointlessly around the idea, she heard a sound. The door. Fear held her motionless, barely breathing – what if it was Cardston?

The door clicked shut. Footsteps, barely heard on the rich Aubusson carpets which covered the floor, moved into the room – towards the other chairs she had seen, which were placed fortuitously out of sight from where she sat. Two people, she thought. Helpless to do anything else, Marion sat there – she could not show herself until she was sure it was safe, and even then, she could not do so if the people were here for more… amorous… reasons – for that would be utterly embarrassing. And then they began to speak.

"So, Faith, what is it that you feel such an urgent need to discuss with me?"

Marion's thoughts spun – it was his voice, Hungerwood's, and it was obvious that he was speaking to his sister. In that instant, Marion wanted the floor to open up and swallow her. She definitely could not reveal herself! But what might she hear if she stayed here? It was too late to do anything but be an unwilling eavesdropper.

"You probably won't like what I am about to say."

Hungerwood gave a bark of half laughter. "Well, I expected that, as soon as you dragged me away to talk."

Lady Faith made a 'hmmph' sound, then spoke.

"Drummond, I have observed, very closely, the way that people treat you. The way that they have treated you, since you returned to England. People who are normally cheerful and pleasant are cold to you. Lady Scartwick almost runs from your presence, and speaks to you in a voice of ice when she must encounter you, yet she is normally the most delightful, warm, and friendly person. I want to know why. Not some excuse, but truly why. Has it something to do with whatever it was that Hugh did, that you took the blame for, when you left us all those years ago?"

Marion blushed at Lady Faith's words. Both because she had not realised how positively Lady Faith saw her, and because it seemed that her antipathy for Hungerwood had been so clear as to be rather unconscionably rude. For some time, he did not speak, and she wondered if he would answer his sister, or not. When his voice finally came again, it was hesitant, as if he feared his sister's reaction to what he would say.

"I... yes, it has something to do with that. Everything to do with that. But I am not at all sure that I should tell you, that you should know the bald truth of the dishonour that has tainted our family."

"Drummond! Do not try to 'protect' me, by leaving me ignorant. How can I deal with whatever may come, how can I allow a man to court me, even encourage one to do so, if I do not know the truth of what I would be asking him to deal with?"

Hungerwood sighed, and Marion discovered that she was holding her breath. For if what he was about to speak of was what she thought it to be, then the next few minutes mattered as deeply to her as they did to Lady Faith.

"I had not thought of it like that before. I am sorry – sorry that you must bear the burden of this, through no fault of your own – you and Mother both."

"It will be easier to bear if I understand it."

"Then yes, I will tell you. But you must promise me not to reveal this to anyone else – for if you do, then everything I have done, everything I have sacrificed this last six years, will have been for nothing."

"I... I promise – I will not reveal it to anyone, unless you give me explicit permission to do so."

Hungerwood sighed, a sound full of such deep sadness that Marion felt the urge to comfort him, somehow.

"Six years ago, a night shortly before I left the country, Hugh and I were out with the crowd of men we called friends then. Of them all, when I look at them, both as they are now and as they were then, really only one or two were truly friends – but I was too young and foolish to understand that then. Hugh was in his cups, and was arguing, baiting another of the group, about the woman he had taken up with. Hugh claimed that she was nothing but a lightskirt, and that Martin should share her favours with the rest of us. Martin kept telling Hugh that he had married the woman, that she was his Countess, and not to be trifled with. None of us believed him, for we had heard and seen nothing of a wedding. Hugh kept at him, being crude and obnoxious, as did Lord Jasper Sinclair, even more so."

"What happened? Who was the woman?"

"Patience, sister – I will tell you the whole sordid tale. Sinclair was a man who liked to duel, and Hugh knew it – he was intentionally rousing Sinclair to speak ill of her, enjoying watching Sinclair and Martin at each other's throats. In the end, Martin challenged Sinclair to a duel, and Hugh instantly agreed to be his Second, in a whispered conversation with the man. I was close enough to hear, but I doubt anyone else was. Martin accepted – what else could he honourably do? – and the time was set for the following dawn. Most of us attended the duel, although not as many as had been out drinking that night. I stayed close to Hugh, for he was still half-foxed from the night before."

"And? What did Hugh do? What was the result of the duel?"

"Hugh encouraged Sinclair to duel to the death, not just first blood. I think that Sinclair might have hesitated, if it was not for Hugh's encouraging him. They duelled. They were well matched, but Sinclair became wilder and wilder with his blows. I thought then that Martin would manage to disarm him, and that the duel would be done with, for I doubted that Martin would kill. But fate was cruel. Martin slipped on the dewy grass, just as Sinclair slashed wildly, and Sinclair's point went home. There was so much blood. Even though Martin's Second tried desperately to staunch the flow, it was already too late. Martin spoke some whispered words, thrust something into his Second's hands, and was gone from this world. In an instant, everything changed. For Sinclair could be tried for murder, and Hugh for assisting him, which would destroy our family. Hugh looked at me, and I made a decision. I pushed Hugh behind me, and pretended that it was I who had been Second to Sinclair."

"But... why would you do such a thing?"

"Because the only recourse was for both Sinclair and his Second to leave the country. The dishonour of a younger son, especially one who had fled England, might be whispered about, but would not completely destroy the family, whereas the heir admitting to such a thing would have been a monumental scandal. I could not allow that to happen to you, or to Mother, or Father. So I chose to take on Hugh's dishonour, that you might suffer less. I never expected to see England again, certainly never expected to bear the title. I had prayed that Hugh might value my sacrifice, might curb his wildness, and marry, might settle, and get an heir. But, as you know all too well, those hopes were in vain."

"What did you do when our letter finally reached you?"

"I laughed like a madman, and cried at the same time. And I was glad that I had amassed a fortune from my share of the privateer's prizes, for I knew then that I would likely need it."

"So you came home, knowing that they would all treat you like this, for something that you did not even do? I cannot imagine the depth of courage it takes to face them every day. But... you did not tell me – who was the woman that this Martin found worth losing his life for, in defence of her honour?"

"Ah, that is the most difficult part of all. For it seems that he had told the truth, no matter what Hugh believed – Martin had married his commoner love. And she is now well accepted in society, as is her son, Martin's child. That woman is Marion Stafford, Countess of Scartwick."

Chapter Nine

Marion felt faint, dizzy, the world going grey as she struggled to assimilate all that she had just heard. She did not truly hear what was said after that, did not hear them leave the room. She sat, drifting in and out of darkness, as grief besieged her again – grief not just for Martin, for all that she had lost, but grief also for Hungerwood – a man honourable far beyond the average, who had allowed his life to be destroyed for the sake of his family.

A man she had foolishly been hating, trusting the rumours of the *ton*, rather than investigating further. And now that she knew the truth, hating his brother was pointless, for Hugh St. John was more than a year in the grave.

She did not know what to do. She could not simply change her public behaviour towards him overnight, for that would most certainly occasion notice and comment – and more gossip was not something that either of them, or Lady Faith, needed. Yet she could not continue to treat him so icily, not now that she knew. And she could not admit that she knew.

All over again, she was filled with shame at her eavesdropping, however unintentional it had been. Yet she could not regret it. The knowledge she had gained had changed fundamental parts of her life. It would take some time for her to truly absorb it all – she would likely think of nothing else for the next few days, as she struggled to decide how to deal with it, how to go on, from now forward.

Eventually, she rose from the chair, and quietly made her way back to the ballroom, and straight to the Duke and Duchess – she could not risk having Cardston approach her, and the Ball was drawing to a close anyway. The sooner she could leave, the better. The Duchess looked at her closely as she reached them, no doubt seeing far more than Marion would have wished, but she did not ask any difficult questions.

"You look very tired, my dear – perhaps we should take our leave now?"

"Thank you. I think that would be for the best."

~~~~~

The following morning, as Marion sat on the picnic blanket in the Park, the conversation she had overheard replayed itself, endlessly, in her mind. Daniel ran about, chasing his ball, pulling leaves from a nearby bush to fashion into boats to float on the Serpentine, dragging his Nanny with him to see his achievements. Marion was deeply grateful for the woman's patience, for it allowed her to simply sit and think.

She was still as shocked and confused as she had been the night before, and no further towards a way forward.

Her hatred of Hungerwood had been transformed to respect, and she was left with an abiding sense of regret, a sense that she had done the man a great disservice by willingly believing him dishonourable, when everything she had seen of him had spoken to the opposite. The idea began to grow in her, that she needed, in some way, to provide recompense – for, undoubtedly, her harsh coldness to him had been noted, and had encouraged others to treat him similarly.

She did not know how to go about doing such a thing, but she resolved, then and there, to at least begin to be less cold to him each time they met, and to no longer flee his presence, as Lady Faith had described it.

Exhausted from little sleep and too much thinking – for her mind had also replayed, over and over, the description of Martin's death which had been given in a level of detail which she had never been provided before, but which brought some closure to her emotions – she lay back on the blanket, and allowed the morning sun to warm her, and drifted towards sleep. The Duchess watched her, with a gentle smile on her face.

~~~~~

Lord Frederick Cardston was once again leaning against a tree, attempting to look negligently at ease doing so, whilst his whole body almost vibrated with tension. The child was running wildly about, and the Nanny was barely able to keep up. Lady Scartwick appeared to have fallen asleep on the blanket, and was not watching him.

This might, finally, be the chance he sought.

His plan was simple, and therefore most likely to succeed. Lady Scartwick appeared to love her son. The Duke appeared to care greatly for the boy, also, as he was his heir. So, surely, if the price of the boy's continued freedom was Lady Scartwick's agreement to marry him, then she would agree.

He watched the child run, with that boundless energy that the young brought to everything, outpacing the Nanny again and again. Cardston edged forward, from tree to tree, until he was close to the grass where the child played. The boy was running towards him, and he tensed, ready to move.

He took one step, almost out into the sunlight – another few quick steps and he would collide with the boy, could scoop him up as he ran, and make off with him, before the Nanny saw him. He took a second step, his arms out and ready to grab, but, somehow, the Nanny appeared beside the boy, out of breath, but there.

Cardston shifted his weight, desperately turning himself back into the shadows under the trees, cursing the woman under his breath. She did not see him. She was focussed on the child.

"Master Daniel, you really must not run off so far! I'm quite breathless and my poor heart is pounding. Please be good, and stay closer to the blankets!"

"Yes Nanny. I'm sorry Nanny. But running is fun! Why can't you run as fast as me?"

The Nanny sighed.

"Because I am older, Master Daniel, and I haven't had to run for years, until I started looking after you. I'm out of practice."

The boy laughed as she led him away.

Cardston gritted his teeth, and slipped back through the trees towards his carriage. Another day. Another chance would come, and he would make sure that it was soon.

More and more, when riding in the Park in the morning, Sin found himself taking the path which would bring him to the point where he could see Lady Scartwick and her son, with whoever had accompanied them that day.

He could not explain to himself why he did so, but day after day, he ended up there, regardless. He sat each time, letting his horse rest, and watched. It was almost a punishment for him, to see the child which looked so like Martin, to see the happiness he would almost certainly never have, to understand, day after day, what damage his fool of a brother had wrought in the world.

And to admire Lady Scartwick. For he could no longer deny that he did so. She was becoming more beautiful as the spring wore on, as she became more settled amongst the *ton*. If he could in any way protect her, or provide any service to her, he would.

Nothing could bring Martin Stafford back, but every day of his life, Sin could work towards undoing some of the damage that Hugh had done. He refused to consider his feelings about Lady Scartwick, beyond a need to provide reparation for his brother's deeds – anything deeper than that was too painful to contemplate.

This day, as all the others, he sighed, and turned away, never making his presence known, having drunk his fill of the picture of innocent happiness again, having refilled the sense of hope in his soul, just a little more.

~~~~~

The Season continued, and the endless whirl of social events occupied more and more time.

Marion was torn between a desire to avoid them all, so that she need not face Cardston and the others of that group, who watched Cardston's attempts to seduce her to his wishes with amusement, and a desire to attend, so that, she ruefully admitted to herself, she might see Hungerwood, and have the chance to speak to him more kindly.

The first event at which she had not removed herself from his presence, he had looked at her with shock – a shock which was quickly hidden behind his usual charming expression. But his eyes had followed her, their dark blue depths filled with an emotion she did not understand. It had intrigued her, and she had seemed helpless to stop herself from watching him. Their eyes had met, multiple times throughout the evening, and each time a shiver had run through her.

At each event, it had become easier to be less cold in manner towards him, easier to allow herself to be present when he conversed with his sister, and, slowly, easier to let herself be a part of those conversations too. She had the oddest feeling that he had begun to intentionally seek such conversations, to put himself in her way. But surely that was madness on her part – for why would he do such a thing, especially given the way that she had treated him at first?

Now that she viewed him more kindly, she had also become acutely aware of how others treated him. They were, she could see, in many cases intentionally hurtful, vicious in their indirect castigation of one of their own who had strayed.

The *ton* had high expectations of behaviour – or at least of the behaviour which one let become known to the world. And accepting, admitting to, dishonourable acts and fleeing the country as a result, was far beyond the pale. Now that she saw him for the deeply honourable man that he was, the way that others treated him roused her anger, and her protective instinct.

Perhaps that was foolish in the extreme, but it happened, no matter her resolve to be unaffected.

On this particular evening, the mid-April weather was magnificent, the warmth of Spring leading couples to wander on the terrace outside the ballroom, and the entire place filled with great mounded bouquets of richly scented spring flowers. The scent was such that it was almost intoxicating. She stood with Lady Faith, discussing the beauty of the blooms around them, as well as the people in attendance. Lord Hungerwood approached them, having just finished dancing, his face a little flushed from the exertion, and his eyes alight with what Marion was startled to find could be described as mischief.

"Why Faith, how can this be? You did not dance that last set. I thought that the queue of your admirers made such a thing improbable in the extreme."

"There are, my dear brother, occasional moments in which I manage to rest. And indulge in delightful conversation with my friend."

He looked at Marion for a moment, and everything stilled. There was nothing but the deep pools of his eyes, the curve of his lip as he smiled at her. She discovered that she was smiling in return.

His voice, when he spoke, resonated within her.

"And Lady Scartwick's conversation is, I will admit, far superior to that of every other friend of yours whom I have met. I do believe that your taste in friends has improved, dear sister."

Marion felt herself blush at his words, and cast her eyes down, suddenly completely unsure.

A flash of memory came to her then, of when Martin had been alive, of the few times then that she had met his 'friends'. This man had, even then, been more polite, more honourable, than the others. There had even been a day, she now remembered, when he had apologised to her for the behaviour of another man in the group. She also remembered, now that it was so clear in her mind, how very horribly different his brother had been. A shiver ran through her.

A gentleman arrived beside them.

"Lady Faith, I do believe that this is my dance?"

"Why yes, Lord Haleford, you are quite correct."

She placed her hand on his arm, and allowed him to lead her to the floor. Silence seemed to surround Marion and Hungerwood, as Lady Faith and Lord Haleford walked away. Their eyes met, and held, and all capacity for speech seemed to have deserted Marion. Between them, the air almost crackled with a tension that was by no means unpleasant, a tension that Marion almost dared to describe as tinged with desire.

His eyes were not simply deep blue, but, like the ocean he had spent so long sailing, held tones of dark green, and small flashes of silvery light. His lips curved into a wider smile, and she watched them, drawn by the shape and the movement.

Slowly, as if afraid that the moment was as fragile as glass, and would shatter, he spoke, his voice low, a vibration barely heard, but felt deep within her.

"Lady Scartwick, would you do me the honour of granting me this dance?"

Marion felt light headed, knowing that refusing would be wise, yet she discovered that her lips had already formed the word.

"Yes, my Lord."

He offered his arm, and she placed her hand upon it, acutely aware of the eyes which followed them as he led her to the floor. Only then, as the orchestra struck up, did she realise that it was a waltz. Heat flooded her as he took her hand, and brought his other hand to rest low on her back. Everything else ceased to exist as he swept her into movement, and the music became something that she floated on, safe in his arms.

Distantly, she wondered at that thought — why would she feel safe, with this man, of all men — yet she did. Neither of them noticed those around them, or the whispers which ran through the ballroom like wind through the trees, a shimmer of sound filled with speculation and shock. The *ton* had noticed that the two who should, by all things righteous, be enemies, were dancing — and dancing in a manner which made it quite clear that enmity was no longer a possibility.

When the music finally drew to a close, the spell was broken, and Marion blushed with embarrassment as she noted, as he escorted her to the Duke and Duchess, that everyone was watching them. What had she done?

~~~~~

What had he done?

And why had she accepted his request for a dance?

Sin did not know, but even if she never spoke to him again, it would have been worth it. Whilst he held her, everything else had disappeared. For that magical time, he had forgotten all about his dishonour, about the past and the terrible things that his brother had done, and their effect on this woman.

There had only been the feel of her in his arms, and the depths of her green eyes for him to drown in.

When the music stopped, and every eye was upon them, he drew himself up, settled his face into the most dignified expression that he could manage, and ignored the lot of them. As he led her from the floor, he knew, with absolute certainty, that there would come a time, and soon, when he would lay the truth before her, no matter what she did with it. After this moment, he could no longer countenance leaving her believing the lie.

Chapter Ten

By the time she arrived at Lord and Lady Northcott's residence the following evening, for yet another Ball, Marion had regained some semblance of confidence in her ability to remain serene, no matter what whispers happened – for she was sure that there would be some. The ballroom was crowded, and she was greeted by many acquaintances as she moved into the room. Nothing was said, but she could tell that all of them were bursting with curiosity.

She had hoped that the slow change of manner towards Hungerwood might have been noted, and made this moment easier – but apparently, dancing with him had gone quite beyond what they had been ready to accept. She drew herself up, smiled, and chose to act as if she had not noticed their attitude. Soon, as if it was fated that she cause more gossip, Marion found herself near Lady Faith, and drawn into conversation. At that moment, Hungerwood was elsewhere – Marion was part disappointed and part relieved.

"I wish that people did not gossip so!"

Lady Faith frowned as she spoke, almost glaring out across the room at everyone in general.

"I quite agree – but I doubt that they will ever stop."

"I suppose that I am more sensitive to gossip than most, for my family has been subjected to rather a lot of it. Especially since my brother returned from the Americas."

"Indeed, being the subject of gossip makes one far more aware of it. I have suffered that fate as well, although they had mostly decided that I was dull, once the first year or so passed. Until now."

"I wish that would happen for us – but they never seem to tire of it."

"That is true – I hear many whispers about Lord Hungerwood – mostly from ladies who find his history exciting, but I have also overheard the men speak of him. May I ask you... why do some of them call him 'Sin'?"

Lady Faith gave a small brittle laugh.

"It's a contraction of our surname. Spoken rapidly, St. John sounds like 'sinjun'. When Drummond was a boy, the other boys at Eton started calling him that, making jokes about 'Sin the sinner', whenever he did anything wrong. He told me about it, when I, as a small child, asked him why he didn't like going back to school. But, typical of him, he chose to turn it against them – he began to go by that name much of the time, away from the family anyway, and they left him alone because he was no longer distressed by it. I gather that, once he left the country under... dishonourable... circumstances, he felt it appropriate to be that identity."

Lady Faith had hesitated a moment when she said

'dishonourable circumstances' and Marion knew that it galled her to speak of Lord Hungerwood that way, when she knew the truth of it.

"But – if that is the case, why does he tolerate men calling him that, now, when he is Earl, when he is, I gather, taking pains to change the perception of the *ton* towards your family?"

"I think that he is simply used to it. And if he objected, then those of the *ton* who like to discompose others would use it to annoy him. Perhaps he even finds it darkly amusing."

Marion nodded, considering Lady Faith's words – what might it be like, as a child, to have been treated so? That the man could wear such a sobriquet with equanimity was yet another sign of how steady and strong his character was. At that moment a gentleman arrived to claim a walk on the terrace with Lady Faith, and Marion found herself alone.

She edged back, hoping to hide herself in the alcove where palms and flowers shaded chairs. She had barely moved two steps, however, when a hand took her by the elbow. She jerked to a halt, spinning to face the person who had so accosted her. It was Cardston. Her heart sank. His expression was almost gloating, and she repressed a shudder.

"My dear Lady Scartwick, one would almost think that you were avoiding me. But surely not, for you know how... ardently... I admire you. And how much I would wish to demonstrate that admiration in a far more... physical... manner."

Marion forcibly removed her arm from his grasp, and stood straighter, glaring at him.

"However much you may wish it, that, Lord Frederick, is something that you will never have the opportunity to do. I do not appreciate your crude innuendos, or your presence."

The man laughed, as if she had said something flirtatious and amusing, and reached to take her arm again.

"Never is a long time, my Lady. And I am most confident about my ability to change your mind."

"You will not have the chance."

Quickly, Marion wrenched her arm from his grasp, and pushed past him, almost running out into the main part of the room.

~~~~

Sin had, again, tested the waters of acceptance by going to the card room. The men there noted his arrival with frosty stares, then turned back ostentatiously to their games. No one suggested that he join them, and no one greeted him. He stood for a while, watching them play, but found nothing entertaining about it – it reminded him too much of the things which Hugh had enjoyed – and the money he had wasted on gambling. Sin turned away – eventually, he had to hope, they might be less cold towards him.

He stepped back into the ballroom, and simply stood, leaning against the wall, observing the room. As always, now, he looked for Lady Scartwick, somehow unable to prevent himself from doing so. He found her, some distance away, near a decorated alcove with chairs. His sister stood with her.

He was struck again by just how beautiful Lady Scartwick was. The shy young girl whom he had seen with Martin had matured into a stunning woman, who held herself with confidence and grace. As he watched, his sister was claimed by a gentleman, who led her towards the terrace, and Lady

Scartwick was left alone. She turned to step towards the chairs. For a few seconds, his view of her was obscured by people moving between them, then the path to her cleared again.

Lord Frederick Cardston approached her from behind, reaching out to take hold of her elbow. Sin felt a rush of anger rise within him. Cardston was a cad – he had been six years ago, and he still was, just with a little more polish now. His fists clenched, and he found himself moving, without having intended to do so.

As he walked towards them, he saw Lady Scartwick spin around, saw her face as she flinched back from Cardston. It was obvious that they spoke – a few sentences, no more, before Lady Scartwick wrenched herself from his hold and rushed past him, towards the centre of the room, a look of almost fear upon her face. Cardston turned to watch her go, and his expression was not one that Sin liked in any way. It was reminiscent of a wolf viewing its prey.

Sin increased his pace, and turned to intersect Lady Scartwick's path. She almost collided with him, before she came to an abrupt stop, her face colouring.

"Oh, I am sorry, Lord Hungerwood, I did not see you approaching!"

At that moment Faith arrived beside them – Sin wasn't at all sure that he was happy about that.

Before Sin had a chance to speak at all, Faith was exclaiming – he was not sure which of them she intended to address.

"Well! I shall not be dancing with Lord Willston again! He asked me to walk on the terrace, and almost immediately attempted to steal a kiss. I do not like him that much at all. I rejected him soundly."

Sin considered her words a moment.

"Do you wish me to have a pointed word with him?"

"No," Faith shook her head, "I believe that I made my opinion more than clear."

Sin turned his attention back to Lady Scartwick, who was pale, and simply stood, as if their presence was a shield. She glanced behind her, and her tension eased a little when she did not see Cardston. Sin wondered where the man had gone.

"Good. But I will be watching him, lest he try anything inappropriate again."

"Thank you." Faith looked about her, and her face transformed with a smile as Lord Haleford approached and offered his arm. "Is it our dance already, Lord Haleford?"

The man nodded, and led her away. Sin turned back to Lady Scartwick, and found himself helplessly caught in her gaze.

~~~~~

"Let us start the conversation again, now that my sister has been distracted by a man whom she obviously finds more to her taste than Willston. Good evening, Lady Scartwick. I trust that you are well?"

That voice... Marion felt the resonance deep within her, as she always did. But she did not allow her reaction to show. She smiled at him, and sought words which would answer the unspoken question, as well as the spoken one. As much as she was willing to. He referred to the gossip after their dance the previous evening, she assumed – for he would know nothing of her encounter with Cardston.

"I am well, Lord Hungerwood. I am most glad of Lady Faith's presence, for her conversation is far preferable to the surfeit of gossip that most others attempt to dress up as conversation. Or as commentary, thinly veiled, upon who is dancing with whom."

He nodded, his eyes flickering with emotion which did not show on his face. Was it relief, that she was not suffering too badly from the gossip that their previous evening's dance had engendered? Or something more? It seemed a most intense emotion. The memory of that dance rose in her mind, and suddenly she felt overheated, flushed, and unaccountably nervous in his presence. His eyes held hers, and she was mortified to realise that he had most likely just followed the path of her thoughts and reactions. She looked away.

"It is, my Lady, wise to ignore the gossips, for they are never satisfied with a person – they will always find something to disparage and whisper about. Some time ago, I made the decision to do what I needed to do in my life, as honourably as possible, and let them make of it what they would, without allowing that to disturb me. I must admit that I have come to find some degree of amusement in the wild stories which they manage to concoct from tiny grains of truth."

"I am in complete accord with you on that matter. When the Duke first introduced me to society, there was a great deal of gossip, and taking the approach that you describe was the only way that I survived that first few months."

He looked at her again, and his eyes filled with sadness – she wondered exactly why, but resigned herself to the fact that she would most likely never know.

"I can only begin to imagine how difficult that must have been for you. Especially with the attitudes of some who had… met you before."

His hand moved gently, indicating the group of men across the room, gathered around Cardston, who had simply returned to his cronies after accosting her, apparently. Marion felt a shiver of the old fear run through her. So, Hungerwood remembered how they had treated her – and appeared to disapprove of them still.

Now, she thought that she understood what she saw in his eyes – it was, at the least, compassion, a recognition of the similarity of their suffering at the hands of the judgemental *ton*. In that moment, she realised that she felt safe with this man, secure in the idea that, when he was beside her, Cardston would not attempt to approach her again. It was most odd that she should feel so, yet she did. This man, who had for so long been among those she considered enemies, had somehow become a haven of safety. She half shook her head at the oddness of her own reactions.

Then he smiled again, banishing the thoughts of the past, the thoughts of Cardston – how could she think of anything terrible, when such a smile lit his face, directed at her?

The orchestra struck up for the next set. It was almost a repeat of the previous evening – here they stood, alone together, as Lady Faith had already moved off to dance with Lord Haleford. Again, she found herself drowning in his blue eyes, utterly caught, to the extent that everything around her faded away. Her heart beat faster, and her mouth was dry. She licked her lips, unsure what to say.

His eyes lit with a mischievous glint, and he offered her his arm.

"Given our mutually agreed position on the subject of gossips, shall we then be scandalous, and give them further material for their whispers? Will you dance with me again, Lady

Scartwick?"

Words failed her for a moment, and she sucked in her breath in a gasp. But... why not? As they had discussed, she should do as she wished, not let her life be controlled by the gossips. She placed her hand on his offered arm, inclining her head in acceptance.

"Why not, Lord Hungerwood? After all, tis but two dances separated by a day – which surely is nothing so scandalous as would be two dances on the same night."

He turned that smile upon her again, his lips quirked in a wry twist.

"Of course. But should you wish to truly scandalise them, two dances in one evening could be arranged...."

"I do believe, Lord Hungerwood, that you are quite as devilish as they whisper that you are. For to do such a thing would be seen as a declaration of intent..."

"It would. But would we allow their expectations to dictate to us?"

Marion shook her head, astounded that she was actually flirting with this man, of all men, and enjoying it! She could no longer pretend that she did not find him attractive, not just of visage, but of character. That realisation left her confused – for, although Martin was six years in the grave, it felt somehow almost disloyal to him. She had much thinking to do, obviously. But for now, she pushed all thought aside, and allowed herself simply to enjoy the moment. From the corner of her eye, she watched the whispers begin, as people noticed him leading her to the dance floor. It was comical, when she considered it without fearing it. The set was a country dance, and they took their positions in the line, beside Lady Faith and Lord Haleford.

Lady Faith raised an eyebrow at her brother, but did not speak, for which Marion was exceedingly grateful. The dance began, and, as the movements brought them close, Hungerwood spoke softly.

"You have not answered my last question, Lady Scartwick. Does it pose such a conundrum, to require long thought?"

They spun apart again, relieving her of the need to respond immediately – for what on earth could she say? Great care was needed with her words. They came close again, spinning about each other, their hands clasped.

"Why my Lord, that is a question where there is no good answer. For if I declare that I do not care what they think, what they expect, and encourage you to offer such a scandalous thing, then I leave myself and yourself open to having our intent questioned by all. And when I do not truly know your intent…"

He gave a soft laugh as the dance parted them again. She found herself impatient for the moment when he would be brought close enough to speak. She wished that it had been a waltz, not simply a country dance.

"I am not certain, if I am truthful, that I know my own intent. But I would explore that with you, by your leave. I am certain that more time spent conversing with you… and dancing with you… will bring clarity."

"Then by all means let us seek clarity. I would not have you spend your life uncertain, in addition to dealing with gossips and your bro… past history."

The dance spun them apart again, and Marion wondered what might come of this – for she had just effectively agreed to dance with him in future, to speak with him often, had she not? His hand took hers as the dance brought them back together, and a warmth spread through her from that contact. She realised that, with every moment she spent with him, she found it harder and harder to avoid admitting that she knew the truth of his past. Why, she had almost said 'your brother's past indiscretions' rather than simply 'past history'!

But how could she admit to her eavesdropping? For she would have to, if she was to tell him that she knew the truth of it.

The music came to an end, and he offered her his arm again. She placed her hand upon it, expecting that he would escort her to the Duke and Duchess. Instead he led her to the terrace doors. She looked at him, the question clear in her expression.

"I thought that some cool night air might be refreshing."

"I am sure that it will. Even though it will give the gossips yet more fodder for their whispers."

He gave a soft laugh, and she felt it, deep within her. They stepped out and walked along the terrace, finally coming to a halt at one end, where the shadows were deeper and they could look out across the garden below, where coloured paper lanterns created an almost magical effect.

"I find, Lady Scartwick, that your company is worth the price of being gossiped about. Indeed, I must admit that I admire you. Your equanimity in the face of gossip is to be respected, and speaking with a woman who neither disdains me, nor regards me as a thrillingly dangerous flirtation is most refreshing. I feel that I can trust what you say to be honest -which is more than I can say for most people."

Marion's heart beat faster. Now the fact that she had not admitted to her eavesdropping burnt in her mind – he thought her unfailingly honest! Yet she held such a secret from him!

It was untenable. She must speak. She turned to face him. They were so very close – his deep blue eyes caught hers, and the words she had been about to utter failed her. His lips curved into that wry smile, and he raised an enquiring eyebrow.

"I…" what could she say? Anything would spoil this new… friendship… between them, and she found that she very much did not wish that to happen. Her breath caught, and she simply looked at him. He, as if unable to help himself, bent his head to her, until his lips were almost brushing hers. She wanted… she could not allow… not with her dishonesty hanging between them…

Marion turned and fled, before he could kiss her.

Chapter Eleven

Marion barely slept, so much were her thoughts in turmoil. She had enjoyed the time with Lord Hungerwood the previous evening – far too much. If she was truthful with herself, she had wanted him to kiss her, there on the terrace. Yet… that still felt, in some way, as if she was being disloyal to Martin. But now that she knew the truth of that night of Martin's death, how could she regard anything the same way? She could not.

In the end, she was left with confusion – about what was right, about her own feelings, and about what to do the next time that she saw Lord Hungerwood.

She slept but an hour or two, and rose not rested at all. Perhaps the time in the Park would settle her mind. The day was bright and beautiful, and she knew that Daniel would be full of energy, and desperate to be out and playing. That thought was enough to encourage her to start the day, and by the time she took a seat at the breakfast table, she had decided to simply enjoy the morning, and leave deep thinking until later in the day.

The Park was quiet, with few others about – most likely because half of London had been up late attending various Balls and other social events, Marion thought. Daniel was unconcerned by the lack of other children – he had rarely had other children to play with for most of his life, and had become adept at entertaining himself. Even Nanny seemed tired, and simply walked about, watching him as he ran and kicked his ball about. Every so often, Daniel would run to her, and ask her to throw the ball for him, then speed off again after it.

Marion watched, wishing that she had half so much energy, laughing when Daniel, in a playful moment, tugged on Nanny's bonnet strings, before running off giggling. With a smile, Marion lay back on the blanket, and allowed herself to rest in the warmth of the spring sunshine, and the gentle touch of the light breeze.

~~~~~

Sin rode through the Park, knowing that he would wind his way through the shaded paths to the point where, lately, he always paused. The point where he could watch Lady Scartwick and her son. As he rode, his mind replayed the events of the previous evening's Ball. He had been a fool of the worst kind. What in God's creation had led him to believe, for even a moment, that she would let him kiss her? It did not matter that he wanted to, what mattered was that he had begun to forge what he hoped was a true friendship with her, this woman who had been served so badly by his brother's actions. And now, it was most likely that he had ruined it completely, in a single moment where he had allowed desire to overrule sense.

His horse was fidgety, keen to run, obviously sensing Sin's unease and confusion, yet perversely, Sin had taken the ride slowly, needing the quiet that brought to allow him to think. What would he do, if she went back to treating him coldly? The idea of it made him shudder – he very much wanted to continue from where they had been, before he had been fool enough to be tempted to kiss her. The memory of the moment when she had fled from his arms was bitter. Most of his disappointments and troubles in life had come from other people's actions. This time, it could be laid at no one's door but his own.

As he approached the group of trees from which Lady Scartwick could usually be seen, a movement amongst the trees ahead of him caught his eye. It was rare for anyone else to take this path in the morning, and he looked ahead curiously, wondering who it might be.

$$\sim\sim\sim\sim\sim$$

Marion started upright as a scream rent the air. She was on her feet before thought had time to intervene, instinctive fear for her child driving her. Across the grass, near the shady cluster of trees, the Nanny stood, her bonnet loose in her hands. The screaming was coming from her. Marion and the Duke reached her at the same moment.

"Gone! He's gone! I but looked away for a moment, to capture my bonnet – Master Daniel had pulled the ribbon undone, and it blew off. When I turned back, he was gone. Look – his ball lies there in the grass, but he is not anywhere. Oh! Oh! What can I do?"

Cold fear settled in Marion's core.

She chided herself for being silly, for assuming the worst. In all likelihood, he was simply hiding, peeking out at them, and quietly laughing at how frantic they were.

She took a deep breath.

"Nanny, please be calm. Are you sure that Daniel is not hiding somewhere, to be mischievous?"

"I looked my Lady. And he has never hidden for very long before – he is far too fond of laughing at me for not finding him. Where can he be?"

Nanny wrung her hands, to the detriment of her bonnet, which she seemed to have forgotten. The Duke looked at Marion, and she could see as deep a fear in his eyes as she felt herself. When he spoke, there was a tone to his voice which told Marion that he was remembering Martin – and losing him.

"We must all search – how far can one small boy go in a few short minutes? Let us walk all through the trees here – for surely there are many hiding spots big enough for one boy."

They began to search. As they did, on the trail which wound through the trees, a horse thundered past, far faster than was supposed to be allowed in the Park. Marion realised, as her eyes followed the horse, afraid that Daniel might get himself in its path, and be trampled, that the rider was Lord Hungerwood. What was he doing? Why was he here, and riding so fast?

~~~~~

Lord Frederick Cardston was leaning against a tree, again, watching a small boy run about, a pastime which had ceased to amuse quite some time ago.

Today, he was determined, he would take the chance, and capture the child. At the Ball the previous evening, Marion – in his thoughts he would not dignify her with the title of Lady Scartwick – had again rejected him. Her arrogance offended him

– she, who was commoner born – how dare she turn her nose up at the idea of marriage to him! At the time, he had simply smiled, and passed it off as nothing, but her continued rejections annoyed him – more and more. She would do whatever he wanted, once he had the child, he was sure. And the old Duke would pay a ransom to get his heir back. Just the thought of the money made Cardston almost salivate.

The child ran closer, kicking the ball before him. The Nanny was quite a distance away, but watching him. Cardston waited, hoping, gritting his teeth. After this was done, he would be happy never to step off the road in the Park again. The Nanny spun, clutching at her bonnet, which had been lifted from her head by the breeze. Cardston leapt forward, scooping the child up, and getting a hand over the boy's mouth before he could call out. The ball rolled to a stop, unregarded, as he turned and sprinted back towards where his carriage waited.

There was no sound of pursuit. If luck was with him, the Nanny was still running the other way, chasing her bonnet. Reaching the carriage seemed to take ages, but reach it he did. He opened the door, and dragged the boy in, then quickly wrapped him about with the rope that lay waiting. The knot was inelegant – it would not hold a man, but a small boy was a different matter. The child looked at him, shocked silent, as he slipped out, shut the door, and climbed up to take up the reins. Thank God he had chosen to train his horses to stand and wait, even if no one held them. He needed no witnesses.

He drove off, as steadily as he could, not wishing to draw attention, and prayed that the child would stay reasonably quiet.

Sin had watched with dawning horror as the figure ahead of him moved away from the tree he had been leaning against, and surged out to lift the child off the grass in one smooth movement, at a time when the Nanny's back was turned, as she chased after her bonnet. For a moment, shock had held him immobile, then battle hardened reflexes had taken over.

He urged his horse forward, going from a slow walk straight to a gallop in two strides, his focus entirely on the running man holding the wriggling child. He cursed when the man reached a carriage, thrust the child inside, and very quickly reappeared, to climb up and take the reins. The carriage began to move, and Sin urged his horse faster. He could not allow the blackguard to get away, to steal Martin and Marion's child – whatever his reasons for doing so. As he reached the trees and raced through them, he was peripherally aware of people, moving about, calling the boy's name. He could not stop to tell them what had happened, or he might lose the carriage.

As he came out of the trees onto the gravelled road, he was pleased to see that the carriage was not moving fast. Perhaps the driver sought to avoid drawing attention. If that was the case, he had already failed – for Sin was gaining on him. He urged the horse faster again, just as the driver glanced back, perhaps hearing the hoofbeats.

The carriage began to go faster, and Sin cursed under his breath again – he had hoped to get closer before the man realised that he was pursued. He leant low over the horse's neck, urging him to even greater effort, and desperately changed his path when unaware pedestrians stepped out, or other carriages passed. Ahead of him, the kidnapper's carriage was still some distance away, also now finding the need to avoid other traffic. Sin gasped as it narrowly missed locking wheels with a carriage passing in the other direction.

Soon, the carriage ahead was careering about, rocking wildly as the driver tried to outpace Sin. But Sin was gaining on it. He braced himself, studying the carriage as he finally drew abreast of it. There – what he had hoped for. A handhold stuck out, designed to allow the driver an easy grasp as he climbed up. He brought his horse in, dangerously close to the rapidly turning wheel, and leant out.

Kicking his feet free from the stirrups, he grasped the handhold on the carriage side and swung himself, flicking his legs back, over the horse's rump, then forward again, towards the steps. His arms were strained to the utmost, and his muscles threatened to give way, reminding him just how little exercise he had been doing, since returning to shore. His horse dropped back away from the carriage. His feet hit the steps before his hands lost their grip, and he rapidly hauled himself up and onto the box, to land beside the driver.

The man turned his face to him, wide mouthed in horror and fear. Cardston! The man was a cad, but this was more than Sin had thought him capable of. Sin gave him no time to recover from the surprise – he swung hard at him, a solid punch to the side of the jaw.

With his other hand, he just managed to grab the reins as Cardston dropped them. Cardston slumped, half falling, and Sin grabbed him with his aching hand, and pulled him back onto the seat, just far enough to prevent him going over the side and beneath the wheels.

Sin turned his attention to the road ahead, and desperately steered the carriage horses away from an oncoming vehicle. He set about steadying them, bringing them back under control and down to a sedate pace. He barely managed it before they reached the Park gate.

There, he turned the carriage, earning curses from other drivers, and set off back towards where Lady Scartwick and the Duke could be seen standing beside the road, staring in his direction.

~~~~~

Marion kept searching, moving steadily through the trees in parallel with the others, until they reached the road edge, without finding Daniel. She looked along the road, and froze in place. Lord Hungerwood was riding faster now than before – it seemed that he urged the horse to its greatest possible speed. Just ahead of him, a carriage raced dangerously along the road, weaving in and out of other carriages, barely missing pedestrians. It seemed that the carriage was attempting to prevent Lord Hungerwood catching up to it.

Why would he? And what had the person driving the carriage done? Could it have anything to do with Daniel's disappearance? At that thought, terror filled her. If Daniel was in that carriage... the Duke reached her, and for a moment she turned her head against his shoulder, unable to watch. But the need to know what happened overcame her, and she turned back. Lord Hungerwood had reached the carriage, and ridden up beside it. With a feat of agility that stunned her in its demonstration of his strength and courage, he swung himself from the galloping horse onto the racing carriage. His horse immediately slowed, swinging away from the carriage, and turning back towards where Marion and the Duke stood.

The carriage rocked and swayed, shifting wildly about the road, and Marion wished that she could see what was happening. All she could do was pray that both Daniel, if he was in that carriage, and Lord Hungerwood, would be all right.

The carriage slowed, and, in the far distance near the gate, she saw it turn, and start back towards her.

Closer, she realised that Lord Hungerwood's horse was still loose, moving towards her, scaring people who walked along the paths as it ran, although it had slowed from a gallop to a trot. Without considering anything more than the fact that it needed to be caught, Marion moved towards it, her hand extended, and her voice soft as she spoke. It slowed more, its ears flicking curiously at her. Eventually it stopped, and allowed her to approach. Cautiously, she waited while it sniffed at her, before gently grasping the reins near the bit. It did not pull back, so she scratched it in that spot just above the eye ridge, where she had learned that most horses like to be scratched. It lowered its head and nudged at her. After a few moments, Marion turned, and led the horse back to where the Duke stood, where Lord Hungerwood was just drawing that carriage to a halt. Beside Lord Hungerwood on the box, there slumped a man she loathed.

Lord Frederick Cardston.

At that moment, Marion heard a noise from within the carriage – first thumping, and then an enraged yelling which she recognised all too well. That was the sound of an angry and frustrated Daniel. Her fear eased a little – if Daniel was making that particular set of sounds, then he almost certainly was not hurt – simply frustrated in some major way.

She handed the horse to the Duke, and rushed to open the carriage door. She reached it at the same moment as Lord Hungerwood did, almost colliding with him. For one moment, despite everything, she paused, as if time stood still. His deep blue eyes, so full of concern, caught her, and her heart missed a beat – she remembered that moment – was it only last night? – when he had almost kissed her.

Quickly, she turned back to the carriage. He opened the door, and she climbed in.

"Mama! Let me out! That bad man tied me up and I CAN'T UNDO IT!

Daniel's voice rose to an indignant shout at the end of the sentence, and Marion was hard put not to laugh at his expression. At this moment, at least, there was no fear in his manner, only complete annoyance. She bent over him, shushing him a little, and turned him so that she could reach the knot – it was poorly tied, but had pulled tight from Daniel's struggles and took some time to release. When the rope was removed, he flung his arms around her neck.

Lord Hungerwood reached past her, and pulled the rope out of the carriage, coiling it in his hands. Marion looked at him with a raised eyebrow.

"For Cardston."

"Good. I hope your knots are better than his!"

Lord Hungerwood laughed.

"My Lady, after six years at sea, I would hope so!"

He assisted Marion, still carrying Daniel, who clung to her fiercely, out of the carriage, then went to deal with Cardston. Daniel watched as the unconscious Cardston was securely tied.

"Good. The bad man deserves to be tied up."

"He certainly does, Master Daniel, and we will make sure that he can never do bad things again, to you, or anyone else."

Lord Hungerwood's voice was firm, but Marion heard an undertone to it, which made her look at him curiously. Nanny came rushing over to her at that moment, and Daniel, after a minute's consideration, agreed to release his stranglehold on Marion, and allow Nanny to take him. He looked at Nanny's rather twisted and damaged bonnet, then made a little scrunched up face.

"Nanny – your bonnet?"

"The wind blew it off, Master Daniel, after you undid the ribbon, and it got... squashed... before I could save it."

"I'm sorry. I promise not to undo your ribbons again."

"You are forgiven."

Nanny hugged him to her for a moment, and Marion sighed, glad that Daniel had so many people who loved him. She turned back to find Lord Hungerwood standing closer than expected, his eyes upon her. He was rubbing one hand with the other, and the movement drew her eye.

"Are you hurt?"

"My fist is bruised, perhaps – Cardston has an unfortunately solid skull."

A bubble of slightly hysterical laughter escaped Marion. She repressed it. "How did you come to be here, to know what had happened, in time to save Daniel?"

"I was riding – I usually take the quieter paths through the trees, and along the streamside – and from the distance, I saw a movement in the trees ahead of me. I saw the moment when the man sprang from the trees and grabbed Daniel, while the Nanny was chasing after her bonnet. It was obvious that he was up to no good, and I set off in pursuit. He had a long start on me, but I was determined – for I knew whose child he had kidnapped. I did not know that it was Cardston, until the moment before my fist met his face, though."

"How… how did you know it was Daniel?"

He flushed a little and looked away for a moment.

"I ride most mornings. I must confess to you that I have often passed this point, and paused a moment, to watch him run and play. I am glad to see that Martin's child is happy. He looks so like his father."

That was as close to him speaking the truth to her that she had heard, on the matter of Martin's death. For now, it was enough. Marion took one step forward to close the distance between them, put her hand on his arm, and rose up on her toes, leaning forward to brush a petal soft kiss on his lips.

"Thank you."

Chapter Twelve

After a short conversation in the Park, Cardston had been bundled into his own carriage, and, with Sin's horse tied to the back of it, Sin drove it sedately through the streets to Stafford House, following the Duke's carriage with the Duke and Duchess, Marion, Nanny and Daniel. At Stafford House, Sin oversaw the transfer of Cardston, now awake and uttering a string of profanities, to the care of two burly footmen, who were given instructions to take him to the parlour, and hold him there until he could be questioned.

During that short drive, Sin's mind had been in turmoil. She had kissed him! Was it only gratitude? Or was there more to it? It had been the veriest brush of her lips, yet it had burned him like a branding iron, sending heat through every part of him. And now, here he was, invited to Stafford House. The Duke must know of the rumours, of his supposed part in Martin's death, yet he had invited him without question. What should he say? What should he tell all of them? What had seemed a clear choice for his family's honour, all those years ago, no longer seemed clear at all.

As the footmen hauled Cardston off into the house, Sin arranged for the care of his horse, and then stood a moment, attempting to straighten his somewhat dishevelled appearance before facing the others. He knew, deep within himself, that the moment had come – he could not see a way that the next hour could pass, without him admitting the truth of that night, six years before, when Martin Stafford had died.

Marion deserved to know the truth, as did the Duke – what had been a secret for the sake of his family's honour had become a barrier to healing of the heart for people he had come to care for.

Somehow, he needed to find a way to restore his family's honour, to keep them safe, and yet to give these people the truth. He could not yet see a way to do so, but he must try.

As tidied as was possible without mirror or valet, he went inside, following the footman who had waited for him.

The house was large, quietly elegant in a way that spoke of generations of carefully managed wealth and excellent taste. He was shown to a large parlour, where the Duke and Duchess, and Lady Scartwick, waited.

"Have a seat, Hungerwood – and perhaps a brandy? I have asked the men to hold Cardston in the small parlour, so that we might discuss what happened, before I speak to him. But before anything else is said, I must give you my heartfelt thanks for saving my grandson today. I do not think that I could have borne the pain if I had lost him too."

Everything that Sin had heard of this man was good – his previous wife had been a very unpleasant woman, but the Duke had always been spoken of as both kind and honourable.

He took the offered brandy, and wondered exactly how to

respond to the Duke's words.

In the end, he chose simple honesty.

"Thank you, Your Grace. But I could have done nothing less. Having seen Cardston scoop him up and run, the only honourable thing to do was make chase."

The Duke nodded, then turned to Lady Scartwick.

"Marion, my dear, do you know anything of why Lord Frederick might have wished to kidnap Daniel? Is this to do with me? Or with you? Or something else incomprehensible?"

Lady Scartwick paled at his words, and Sin felt an intense desire to go to her and comfort her in some way. He took a large sip of his brandy, and forced himself to stay as he was. Awaiting her answer.

"I... I believe that it is because of me that Cardston has done this. Exactly what he hoped to gain, I do not know, but he has been... unpleasantly... pursuing me this last month and more, since we came to London. You will remember what I told you, when you first discovered who I was, and who Daniel was, of the weeks before and after Martin's death. Cardston was one of the worst then – the most insistent in pursuing me, in believing that I was a lightskirt who could be taken at will. When we returned to London this year, he approached me, and made... indecent... although politely phrased, suggestions. He, to be very blunt, wanted me. And he had the gall to suggest that I should be grateful, especially as he was 'willing to offer me marriage, rather than just take me as a mistress'. I told him that I did not wish to marry at that time, and even if I had wished to, that he would never have been considered."

The Duke's face had flushed with emotion, and his hands had closed to fists as Lady Scartwick spoke.

"The man is obviously the worst kind of cad!"

"He is. He did not take my refusal as serious. He continued to press me, at most Balls we attended, if I was unwise enough to allow him to get near me. I knew that he was becoming more and more angry with me, but I never thought that he would do something quite so mad as this!"

"Indeed, mad is, I believe, the correct word here," the Duke turned to Sin, "and you, Hungerwood, how came you to be in place to carry out such a dramatic rescue?"

"Your Grace, I ride in the Park each morning, and have often seen your party from a distance – so I was aware of the identity of the boy. As I rode along my usual path this morning, through the trees along the stream, I saw, from the distance, a man among the trees. It caught my eye as unusual, and, as I watched, he leapt out, when the Nanny's back was turned as she chased after her bonnet, scooped up the child, and ran. I knew that could not be right, so I gave chase. I did not know his identity, until the moment just before I punched him, as the carriage careered along. But I do remember him, from... before I left England. It is as Lady Scartwick says. He was amongst the worst of the group who went about with Martin, and he envied Martin's relationship with Lady Scartwick."

"I see. It is best, then, that we go and question the man, with respect to his reasons for his actions today."

"I would come with you – not that I ever wish to see that man's face again, but I must understand why he kidnapped my son."

The Duke looked at Lady Scartwick, concern on his face.

"Are you sure, Marion? If he has been so impertinent to you, so utterly rude, are you certain that you wish to be exposed to whatever he says now?"

"I am quite sure. I must know. There is far too much of what happened back then, of what happened when Martin died, that I do not know – and the not knowing haunts me, always."

The Duchess quietly took Marion's hand, her expression kind and caring. At Lady Scartwick's answer to the Duke, Sin felt the urge, again, to tell them the truth. But first, perhaps, hearing what Cardston had to say would be best.

They rose, and the Duke led them to the small parlour where Cardston was being held.

As they stepped through the door, Cardston looked at them, his face contorted with anger.

"Release me! How dare you hold me!"

"You will not be released, and you are a fool to even think that I might allow it. When you have attempted to abscond with my grandson, my heir, why would you expect any forgiveness from me?"

"You are a fool, just like your son was, taken in by that commoner fancy piece's pretty face. How did she convince you that he married her? A fine set of lies that is – the child is probably not even his! And you," Cardston almost spat the words in Sin's direction, "you've done a fine job of lying too, but I can't see why you've taken against me now – were we not all of the same friendship, back then? But then, you're a fool – I should have understood that. Any man who takes on his brother's dishonour, and lets the world destroy his life for it, is as likely to do anything, isn't he?"

Sin swallowed hard. So Cardston knew.

The Duke turned to Sin, a look of confusion on his face.

"Hungerwood, what is he raving about? What lies does he speak of, and what is this of your brother's dishonour? And what has that to do with what he did today?"

"He speaks of the night of your son's death, Your Grace. Although I was never truly this man's friend – an acquaintance, yes, but not a friend – for even then, his attitudes and manner were a bit more than I could stomach, on many occasions."

"More lies – you are obviously quite mad, Hungerwood."

Cardston's voice was shrill, and his eyes wild. Sin sighed – there was nothing for it but to relate the whole sordid tale, and risk what might come to his family. He could not allow this madness to continue.

"Perhaps I was mad, back then, to do what I did – but I saw only the threat to my family – I did not realise that I would ever be in the position I am today. Your Grace, I am quite certain that you will have heard every rumour. That you will have been told that I stood Second to Sinclair, on that fateful night, and that, as Sinclair did, once it was clear that Martin was dead, I fled the country. I must tell you now that only part of that is true."

Behind him, he heard a small gasp from Lady Scartwick, echoed by one from the Duchess.

The Duke looked at him steadily a moment before speaking.

"Then tell me what is true, and what is not. I would not have one detail of my son's last hours lost to me."

Cardston made a derisive noise, mocking, as if glad that someone else was the focus of the Duke's attention at that point.

Sin ignored him.

"Your Grace, what I am about to tell you has hitherto, as far as I know, only been known by my family – and even that only recently. Initially, only my brother and I knew. On the night of the duel, my brother Hugh, then the heir to the title, was the man who was second to Sinclair. I was present, and standing not far from him. We were quite alike to look at, and in the darkness before the dawn, an onlooker could easily mistake us. My brother was, I am sad to say, a rabble rousing, hot headed fool," Cardston laughed raucously and Sin ignored him again, "I had tried to talk him out of being Second, but he had insisted, even urging Sinclair on, in a way that I could not like. But when the moment came, and I saw Martin's life fade before me, I realised that I had only one choice. If it was known that Hugh had been Second, had encouraged the duel, our family's honour would have been damaged beyond redemption. He was the heir, and I knew that society might not accept him as Earl, when the time came, if he had dishonour so sordid attached to him."

The Duke looked at him calmly, listening without apparent judgement, and Sin was grateful.

"So, Hungerwood, what did you do?"

"I believe you will already have deduced that, Your Grace. I stepped in front of Hugh, pushing him back, and pretending that I had been Second. Dishonour of a second son would not hurt the family anywhere near as much as dishonour of the heir. Hugh let me do it – I think that, in that moment, he realised why it was necessary. Within days, both I and Sinclair had left the country. Only he and Hugh knew the truth for certain. And now, both of them are dead. I never expected to return to England, never expected to bear the title. But now that I do, I must face the consequences of that decision, every day."

Cardston spoke, quietly this time, and it was all the more chilling for it.

"But I knew. As soon as I saw you again, when you returned, I knew. For whilst the two of you were alike, you were not identical. You were a fool to throw your life away for your brother – for he did not value it. I've watched you, since your return, trying so hard to please them all, while they treat you coldly, barely better than the cut direct. And it wasn't worth it in the end, was it? For Hugh went and died with dishonour himself, making all your effort for nothing. I don't know why you bothered to interfere today – or do you want Martin's strumpet for yourself?"

Sin stepped forward and slapped Cardston across the face, hard.

The man fell silent with a whimper.

"You will not speak of my daughter-in-law like that again." The Duke's voice was glacially cold. "But... I still do not entirely see why you kidnapped my grandson?"

Cardston glared at everyone.

"Well, it seemed to me that, if she wouldn't agree to wed me, bringing that nice dowry its rumoured you've settled upon her, willingly, then I needed to provide a reason to... convince... her to agree. The boy suited that purpose admirably. For she would do anything to ensure his safety, as would you. Had Hungerwood not intervened, you would have received a note tomorrow morning, laying out my requirements."

Sin looked at the man in shock – Cardston must be mad, to think that a woman would marry him under such conditions – yet he seemed to be speaking the truth, as he saw it.

The Duke was silent a moment, then fixed Cardston with a glare that would make any sane man quail.

"I see. You have just, I believe, admitted to kidnapping with the intent to blackmail, in front of multiple witnesses. I could see you charged, and your disgrace dragged before the view of everyone – but I believe a better solution would be for you to simply disappear. It seems fitting that you suddenly discover a deep need to remove to the Americas and seek your fortune there. I will arrange your passage on a ship of good repute – one where the crew cannot be bribed… and I will even be so generous as to provide you some funds – to be handed to you once you have left the ship in America. If you ever attempt to set foot in England again, after that, you will rue the day that you were born."

Sin spoke into the silence that followed the Duke's words, while Cardston was still gaping at them, shocked.

"I believe that I can assist with both a suitable ship, and appropriate contacts in the Americas – in addition to whatever contacts you have yourself, Your Grace. Six years as a privateer has left me with some… unusual… connections."

The Duke nodded, and turned to the footmen who had stood silent, holding Cardston in place, throughout the entire exchange.

"Take him, and lock him in the deepest, most secure cellar. Give him only what food and drink is required to keep him alive, and nothing more. And forget that you ever heard a word of what has been said here today."

"Yes, Your Grace. I will see to it."

They watched Cardston led away, only then coming out of his shocked silence to rail at them as he realised the truth of his fate. Only once he could no longer be heard did anyone move or speak.

"I believe that we have much to discuss. But let us repair to the main parlour, and call for refreshments before we begin. I would be away from this room, for at present it echoes with Cardston's foul words, even if only in my mind."

The Duchess looked at her husband as she spoke, and something seemed to pass between them. Beside her, Marion looked pale and very shaken. Her eyes sought Sin's, and again, he felt the extreme urge to go to her, to hold her close. He did not move. After a moment, the Duke spoke, his tone sad.

"You are correct, my dear Sylvia. I had hoped never to need to discuss that dreadful night again – but it seems that I must."

Chapter Thirteen

Once they had settled in the parlour, and tea and biscuits sat before them, the Duke looked at Lord Hungerwood. Marion wondered what he was thinking. Her mind was still reeling from the events of the day, and from her reaction to Cardston's vile attitudes. She had, due to her eavesdropping, had some weeks to come to terms with the fact that Lord Hungerwood was not the villain he had been painted as, with respect to Martin's death – but the Duke had not had that benefit. Hungerwood seemed calm, but Marion could see the uncertainty in him, that tension which comes with expecting unpleasantness. She put her faith in what she knew of the Duke – the most unfailingly kind and fair-minded man she had ever met. His first words confirmed how right she was to trust him so.

"Hungerwood, I must understand, must know all of it. You are telling me that it was your brother who incited the duel that took my son's life, and that you took on your brother's disgrace, for the sake of the good name of your family, accepting what seemed likely to be permanent exile?"

"Yes, Your Grace. That is the heart of it."

"Then you have been done a grave disservice. It is obvious that you are far more honourable than a cad like Cardston could ever be – and all should know that. It is unconscionable that Cardston has been welcomed amongst the *ton*, whilst you have been barely tolerated."

"I would be delighted to have my honour proved to the *ton* – but how could that be achieved? For if I blacken my brother's name, my family will be the worse for it, no matter what the circumstances now. Many would not believe me – they would claim that I spoke from self-interest, blaming a dead man who could not speak in his own defence."

The Duke regarded him, and shook his head.

"I do not have an answer to that difficulty, much though it pains me to admit it."

Marion felt a rush of disappointment – to her, the Duke had always seemed capable of resolving almost any problem.

"Surely there is a way? Some way to restore Lord Hungerwood's honour in the eyes of the *ton*, without damaging his family in the process?"

As the Duke shook his head, frustration clear in his expression, the Duchess spoke.

"I have an idea. I believe that it is possible." Three faces turned to her, each full of hope, tempered by the improbability of there being such a solution. "It will involve the assistance of quite a few of our trusted friends, in a way that we have used before. When we acted to change the *ton's* perception of Lord Porthaven. Many of the same tactics will work in this case."

The Duke raised an eyebrow at his wife.

"My dear Sylvia, yet again, you surprise me. What is this manipulation of society's perceptions that you refer to?"

The Duchess flushed, which was such a rare occurrence that Marion was startled to see it, and then she set about explaining.

"Well, Julian, it was before we met, so, of course, you were not aware of it. At that point, you were still rather a recluse... This could be a very long story, but I will attempt to summarise it effectively. The man who is now the Earl of Porthaven is Raphael Morton. He is one of the group of men often referred to as 'His Majesty's Hounds' who served with my son during the wars, in France and Spain. He was, and still is, an inordinately successful merchant, following on from his father in that success. When the Prince Regent saw fit to have him granted a title, in recognition of his service to the crown, the *ton* did not respond well. There were nasty caricatures and worse. One of his businesses is an art gallery – and we used that as the starting point to changing the *ton's* opinion, not only of him, but of the woman who is now his wife – a woman whose own family were the subject of a scandal."

"Fascinating my dear – how on earth did you overcome the prejudice and gossip which that combination of events would have created?"

"We arranged an event at the gallery, and had every person of high rank of our close friendship attend. We made quite certain of the exact timing of their arrivals on the day, so that it presented a dazzling parade of important people, each showing obvious approval. Lord Setford even managed, somehow, to get the Prince Regent to make an appearance."

Marion almost gasped at the audacity of it – it seemed unlikely... yet the Duchess was, if she had it aright, telling them that this had worked.

"And this worked? The *ton* changed their attitude? But why? What made that so?"

As he spoke, Lord Hungerwood's face, for one moment, displayed a look of raw desperation, before he quickly calmed his expression.

"It worked. After so many people of importance had greeted the Earl and his then wife-to-be as valued and respected friends, even the Prince Regent, how could the *ton* cut them? The toadies who follow the Prince Regent's every whim actually helped, in a sense, for they simply did as he did – if he approved of someone, and of their business, so did they, even if that person was titled, previously scandalous, a merchant, or worse, all of those together. Over the next month or more, after that event, we kept ostentatiously being friendly to Raphael and Sera, at every social event we could, until the *ton* grew weary of attempting to see it as scandal, and moved on to more titillating gossip. I am sure that we could arrange something similar in this case."

"But... that might make the *ton* less frostily cold to me, and my family, I agree – but how might it allow the truth to be known, allow my honour to be restored, without damage to my family?"

"It will restore your honour, because we will start with some carefully crafted rumours. We will give them something to gossip about – but something which is to your benefit, rather than to your detriment."

"Rumours?"

"Yes, rumours – about how things have come out which indicate that perhaps your brother was not quite as well behaved a gentleman as others had thought, about how his final demise in a duel over an actress led some to dig deeper, and discover that, whilst he mostly acted as many other men of the *ton* do, he was not of ideal character. And we will lead from that, in tiny increments, to our 'mysterious unnamed investigator' having realised that the issue of having been Second to Sinclair in the duel which took Martin's life was something far more in character for your brother, than for you. And then we will introduce supposition that perhaps you did the honourable thing, and took the blame, to allow him, as heir, to remain unsullied. At which point the rumours will move on to sympathising with how you must have felt, when he died and you returned to England, to see that your sacrifice had been wasted. And all the while that these rumours are circulating, leading people steadily to the conclusion that we want in the whispers, in the open, at every event, many of us will be speaking with you and your family, and generally proving that there is no reason to be cold to you."

Lord Hungerwood was silent, absorbing the remarkable plan which had been laid before him. Marion watched him, unable to look away, remembering all of the moments at Balls where he had suffered the disdain of his peers. She discovered that she wanted this for him, intensely. Finally, he asked the question which had also been in Marion's mind.

"Your Grace, when you speak of 'we' who do you mean?"

The Duchess laughed, a bright silvery sound.

"Oh dear, I did leave that bit out, didn't I? I believe, at a quick consideration, that we can bring four Dukes, two Marquesses, three Earls, two Viscounts and two Barons to this project immediately, and a number of well-known heirs to titles, plus any friends of theirs who may be persuaded to indulge us. And, whilst it cannot be promised, I do believe that Lord Setford may be able to influence the Prince Regent to perhaps be in the right place at the right time – although if that happens, I am quite sure that your pretty sister will have to accept the Prince Regent's flirtation, even if only for a few minutes. He can be quite... blatant... when he admires a woman."

"I am sure that Faith would manage – she is of quite strong character. But... I have just realised – if I agree to this plan, we will not be able to tell my mother or my sister – I would not want them to hope, and then have that hope dashed if it all came to naught. Nor, for that matter, would I wish them to know what sort of rumours were circulating about Hugh. That would be far too embarrassing for them. Although, I suppose that they will hear some of it, regardless. But I would prefer to limit how much they must suffer."

The Duke spoke for the first time since his wife had begun to describe her plan.

"I do believe, my dear Sylvia, that what you propose is possible and practical. And just might work. We can most certainly implement a plan of that nature, and also keep it from Lady Hungerwood and Lady Faith. We would, Lord Hungerwood, need your assistance in composing these rumours, so that what is said of your brother is based solidly in truth, and impugns his character only so far as necessary for your own honourable nature to shine by comparison."

"Of course – I will do whatever is needed – for this is a gift beyond measure that you offer me."

The Duke studied the man before him for a moment, then smiled. "For the man who saved my grandson, I will do my utmost. And for the man who has given me the last pieces of the truth about my son's death, I have eternal gratitude. We have all suffered far too much, for more than six long years, as a result of that one fateful night – I would see the wrongs righted, and the painful memories released, so that we might all move on in our lives, unburdened by the past."

"Thank you – I can only agree with your sentiments. To free us all from the past would be a wondrous achievement. A life in which I might live without being reminded every day of the mistakes of the past is something I have only dreamed of."

As Lord Hungerwood uttered those words, his eyes met Marion's and she felt as if he wished to say something more, something for her alone. She smiled, holding his eyes for some time, before turning away. The Duchess observed it all, her eyes bright and perceptive, and nodded quietly to herself.

"Then we must plan in detail. Lord Hungerwood, are you able to call upon us tomorrow, that we might begin? I expect that we can, with care, have the first rumours circulating within the week."

"Your Grace, I can. I will make myself available at your command, for as long as this takes, and hope that, by the end of it, I will see my honour restored, and my family's situation improved as a result. I will also, I confess, look forward to the chance to get to know your grandson, if you will permit it, Your Grace?"

The latter question he addressed to the Duke.

Marion discovered that she was holding her breath, awaiting the answer.

"Of course. I suspect that the boy will like you. That is, of course, if you are also in agreeance, Marion?" At her nod, he went on, "I think it a good step towards removing the false beliefs of the past."

"Thank you, Your Grace. I will depart now, and leave you to your day. But, before I do, might I have a short word with Lady Scartwick, in private?"

The Duke and Duchess looked at each other, and as so often happened, something unspoken passed between them.

Marion watched, unsure – part of her desperately wanted to be alone with Lord Hungerwood, and part of her feared her own reactions in such a situation – after all, in the Park, she had kissed him, where anyone might have seen – and she did not know if he thought badly of her for that. Or if, indeed, he might be inclined to kiss her in return....

~~~~~

Sin held his breath, for what he asked might be seen as significant impropriety – although widows had far more leeway than unmarried young women.

But after one quick look between the Duke and Duchess, the Duke turned to him.

"Of course. We will leave you – do call for more refreshments if you feel the need. I will see you on the morrow, to further our plan."

They left the room, and closed the door as they went. Lady Scartwick – Marion, as he more and more allowed himself to think of her – sat, unmoving, waiting. He stepped towards her, unsure of his welcome, but she made the tiniest of gestures to the space beside her on the couch. He sank down, acutely aware of her warmth, such a short distance away. Suddenly, he had no idea what to say – yet he needed to know where he stood. The previous night on the terrace at the Ball, she had fled his embrace, yet this morning, in the Park, she had pressed her lips to his, however fleetingly. He swallowed. She watched him.

"I… I wanted to apologise."

"Apologise?" She looked confused at his words.

"Yes. For… for whatever I did or said last night, which caused you to abandon me so precipitously, on the terrace."

"Oh!" She flushed a little, but met his eyes. "That was not what you did, but rather my own state of mind. You spoke of your belief that I would be honest in conversation, and... I was struck with guilt."

"Guilt? But..."

"Oh dear. I am making a mess of this. But, after the events of today, and after your admission of your secret, it is only fair that I do tell you the truth of this, however embarrassing it may be. Some weeks ago, at a Ball, I had fled the ballroom to hide – from Cardston. I found a library, and settled in the furthest darkest corner, so that I might rest and avoid him. But I had not been there long when I heard the door open, and footsteps. I could not see that part of the room, and I froze, lest it be him."

Sin nodded, understanding in a flash of insight.

"But it was not him, it was me, with Faith, wasn't it?"

"Yes – and I heard your whole conversation. For, by the time I knew it was not Cardston, it was far too late to reveal myself. So, since that night, I have known your secret. And it changed how I saw you. From the moment I met you, I had struggled to reconcile the rumours and tales with the honourable man I saw before me – and once I knew the truth, I could no longer allow myself to believe any of it, nor to be cold to you – for you were not the man I would have had cause to hate. But I did not tell you that I had eavesdropped, or that I knew. And when you spoke of my honesty..."

"You fled, rather than explain, in such a public place, where others might come upon us at any time." She nodded, her green eyes unhappy. "Then... might I resume at the point where our... conversation was so sharply broken off?"

He reached for her, and gently pulled her to him, bringing his lips down upon hers. She did not pull away, but, after a moment, relaxed and leant into the kiss. Time slowed, and there was nothing but this woman, the scent of her intoxicating, the feel of her lips against his sweeter than anything he had ever felt. Her lips parted, allowing him access, and a tiny sigh escaped her. Then her lips moved against his, and she pressed into his arms, as hungry for the moment as he was. It lasted forever, and barely a moment. He drew back, and held her eyes. She smiled, tremulously, then burst into tears. He pulled her against him, cradling her as she cried, releasing all of the fear and stress of the day, and most likely of the last six years as well.

Chapter Fourteen

For the next few days, Marion did not attend any social events. She concentrated on spending time with Daniel, making sure that he was none the worse for his adventure, and on the planning for their grand scheme to restore Lord Hungerwood's honour in the eyes of the *ton*. Each day, she found herself awaiting his arrival eagerly, and secretly hoping for a chance to arise which might lead to another kiss. It did not, until the second day, on which day Cardston was finally removed from the cellar, and taken away in a carriage sent by Lord Setford, to be placed upon a ship which sailed on that morning's tide.

Knowing that Cardston would be gone from the country lifted a great weight from Marion's soul. He had been persuaded to write and sign a note, which was sent to his family, informing them that he had chosen to sail for the Americas. For a week or two, Marion was sure it would be speculated about amongst the *ton*, but soon, she hoped, their carefully constructed rumours about Lord Hungerwood's brother would overtake Cardston's disappearance as the favoured gossip of the day.

As Setford's men led Cardston away, Marion had stood in the parlour, behind an almost closed door, and watched as he was removed from the house – she needed to see it, to know that it had happened, that he was truly gone. Just before Cardston was removed, Lord Hungerwood had stepped into the parlour, having just arrived.

They were alone, and he had not said a word when she mostly closed the door and watched. He had simply stepped up behind her, and gently settled his hands on her hips. She had leant back against the hard strength of him, as if it was the most natural thing in the world. When Cardston was gone, he had reached past her shoulder, and pushed the door shut.

She turned in his arms, and looked up at him.

This kiss was an exploration, in some ways a celebration of the removal of something bad from her life. It sent warmth through her, and left her aching, wanting, as she had not, since the day of Martin's death.

She did not yet know what she desired with this man, but she knew, without doubt, that it was worth pursuing.

When they finally drew apart, he smiled, that brilliant smile which transformed his face, and tugged at her heart.

"My Lady, dare I assume that you wish to further our acquaintance, that you feel an intensity of connection between us, as I do?"

"I… I do not know what I want, in truth, not yet. That I wish to spend time in your company, that I enjoy your kisses – that much I know. But where that might lead… there is far too much to deal with at present for me to think clearly on the matter."

"Then we will go slowly, and find clarity together."

"I think so. let us not overly scandalise the *ton* all at once. While the rumours are set, and the change in your reception amongst the *ton* is orchestrated, let us talk at Balls and other events, let us dance, and walk on terraces and in gardens, but nothing more. Once that plan is well advanced, perhaps then, you might wish to call upon me, and... discuss... what we each want."

He lifted his hand, and cupped her cheek, and Marion felt his touch as heat, and yet as gentle care. It shocked her, then, just how much she cared for this man, how much she wanted to explore what might be possible for them, once the spectre of the past no longer haunted either of them.

"As you wish, my Lady. But I do not promise not to steal a kiss, every so often."

He brushed his lips across hers again, gently, the touch a commitment to his words, yet arousing to a far greater degree than such a simple touch might be expected to be.

They stepped apart, by unspoken consent, and settled to discussing the ongoing plan, awaiting the Duke and Duchess to finalise their ideas.

~~~~

A week later, when Sin stepped into the ballroom at Lady Croftonleigh's townhome, the whispers began, as always. But this time, there was something different about it. The young women eyed him with even more interest, and more flirtatious looks, their mothers pushed them forward with more enthusiasm. The men eyed him with barely concealed curiosity.

And, every so often, as he moved about the room, he overheard a word or two – his brother's name, and snippets of speculation – one memorable one was a lady who obviously thought herself a wit, contemplating whether 'Sin the sinner was wicked in the 'right' way, or in a dishonourable way...' Sin flinched a little, then forced a non-committal smile onto his face, and pretended not to have heard at all.

Soon after, the Duke and Duchess of Windemere arrived, with Lady Scartwick at their side. His eyes went to her, and he admired, yet again, what a beautiful woman she was, and how gracefully, elegantly so, with none of the posturing of the younger women. As they had agreed, he went forward to greet the Duke, and they fell into an obviously friendly conversation.

As they spoke, they moved about the room, and the Duke introduced him to other men and women – people of significance, who also treated him warmly. At each event they attended, he would meet more people, like this, introduced from person to person, through an extended web of connections. He discovered that he liked the people who he was introduced to, in almost every case, and hoped that continued to be the pattern.

He had not realised just how empty the continual coldness of the *ton* had left him feeling, until the first time that he was greeted with warmth. It was as if an aching void was slowly being healed within him. He could so easily have stayed by Lady Scartwick's side for the entire evening – but he did not, he did not have the right to do so, not yet. Instead, he danced with hopeful young women, saving the waltz for Lady Scartwick, and concentrated on being seen to have the right friends. It was far more exhausting than he had expected.

When the time for the waltz finally arrived, he took Lady

Scartwick in his arms with a sense of relief. For the span of the dance, he could cease pretending, cease needing to be utterly careful of every word he said, and simply enjoy the moment. And enjoy it he did – far more than he could ever remember enjoying dancing in his life before.

She looked up at him with those soft green eyes, her fingers tightened on his, and everything else faded away. They moved without thought being required, completely in tune with each other. He smiled, lost in the wonder of a moment when all stresses were forgotten.

He came back to himself when she spoke – her words so soft that they were barely audible.

"They whisper about your brother, which is good. But... they also whisper about Cardston, and not in the way that we expected. Someone saw his wild driving in the Park, someone who recognised both him, and you. They whisper about his odd behaviour, and your daring act – and they wonder what caused it all, and why you did it. They perceive you as a hero, having saved everyone from his mad driving, and the accident which was certain to happen if he had continued. At least none of them seem to have seen us remove Daniel from the carriage. And from the tone of their whispers, being seen as a hero is doing no harm to your image."

Sin looked at her, shocked – it was not a result that he had expected – at the time, all he had cared about was saving Daniel.

"That is a... surprising... piece of news."

All too soon, the music ended, and he was forced to let her go – he found that he did not wish to – not then, not ever.

That thought made him falter, as they walked back to the Duke.

'Not ever' – did he really mean that? For there was only one conclusion to be drawn from such a thought. He pushed the idea away – there would be time to consider it later – when he was not in the midst of a crowd of people, all avidly watching his every move. That they now were conflicted, some calling him hero, and some still calling him blackguard, amused him darkly, but made their attention all that more focussed.

By the end of the evening, he was more than glad to leave, although there was a part of him that wished to stay with Lady Scartwick. On the way home in the carriage, as their mother half dozed on the opposite seat, Faith leaned close against him and whispered to him.

"Drummond, what has happened? For something has changed, do not try to deny it – they are treating you differently. And I hear whispers, although they all stop as soon as I get near. Do tell me, oh frustratingly secretive brother."

Sin looked at her, and schooled his face to impassive calm.

"No, dear sister, I will not tell you anything. I will not even confirm that there is anything to tell. I will leave everything to your powers of observation."

"Hmmph! You are so annoying sometimes!"

But she left it at that, for which he was grateful.

~~~~~

The next few weeks passed quickly, and the plan proceeded as it had been designed to. Marion began, just a little, to relax.

It fascinated her how easily the *ton* could be manipulated, and she regarded her now mother-in-law with awe. She had known that Sylvia was most intelligent, outspoken, and determined to do good in the world, but Marion had never before truly understood the depth of her skill with people, and the complexities which her mind unravelled easily. Ball after Ball, dinner and soiree passed with the flow of expertly started rumours drifting around the *ton*, tangled with, and augmented by, the rumours about Cardston, and Lord Hungerwood's heroics in the Park. And each time she heard them, they were a little more favourable to Lord Hungerwood, and a little less so to his deceased brother.

It seemed that people were quite ready to believe ill of the dead, and good of the living, when encouraged the right way. The friendship of Dukes and other significant persons had not gone unnoticed either, and Marion was delighted to see the attitudes to Lord Hungerwood shift, as people greeted him more warmly, and invited him to more events than before. He seemed less tense, less on edge now, too, and even sometimes laughed with friends, rather than standing aloof.

Best of all, apart from the improvement in Lord Hungerwood's status, it seemed that Cardston's fall from grace and disappearance had made an impact upon the rest of the 'old crowd' who had been there, pressing themselves upon her, just after Martin's death. Now, they no longer attempted to speak to her. They did not cut her, but they did avoid her, especially when Lord Hungerwood was near. Her fear of them was fading with every evening spent free of their impolite presence.

She danced with Lord Hungerwood, walked in gardens with him, and allowed him to kiss her, more than once.

And with every day that passed, she became more certain that her feelings for him were deeper than she had ever expected, far deeper than just gratitude for his saving Daniel.

But what was the character of his feelings for her? She did not truly know – not yet, at least.

Finally, as the Season was drawing to a close, there came the point when the last of the rumours had been released quietly amongst the gossips. And, true to the pattern of the weeks that had gone by, it was soon being whispered at each occasion when people came together – it was simple – the idea that, with all that had been revealed, the only conclusion possible was that, in fact, the current Lord Hungerwood was a deeply honourable man, one who had sacrificed himself for his family's sake.

Just hearing it whispered made Marion happy. Soon, perhaps, they might explore what they felt for each other, now that the world had begun to see him differently, now that the ills of the past were well on their way to being healed. As Marion dressed for a Ball at Lady Chesterton's, to be one of the last Balls before the Season wound down into summer, she wondered what might happen next. And, perhaps for the first time in ten years, all of the options which she could picture were at least pleasant, rather than bad.

~~~~~

Sin stared at himself in the mirror. Carlton had worked his magic with cravats and hair again, making Sin look the perfectly turned out gentleman. And, as a reflection of his growing optimism, for the first time, he had added colour to his attire.

The deep blue of the brocaded waistcoat brought out the blue of his eyes, and made him wonder why he had avoided colour for so long. From now on, he vowed to indulge in it often.

The carriage trip was short, this evening's event being held not far from his home, and the warmth of the summer twilight made him happy to leave the carriage window open, to catch whatever breeze there might be. He looked out as they travelled the streets, and realised that, somewhere in the last few months, London had become normal again – he no longer expected the brightly coloured houses of the West Indies, or the colonial style of the Americas. London had become, somehow, against his expectations, home again.

Once they arrived at Lady Chesterton's, the evening proceeded as expected – he was greeted by friends, flirted with by young ladies, and generally welcomed. And, of course, gossiped about. It had become ordinary to him, for that to be so, but there was a new pleasure in hearing the whispers, for they spoke of his honourable nature, of his heroic character. He cared not one whit whether they thought him a hero, but he cared beyond measure that they thought him honourable.

He danced, as always, with an assortment of increasingly hopeful young women, and waited for the moment when he might waltz with Lady Scartwick. For she always kept the waltz on her dance card for him. When that moment came, he swept her to the floor, and into his arms, and she laughed at his enthusiasm. He laughed with her, as the music carried them into that place where all else became irrelevant.

"My Lady, I do believe that the plan can be said to have worked, well beyond my hopes and expectations – do you agree?"

"I do, my Lord."

"Then may I ask, my Lady, if I might call upon you, if I might allow the world to see that I care for you?"

Her eyes widened at his words, and for an instant, he feared her answer, feared that she would not permit it – he knew, quite certainly in that moment, that he would do anything to spend more time with this woman – anything at all. And that was quite the most terrifying thought that he had ever had in his life. Then, freeing him from his immediate fear, she smiled broadly, and answered him.

"I believe that I would enjoy that, my Lord."

He pulled her a little closer to him, so close that it was almost scandalous, and inhaled the clean scent of her hair as he whispered in her ear.

"Then you may expect me tomorrow, my Lady, most likely at an hour far too early for polite morning calls."

She said nothing more, but her smile was enough. When the music ended, he led her back to the Duke, and stood talking with the Duke and Duchess for some time. As they spoke, there came a commotion at the door. Looking up, Sin almost gasped. There, in the entry, stood the Prince Regent, accompanied as always by those who clung to his coattails, hoping to achieve vicarious importance.

The Duchess made a small sound, and Sin looked to her. She smiled, and whispered, "Setford has achieved miracles, as usual. I am pleased."

"Setford?"

"There, near the Prince – the inconspicuous one."

"Ah, yes, I remember seeing him before – in the Park with you?"

"Yes."

At that moment, the Prince Regent and his entourage began to move into the room, having greeted the host and hostess.

It appeared to Sin that Lord Setford had said something to the Prince, and indicated their direction. Sure enough, the Prince Regent was coming towards them.

Time slowed - the moment was almost as frightening as the moment before a ship went into battle – a stillness within which anything might happen, no matter how well planned the approach had been. Then the Prince Regent was upon them, and Sin bowed, the deep court bow that he had been schooled in, but never expected to use, as Lady Scartwick beside him sank into a deep curtsey, her movement fluid and elegantly controlled.

"Up, up. Let me see you, Hungerwood. I have been hearing much of you lately – most interesting gossip indeed. And Setford informs me that it is, in the vast majority, true. If that is the case, then you are a man of rare honour and ability. Tell me – are the descriptions of your athletic leap from horse to speeding carriage accurate? Or do these fools exaggerate?"

Sin swallowed – what on earth could he say?

"Your Highness, as I have not heard, myself, the descriptions you speak of, I cannot be entirely sure of their veracity. But yes, I did leap from my galloping horse onto a speeding carriage, which was being driven rather erratically at the time, by a man intent on mischief of the worst kind."

"Hah! Excellent! No wonder the women flock to you." Sin blinked, unsure how to respond to that, but the Prince Regent went on. "You have far more style and character than the fops who surround me, well matched with looks and honour." The Prince Regent's eyes turned to Lady Scartwick, who stood quietly beside Sin. He regarded her a moment, appreciatively. "But I see that you have good taste in women too. Lady Scartwick, is it not?"

Lady Scartwick curtseyed again, rising quickly.

"Yes, Your Highness."

"You could do worse than Hungerwood, far worse, my Lady. Your son would do well with a man like him as a parent. But, of course, you will do as you will, sensible or not – for women are fickle creatures."

Lady Scartwick blushed, and the Prince Regent's toadies all laughed at his jest, but the words struck hard to Sin's heart. For the very idea that she might ever marry – anyone but him, that is - caused him deep pain. His path became utterly clear in that moment. Lady Scartwick waited for the laughter to die, then spoke again, her voice quiet but clear.

"I do believe that you have the right of it, Your Highness – about Lord Hungerwood, that is, for I may perhaps take exception to the implication that I am fickle."

The Prince Regent looked at her, startled and delighted.

"This one has courage. I'd heard that, but it is good to see it proven. A good match, I think. Do remember to invite me to the wedding."

Both Sin and Lady Scartwick stood, stunned.

The Prince Regent turned away, obviously finished with what he had wanted to say to them, and spoke to the Duke and Duchess.

Sin said nothing, but could not help but reach out and take her hand. She threaded her fingers through his, and he tightened his hold for a moment. Words had become unnecessary. Then he released her, and they simply stood, as the Prince Regent moved on about the room, speaking to various people.

In his wake, people began to come to Sin – people who had still not overcome their reserve about him, until now. It seemed that the Prince Regent's obvious favour had broken down the last barriers.

An hour or more later, after the Prince Regent had departed, and the schedule of dances and supper had been re-established, Sin turned to Lady Scartwick, as the orchestra struck up for the second waltz of the night. Her green eyes drew him in, and he knew now that the Prince Regent was utterly right. They were a good match – but did she agree? Could she accept him as a serious suitor, after all that had happened?

There was but one way to find out.

"My Lady, we spoke long ago about the comparative scandalousness of me dancing with you two nights running, or twice in one night. I feel that I am ready to explore that to the full – will you grant me this dance?"

Her eyes sparkled, and she tipped her head slightly, studying him, before she spoke.

"I seem to remember, my Lord, that you said, then, that you were not certain of your own intent. Are you certain now?"

"Quite, quite certain, my Lady."

"Then yes, I will grant you this second dance of the evening."

ARIETTA RICHMOND

Chapter Fifteen

When they reached home that evening, Sin was ready to simply collapse into bed, but his mother stopped him as he went towards the stairs.

"Drummond. A word, if you will." She led him into the parlour, and Faith followed. "How did you do it? For I am sure that you arranged it. How did you cause this change of attitude from the *ton*, over these last weeks?"

Faith looked on, obviously as keen to hear his answer as their mother was. Sin sighed, unable to blame them for asking, but wondering exactly what he might say. As he hesitated, Faith spoke.

"It started when those rumours started – about Hugh. Where did that come from? For what was said was truthful – embarrassing, but truthful – bad enough to be mildly scandalous, given the way that he died, but not so bad as to tarnish our reputation much further."

"It did start then."

She looked at him, her eyes narrowed.

"You know where the rumours came from, don't you?"

Sin gave in – Faith would not let it rest, he was quite sure.

"I do, although I will not tell you the details. We have friends – people that I never, ever, expected could be our friends – and circumstances meant that they needed to know the truth of that fateful night. I expected nothing from them, but they chose to help me, to help us."

"That drama in the Park – that you brushed off as simply doing the right thing – there is more to that too, isn't there – it's all connected, isn't it?"

"It is. Faith, you are far too astute for my peace of mind!"

Their mother laughed at his words, then asked the question that had hung unspoken in the room until then.

"Who? Who has done this for us? Or perhaps I can guess, based on the first people whose attitude seemed to change towards you. It was the Duke of Windemere, wasn't it? Yet… I do not understand why he might care to assist us, after all the duel that sent you from England brought his son's death – I would expect him to hate us, and rightly so."

"Why? Because that carriage that I stopped in the Park – it contained his grandson, and the man who drove it had kidnapped the boy."

"Oh! That does make far more sense of it all. But even so, for him to do this – for he introduced you to others, did he not? Others who treated you as friend, for all to see?"

"He did. He is a kinder man than I deserved to ever meet."

Faith eyed him, her mind obviously working rapidly.

"There is more, isn't there. You have come to care for Lady Scartwick, that much is obvious, and you saved her son. So I must ask – has she come to care for you?"

"I hope so. What will come of it, I do not yet know, but I call upon her tomorrow."

"Good. For she has become a friend I do not wish to lose."

~~~~~

Marian woke slowly, as the early summer sun filled the room with golden warmth. Had it been a dream? No, she was sure that it had been real. The Prince Regent... and what he had said... it had almost been a command, coming from him.

To marry Lord Hungerwood... she had shied away from even thinking about their relationship going so far. Yet, when it had been so baldly placed before her as an idea, she had felt no rejection of it. Rather, a pleasant warmth had run through her at the thought. But... if it should go so far, what would Daniel think?

That concerned her, for she could never marry a man that Daniel did not like. At that she laughed – here she was, considering it as if, just because the Prince Regent had said it, it was a given – Lord Hungerwood had not asked her, and might never do so. Yet... he had asked for that second dance last night, and it had not gone unnoticed by the assembled cream of society.

She rose, and went to dress. There was no point maundering on about it in her mind. If Lord Hungerwood was true to his word, he would call upon her today. And Daniel would see him then, she would make sure of it – he had, after all, on that dreadful day when Cardston had nearly stolen Daniel, asked that he might see the boy again.

They did not go to the Park that morning, for everyone had overslept, after the eventful evening before. Everyone, that is, except Daniel, who was, she discovered, running madly around the garden, while Nanny sat on a bench in the middle, watching him, and attempting to prevent the worst damage to the flower beds.

She joined Nanny for a while, then went to break her fast. She found herself eager for Lord Hungerwood's arrival, yet nervous – for after last night, things could never be the same again. Not that she wanted them to be – she was ready for change – but would the change which came be what she wanted? Did she, for that matter, even know what she really wanted?

After eating, she selected a book from the library, and settled herself in the parlour. But she could not concentrate. The previous evening replayed itself in her mind, and every nuance of Lord Hungerwood's reactions came back to her. Did he mean...? Did he feel...? Was she correct if she assumed that...? It was pointless, for she had no answers. In the end, she laid the book down upon the side table, and simply stared out the window, idly watching people come and go in the street below.

Eventually, she saw an elegant phaeton turn the corner, and draw up before the house. She rang for the maid.

"Please ask Nanny to bring Master Daniel to the parlour in about ten minutes."

"Yes, my Lady."

The maid bobbed a curtsey and went. Marion walked back to the window – the phaeton stood, a footman holding the horses – Lord Hungerwood was nowhere in sight.

She turned to go back to her seat, when a tap came at the door.

"Enter."

"Lord Hungerwood, my Lady."

The footman showed him in, and closed the door after him.

Marion stood, suddenly unsure of how to go on. He came to her, took her hand, and bowed, his fingers pressing hers tightly. When he rose from the bow, their eyes locked, and they stood, silent, yet so much passed between them that it left Marion utterly breathless.

He leant forward, and brushed his lips over hers, softly, yet with an intensity which seared Marion to her core. Then he moved back, releasing her hand, everything that was proper, in a moment. She felt the loss of his touch acutely. As she searched for words, there came another tap on the door. Before she could speak, it opened, and Daniel came rushing in. He had almost reached her when he realised that there was another person present.

He skidded to a stop, regarding Lord Hungerwood with wide eyes – eyes which, despite his age, assessed the man before him keenly. Marion waited, barely daring to breathe, to discover what Daniel's decision would be. Lord Hungerwood, wisely simply stood waiting.

The moment stretched. Then Daniel's face lit with a huge smile, and he flung himself forward, to hug Lord Hungerwood about the knees and upper legs (which was as high as he could reach). Lord Hungerwood swayed in place, recovering his balance quickly, and reached down to brush a hand over Daniel's head, his eyes meeting Marion's. At the touch, Daniel looked up.

"You. You stopped the bad man from taking me in the horrible carriage. Thank you. I like you!"

"Daniel, might you release Lord Hungerwood from your grasp a moment, so that he might sit down?"

"Oh! Sorry."

Daniel released him, and Lord Hungerwood sat on the nearest couch. At which point Daniel climbed up beside him. Marion's heart swelled with joy. Not only did Daniel like Lord Hungerwood, it appeared that the liking was mutual, for the man seemed unperturbed by the energetic greeting.

"And what have you been doing this morning, young man?"

"We couldn't go to the Park, because everyone else was asleep," he accompanied this statement with an accusatory look at Marion, and she fought not to laugh, "so I played in our garden. I didn't squash too many flowers."

"I see. Perhaps you will be able to go to the Park tomorrow."

Daniel looked at him a moment, obviously thinking carefully.

"Yes. Will you come to the Park with us? In case there are any bad men there?"

Lord Hungerwood's eyes met Marion's. He smiled at her, a smile that seemed a promise, then turned his eyes back to Daniel.

"I will come to the Park with you, if you want me to. Every day that I possibly can, if that is what you want."

"Yes, it is!"

Daniel launched himself onto Lord Hungerwood again, hugging, and Lord Hungerwood simply folded his arms around the boy and held him. Marion blinked the tears from her eyes.

After a little more conversation, Daniel was persuaded to go with Nanny, given the promise of food and toys thereafter, and Marion dropped onto the seat beside Lord Hungerwood. He took her hand, and drew her to him. She went willingly, needing, in that moment, to be held, as much as Daniel had needed it. Her head rested against his shoulder, and the vibration of his voice reached her through his body, as much as her ears.

"I would do whatever you will permit, to help him be happy. After the part that my brother had in Martin's death, how could I do any less for his son? I saw too many children, in my years as a privateer, whose lives were destroyed, who were half starved, who had no home, or no-one to love them – I swore then that I would help any child that I could. And... I find that the boy has captured my heart, as surely as you have."

Marion looked up at him, his words echoing in her mind. She had captured his heart? Did he truly mean...? She discovered that she hoped so, that all of her swirling thoughts, since the moment that the Prince Regent had made the suggestion, coalesced into certainty at that moment.

"Your heart...?"

"My heart. It is yours. Lady Scartwick... Marion, if I may be so bold as to use your given name. I have come to care for you, more than simply care – I love you. Whether you can care for me or not, that will not change. You are everything that I could ever desire in a woman, and more."

Marion licked her lips, her mouth drying at the enormity of the moment. This man, who she had once believed to be worthy only of hate, had become the key to her happiness, and he had just said... A smile lit her face, and she leaned close again, bringing her lips to his for a moment.

"Then I must tell you that your feelings are returned. I love you – I think that I began to love you the first time we met, when you proved to be so very different from what I had expected. And now... I cannot imagine my life without you."

He crushed her against him, and brought his lips to hers in a deep passionate kiss, a kiss that left her melting against him, her body singing with desire. When they finally drew apart, he gazed into her eyes, and spoke, his voice husky with emotion.

"Marry me? Please say yes, Marion, for I do not think I could bear it if you refused me."

There was no hesitation.

"Yes, oh yes, I will marry you, and if that scandalises the *ton* all over again, so be it – I do not care!"

Epilogue

They had spent the week after he had proposed talking – at Stafford House, during drives in the Park, in the Park while they watched Daniel play. For the first time, Marion spoke of everything that had happened to her, from the moment that she first met Martin. She spoke of things she had not told anyone else – not her mother, not the Duke and Duchess. The weight that it lifted from her heart was immense.

In return, Sin spoke of his years away, of the joys and the horrors of the sea, and of his own struggle to come to terms with it all, once he had returned to England. Greatly daring, one day she asked him about names, about why he allowed people to call him Sin, with all that it implied. The answer half shocked her, and yet seemed so very in tune with his character.

"It has become a part of me. When the boys at school first called me that, I hated it – but I soon discovered that if I chose to own it, they left me alone. But they still called me that. And over the years I came to think of myself that way. It's rather shorter and quicker to say than 'Drummond'."

Marion had laughed a little, and he'd shared her amusement.

"But it became more part of me when I took on Hugh's dishonour – for that night, by doing so, I truly became 'Sin the sinner' in so many ways. I kept it. I kept it as a reminder of what I was, and what I wasn't. In a way, it became a badge of the honour I could not admit to. If it appeals, I don't mind if you call me that – just not in front of Mother and Faith, please."

"Perhaps I will. Let it remain a badge of honour, a thing that only we understand the true significance of."

She thought back on that morning now, as she dressed for her wedding. Lady Hungerwood had, on almost first introduction, become fast friends with the Duchess – which did not surprise Marion in the slightest – for the Duchess was kind, and unconventional, and far more clever than most women of the aristocracy – characteristics which she had come to realise Lady Hungerwood shared.

Between them, they had arranged the wedding, and she was quite certain that everything would go exactly as intended, just as all of the Duchess' plans seemed to. She studied herself in the mirror, the shimmering silver lace overlaying the rich blue silk of her gown, the sapphire pins in her hair, and the sapphire drop which hung about her neck. So very different, she thought, from her first wedding, where she had been dressed in a worn woollen day gown, with her hair in a simple knot, as she stood in Gretna Green with Martin after days on the road.

If his spirit was watching her, she hoped that he wished her well, that he was pleased with this unravelling of the wrongs of the past.

Briefly, she touched the tiny pocket sewn into the bodice of her gown, where the small gold heart on its tarnished chain rested. The heart that Martin had given her, as a wedding gift, all those years ago. There would come a time in the future when she would give it to Daniel. But for now, she carried it, to remind herself that love is never truly lost, no matter what happens.

~~~~~

Sin watched her approach him, where he waited at the front of the church. She was stunningly beautiful, and for a moment, he could barely believe that she was his. Had anyone suggested to him, less than six months before when he had set foot on English soil again, that he would marry within the year, to this woman, especially, he would have laughed in their face. But things had a way of setting themselves to rights, no matter what one expected.

She reached him, and stood beside him. From that moment, the ceremony passed in a blur, his awareness centred on Marion and his heart full of joy. On the front pew, sitting between the Duke and the Duchess of Windemere, Daniel tried very hard to be still, and simply to watch. He lasted until the very end, when they had been declared man and wife, before it became too much, and he launched himself forward, trying to hug both of them at once.

Laughing, Sin lifted him into his arms, and settled him against his hip. Holding Marion's hand with his other arm, he walked out of the church, to be greeted by a storm of rose petals. He looked at those gathered to celebrate with them, and felt, for the first time, that his honour was truly restored, that the past was gone, and that the future was full of hope and happiness.

The wedding breakfast was a whirl of people, and dancing, and congratulations which went on all day, and into the night. As had been asked, an invitation had been sent to the Prince Regent, and he had made an appearance for a short while, flirted outrageously with Faith, and then left, to no doubt attend another event.

Somewhere in the late afternoon, Daniel finally succumbed to all of the excitement, curled up on a chair, and went to sleep. Nanny lifted him carefully, and took him up to bed.

Sin led Marion through the crowded room, and out onto the quiet terrace. The scent of roses drifted up from the garden below as he drew her into his arms. She looked up, smiling.

"I realised, as we left the church, that I am no longer afraid. For seven years, I lived afraid, and now, you have taken that burden from me. I feel as light as air, and so full of happiness."

"I promise, my darling Marion, that I will do my utmost to keep you feeling that way, every day of our lives. From this moment, the past has no hold on us – let us live with joy, always."

He bent to kiss her, and all else faded from his awareness, save the intoxicating scent of roses.

The End

I hope that you have enjoyed these Spring and Valentine's Day stories!

After the 'About the Author' section of this book, you will find a preview of the first book in the His Majesty's Hounds series

'Claiming the Heart of a Duke'

Try the whole series – start and the beginning and discover how every story builds on the one before!

About the Author

Arietta Richmond has been a compulsive reader and writer all her life. Whilst her reading has covered an enormous range of topics, history has always fascinated her, and historical novels have been amongst her favourite reading.

She has written a wide range of work, from business articles and other non-fiction works (published under a pen name) but fiction has always been a major part of her life. Now, her Regency Historical Romance books are finally being released. The Derbyshire Set is comprised of 10 novels (9 released so far). The 'His Majesty's Hounds' series is comprised of 17 novels, with the last having just been released.

She also has a standalone longer novel shortly to be released, and four other series of novels in development. She lives in Australia, and when not reading or writing, likes to travel, and to see in person the places where history happened.

Be the first to know about it when Arietta's next book is released! Sign up to Arietta's newsletter at

http://www.ariettarichmond.com

When you do, you will receive two free subscriber exclusive books - **'A Gift of Love',** which is a prequel to the Derbyshire Set series, and ends on the day that 'The Earl's Unexpected Bride' begins, and **'Madame's Christmas Marquis'** which is an additional story in the His Majesty's Hounds series.

These stories are not for sale anywhere – they are absolutely exclusive to newsletter subscribers!

Connect with Arietta:

Follow her on Amazon - https://www.amazon.com/Arietta-Richmond/e/B016GG1KJ6/

Like her Facebook Page - https://www.facebook.com/AriettaRichmondAuthor

Follow her on Twitter - https://twitter.com/AriettaRichmond

Follow her on Instagram - https://www.instagram.com/AriettaRichmond/

Follow her on Bookbub – https://www.bookbub.com/authors/arietta-richmond

Follow her on Goodreads - https://www.goodreads.com/author/show/14508806.Arietta_Richmond

Here is *your* preview of

Claiming the

Heart of a Duke

His Majesty's Hounds– Book 1
Sweet and Clean Regency Romance

Arietta Richmond

Chapter One

Having broken his fast at the inn that morning, Hunter Barrington, tenth Duke of Melton, had decided that he would ride for the last leg of his journey, because he was heartily sick of the stuffy carriage and of his valet's mournful mien.

This worthy, whom he had hired following his friend Raphael's advice (for it seemed that his business was a source of excellent information, not just imported goods), had vainly tried to turn him into a dandy during their short stay in London. Hunter smiled thinking of Bulwick's dismay when he had flatly refused to use the cane that Bulwick had tried to foist upon him, or to buy the inordinate number of fobs, which it was fashionable to attach to one's watch chain. After years in the field, his taste in dress was so simple that it could be called austere. Not so long ago, a day with clean clothes had been worth savouring, so all of this fuss seemed rather ridiculous to him.

Poor Bulwick had been horrified when he had declared his intention to ride.

"You can't possibly do that, my Lord," he had whispered.

"You will reach Meltonbrook Chase in a dishevelled and mussed condition. You will get a head cold, of a certainty. And, my Lord, if I may presume to comment further, the road is in very bad condition and frozen all over."

"Fustian!"

Hunter had exclaimed, shrugging away his valet's concern.

"It will do me good. Look after my luggage, Felton. I'm off."

The road, in his opinion, was quite good – certainly a vast improvement on trampled battlefields and roads in a war zone!

So, without further ado, he had swung onto his horse, leaving the bewildered valet with his mouth still open in protest.

For the first few miles, the ride had been exhilarating. Warmly clad in his greatcoat, beaver hat and fur lined gloves, astride his dapple grey stallion, he had delighted in the cold wind and in the speed-blurred landscape, as he let the stallion run off his energy.

The feeling of freedom, however, did not last long and had already vanished when Meltonbrook Chase appeared in the distance.

It was the first time he had seen his family estate since his father, the late Duke, had purchased a commission for him, as was traditional for a second son.

Hunter could remember, perfectly well, his father's stern admonitions, imparted before sending him on his way to London, and hence to the Peninsular and war.

"Honour first of all, my son. Honour means more than life to our family. Never tarnish it, never demean yourself, never show a streak of the yellow. Remember, an officer and a nobleman must be an example for his men. England must stand against the French tyrant. Your commitment must be wholehearted. Your days as a dissipated and wild young buck have ended. Do you understand?"

'I thought I understood, Father, but I didn't. Only later, I did. Oh, yes, later I understood, all too well, what you meant.' Hunter's thought was wry, and a little sad.

He was so absorbed in his musings that he was barely registering the landscape. It took some time for him to realise that he was inside Meltonbrook Chase's expansive park. He reined in his horse, and stopped to look at the wintry landscape around him.

The silence was profound, broken only by the cawing of a crow, somewhere in the woods, and by the soft murmuring of the nearby brook.

The grounds were immaculate under the heavy pall of snow, the ice-traced tall poplars, which surrounded the lake, shining like silver filigree under the setting sun's slanting rays.

"I'm home." he thought, steeling himself for his first meeting with his family, after so many years.

Riding into the deserted stable yard, it seemed surreal that he was actually here – and even more surreal that his father and brother were gone, that all of this was his now.

He dismounted, the icy gravel crunching under his feet, as a brawny groom, in a leather coat, came running toward him.

"Master Hunter! Master Hunter! Is it you? Is it really you? At long last you're home again!" The man suddenly checked and lowered his head.

"Begging your pardon, Your Grace. I've been overfamiliar, but me happiness made me tongue run away with me, it did, old fool that I am."

"Never you mind, Nick. Master Hunter it is, if you wish it, as long as you keep it just between us. You know how stuffy my mother can be... Now, this is Nuage...." he gestured to the horse, which snuffled curiously at the old groom. "I bought him in France, and a valiant fellow he is. Take good care of him, will you? Go with Nick, my boy, he's a good one."

Nick stroked the horse's silky coat and took the reins.

"Always been a good judge of horseflesh, Master Hunter. Since you was a stripling, you was. Come along Nuage, a good rubdown is what you need right now. And what about some clean straw to lie on and some oats to chew?" Talking to the horse, the head groom disappeared around the corner toward the stable, as the carriage, bearing his valet, and his meagre luggage, drew up before the house.

~~~~~

Nerissa looked at her reflection in the tall mirror and sighed.

She would never be an Incomparable, and that was that. Her colouring was all wrong, she was too tall and her face was too angular.

In the pale pastel colours that were deemed fashionable for young ladies, she faded into insignificance.

She sighed again, thinking of her sister Maria, an acknowledged Beauty, who had cut a triumphant swathe through the *ton* during the previous Season. It had been fashionable to be in love with Maria, with her flashing amber eyes, rich auburn hair and flawless creamy complexion.

Thus, Maria had had the opportunity of choosing from amongst a veritable army of suitors and was now betrothed - very advantageously betrothed, to be sure, to a wealthy Earl, to their parents' delight.

Donning her fur lined pelisse and her velvet bonnet, Nerissa crossed the hall and stepped into the carriage with her maid, bound to Meltonbrook Chase, where she was to have tea with her bosom bow Alyse, the Duke of Melton's daughter. No, not daughter, sister, she amended her thought. Hunter was Duke, now, after the untimely demise of his father and his elder brother. She blushed. They hoped that Hunter would be home soon, for he had sent his family a message from London, but with the deep snow on the roads, he was likely delayed.

Would he recognise her? She did not think so. He had had scant interest to spare for her, to begin with, when he was a young man just back from his term in Oxford, and she was just a shy ten-year-old, all angles and elbows and not even a promise of feminine allure.

Nerissa leaned back on the carriage seat, closing her eyes. *'Much good it does me to wool-gather like that'*, she chided herself. *'I'll be lucky if I don't find myself married to some gouty old man before the Season is over.'* She shivered, and not because of the sharp wind blowing and howling through the naked trees.

~~~~~

As Hunter approached the door, the butler, a delighted expression lighting his usually impassive features, opened it. Immediately regaining his formal demeanour, Jermyn schooled his expression to a more serious face, better suited to the Butler of a great house.

"Welcome home, my lord. The ladies are in the drawing room. Follow me, please."

"No need, Jermyn, I know the way", answered Hunter, secretly amused by the butler's display of self-restraint, and almost ran to the drawing room doors, suddenly unable to wait any longer to see his family.

He opened the doors, and an instant of shocked silence followed his entrance.

Hunter scanned the tableau – a morning visit frozen before him. All of his family were there (although part of his mind still expected to see his father and Richard as well), and there was someone else.

A woman he did not know, a woman who was more beautiful than any he had seen.

She had burnished golden hair, surrounding her face with a profusion of waves and ringlets, a honey and gold complexion; long, almond shaped green gold eyes, fringed by thick burnished golden eyelashes and emphasized by high cheekbones, and a tall, shapely body.

The only feature detracting from perfection, but greatly adding to character, was a rather large, mobile mouth, much more capable of expressing feelings (and temper, he suspected!) than a proper prim little rosebud. He was captivated. Her eyes met his across the room, and for a moment, everything else faded away.

He was brought back to the moment when the silence was broken by his sister Alyse, who cried out: "Hunter! Hunter, you are back! Is it really you, Hunter?" and, without any further ado, threw herself at him. His eye contact with the woman was broken, and he forgot her in the chaos that followed.

Hunter's mother, the Duchess Louisa, half-fainting, reclined on the sofa, fanning herself and calling for her vinaigrette. His sister Sybilla, almost jigged around the table, before forcing herself to behave with greater propriety. His brother, Charles, obviously tried to be the cool gentleman, but could not help but step forward and embrace Hunter, his eyes shining with held back tears.

"At long last, my son," sobbed his mother.

"Come here, and let me look at you. Last time I saw you, you were a boy. Now you are a man. And what a man! Your father, God rest his soul, would be so proud of you..."

Moved despite himself, Hunter gathered his weeping mother into his arms.

"Shush, Mother, I'm here to stay. I'm so sorry I was not here when it would have really mattered. I feel that I have failed you all, yet it was at the time of Waterloo, and I did not even hear the news for months! I'm so sorry..."

The Duchess brushed her tears impatiently aside.

"I'm a foolish old woman, my son. This is not a time for weeping, but a time for rejoicing. God knows, we have been mourning long enough. And look who is here, Hunter. Do you remember Lady Nerissa Loughbridge, Lord Chester's youngest daughter?"

A faint recollection of a meddlesome brat, always trying to follow him around, vaguely stirred in Hunter's memory.

He turned his head and froze again, caught by her appearance. Brat? She was not a brat anymore, she was a woman, and a very beautiful woman at that, more so because of her unusual colouring.

It was all he could do not to stare at her with his mouth agape. He tried to react in some polite way, and smiled, suddenly recalling one of Nerissa's youthful misdeeds.

"Nerissa? Was it you who hid inside your brother Kevin's portmanteau, because you wanted to come with us when we went to our hunting lodge near Cottesmore? And did we not discover you because you sneezed? Do you remember, Charles?"

Nerissa had not heard a single word.

Hunter's sudden appearance had completely stunned her.

All her childhood emotions flooded back, crowding her mind, amplified with new meaning and significance. A rosy blush washed upon her face as she dared to smile back.

"She's not a child anymore, Hunter," broke in Alyse.

"She is a dear friend to us all, and I really don't know how we would have managed without her. She is a sensible young woman, with a good head on her shoulders, and she gave us invaluable help when Mother was so ill after..." Alyse's voice faltered "...after the accident..."

Hunter looked at his family: his sisters, pretty, vivacious, eager to try out their wings during the London Season, his mother, with her gentle face marked by loss and sorrow, his brother, suddenly scowling and dark browed, and the enchanting stranger in their midst. He felt rather like he had stepped into the centre of a whirlwind.

Suddenly he felt mortally tired, in dire need of rest and solitude.

He went to his mother and kissed her gently on her cheek.

"Will you please excuse me, Mother? I have had a long and

tiring journey and I'm much fatigued. I believe that, if you will forgive me, I will have a bath drawn and a tray sent to my room. I am not really up to a formal supper. Tomorrow, we can all begin to catch up."

"But of course, my dear. How thoughtless of me not having foreseen your needs... my happiness at seeing you again quite overwhelmed me. I have not all my wits about me, I'm sure... Jermyn, please, see His Grace to his apartments and make sure that his valet attends him."

"Yes, my lady. Please follow me, Your Grace."

To his chagrin, Jermyn did not lead Hunter to his bachelor's quarters as he had unthinkingly expected, but to his father's apartments.

That was the precise moment at which the full import of his new condition crashed in upon him like a dark and overwhelming wave.

He was the Duke of Melton.

Not his father, nor his elder brother, both now dead after a freak carriage accident. Himself.

He had not wanted it, he had not coveted it, truth to tell, he had no idea how to go about being a Duke, but there it was, with all its implications and obligations, including the need to marry, and to sire heirs to the title.

It was like a bad dream, but it was not going to disappear at dawn.

ARIETTA RICHMOND

Chapter Two

Hunter rode along a rutted track, across a barren and ravaged landscape, under a dark and menacing sky. The stench of burned and rotting flesh, of death and decay was all pervading, a leaden overcoat on his shoulders. Far away, one could hear the great, long-distance artillery guns roaring, more like a muted vibration than a real noise.

Around him, there was nothing but destruction - bloated carcasses, untended fields, ruined buildings and skeletal trees - where once cattle had grazed, wheat had ripened and orchards had blossomed. Suddenly something, a white rag fluttering in the rank wind, half-hidden by the ditch, attracted his attention. He was drawn toward it, almost without volition, but stopped dead in horror when he was near enough to see.

Beatriz lay lifeless, among rubble and sundry discarded items, her skin beaten and bruised with the imprint of vicious hands, her body broken and bloody, her mouth still half open in a hopeless scream, her lovely dark eyes fixed, and staring in a desperate appeal into the eternity of death.

Beatriz. His love.

Beatriz, on whose grave he had cried until his throat was raw. Beatriz, whom war had wrenched from him and who had died alone, in shame and terror, ravished by French troops in rout after the battle of Vitoria.

Beatriz, one of the countless casualties of war.

Suddenly, something shifted, and a flickering image of another face, in a soft green and golden light, like a sunbeam on new leaves, flashed into his mind, and broke the grip of the dream.

Hunter woke, drenched in cold sweat, lurching to his feet, his heart beating wildly against his ribcage.

At first, he stood bewildered, unable to recognise his surroundings, still gripped by the horror of his recurring nightmare, then, gradually, he calmed down, his heartbeat steadied and his anguish receded.

It was not real. He had never seen Beatriz like that, he had only seen her grave, been told of her death. He did not know, could never know, how terrible that death had been – but his imagination was all too able to present him with the ghastly possibilities. As it did – almost every night.

Completely awake now, he drank deeply of the water, which Bulwick had thoughtfully provided, in a carafe on the side table. He went to the window, opened the heavy velvet drapes, and peered outside.

It was still dark, but a faint rosy shade began to colour the East. No question of going back to sleep, now. Hunter was sure that Nick was already up and going.

He would look for the old groom and wipe away the last of

the nightmare, listening to Nick relating everything that had been going on here, during his long absence from home.

~~~~~~

Louisa Barrington, Duchess of Melton, looked critically at her face in the mirror, while her young maid, Prudence, was arranging her hair under a flattering beribboned lace cap.

"You look yourself again, my lady, if I may say so. You have filled up a bit and your eyes... But now", she went on briskly "his Lordship is back home again and everything will be all right, will it not, my Lady?"

Lady Melton smiled. She had known Prudence since her birth, the daughter of a respectable but impoverished family, and was used to her artless demeanour. And the girl was right. For the first time since the accident, she could look at herself with some satisfaction, and at the future with some hope.

She closed her eyes, remembering the mindless terror that had gripped her when the careening coach, driven by some drunken lout, had suddenly appeared around the bend. The horses had reared, neighing, and the heavier vehicle had smashed full into their light travelling carriage, with a sickening noise of crushed wood. That sound was the last thing she could recall before oblivion had claimed her.

Louisa shook herself out of her brooding. Time to start the new day and to get to know, again, her own son – so much time had passed - she wondered what sort of man he had become.

There was so much to be said and done.

She sighed. Some of what had to be said would not be pleasant. Her late elder son, Richard, heir presumptive to the title, had not been wise.

Handsome and debonair, always exuding charm, a redoubtable Corinthian, able to spar with Gentleman Jackson himself, and to feather angles with his curricle, he had also been a reckless gambler and had entertained questionable relationships with ladies of dubious virtue. His father, the late Duke, had been so inordinately proud of his heir, that he had never checked or restrained him.

"Don't you fret, my boy" he had indulgently told Charles, his hard working, serious third born, when he had shown his father the heavy dent that Richard's expenses were making in the estate's revenues.

"Let him be, he will calm down in time and, anyway, we can afford it, can't we?"

'Well, we are not destitute,' she thought, 'and the estate is vastly profitable, thanks to Charles' thrifty management, but, with two dowries to provide for, a mansion in London to keep up, and a living to arrange for Charles, if he decides to enter the Church (although that seems rather less likely now)... things need to change. It is, truly, not seemly for Charles to act as his brother's steward – regardless of the cost, an estate manager must be employed. And, as Hunter really must marry, and get himself an heir, a good dowry would not come amiss, now, would it?'

~~~~~

In a few days, a routine, of a sort, had been established.

Hunter would wake at dawn, after a restless night plagued by nightmares, go down to the stables and have a chat with Nick, take a brisk walk in the park and then break his fast, with his family, in the small dining room.

It was a cosy and intimate room which he liked infinitely better than the formal dining room, with its long table, musty hangings and depressing centrepieces.

His mother would tell him about his neighbours, and expound on her plans for the coming Season; his sisters would laugh and chatter and talk of French couturierès, balls and routs; his brother would prose on about the estate, the tenants and the improvements he had thought of. Hunter would listen to everybody, nod genially, let the flow of conversation dance around him, and reprove himself for his lack of interest.

After having dealt with decisions which entailed life or death, for much of his adult life, he could not help but feel that there was a slight lack of import, or even sense, in the topics in which his family – as dear as everyone was to him – seemed so absorbed.

Life as Colonel Lord Barrington had been much harsher, but much simpler, than life as His Grace the Duke of Melton.

Hunter soon realised that his mother wanted him married tout de suite, possibly before the Season ended, and preferably to a young lady with a fat dowry.

He found this an appalling prospect, because, even if not averse to marriage in principle, he did not want to be rushed, neither did he want somebody else to choose for him.

His mind felt scarred, still torn by everything that he had seen and done – and he was not about to explain anything of that, to anyone. It was still too sensitive a topic, and his nightmares unsettled him more than he cared to admit.

Perusing his library, he had found a book of Ancient Greek poetry, and read a fragment by Sappho, with which he felt a total affinity:

"Like wild gales, sweeping desolate mountains

uprooting oaks

Eros harrows my heart

sweet, bitter, indomitable wild beast…"

Beatriz was still an indelible, aching wound. He did not want to suffer again. He did not want to lose his heart to somebody who could tear it asunder.

He wanted an affectionate, companionable marriage. He wanted to be friends with his wife. He wanted a sensible, cool-headed young woman, not some vapid, giggling miss or some haughty high-flier.

One afternoon, while he was walking, brooding and trying to sort out his feelings, full of a sense of guilt, that he, as the Duke, could not bring himself to care, more, for the management of his estates, he wandered away from his usual path and found himself deep inside his neighbour's park.

Looking around, at first he did not understand where he was: the natural woods of the park had progressively given way to a more structured growth.

The park seemed larger than he remembered, with cunningly planted thickets, graceful avenues flanked by stately trees, cosy nooks, elegant fountains, well designed flowerbeds and herbaceous borders. Even now, in the depths of the winter, it was not difficult to imagine a profusion of bright colours vying with each other to the beholder's delight.

He remembered the park as he had known it during his childhood: a fascinating tangle of trees, creepers and weeds, which could well become a mysterious jungle, where his friend

Kevin, Lord Chester's son, his brothers and himself, would hunt for wild beasts, find hidden treasures and fight warlike natives.

Lord Chester must have hired a new head gardener, Hunter mused. The place had improved beyond recognition.

His senses, honed by times when the ability to hear insignificant noises could make the difference between life and death, perceived a slight rustle, as if something were moving between the winter bare bushes, and he stepped abruptly past the branches.

To his chagrin, he found himself at less than a foot's distance from Lady Nerissa, who could not hold back a soft whimper of startlement at his sudden appearance.

"I am sorry, Lady Nerissa", he spoke softly, almost as startled as she appeared to be. "Did I scare you?"

She smiled, lowering her eyes. He found himself disappointed that she had veiled their green-gold depths from his sight.

"Not at all, my Lord. However, I should not be here on my own, without a chaperone. Please excuse me, I must go back at once."

Her beauty seemed to burn like a flame against the frozen background, composing a jewelled symphony of brilliant shades: gold, silver, coral, aquamarine, mother of pearl, as the cool winter light reflected from the warmth of her skin.

"Nerissa!" Hunter exclaimed, loath to let her go. "Lady Nerissa, we are old friends and neighbours, are we not? Surely nobody could object to our exchanging a few words in an open place, during a casual meeting. I am the meekest and most inoffensive of gentlemen, I do assure you!"

Nerissa looked at Hunter under her lowered lashes. He gave an impression of energy and passion kept on a tight leash, like a wild horse straining at restraints. His deep sapphire eyes flashed in a countenance darkened by many seasons spent in warmer climates, his firm mouth and strong chin bespoke character and courage, his lean, hard body and his long, sensitive fingers, made her feel… she could not even name those feelings.

No, he was not inoffensive, he was very dangerous, much too dangerous for her own peace of mind, for she had discovered, to her chagrin, that she found him just as attractive now, as she had as an infatuated ten year old.

She should go away, but she could not. Mesmerised by his smile, she smiled in return.

"Just a few minutes, then. Let's walk, it is too cold, and the ground too damp, to sit anyway…"

They walked for a while, making small talk, stealing surreptitious glances at each other, laughing without a real reason, somehow prisoners of the strange enchantment of their unexpected meeting.

Nerissa felt as if they were inside a fragile, iridescent bubble and, at the same time, she clearly perceived the terrible impropriety of their situation. Even so, the rebellious mood which had made her fly from home and seek the haven of her beloved park persisted, and made her feel stubborn and daring, enjoying Hunter's company with a carefree elation.

But, while she was tucking a stray, wind-tossed tress under her bonnet, the portfolio she was carrying opened and the sheets inside fluttered and fell to the ground.

Hunter was quick to stoop and help her to collect them, but was very surprised when he discovered that they were not the kind of artwork that one was used to expect from a young lady - pastels, gouaches, flowers and landscapes, painstakingly rendered, dull and respectable - but something completely different, something resembling, strangely enough, the neat battle plans he had so often pored over during his soldiering days.

Nerissa blushed a deep crimson, and almost wrenched the sheets from his hand. The laughing, relaxed mood of the last hour disappeared in a moment, and she was suddenly tense and distant.

"Thank you, Lord Melton," Nerissa whispered.

"I must go now. Goodbye..." and turning quickly, she almost ran away, leaving Hunter bewildered and wondering what all that had been about.

Continued……

Read the rest at:

http://www.amazon.com/dp/B01K7SFHEI

Books in the

His Majesty's Hounds Series

THE REGENCY SPRING AND VALENTINE'S HEARTS COLLECTION

Claiming the Heart of a Duke

Intriguing the Viscount

Giving a Heart of Lace

Being Lady Harriet's Hero

Enchanting the Duke

Redeeming the Marquess

Finding the Duke's Heir

Winning the Merchant Earl

Healing Lord Barton

Kissing the Duke of Hearts

Loving the Bitter Baron

Falling for the Earl

Rescuing the Countess

Betting on a Lady's Heart

Attracting the Spymaster

Courting a Spinster for Christmas

Restoring the Earl's Honour

From Soldier Spy to Lord (Books 1 to 3 as a set)

To Love a Determined Lady (Books 4 to 6 as a set)

Love Heals a Lord (Books 7 to 9 as a set)

Books in The Derbyshire Set

The Marchioness' Second Chance

A Viscount's Reluctant Passion

Lady Theodora's Christmas Wish

The Derbyshire Set Omnibus Edition Vol. 1 (the first three books all in one)

The Derbyshire Set Omnibus Edition Vol. 2 (the second three books all in one)

Books in the Nettlefold Chronicles

Books in the A Duke's Daughters – the Elbury Bouquet Series

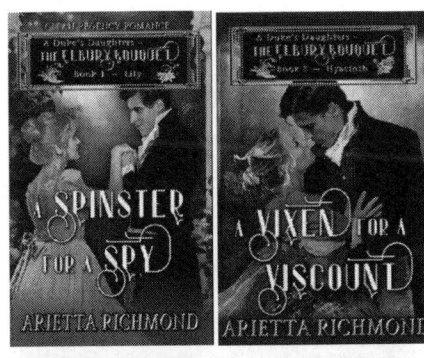

A Minx for a Merchant (Primrose) (coming soon)
An Enchantress for an Earl (Violet) (coming soon)
A Maiden for a Marquess (Iris) (coming soon)
A Heart for an Heir (Thorne) (coming soon)

Books in the Regency Scandals Series

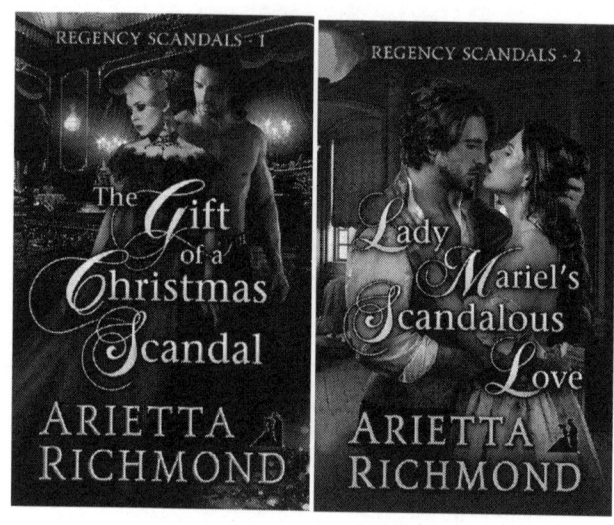

Book 3 – Christmas with *THAT* Duke (Coming Soon)

Other Books from Arietta

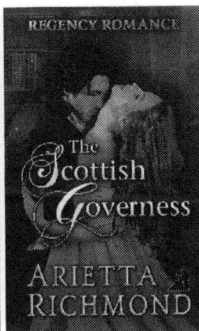

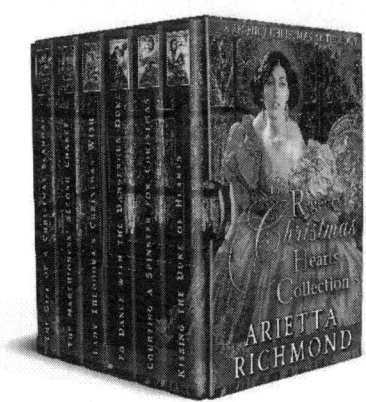

ARIETTA RICHMOND

Regency Collections with Other Authors

Made in the USA
Middletown, DE
10 April 2022

63990278R00413